I0736232

THE UNDEAD CHRONICLES VOLUME 2

Darker Days

PATRICK J. O'BRIAN

Copyright 2020, Patrick J. O'Brian

All rights reserved.

Except as permitted under the U.S. Copyright Act of 1976, no part of this publication may be reproduced, distributed, or transmitted in any form or by any means or stored in a database or retrieval system, without the prior written permission of the author or publisher.

ISBN: 978-1-948638-23-4

Cover by John Herrick.

Published by

Fideli Publishing, Inc.
119 W. Morgan St.
Martinsville, IN 46151

www.FideliPublishing.com

PRINTED IN THE UNITED STATES OF AMERICA

Special thanks to Brad Wiemer, Korby Sommers, Jobina Wiemer, Kevin Sommers, Jeff Groves, Dave Blackford, Kendrick Shadoan, and John Herrick.

*This book is dedicated educators across the world.
Our future depends on you folks more than ever, and you deserve
so much more than you receive.*

Other novels by
Patrick J. O'Brian include:

The Fallen

Reaper (Book 1 of the West Baden Murders Series)

The Brotherhood

Retribution (Book 2 of the West Baden Murders Series)

Stolen Time

Sins of the Father (Book 3 of the West Baden Murders Series)

Six Days

Dysfunction (Book 1 of the Terry Levine Detective Series)

The Sleeping Phoenix

Snowbound (Book 4 of the West Baden Murders Series)

Sawmill Road (Book 2 of the Terry Levine Detective Series)

Ghosts of West Baden (Book 5 of the West Baden Murders Series)

Red Rain (Book 3 of the Terry Levine Detective Series)

Sin Killer (Book 4 of the Terry Levine Detective Series)

The Doomsday Clock (Book 6 of the West Baden Murders Series)

Hallowed Grounds

Home and Back Again (The Undead Chronicles Volume 1)

Uncertain Terms

Non-fiction works by Patrick J. O'Brian include:

Risen from the Ashes: The History of the West Baden Springs Hotel

Pluto in the Valley: The History of the French Lick Springs Hotel

Learn more about Patrick and his projects at:
www.pjobooks.com

One

Join the Navy. See the world. Survive the zombie apocalypse.

While the United States Navy changed slogans over the years to appeal to younger generations, one never held truer than the one a lieutenant commander jotted down in his personal notes.

During his childhood, Bryce Metzger often assumed responsibility in clubs, sports, and other school activities, knowing he wanted to make something of his life one day. He explored various options, knowing he eventually wanted to be his own boss, but doing so meant working for someone else first. Eventually he settled on the Reserve Officers Training Corp (ROTC) program, thinking he might as well have his college paid for by someone else to reach his ultimate goal of managing or owning a business.

He attended his first two years of college at University of Rochester, only an hour away from his parents and younger brother, knowing the decision that lie ahead. With his general studies mostly finished and a degree in business underway, Bryce knew he needed to commit to the United States Navy or pay for the remainder of his schooling on his own. Seeing the world on a fully weaponized ship appealed to him, so he completed intensive schooling, spending time in Norfolk, Virginia, and San Diego, along with summers aboard ships learning trades.

His first summer aboard a ship taught him valuable lessons, like lifting his feet when crossing thresholds, or receiving injured, bloody shins in return. Although the concept of how tons of steel floated wasn't lost on him, Bryce still couldn't believe how solid warships looked and felt in person. He might have questioned whether they could be sunk if history hadn't already taught him the answer through his numerous classes.

Graduating from the University of Rochester simply led to another year of military schooling before he became a commissioned officer aboard the *USS Mahan* (DDG-72) for the better part of three years under two different skippers. During this period, he married Isabella Swanson, a young woman he met during his studies in Rochester, who studied history, hoping to eventually become a college professor and obtain her doctorate. Her career started well enough, but the discovery of her pregnancy almost immediately after her husband departed on a mission with his fleet temporarily derailed her ambitions.

Beginning as an ensign, Bryce worked as a division officer, splitting his time between operations and engineering. He worked his way up to lieutenant junior grade before an assignment that led to four years aboard the *USS Gravely* (DDG-107) where he was eventually promoted to lieutenant. During this period, he became a department head, assuming more responsibility that set him on the course to eventually captain a ship if he attended certain schools and kept his record clean.

Reaching a crossroads of sorts, Bryce needed to decide whether to return to civilian life and try his hand at business, or re-up with the Navy. Given an opportunity to work on shore, Bryce decided to extend his time in the military with Isabella's blessing, knowing their son longed for more time around his father.

Subconsciously he sought to stay in the military long enough to draw a pension, which provided him with income while Isabella decided on what endeavor she wanted for her future. He'd handcuffed her to military life long enough, so Bryce was willing to relocate wherever she wanted after his retirement to fulfill her career ambitions. Isabella landed a job at Norfolk State University as a professor, working on her doctorate, but Bryce knew her dream job wasn't tethered to a military base.

Although he didn't detest shore duty, Bryce grew antsy to be on the water again, knowing he possessed the skills and the mindset to captain a ship someday. Luckily, all of his previous captains and senior officers took a liking to him, and he spent part of his time on land studying to move up the ranks. Returning to the *USS Mahan* as a lieutenant this time, Bryce recognized only a few faces from his first assignment still aboard the ship. He grew accustomed to very little sleep once again, worked his ass off, and eventually took a few more courses after his last tour with the ship.

Both timing and schooling worked out in his favor when he attained the rank of lieutenant commander and became eligible to work as an executive officer (XO). The *USS Ross* (DDG-71) took on a new commanding officer (CO), barely Bryce's senior, who needed an XO after the woman who held the post opted to retire.

Bryce adjusted well to the move because the *Ross* ran much like any of the other Arleigh Burke-class destroyers he'd worked on previously. Many were commissioned and built during the 1990s, some with newer weapons systems than others. Named for Donald K. Ross, a Medal of Honor recipient, the ship launched in March of 1996, typically changing captains every two years like most Navy warships.

Adjusting to his new role required a few months, though Bryce refused to let his discomfort show around his new crew. Leading a division or a department placed him squarely in charge of a particular number of men and women, but now he dealt with every crew member at some point in time. While the CO dealt with the fighting aspect of the ship, the XO drowned in paperwork, dealing with personnel issues, maintenance, scheduling leave times, logistics, and acting as a firewall for anyone who wished to speak with the captain directly.

It turned out working under Commander Mark Dascher wasn't too bad once they passed the initial feeling out period. A bit more standoffish than some officers, Dascher felt a need to assert his authority before allowing any of the officers to speak freely to him. His process almost put a wedge between Dascher and the other officers because most destroyers weren't large enough for the captain to have his own cook.

Instead of eating with the other officers, however, Dascher chose to eat a bit earlier in the day for the first month. Gaining a little bit of trust with the man, because they dealt with one another often, Bryce suggested a little comradery might go a long way in establishing a rapport with the officers who worked often with the CO on the bridge. While they never openly said too much around Bryce, fearing he might have Dascher's ear, they hinted that things were sometimes rigid during their time on watch.

Regardless of rank, the man who ran a Navy ship was always called 'captain' or 'sir' by anyone who addressed him.

Sailors inherently obey orders and respect their ship's captain, so once Dascher loosened up a bit around his crew, morale aboard *Ross* took an upswing. Nearly half the ship, including its two highest ranking officers, carried out duties they hadn't previously performed on a regular basis. Various drills helped develop confidence, and once Bryce discovered which methods of organization worked best for him, he excelled in his new role.

Ordered away from its squadron to train with the Japanese navy for two weeks, *Ross* set sail from the middle of the Pacific Ocean where the fleet monitored recent unrest in North Korea and China. Another ship took its place in the squadron, and Bryce wore his formal white uniform for the very last time during a gala in Japan when the ship reached port. Dascher shared his intrigue about working with a foreign navy with Bryce, and the XO felt much the same. No language barrier hindered operations because the Japanese spoke reasonably fluent English, and the exercises occupied the various departments during all hours.

Occasionally the ship was docked, allowing the sailors some time ashore to explore the towns, which resulted in alcohol consumption and intercourse for many of the seamen. Bryce took in some of the sights occasionally, but for the most part he remained with the ship to carry out his duties. He used his alone time to contact his wife and son, who neared his tenth birthday, wishing for a more conventional family life more than ever. He felt terrible that his brother and parents needed to travel to Norfolk to visit him when he returned home, because time didn't permit for much family travel. When Bryce took Isabella and Nathan on trips, they were usually a day or two away at most, often to a museum, theme park, or the occasional camping trip.

Five days into their training exercise, now closer to the Middle East, the captain received a message from the radio shack where all incoming transmissions were received. He shared the information with his XO that dozens, possibly hundreds of explosions occurred throughout the world, as the result of a suspected terror attack. All of the attacks took place in populated areas, often in factories, schools, or downtown districts in cities. Even worse, chemical agents were released from the detonated trucks that sickened thousands of people immediately.

Panic, anger, and sympathy took hold of the world population immediately, and the timing of the attacks wasn't lost on Bryce.

In a sweeping move, all Navy ships were ordered away from shores across the world for fear that they might be attacked, or the chemical agents might infect the sailors. Bryce initially believed the government's concern about the toxins seemed like overkill, but he soon discovered they knew more than he did about the chemical's effects. Additional messages were received, and both Bryce and Dascher knew they couldn't hide the disastrous aftermath of the attacks from their sailors. Many of the crew members possessed cell phones or access to the ship's computers on a sign-in basis, so someone would eventually see the news and spread it like a different sort of virus across the destroyer.

"There's no hiding this from the crew," Dascher groaned when his XO visited the captain in his quarters.

Less than four hours after the explosions, news spread that some of the infected people were attacking and biting survivors. The government reiterated that ships needed to keep a safe distance from all shores for the time being.

"Whatever happened is spreading," the captain added. "And it's everywhere. Our leadership isn't saying much except this virus is spreading and anyone infected attacks healthy people. When people get bitten, they also get sick."

"This is a clusterfuck," Bryce stated, already wanting to contact his wife to ensure that she and his son remained safe.

Both men knew the ship couldn't last incredibly long in isolation because they met up with oilers and other supply ships a few times each week to receive food, fuel, and everyday necessities like toilet paper. Unlike previous mass terrorist attacks, this one wouldn't cease within a few days, or a week, because the released chemical agent brought about an entirely new set of problems for the military and first responders to handle.

"How do I ask these kids to continue like nothing's happening when I'm just as worried about my family back home?" Dascher questioned aloud, uncharacteristically lost.

"Sir, you're their captain," Bryce said. "Hell, to a lot of these sailors you're the only father figure they've ever had. If this gets worse, and it likely will, I suggest you be firm, but fair, and give them opportunities to contact their loved ones. It's hard for any of us to carry out our duties if we're preoccupied."

Despite any initial tensions easing between the two men, Bryce always referred to his ship's captain with 'sir' or 'captain' because Dascher had never given him permission to do otherwise.

Dascher provided a look of resolve, because he knew his XO provided good counsel as always. Only a year older than Bryce, at age 36, the captain possessed a full head of black hair, hazel eyes, and a clean face. His nose appeared ever so slightly offset, as though he'd been struck there during a skirmish or some high school sport years prior. Still a good athlete, the captain tended to jog outside during fair mornings, and inside when the weather didn't agree with him. He took to making rounds and speaking to his officers, and some of the enlisted men, during such days, earning their respect.

Many of the sailors stole opportunities to view footage on their phones or the ship's computers, learning about the events unfolding around the world. Deciding to reduce anxiety, Dascher posted news footage in the cafeteria and break areas, making certain his officers kept their enlisted personnel from slacking off. Bryce felt the same tingle throughout his body that he experienced during 9/11 and subsequent worldly events carried out by people without souls. He watched in stunned silence with his shipmates as the terrible event sent ripples throughout every corner of the globe. The epidemic grew worse as the people sworn to protect citizens and country alike could only stare helplessly.

Questions ran through the minds of every survivor, and in the case of those aboard *Ross* the captain couldn't provide answers. If he possessed answers, he might have put his crew at ease, but the only messages he received from the government, so far as Bryce knew, contained strict orders. Either the government didn't know exactly why people were getting sick and attacking survivors, or they didn't want panic spreading across their bases and vessels.

Watching the news provided the sailors with some answers, while opening up many new questions. Some of them managed to reach family members and others did not, leaving them concerned and upset. For his part, Bryce managed to reach his parents soon after the onset, and his brother shortly after them. The captain informed him that the personnel left on the base were checking on the families of their own loved ones and those of the men and women at sea. Bryce attempted to call Isabella once, receiving no answer, and he refused to monopolize the satellite phone when other sailors desperately awaited answers.

Within a few days, when the world realized the global crisis couldn't be curbed, Dascher received orders to plot a course back to Naval Station Norfolk. To alleviate fears among his sailors, the captain reported that teams were being sent into town to gather up family members of enlisted personnel. Many families lived in apartments or rental houses outside of the base, but the station was being converted into a shelter to keep everyone safe. The epidemic continued to spread as the news outlets reported that the recently deceased returned to a rudimentary form of life to hunt down and consume the living.

Sacrifices were made during the trip home, and sailors were happy to comply for the reward of seeing their family members sooner. Food and fuel ran low until they caught up to their old strike group, receiving supplies from the aircraft carrier *USS Dwight D. Eisenhower* (CVN-69). With communications in disarray from the United States to allied nations, Navy personnel found their orders changing somewhat routinely. During the fifth day of travel, Dascher received permission to slow his ship to 10 knots from the admiral to conserve fuel, though it put them further behind the fleet. They were destined to meet up with a supply ship in a few days, and he needed to ensure they didn't get stranded in the middle of an ocean.

Realistically, the country wouldn't be able to manufacture fuel much longer. Living and breathing people quickly became the minority, and infrastructure had already begun to crumble, as the crew could attest to. Abandoning the *Ross* to assure every sailor made it home sounded like a fair trade to Bryce, but it didn't become a necessary sacrifice.

Able to plot courses for ships carrying fuel and supplies, the government didn't rely on allied help, because other nations shared the same problems. The journey home came with complications, and it took the better part of four weeks before the men and women aboard *Ross* saw their home port on the horizon. Bryce personally felt a sense of relief, ready to see his wife and son, though the captain provided him with the news that the military commanders at Naval Station Norfolk had an assignment for him that required additional travel. From what he understood, personnel from every military branch convened at the base, creating a disjointed but unified military coalition. Still a few days out from the base, Bryce was able to call his brother one last time, urging him to hurry in his travels.

"I'm sorry about the orders," Dascher said quietly to his XO while both men stood in the bridge with the base growing closer by the minute.

"That makes two of us, sir," Bryce responded. "Duty calls."

"I spoke with one of the other captains. They're trying to relocate all military personnel to strategic bases, which includes ours in Norfolk. It won't be long before we're one big consolidated military."

Realizing their words might be overhead by the number of enlisted personnel and the junior officer on the watch, Dascher pointed toward the door.

"Let's get some fresh air."

Both officers stepped outside, finding clear blue skies greeting them with warm weather and a stiff breeze. They walked to the closest railing, leaning over to look at the water as their ship created a foamy trail in its wake.

"I don't know what's to become of our armed forces," Dascher confessed. "I think our currency is about to become food and security, but even that won't last forever."

"What exactly are you saying, sir?" Bryce questioned.

"I'm saying to watch your back, because the writing on the wall says this is the apocalypse and it's every man for himself."

Bryce smirked, and Dascher caught it as intended.

"I know," the commanding officer said. "It's not very loyal of me to speak of our beloved government in such a way, but the society we knew is *gone*. Mark my words, Metzger, it's only going to get worse from here."

As though on cue, the ship began to slow near the harbor and Dascher fully intended to get inside to make certain his personnel guided her into port without a scratch, but a throaty growl from the water caught the attention of both officers. Floating alongside the ship, several clothed undead with waterlogged, bloated flesh, growled, reaching upward towards the ship at the prospect of seeing live prey. Their skin appeared gray, as though saturated from within, with numerous folds and wrinkles. Without the ability to swim, the undead simply floated in place until the ship's propulsion pushed them away. Bryce noticed one of them wore a Navy enlisted man's uniform, wondering how one of his own ended up in the water, among the undead.

Neither had laid eyes on an actual zombie, having been at sea for so long, and the news footage failed to bring justice to the experience. Bryce felt a shiver through the small of his back, knowing the people in the water once carried out normal lives, now reduced to mindless shells of their former selves. He exchanged an uneasy glance with Dascher before both men turned to enter the bridge to take their ship home.

***

Much of what occurred after that felt like a blur to the lieutenant commander. After a brief, emotional reunion with Isabella and Nathan, Bryce was summoned to a meeting that involved leaders from every branch of the military within one of the buildings on the base. Much of the base appeared to be a refugee camp with tents, clotheslines, and people cooking outside. He suspected the senior officers received the permanent buildings for bunk space, indicating some things *didn't* change in the new era. Several times he noticed what appeared to be people pawing at the base's security gates, but a closer examination caused him to realize a number of the undead wanted inside to attack the living.

Entering the building, Bryce shook hands with several high-ranking officers from every branch except the Coast Guard, which had representation on the base, but not in this meeting. Every shred of natural light was allowed to flow into the room, because the military didn't want to waste resources running generators or using up their batteries. Ironic, Bryce thought, that it required an apocalypse to keep the government from being wasteful. Being a nuclear ship, the *USS Dwight D. Eisenhower* could easily power the port once plugged into the grid, but for some reason it wasn't being utilized. Reworking the existing grid required time and the correct personnel, and it certainly wasn't an overnight fix.

Captain David Parry, the man in charge of the base, introduced Bryce to an Army colonel and captain, a major from the Marines, and a major from the Air Force. He shook hands with each man, having met Parry only a handful of times during his brief stays at Naval Station Norfolk.

Considering Dascher wasn't invited to the meeting, and no admirals and generals were present, Bryce took notice that the government moved forward without relying on previous policies. He took a seat near the end of the large table that seated almost two dozen when the room reached capacity. The various leaders explained to him that he was flying back to his home state to assist with a mission to discover who delivered and triggered the various explosive devices across the United States. He felt a surge of excitement at the opportunity to discover who caused the apocalypse, killing millions of innocent people.

"While you're the highest-ranking officer on this mission," Marine Major Thom Faulkner said, "we want our guys to take point. We don't have electronics to guide us, and we need to reach the Hemingway Factory, the primary target in Buffalo the day this mess started."

"I know it well, sir," Bryce replied, recalling the company manufactured electrical components for numerous motor vehicle and tractor companies. His father once said they produced parts for the locomotives he worked on before his retirement. "I can get us there."

"We're sending out units like this across the nation," one of the Air Force officers stated, "hoping to find the common link between the explosions."

"Are we doing this with the hope of finding a cure?" Bryce dared ask since he was risking his life almost immediately after setting foot on dry land.

"In part," Faulkner answered. "If we can find the person or group responsible, we hope to learn the extent of their plan, along with the science. A cure would be ideal, but we also want to know if there's any corner of the Earth that isn't affected."

Bryce nodded.

"We're providing you with a C-130 and ground vehicles that should get you where you're going, short of an entanglement with an invading military force," the major added. "We're giving you a unit out of MCB Quantico who work together regularly. The unit has been briefed on what to look for, and they'll work out the logistics with you en route."

He slid a folder across the table to the lieutenant commander.

"Inside are your mission parameters. We'll equip you, because we need all hands on deck to get inside, extract the information, and get back here with it ASAP."

Bryce nodded, knowing he could read through the folder during the flight. He hesitated slightly, and everyone in the room took notice.

"My brother is on his way here under my direction," he added.

"We'll take him in," Parry offered immediately. "I can give the guards his name so they don't turn him away."

"If he arrives before my team departs, I'd like permission to bring him along," Bryce said, looking at the eyes of every officer.

In unison they balked at the notion of a civilian tagging along on such a crucial mission, but their thinking originated in the old world.

"Dan knows the Buffalo area as well as I do, and he's been on the road for a month," Bryce added. "He knows how to deal with what's out there, and he can offer some insight regarding how to handle the infected."

Reluctantly the officers agreed, looking to one another and giving slow, affirmative nods. Likely believing Dan Metzger possessed little to no chance of meeting the timeline, they rolled the dice, giving permission for the lieutenant commander's brother to join the group.

"The team is ready to go, but we wanted to give you a night with your family before you depart," Parry said, and Bryce felt as though the captain lobbied to get him the courtesy. "We'll get everything loaded, and you'll depart with your team tomorrow."

Bryce nodded before standing. He shook hands with the officers once again before heading outside to spend quality time with his family. Again, he observed the undead at the fence after hearing their growls and moans. Several soldiers took knives and sharp weapons to their skulls through the mesh wire fence, putting them down permanently. With Norfolk and the base closed off by water, the undead could only reach town limits via waterways or through the town itself.

Accustomed to the smell of fresh sea air, Bryce's nostrils took in body odors, fecal matter, and the stench of decay. Part of him missed the sea already, almost wishing he could stow away on a ship with his family. Nothing about that scenario ended dreamily, because the same problems on land eventually caught up with anyone sailing across blue waters.

Staring at the fence, he figured eventually the undead numbers would thin out, leaving the base safe from attack to deal with other problems. Food, fresh water, and medical supplies were due to run out with so many people staying at the installation, leaving the survivors to fend for themselves, which might lead to the dissolution of the government as they knew it.

"Penny for your thoughts," Isabella said as she and Nathan met up with him near the makeshift camp.

"This isn't fair to either of you," he said, scooping up his son and holding him in a hug for close to a minute.

"How can they ask more of you?" Isabella asked with a heavy sigh. "They tried explaining it, but how does this mission do anything except put more of you in danger?"

"We might get answers," Bryce replied. "That doesn't necessarily make it right, but they need someone who knows the Buffalo area."

He turned to Nathan.

"How are you holding up, champ?" he asked.

"I'm okay."

"This is like one big summer camp, isn't it?"

"Yeah."

Bryce set his son down once his right arm began to grow numb. Whenever he returned from a tour at sea, he found Nathan a bit taller and heavier than when he left.

"How are the accommodations?" he asked his wife as she took his hand, leading him toward the camp.

"They could be worse," she answered. "Most of us stay in the buildings, or aboard the ships, while the scouts stay in the tents and listen for activity. The dead haven't breached the fences yet, so that's good."

He wished the small talk would cease as his mind wandered, thinking he wanted to bed his wife for the first time in six months before leaving on a perilous mission. As a respectable father, he knew to never say anything in front of his offspring about wanting to have sex with his mother like a wild animal. He and Isabella would play the game through and figure out a way to distract their son or busy him for adequate alone time.

"They say the President is aboard one of the ships," Isabella stated as they walked, holding hands while Nathan skipped around in front of them.

"I saw him!" Nathan exclaimed, not missing one step as he continued to burn calories with the excitement of his father being home.

"You did?" Bryce asked with an arched eyebrow, questioning the accuracy of his son's claim.

"He waved to me from one of the ships."

Isabella shrugged when he looked to her, which meant the statement couldn't be disproven.

"We get two or three meals a day," Isabella said, returning to the original topic. "Everyone pitches in, so we have clean laundry, the occasional shower, and enough meds for now. I just wonder how long we can sustain all of this unless they get the plague under control. People are the biggest resource we have now. Without them, we'll never reopen factories, have electricity, or use phones again."

"We got there once before," Bryce said, hoping he sounded more optimistic than he felt. "It's hard to believe everything around us could just turn to relics."

He envisioned a sepia tone world like the movies always depicted where dust and sand covered everything, though the beautiful weather around him spoke to the contrary. Both avoided talking about serious topics until Isabella encouraged Nathan to run over and play with one of his new friends.

"His world opened up when they brought us inside," she said. "Lots of bored kids with nothing except books and each other."

Bryce stared her in the eyes.

"I'm pretty sure I can get a seaman apprentice to show Nate the ship if you know a private setting for a quickie."

If not for his devotion to his trade, Bryce might have suggested his living quarters on his ship. Such behavior got any sailor dismissed from the ship, facing harsh disciplinary action, and Bryce didn't feel that using the apocalypse as an excuse was kosher just yet.

"You're a hopeless romantic," Isabella said with a laugh. "But, yes, I'd like to fuck, and I'm getting sick of all of these horny assholes undressing me with their eyes."

"I'll show them how it's done for real," Bryce promised. "And if any of them get handsy after I leave, you know how to use a gun."

"I certainly do," Isabella answered with a confident nod.

Bryce gave her a quick kiss before they continued their stroll, putting off their alone time until after things settled down around the base.

"How's your family?" he inquired.

"They're fine, last I knew. You know they're tough as nails."

"I'm worried about my folks," Bryce admitted, having last spoken to his mother only days after the terrorist events changed the landscape of the world. "I worried that I sent Dan straight into a trap, but he got out of New York."

"Did he make it to their house?"

"I think so, but we didn't exactly have time for lengthy conversations. He would've said something if he found them, so I'm fearing the worst."

Isabella pulled him into a hug, neither of them concerned that military personnel and their spouses might be looking in their direction. Somehow, despite everything around them smelling like trash, her scent reminded him of his mother's flowers whenever he visited his parents.

"Where on earth did you find perfume?" he inquired with a whisper into her ear.

"Just for you, I managed to dig some up."

"I could take you right here," he admitted, feeling an erection forming, which he quickly ebbed by deflecting his thoughts elsewhere.

Bryce knew from experience that stereotypes told about sailors often held true. While at sea he never stepped out on his wife, though he did so once before they were married with a stranger one night he met at a tavern. He and Isabella were on a hiatus of sorts with their relationship, but looking back, he wished he hadn't given into temptation so easily. Enlisted men often dashed off the ship in search of a good time during their leave, but officers were held to a higher standard. Particularly as XO, Bryce knew he needed to set a good example, even if his sailors didn't always follow it.

Intentionally walking past his ship with Isabella, he noticed unfamiliar soldiers unloading cargo from the ship while most of his sailors set foot on dry land, resting or getting a bite to eat. Bryce decided to grab an early dinner with his wife and son, which he found to be incredibly informal compared to the routine aboard a ship. Following that, he snagged a seaman's apprentice, requesting the man provide his son with a tour aboard *Ross*, particularly the areas any kid would love. Nodding affirmatively, the young man took young Nathan aboard the ship, and Bryce let Isabella lead him to a private room within a building where foreplay lasted less than two minutes, basically consisting of the couple undressing one another.

Once the couple finished making love, they talked for only a few minutes before Bryce got dressed to find the seaman's apprentice aboard *Ross* so he could show Nathan where he worked personally. He thanked the man and finished the tour, which contributed to his son falling asleep in his arms later that evening inside his quarters on the ship. While the military provided some form of housing for everyone on the base, Bryce opted to stay on his ship so he and Isabella could converse before he departed the following morning.

***

Some of his wife's words stayed with him when he entered the transport aircraft the following morning, leaving his family on the landing strip outside. She made him promise to return safely the previous evening, and he did, because no military man wanted to appear pessimistic about his chances of survival.

Just before takeoff, Bryce spied his younger brother approaching him inside the aircraft. Despite the growth of a beard, he recognized Dan Metzger immediately, embracing him with a powerful hug before the two exchanged a few words. Informed that his parents hadn't survived the apocalypse, the lieutenant commander didn't ask for details because time didn't permit. His brother offered no elaboration, as though both understood such a deep discussion required privacy and their full attention at a later date.

Once they were safely in the air, heading for Buffalo, the Metzger brothers sat beside one another to converse. Noise inside the C-130 proved deafening, much like the center of a major factory, making regular conversation impossible. Everyone in the cargo section of the plane put on headsets that allowed them to speak to one another, but not to the pilot or the aircraft's crew. Most of the Marines onboard turned their volume down, simply using the headphones as noise-canceling devices while they closed their eyes. A row of seats lined each side of the cargo plane, with two Humvees strapped down in the center of the aircraft, ready for use once the group landed.

"Where the fuck did you pick up swords?" Bryce asked his brother, spying the two blades intersecting within a pack on the ground.

"Early on I found them in a high-end pawn shop. They were already sharpened and ready to go."

Bryce sensed a bit of sadness in his brother's eyes, stemming from his time on the road.

"What is it?" he asked, digging deeper.

"The guy who owned the pawn shop was Japanese, or maybe half-Japanese. His family was already dead inside the building from gunshot wounds to their heads, and he used one of the swords to kill himself."

Hurt showed in his brother's eyes as he told the tale.

"He was walking around, sword still hanging from his guts, and I had to use the other one to put him down."

"What kind of shit have you seen out there?" Bryce asked, not certain he wanted to know the answer.

"It's a hard world, Bryce," Metzger answered. "Definitely not a place for someone traveling solo."

As much as the lieutenant commander wanted to catch up with his brother, duty called, so he opened the file and passed each page over to him once he finished reading it. Mission parameters called for them to examine the truck that caused the explosion, if possible, and if not, to look through the company's manifests. Paperwork would prove much easier in their search, but if necessary, they could extract the company computers and let the intelligence people sort through them at the base.

Basically, trained soldiers were playing detective, and the mission felt a little too straightforward for the elite skills of SEALs and Green Berets. The lieutenant commander simply wanted to contribute, though he wasn't certain how overrun Buffalo was going to look compared to the global news footage, and what little he witnessed at the base.

"How dangerous are the infected?" he asked his younger brother once they finished the file.

"A few at a time isn't a big deal. It's when you run into a cluster that they become dangerous. A single bite is enough to infect a person and kill them, and there's nowhere to run once they surround you."

"Buffalo?"

His brother responded with wide eyes, as though they were literally entering the lion's den to retrieve information.

A man dressed in fatigues walked over to them, armed rather lightly compared to the other soldiers aboard the plane. He wore only a sidearm, but he carried needles and a small case with him. In order to speak to them, he donned a nearby headset not currently being used.

"Need a blood sample, fellas," he stated, standing over them, waiting for them to roll up their sleeves.

Using a fresh needle for each of them, he stuck the sailor first, followed by his brother, who showed the curiosity of a civilian.

"What's this for?"

"They want before and after samples for comparison from each of us," the man said. "You guys are walking into ground zero, so they want to make sure there's no physiological changes."

"Sounds promising," Dan muttered after the man removed his headset and returned to his regular seat.

"We have masks and gear," Bryce promised. "Hell, the air is probably clear now anyway."

Considering the brothers hadn't seen one another in almost a year, the two spent another two hours catching up before Metzger finally brought up the sore topic his brother avoided completely.

"What happened to Mom and Dad? Did you find them like...those things?"

"No. They were kidnapped and brought to some weird prison camp."

His brother explained how a group of armed men took over a school, abducting people off the street and from their homes for use as laborers. Even as a retiree, their father rebelled against their captors, causing the leader to publicly execute Donald and Connie Metzger as an example to the other prisoners. He added that a group of people trying to free their loved ones from the school turned labor camp killed most of the kidnappers.

"Their ringleader followed us to the airport in some armored car," Dan added. "We killed his buddies, and I watched him get surrounded by the undead."

"Did they rip him apart?"

"I didn't get to see what happened to him. We still had danger around us, so I was busy jumping on a plane."

As much as Bryce wanted to make certain the man who killed his parents was a rotting corpse, he asked his next question with loyalty to his mission in mind.

"Which airport?"

"The small Lancaster airport."

Lancaster wasn't incredibly far from Buffalo, and he imagined the larger airports became a hotspot for people desperate to fly out of their states, or the country. Many people likely died at those airports, and other undead were attracted to them for numerous reasons.

"Was that airport reasonably clear when you left it?" he asked his brother.

"Well, yes. But it's not very big."

"I know."

Bryce stood, removed his headset, and carefully walked up to the cockpit of the plane so he could address the pilot. A man with graying sand-colored hair and a thick mustache named Timmons, according to the nameplate on his flight suit, turned to address the lieutenant commander. He pointed to an empty headset, which the lieutenant commander placed over his ears.

"What can I do for you?"

"Where were you hoping to land, sir?"

"I'm under orders to get us as reasonably close to the site as possible."

Outranked by the pilot, a Navy captain who likely accepted the mission due to a lack of qualified personnel, Bryce decided to appeal to the man's logical side.

"If the larger airports are overrun, I may have a suggestion, sir."

"And what is that?" Timmons asked, as though unconvinced *any* landing spot might prove safe.

"My brother was at the Buffalo-Lancaster Regional Airport a few days back. He says it was reasonably clear of infected."

"That would be a haul for your group to travel into Buffalo, son."

"Thirteen miles or so, sir. Mostly interstate, which could be good or bad."

"I'll keep that in mind, but I'm going to fly over the larger airports first. I need to get you boys as close as I can to the target zone."

"Understood, sir."

Bryce removed his headset and returned to his seat.

"What was that about?" Dan asked.

"Presenting the Lancaster airport as a possibility," Bryce answered once able to speak into the headset's microphone.

"He has to be dead, Bryce. And we don't have time to go hunting him down anyway."

"This isn't personal," Bryce told his brother. "I'm simply providing an optional landing spot that may conveniently give me an opportunity to spit on the asshole who killed our parents."

"No, that doesn't sound personal at all."

Within the hour, Timmons flew them over the two largest Buffalo area airports, finding them swamped with the undead, which looked like a swarm of bees in a honeycomb on the pavement below.

Bryce studied the faces of his fellow travelers, each ready to carry out the mission in their fatigues while armed to the teeth. A man named Cory Nestler introduced himself to the brothers within the first hour of the flight. Somewhere close to the elder Metzger in age, the Marine second-lieutenant made it abundantly clear he was heading up the mission, deferring to the lieutenant commander in all local travel decisions. The man didn't act haughty or like a person who loved being in charge, but rather a soldier who wanted to follow orders, complete the mission, and get home to his family.

Bryce could relate.

After circling the Buffalo area for about five minutes, Timmons summoned both Nestler and Bryce to the cockpit area.

"Boys, I can't land at the major airports because those things are everywhere. They'd either fuck up my landing gears, or they'd swarm us the minute we touch down. I'm going to try the lieutenant commander's recommendation and shoot for Lancaster. It'll be tight, but if it's halfway clear, I can stick the landing."

"That's fine by me," Nestler said. "We're no good to anyone if we get killed or stuck here."

Everyone except the man that drew blood samples, Timmons, and the copilot, readied themselves for work on the ground. In all, ten people were going to exit the plane, five in each of the Humvees, with mounted M240 machineguns. Bryce looked to his brother, who carried only the two swords and two handguns, unfazed by what the group was about to encounter. He wondered exactly what his brother witnessed during a month on the road, and as Timmons circled to land at the small airport, Bryce questioned what awaited them on the ground once they landed.

Two

Dan Metzger looked to his brother while the plane circled the small airport for the best landing scenario. Like most brotherly scenarios, Metzger never told Bryce that he looked up to him during their childhood years. He also withheld his feelings that he felt abandoned and devastated for a nearly a week after his brother formally left home for college, and the military following that.

Bryce provided an excellent model for him to follow during his formative childhood and teenage years, steering clear of drugs and wayward friends. Every so often they fought, as brothers do, but only once did they come to blows, and a mutual friend broke up their skirmish before any real damage was done. While Metzger set his course early on for his college studies, Bryce didn't seem as certain about his path, opting to join the Navy, never knowing it would become a career entrenched with his college studies.

Now his brother wore military fatigues, fitting the part of a responsible leader with neatly trimmed hair and a mustache that appeared meticulous, despite the end of the normal world. Bryce knew how to lead men, handle firearms, and operate machines Metzger couldn't begin to understand. Despite Bryce's strengths, he wasn't ready to confront a wall of undead that looked like the front rows of a rock concert when they drew dangerously close.

Timmons landed the plane reasonably smoothly, informing everyone aboard that the runway wasn't devoid of undead. He tried avoiding the slow-moving bodies as best he could, but the plane still smashed through a few zombies as thumps against the plane's exterior were heard by everyone inside.

Dan Metzger envisioned what the airstrip looked like several days prior when he flew south with a group of people he barely knew. Taking up the modified backpack that held his weaponry and a few supplies, he stood beside his brother, waiting for everyone to file into the two armored vehicles. Nestler verbally assigned each person to the front or rear Humvee, balking slightly when it came to Metzger and his brother, as though he wanted to separate them.

"He stays with me," Bryce stated firmly, drawing a nod of agreement from the second-lieutenant that both brothers would take seats within the lead vehicle.

Without any windows to look through, Metzger could only envision what he last saw. He expected a few dozen undead wandering aimlessly, an armored car, and Xavier's body ripped apart and left unceremoniously beside the car. No last name given, Xavier was the man responsible for the deaths of any number of people at the reconfigured school where people were used as slave labor.

Nestler opted to drive the vehicle the brothers were assigned to, letting Bryce ride shotgun for full visibility when navigating them to the factory. Metzger crammed into the back seat with a muscular black man whose tag indicated his surname was Bryant, and a man who assumed the firing position of the M240 machinegun, whose name he didn't get to read. The Marine stood in the center of the backseat, his upper body out of sight because the gunner position placed him out the top of the Humvee. Metzger stared at a pair of feet and legs covered in traditional fatigues, wanting to warn the soldier that the undead weren't especially nimble, but they could climb.

He said nothing, however, considering himself a guest who shouldn't be handing out advice to capable military personnel.

When the rear hatch of the cargo plane opened, both vehicles backed out with precision speed and technique, immediately ramming a few zombies to the ground as the three men left on the plane used their pistols to calmly shoot any undead that drew too close to the plane. Metzger spotted the loadmaster calmly pushing a large button to close the hatch once both armored vehicles were clear of the plane. He quickly turned his head to see if the armored vehicle, or a ravaged body, remained near the airstrip.

Neither could be seen.

"No," he muttered, bobbing his head to look out every available window to cover every view, fearing he hadn't avenged his parents at all, short of winging the man during the airfield skirmish.

"What's wrong?" Bryce asked, turning to look at him.

Metzger returned a sour expression, along with a negative shake of his head, and his brother immediately understood.

He spied the car he'd driven to the airport still sitting near the hangars, appearing undisturbed. Metzger still had the keys to that car in his pocket, hoping when he left that he might see it again someday because the last of his family memorabilia rested within the trunk. As the Humvees sped out the downed airport fencing near the entrance, he felt his heart sink a bit because he never got to say a proper goodbye to his parents, or even bury them.

Although he tried to stay in the moment, his thoughts wandered to the group of people who escorted him to Naval Station Norfolk only to be turned away by the soldiers guarding the gates. He wanted to think he'd see them again, and he left the means to contact the group with one of its members, but the odds felt incredibly long as the world grew large again without technology to connect people.

Riding in the mammoth plane felt much more comfortable than his current situation. At least the plane smelled of synthetic materials, like opening an action figure for the first time as a kid, discovering that fresh plastic odor. Now enclosed with four other people, Metzger reunited with body odor and the discomfort of being crammed in a seat with people and equipment all around him.

Traveling along county roads and state highways, the vehicles made good time, occasionally swerving around the undead or stalled vehicles. Not until they reached the interstate did the group discover thicker traffic with numerous cars and trucks parked along the road, sometimes blocking the interstate completely. At first, Nestler veered off the road when necessary, but eventually they came across a string of cars parked so tightly together that a bicycle would barely fit through.

Parked every which way, the grouping of cars presented no means of squeezing through because of the barricades lining either side of the interstate. Nestler stopped the Humvee, knowing someone needed to get out and begin the arduous task of moving the vehicles. Not one to use his rank to excuse himself from work,

Bryce jumped out of the passenger's side as Bryant and the gunner followed suit. Metzger scooted over, toting his pack with him, prepared to assist with the labor.

"You don't need to go," Nestler said.

"This will go quicker if I help," Metzger insisted, making his way out the door as the military men began approaching the cars to see how best to clear a path.

He clutched the handle on the shorter of his two swords, making his way up to one of the cars for a look inside. Tapping on the window, he used a trick from previous vehicle encounters to see if any undead were lying dormant inside. No deceased monsters popped up against the windows, so he tried the door, finding it unlocked. Taking notice of his technique, the others cautiously studied the vehicles they approached, each using his trick while their shooting hands clasped firearms.

Metzger looked down the road, seeing additional clusters of vehicles similar to the one they currently handled, knowing their trip wouldn't go as smoothly as anyone hoped. About to jump inside the car to see about starting it, or throwing it into neutral as a second resort, he heard a throaty growl coming from his left. The military men, including his brother, drew their firearms, anxious to notch their first undead kills, but Metzger put up a hand, indicating he would handle the situation.

Regardless of sex, all zombies tended to sound very much alike once they returned to life. This one, a woman wearing a faded, dingy yellow dress with floral printing staggered along, seeing Metzger as her next potential meal. He let her draw within a few feet, his right hand already clasping the wrapped handle of the sword, before letting loose horizontally with the weapon, slicing the zombie's skull in half, sending the top portion of her cranium flying while her body slumped to the ground.

"Watch your feet," he warned the others as loudly as he dared speak. "Sometimes they lurk under cars."

Rather efficiently, the group worked out a system where a few of them kept lookout while the other two jumped into the vehicles, either moving them aside or using them to shove other vehicles out of the way. After the first batch was cleared, Metzger walked with his brother the short distance to the next unintentional roadblock created by gridlocked traffic during a time people desperately wanted to get somewhere else.

"Don't be afraid to speak up," Bryce told him. "You've seen what happens out here. We haven't."

"I'm a guest," Metzger replied, "so I'm trying not to make waves. But it just takes one bite from them, maybe even a gouge, and it's game over."

"These guys think on a different wavelength," Bryce admitted. "They're capable, tough, and they'll get the job done, but they also think the infected aren't much of a threat."

Metzger walked along one of the cars, turning to see if Nestler could skirt past the current opening between vehicles. Both vehicles were able to follow, so Metzger turned to his brother as they continued walking.

"They're easy to deal with in situations like this when they're spread out, or alone. It's when you start making noise, like gunfire, when they're congested, that it becomes an issue. You realize it's suicide if we do this kind of thing inside city limits, right?"

His words indicated the convoy couldn't simply hop out of the Humvees once dozens, hundreds, or thousands of zombies surrounded them.

"Will traffic be this much of an issue once we're in the city?" Bryce asked.

"Not so much. Most people were trying to leave, but those who couldn't were stranded there, and it's not pretty."

During the movement of the second batch of cars, Metzger wasn't quick enough to keep the gunner from shooting an incoming zombie in the skull. Everyone looked at the man, who simply shrugged as though his hand was forced, even though the walking corpse posed no immediate threat from nearly five car lengths away.

Metzger caught a glimpse of the man's nameplate this time, seeing the sergeant was named Wheeler. He didn't particularly show emotion over putting down a zombie, but the echo traveled for miles over the otherwise quiet region. Although Metzger didn't know exactly why, zombies tended to know exactly where loud noises originated. Perhaps because their second coming left them with *only* rudimentary senses, the undead possessed heightened abilities in sight, smell, and hearing, but Metzger lacked the scientific skills to narrow down the possibilities.

After a few seconds everyone simply moved along, testing more vehicles before moving them accordingly.

"What did the government say about all of this?" Metzger asked his brother, referring to the apocalypse.

"I wasn't privy to a lot of things, but the little bit I was around the brass, they indicated they were working on solutions. It sounds like the government managed to save a lot of top scientists, along with our nation's leaders."

Metzger wasn't convinced politicians proved very useful in the current world, either in their old jobs or dispatching zombies. He said nothing, allowing his brother to elaborate further.

"I know they plan to aggressively attack the problem," Bryce continued. "If we're able to eliminate the undead, and keep anyone else from getting sick, they think we have a chance of restoring the infrastructure before everything is lost."

Excusing himself momentarily, Metzger cut through another zombie skull before the assailant reached anyone else. Simply beheading them didn't kill them because the head of a zombie continued to function, even when detached from the body. He didn't like leaving potential hazards lying around, so he usually finished the job with one precise cut.

Returning to his brother, he helped the group move the last of the clutter aside for the Humvees, taking notice that their straightforward objective hit a snag. Emerging from the nearby woods, and from between vehicles, a dozen or so undead likely heard the running motors and gunfire, stumbling forward in search of prey.

"We need to get through this quickly," Bryce announced before Metzger could basically utter the same words.

Everyone jogged forward to the next batch of vehicles, virtually ignoring the undead for the time being. Metzger felt thankful the gunner in the second Humvee hadn't developed an itchy trigger finger and started laying waste to the undead threat. Rapid gunfire would assuredly draw more trouble their way, and as they drew closer to Buffalo, the group needed to remain quiet. While noise attracted the undead, it also caught the attention of survivors who would seek aid or attempt to steal what the group possessed.

Such a move likely wouldn't end well for any would-be thieves when they faced down nine men trained by the government and one man who defied the odds by surviving. Metzger approached a beige car, about to tap on the driver's side window when a zombie reached from beneath the vehicle, grabbing his ankle. Immediately upset that he didn't observe his approach more carefully, he yanked his leg back, dragging the female corpse out from beneath the car because she refused to let go. Her jaws were already poised to take a large chomp from his leg, and Metzger didn't have his sword in position, so he used his other foot to punt her in the side of the head, knocking her grip loose. She tumbled a few feet away, and he ended her suffering by putting the blade through the side of her skull as everyone took time from their duties to watch him ignore his own advice about approaching vehicles.

Now he shrugged in turn, tapping on the window to find the car clear of any passengers before opening the door. Able to start the car, he drove it to one side, emerging to find some of the undead drawing dangerously close to the group. While the military moved more of the vehicles, he went to work, cutting through skulls with practiced efficiency, wishing he'd eaten more than just a protein bar on the flight. Because of his movements, most of the undead drew toward him, and as a precaution, he climbed into the bed of a truck, giving him a great vantage point. The clumsy fingers and clouded minds of the undead didn't allow for them to grasp objects and pull themselves upward immediately. Like toddlers, they learned how to use their motor skills whenever the need arose.

Most of the time, they simply stood on the ground and swiped at whatever object caught their attention.

Careful not to stick any limbs out too far, Metzger either stabbed or sliced with the sword, dispatching the group rather easily. From the corner of his eye, he saw the military men deal with the few remaining undead once they finished moving the vehicles out of the way. Trying out their knives for the first time, each of them appeared a bit apprehensive about stepping in so close for the kill. Part of dealing with zombies up close, in Metzger's estimation, was being forced to see the shred of their former humanity staring at you with cold, pale eyes.

Everyone quickly filed into the Humvee, anxious to reach Buffalo's official town limits and the Hemingway Factory.

Nestler led the way, weaving through parked cars, occasionally finding clear patches along the interstate where he took the Humvee up to normal speeds before finding more packs of stranded vehicles. Metzger recalled many of the local landmarks from his travels in and out of the Buffalo area.

"Are we better off staying on the interstate as long as possible, or getting into town?" Bryce asked him once they saw signs for exits ahead.

"I didn't see much of the city during my time there, but from what I've seen, local streets are much better."

"If you've got an exit in mind, just tell me," Nestler said from the driver's seat.

Looking out the window, Metzger saw a sign that caught his attention, and a large building not far from the exit they were quickly approaching.

"We need to go there," he said, pointing out the building to the second-lieutenant.

Taking a look at the old structure, and the sign looming above it, Nestler shook his head incredulously.

"Boom Town Fireworks?" he questioned aloud. "We don't have time to deviate from our mission."

"If we don't make it back alive, the mission is for nothing," Metzger stated. "Believe me, it's a worthwhile stop."

Nestler looked to Bryce, as though asking for a second opinion.

"If he thinks we need fireworks, I'm inclined to believe him," Bryce said. "If it's as bad as Dan thinks, we're going to need a distraction."

Taking the exit, Nestler went down to a dead stoplight, making the appropriate turn as the second Humvee reluctantly followed him. All of the mechanical arms at each of the toll exits were long since shattered by vehicles that no longer adhered to the laws of man.

"Right in and right out," Nestler said as he glanced back at Metzger. "This is a big risk for something we can probably handle ourselves."

Metzger didn't agree, but he held his tongue on the subject.

"If it makes you feel better, I can run in there and grab what we need myself," he said instead.

"I'm not putting a civilian at risk, especially one related to my tour guide."

"This should only take a minute," Metzger said, though he didn't consider himself an expert on fireworks, or which types produced the effect he sought.

Nestler navigated around a few vehicles, pulling to a stop within a vacant parking lot beside the rather large fireworks warehouse. It occurred to Metzger that Independence Day occurred a full two months before the apocalypse, but he suspected the store hadn't put a clearance sale on its inventory. With a building dedicated to selling one thing, and signage that indicated people could pull off and purchase fireworks, the owners surely sold their product all year round.

Scooping up his handheld radio, Nestler informed the driver of the other Humvee that the group was heading inside for a look around. Wheeler and Bryant didn't seem to have an opinion about the detour one way or the other as everyone climbed out from the armored vehicle. Everyone from the second Humvee also jumped out, likely anxious to stretch their legs, and as they studied the perimeter of the building, an unusual noise broke the otherwise quiet surroundings.

Metzger barely distinguished the sound as the siren of a police squad car before a black and white Dodge Charger drove in their direction at a high rate of speed. Blue and red lights spun within the lightbar atop the cruiser, and its brakes were easily audible as it screeched to a stop at the edge of the parking lot, as though trying to prevent the military vehicles from leaving.

"What the fuck?" Nestler asked, stating each word slowly and clearly, his eyes focused on the bizarre and unexpected sight before the group.

Three

Jillian Varitek felt an impending sense of danger to her group, caused by one of its members. She understood protecting what one possessed, because food, water, and weapons, were important in the new world. In some ways they served as currency, because most people couldn't forge weapons or grow food on their own. Much of the generation that relied on their computers, phones, and tablets didn't survive past the first week, and those who did were left in a hell on earth.

After crossing several bridges and departing the greater Hampton Roads area where Naval Station Norfolk didn't welcome them, the group stopped to swap vehicles momentarily. Upon discovering a newer van, like those used on trips by churches and schools, they left their two trucks roadside because the vehicles ran low on fuel. The white van comfortably held four of them, and their gear, while Gracine Tucker and Colby Sutton planned to ride in the box truck that Sutton monitored like precious cargo at all times.

"That's some bullshit that the Navy base wouldn't take us in," Gracine muttered while she helped transfer items from the two trucks to the van.

A black woman somewhere near middle age by Jillian's estimation, the group found her with Sutton when they crash landed their Cessna plane in Virginia several days earlier. The newly larger group traveled to a camp where Sutton hoped to find his two sons at their family camping spot. Undead ruled the area, and Sutton found no signs of his sons having visited the property, so he wanted to double back.

Currently, Sutton walked with his dog, Buster, along the road while they both searched for somewhere to relieve themselves.

"So, you and him," Jillian said, her eyes shifting toward the dog owner, questioning if Gracine and Sutton shared bedroom relations.

"Oh, hell no," Gracine answered firmly. "We just met a few days before we met y'all, like I said. The dog treats me a hell of a lot better than he does."

Gracine moved a box of food from one of the trucks to the van, addressing Jillian again once she knew everyone else took items from the other truck, too far away to hear their conversation.

"You and the school teacher guy seemed to hit it off," she noted, speaking of Metzger, who had just left the group in Norfolk to join his brother. "I know you didn't let him go without a farewell present."

Jillian blushed, figuring everyone knew because one of their group members made it known to her and Metzger that their attempts to make love quietly failed utterly. She decided Gracine hadn't found time to speak with Vazquez, the one who heard them, so she remained mum about the topic.

"You go, girl," Gracine said with a knowing nod, picking up another box.

Jillian took up her personal backpack, along with a notebook and pen from the front seat of the truck she'd been riding in since departing Norfolk.

"What do you do with that?"

"I keep a journal of sorts about what we see each day," Jillian answered.

"Why bother?"

"I was a history major. How do I know if anyone else is recording history these days?"

"You don't, because it doesn't matter."

"You honestly think we'll never get back to a normal civilization?"

"If we do, the government spooks will spin whatever version of history they want us to know, just like always."

"You're a very pessimistic person, Gracine."

"I'm a realist, girlfriend. If we were smack dab in the middle of something important, I'd say write away, but we ain't."

"Are you kidding? Dan just left us to visit a military base. One of ours could be witnessing the heart of the problem right now."

Gracine's look softened, as though bad news resided on the tip of her tongue.

"I hate to tell you this, but we probably ain't gonna see your man again. He'll get cozy and soft inside those walls, and he won't want to slum it out here with us common folk."

Jillian said nothing, believing for some reason she would see Metzger again. She didn't possess a crush, or some naïve love for him, but she wanted to reconnect with him at some point. The man appeared torn when forced to choose between his group and entering the military installation without them. If not for the allure of seeing his last, close living relative, Metzger might have turned his back and stuck with them.

Within a few minutes everyone convened beside the van, which Vazquez had already started to ensure it functioned before they transferred all of their belongings. Buster squeezed within their circle, walking from person to person until they each scratched his head or neck. He often sniffed the air for any signs of the undead, and several times over, proved his worth by detecting the foul creatures before any of the living saw or heard them.

"What's the plan?" Luke Johnson asked, standing beside his adopted daughter who became his responsibility early in the apocalypse.

"I need to backtrack to my cabin to see if my boys got there," Sutton said.

"And after that?" Vazquez asked. "The rest of us have people we want to find, too."

His statement rang true for Jillian. Her sister died at the hands of the people who turned the school into a work prison, but the remainder of her family wasn't incredibly far from Naval Station Norfolk. She also knew Vazquez's sister worked in Washington, D.C., but he held out little hope for her survival in his own words.

After seeing what Metzger and several others endured, she wasn't entirely certain she wanted to know the fate of her family. Not knowing left an image of them surviving and enduring in her mind, providing a glimmer of hope. Seeing them as walking corpses, gnashing their teeth while stumbling towards her, might leave her too devastated to carry on with her life.

"I need to know if my family is alive," she spoke her decision before losing the courage to see for herself.

Sutton looked at her with curiosity, possibly not knowing or remembering about her family ties in Virginia.

"We can do both," he said.

"Where is your family?" Gracine asked for the sake of everyone else, so the group could make a collective decision.

"South Hill."

"That's a few days from here if the roads suck," Sutton stated.

"We *just* came from your campsite," Gracine said evenly. "We should give your boys a few more days before we head back there."

Jillian noticed she often talked in such a way to the man who claimed to have saved her from soldiers who were about to accost her. Metzger relayed the story to her in confidence after Sutton told him, but she and Gracine never discussed any details related to the event. Gracine, feisty in her own right, wasn't afraid to speak up to Sutton, or lay down the law when necessary. It seemed as though she gave him chances to do the right thing, and if he didn't, she brought out her claws like a feral cat.

"We can try it," Sutton conceded, "but if the roads are blocked for miles, I'm turning back."

Jillian seriously doubted the smaller highways would prove difficult, and Sutton simply needed to say something to save face. By far the most experienced with firearms and tactical techniques, he knew the group needed him, and when he didn't put his own needs first, Sutton wasn't entirely unpleasant to be around.

Almost directly west of Norfolk, South Hill was a small town of less than five-thousand before the world fell apart. Jillian never cared much for the quaint little village until she left for college. She soon discovered the hustle and bustle of cities was overrated, and while some of her friends loved urban life, she wasn't completely sold.

Everyone appeared ready to leave Norfolk and its bitter aftertaste in their rearview mirrors when a humming, almost buzzing kind of noise pierced the air. At first, Jillian thought some sort of bug might have flown close to her ear, but the sound didn't single out one particular eardrum. The entire group looked to the air at once, curious what creature or device hovered nearby, but Sutton drew a scowl, already suspecting what stalked them.

"Drone," he muttered, making a move toward the box truck.

He returned within a few seconds, carrying a sniper rifle, holding it down along his waistline while he listened for the machine's location. It appeared just above a trailer detached from the semi that once pulled it, already looted with its doors open, like some alien spacecraft studying its human prey. About half the size of a conventional car, the drone wasn't especially good at masking its presence. Equipped with cameras and accessories that let the cameras see in complete darkness and various other scenarios, it needed to travel quickly while carrying bulky equipment. Jillian felt certain it belonged to the military, because no citizen was going to waste time flying a large drone along an otherwise deserted interstate.

"Everyone keep talking like we haven't noticed it," Sutton said just above a whisper, and the group members exchanged uneasy glances as they tried to mouth words they didn't actually speak.

From the corner of his eye, Sutton marked the location and distance of the drone before pulling up the sniper rifle and firing a shot within a five second span. Struck by the precise round, the drone sparked once before whirling out of control in a nosedive toward the pavement. Sutton took a step forward, assured his shot fulfilled his intentions, before turning to the collective.

"You all need to head to South Hill," he stated.

"What about you?" Gracine questioned with suspicion in her voice.

"I'm staying here to deal with these military assholes."

"That's suicide," Luke stated with a hint of a lisp.

Sutton wasn't backing down.

"I just need to slow them down and discourage them."

"We can outrun them," Vazquez said.

"Until they send up another drone, or maybe a plane?" Sutton countered. He turned to Gracine. "Take the box truck, take Buster, and head with them to South Hill. Wait for me a day, maybe two, if you can spare it, and I'll meet you there."

Gracine visibly grew concerned, seeing him willing to sacrifice the most important things in his life to buy the group some time.

"You don't have to do this," she said, touching his cheek.

He didn't turn away, but his gaze didn't soften, either.

"I caused this, so I'm going to fix it."

No one moved, and their eyes looked to one another as though asking what they should do.

"We need to go," Gracine finally said to the group, though she didn't immediately move from Sutton's side, or look anywhere except his direction. "You come back to us, Colby."

"I'm not planning a suicide mission," he assured her.

Jillian observed the two touch hands for the briefest of seconds, wondering if Gracine played off her feelings for the man. Perhaps she harbored gratitude, rather than any form of love, but the two certainly shared *some* kind of bond.

Gracine coaxed Buster into following her, and the dog didn't realize they were leaving his owner behind until he found himself trapped in the cab of the box truck. Jillian jumped into the van, which Vazquez drove as everyone else piled in the back. Left with a sniper rifle, a sidearm, and a survival knife, Sutton had something in store for the National Guard soldiers when they drew closer, and Jillian didn't want to be one of those unsuspecting grunts.

When the van pulled past the box truck, she saw the distressed look on Buster's face as Gracine put the truck into drive and pulled away without his owner. No one liked the idea of leaving Sutton behind, because they'd done well as a group, but the man chose a terrible time to develop a conscience.

Opening her notebook, Jillian made notations about the day's events, questioning what the future held for her group, and for Sutton.

***

Sutton stood and watched the two vehicles leave the area, knowing full well he might not see them again. One, they might leave him behind, particularly if he took too long reaching their destination, or worse, he might not survive the encounter with the National Guard members coming his way.

Clasping the sniper rifle, he searched the area for high ground, finding the woods on either side of the interstate about the same grade, and too far back for him to effectively slow the military vehicles. Less than a hundred yards away, he found a yellow school bus that offered both cover or a higher vantage point if he chose to clamor atop the vehicle. Inside, several preteen zombies clawed at the windows, wanting to chomp into his flesh. Barely visible through windows covered in dried blood, human skin particles, and a variety of fluids, they obviously took notice of Sutton. He couldn't imagine the events that led to a handful of kids on a bus outright dying, or worse, one dying and turning on the terrified living one at a time.

Not left with much time, Sutton forced open the main door on the bus, immediately finding the bus driver still strapped into the driver's seat, trapped for eternity by a seatbelt. A red gouge prominently showed along the man's neck, indicating he was bitten at some point, possibly bleeding out in that very spot. Forced to ignore him momentarily, Sutton waited for each of the smaller zombies to amble toward the front of the bus, making easy prey for him as they lurched forward, receiving a knife to their skulls, one at a time.

Prepared to enter the bus after dispatching four child zombies, Sutton was surprised when another came forward from one of the front seats, toppling down the stairs and landing awkwardly on him. Growling and hissing, the small zombie snapped its teeth at his face while Sutton managed to hold it back by lodging his forearm beneath its neck where it couldn't bite his arm, or his face. During the fall, Sutton lost the knife, which bounced several feet away from him. As he tried keeping the zombie at bay, using his legs to shove his body toward the knife, he heard another sound from beneath a nearby vehicle. Turning his head, he spied a female zombie crawling in his direction, attracted by the noise.

"Shit," he muttered, quickening his pace because he couldn't afford to fire a shot with the military closing in.

Sutton used his free arm to help maneuver his body toward the blade, and the female zombie came within inches of biting one of his fingers as he lifted his hand from the ground. He might have simply thrown the smaller zombie away from him, but now Sutton found himself trapped halfway beneath the bus, not leaving him much room. Still moving, he thrust his forearm upward, knocking the child zombie's skull against the bottom of the bus until blood showed against the undercarriage. He continued shifting his body to the knife, occasionally ramming the small zombie's head upward until it stopped making noise and its eyelids remained fixed halfway down, indicating any rudimentary life left its body.

Still grasping at his feet, the second zombie wanted nothing more than to taste the meaty part of his lower leg. Sutton kicked it in the skull twice, but the ravenous creature kept crawling at him, trying to clasp the blue jeans he wore to establish a solid grip. Feeling relieved the others didn't see him struggle so mightily against one member of the undead, Sutton felt his fingertips graze the knife's blade. Luckily the metal didn't cut him, and as he grabbed the handle, he swung the knife at an awkward sideways angle to avoid striking the bus's metal frame. The blade struck home, leaving him safe from the zombie's attack as it fell limp atop the pavement.

Wriggling his way out from under the bus, Sutton looked around, hearing no danger nearby. The wreckage of the drone lay atop the pavement between a few vehicles, one of its green power lights still blinking intermittently. Its front, where the camera would normally be, faced the ground, so Sutton imagined the military couldn't see video feed of him from their position.

Collecting the sniper rifle from the ground, he entered the bus, using the knife to swiftly stab the bound driver in the side of the skull, silencing him. At this point, Sutton wasn't sure if the lieutenant he confronted earlier went rogue and pursued him individually, or the man somehow convinced some of his men to assist. Suspecting the latter, Sutton didn't imagine the man could track him, deal with the undead, *and* operate a drone simultaneously.

Before taking any action, he needed to lay eyes on his enemy and decide if he could neutralize the threat alone, or if warning the group might save their lives. Knowing that Lieutenant Keppler held a grudge against him, Sutton wanted to own the responsibility and deal with the threat personally. While the others were present when Sutton reclaimed his box truck from the thieving officer and his lackey, they certainly didn't initiate the embarrassment the lieutenant suffered when Sutton bound him and left just outside of his post.

Moving to the back of the bus, Sutton found several youthful bodies on the floor, and in a few of the seats, too badly devoured to reanimate. Turning away from both the ghastly sight and the odors produced within the formerly sealed bus, he poked each of the bodies while covering his nostrils, making certain none of them could ambush him later.

Sutton reached the emergency door at the back, facing the direction he anticipated the military men could be spotted from when they drew closer. Sutton used his shirt sleeve to wipe dirt and blood smudges from the rear window. He stared out the square surface, seeing no movement for a few minutes. Only the sounds of his breathing accompanied him as he wondered if his dog missed him, and how the group might fare without his survival instincts.

Wanting only the responsibility of caring for himself, and his sons, if he found them, Sutton didn't particularly like being saddled with the group. They delayed his search, though they provided extra eyes and ears, which never hurt when the dead were adversaries in great numbers, and the living couldn't always be trusted.

Some of his view was obscured by vehicles, but Sutton knew he'd see movement through the dingy glass. A few minutes later, he heard gunfire in the direction his group had come, and he figured the National Guard people were dealing with some of the undead. He waited a moment longer, seeing a Stryker vehicle make its way around a few stalled cars, likely carrying at least half a dozen soldiers within its armored plating.

Knowing he couldn't kick open the emergency door, because he'd ruin his cover, Sutton decided to exit the bus from the front to find a better vantage point with cover.

He walked to the front of the bus, making a mistake by glancing at the down bus driver once again, because when he turned to exit the main door, Sutton found five guns pointed at him by angry soldiers. Obviously, they'd scouted ahead and seen his position, creating a diversion so he never saw the real threat coming.

"You're coming with us, asshole," one of them said, snatching the sniper rifle from his right hand. "Our lieutenant has plans for you."

Four

Daniel Metzger couldn't believe his eyes when two Buffalo police officers stepped from the patrol car, and immediately put their hands halfway up, indicating they didn't pose a threat, and didn't want trouble. The car's light bar remained flashing, which didn't seem like the best idea since the undead were attracted to virtually anything loud or bright.

Both wore the navy colored uniforms and black tactical boots from their patrol days, including the armored vests worn over their shirts. Each possessed a sidearm, but neither appeared interested in aggression towards the military convoy.

"We aren't looking for trouble," the one from the passenger's seat stated.

His sewn nameplate indicated his last name was Mullins, and he was the thinner of the two. A shaved head and eyeglasses completed his look, and Metzger couldn't help but wonder if the two men were actual cops before the apocalypse or donned the uniforms and stole a squad car after things went bad.

Both men appeared to be in their forties, closing in toward the young retirement age many modern cops utilized before working in the private sector.

"Stay frosty," Nestler ordered his troops, not hiding his distrust for the two men parked before them.

Every gun remained trained on the two men, and every soldier except Nestler looked from side to side, scanning for possible enemies and ambushes.

"We're just curious what brought the military to our town," Mullins said defensively. "We'd pretty much given up hope of anyone coming to help us out."

"This isn't a mercy mission," Nestler stated. "We're here to carry out an op for the federal government."

"There's still a government?" the second officer asked with genuine surprise. "We've had radio silence since the end of the first week."

Metzger noticed the man's name on his uniform, which revealed his surname as Weir. Just a tad husky, the man possessed a beard of reddish-brown, peppered with some gray around his chin. His hair remained close to the scalp, a police flattop of sorts, which raised the question how he kept up grooming habits in the apocalypse.

"We aren't here for you, or anyone else," Nestler reiterated. "You need to clear the area."

Both cops looked to one another, refusing to simply turn and leave before they received some answers or assurances.

"We've been stuck here for a month, waiting for something, someone, to show up and tell us what the fuck we're supposed to do," Weir said firmly. "I sent my family ahead to South Carolina with friends, and I have no idea if they survived."

"Why did you stay?" Metzger asked out of curiosity, receiving a cross look from Nestler, who obviously didn't want to suffer any further delays.

"Duty," Weir answered, "and to help my buddy here figure out what happened to his two children."

"My ex had them when everything went bad, and I couldn't locate them," Mullins added, though his tone indicated the story didn't have a happy ending.

Metzger's brother leaned in close to Nestler so the cops didn't hear his words.

"We might be wiser to keep these two close to us," he suggested. "They might be able to navigate us through this shit quicker, and if they're up to something, we deal with them up close and personal, rather than wonder where they are."

"It's bad enough we have one civilian tagging along," Nestler replied, giving the Navy lieutenant commander a bit of a dig. "You willing to take responsibility for these two?"

"I'll keep an eye on them. We don't need to take everyone inside that building."

"No, but it's your brother's idea, so I'm taking him."

"I heard that," Metzger chimed in. "Can we get this over with and argue about civilian participation later?"

Nestler looked to the lieutenant commander.

"He's not so bad. Get those two disarmed, though."

Next, the Marine addressed his team.

"Bryant, Wheeler, Stanley, look alive. We're accompanying our guide inside the facility. Everyone else stays with the squid and our two city employees."

His 'squid' comment, directed at Metzger's older brother, came from the old days in the military, much like Marines might be referred to as jarheads to instigate a bar fight. Much like his brother, Metzger ignored the barb, ready to head into the warehouse to retrieve some useful items. He turned to the three Marines, figuring they were itching to lead the way, and his intuition proved correct as the three held their rifles in ready positions and marched to the front entrance.

Likely ranking near the end of anyone's priority list of places to loot, the fireworks warehouse didn't appear barricaded or secured beyond regular locks. The Marines assumed either side of the door, putting forth much more effort than Metzger would if he were alone, and Stanley gave the metal door a firm tug. Refusing to give, the door forbade them entry, and the building had no windows visible from the two sides Metzger viewed when the group entered the parking lot. He imagined any rear entryway wouldn't grant them ready access, so he thought of ways to break past the metal door when Stanley dropped his pack to the ground.

Metzger imagined the man pulling out some C4, or another sort of explosive to blow up one side of the entry, just like he saw in the movies, but instead he pulled out a small sledge hammer and a prying tool.

"What did you expect?" Nestler asked when Metzger glanced at him.

"Something cooler than that, I guess."

Nestler grunted, finding a bit of humor in the statement.

Built somewhat like the vehicles the group used to enter the city limits, Stanley required only three strikes of the hammer and four slight maneuverings of the prying tool to get the door open. He worked the tools around the doorknob itself, compromising the frame around the latch until the door swung open.

"We're in," he said as he pocketed the tools and took up his rifle.

Based on personal experience, Metzger knew the building likely held absolutely no undead, or dozens, because someone tried locking them up so the living could remain safe. Being respectful, he let the Marines enter first because they certainly weren't going to let a civilian go before them. Once inside, Nestler pulled out a light stick, snapped it, and shook it until it glowed like an LED flashlight. Certainly not the lower grade light stick kids used for Halloween, it illuminated a large area around the men, revealing a number of shelves with reachable tops, and several that climbed almost to the ceiling.

"What are we looking for?" Nestler asked, deferring to his civilian guide.

"We want something that fires a good distance," Metzger replied. "We want them to chase after it instead of focusing on us."

"Look around, and lock it down, gentlemen," Nestler ordered.

Metzger found a hammer lying on the ground and struck the metal frame of one of the industrial shelves with it several times, drawing almost hostile stares from his companions.

"If they're in here, better to deal with them first," he explained.

None of the Marines argued the point, and after nearly half a minute with no noise from any direction, they resumed their search.

***

"Why are you two still here?" Bryce Metzger asked the two police officers. "And why the hell are you still in uniform?"

"We aren't all the time," Weir explained. "But we're using the department weapons and vehicles, so we figure we might as well represent."

Sidearms from both men were lying on the ground, too far for either of them to reach without being shot by the military men.

"Not much left to protect these days," Bryce noted. "Why stay here? Are your families still around?"

Both remained silent a moment.

"His son and daughter didn't make it," Weir said slowly at last. "We held out hope that his ex got them to a safe spot, but it turned out their community got overrun. I sent my wife and kids ahead to South Carolina with some friends. If they make it, we've got a good spot picked out where we can make a go of it."

Mullins said nothing during the explanation, but his pained expression said what a thousand words could not. Bryce understood leaving loved ones in the hands of trusted people, so saying anything contrary made him a hypocrite.

"We were gathering the last of what we needed before heading south when we saw your vehicles roll into town," Weir explained. "We hoped maybe there was some salvation coming for the survivors after all."

"We're still looking for answers," Bryce said, noticing the nearby Marines weren't exceptionally thrilled that he took time to converse with the two cops.

"Where are you guys from?" Mullins inquired. "I mean, what base?"

"Norfolk," Bryce answered without elaboration.

"I was active four years in the Army," Mullins said as though it might gain him further access to the mission parameters.

Bryce nodded appreciation instead. Before the conversation grew any more personal, he decided to ensure he wasn't talking to imposters.

"Do you two have any credentials on you?" he inquired, drawing quizzical stares.

Both men reached slowly behind their backs, tossing him their wallets, which they still carried for some reason.

"Force of habit," Mullins explained before anyone asked.

Opening them, Metzger found both driver's licenses and formal identification from the Buffalo Police Department for each, which certainly couldn't be forged after the apocalypse without some divine intervention. They each held family photos, and Weir still had money tucked away, as though it might come in handy one day. Not disturbing anything more than necessary, the lieutenant commander finished and tossed their property back to each man.

He took a moment and decided to see what the two officers knew that might aid with the impending trip to the factory.

"Were you two working the day the Hemingway Factory went up?" he asked, drawing questioning stares from the Marines who stood around the Humvee.

He held up a finger, telling them to stay put and keep quiet without even speaking.

"I was," Weir said. "I was working on the other end of town, so when the explosion happened, just about everyone else headed there while I was left to protect the remainder of the city. Turned out that was the luckiest thing that could've happened to me."

"How so?" Bryce asked, noticing even the Marines took interest in what the officer had to say.

"Just about everyone who went there came down with the sickness. Our guys, deputies, firemen, medics, and definitely anyone who was working at that place. We couldn't have known."

Weir shook his head slowly, and Bryce tried to imagine how many colleagues and friends the man lost that day. He recalled the news broadcast on the ship saying something in the following days about particles in the air from the multiple explosions that people inhaled. Scientists believed the substance was actually part of the terrorist attack itself, and not some incidental secondary effect caused by the explosions.

"That day was pure chaos," Weir continued. "The following days were worse, because it was just call after call with these things attacking people. At first, we thought it was some kind of new drug fucking people up, but our rounds weren't dropping them. We discovered headshots took them down half a day before the news confirmed it." He paused. "I could've been bitten half a dozen times that first day before I knew what the fuck was going on."

A moment of awkward silence filled the parking lot with the only sound being the wind coming off nearby Lake Erie.

"I was off that day," Mullins said after a few seconds. "By the time I realized what was going on, my ex-wife had already moved the kids to her parents' house without telling me. Getting around the city was no easy task once people started getting sick after the explosion. People were everywhere in the streets, either looting or running for their lives, and I ended up shooting a few of those things when I got out of my car to look for my kids.

"At first, I thought I'd be in trouble, maybe even lose my job, but as things escalated, I realized there wasn't going to be a normal world anymore. I ended up at Brad's house," Mullins said nodding toward his buddy, "and he was already on the ball, getting his family sheltered in place to ride out the storm."

"It wasn't until a few days passed without any assistance from anyone that I realized we needed to make future plans," Weir added. "I sent my wife and kids ahead with some buddies who owned firearms and told Mike I'd help him find his family before I headed south. I wanted them to come with us if we found them safe."

Bryce knew from their silence that what they found likely gave both men nightmares in their overnights.

"I'm not sure anywhere is safe," he stated, "but being around other people is the important thing. None of us can make it in this world on our own for long."

A question crossed his mind, but a member of the undead drew close to the group, making its presence known with throaty noises. One of the Marines stepped forward to stab it forcefully in the skull with his knife before looking around for additional danger before returning to his post.

"It surely didn't take you a month to do what you needed to do up here," Bryce said, addressing both men. "So why are you still in the area?"

"We ended up helping a few other buddies from work," Weir answered. "Believe me, I'm ready to find my family, but we helped strangers, too. People saw the uniforms and just asked for help."

Bryce might have questioned his own devotion to a job that basically went to the wayside, except he was several states removed from his family on a mission that might cost him his life.

Presumably for no government paycheck.

"You're going to Hemingway, aren't you?" Weir finally asked, his tone indicating travel in the opposite direction might prove wiser.

Bryce didn't immediately reply, evading eye contact instead, which provided the officers with an answer.

"It's nothing but death," Mullins spoke his opinion. "You're going into the epicenter, where there's surely going to be remnants of the chemical agent, but more zombies than you would've seen at Woodstock."

"Zombies went to Woodstock?" Bryce kidded, drawing a thin grin from Mullins.

"You know what I mean. We've survived this past month by staying as far away from that place as possible."

Bryce led the two cops away from the Marines slightly, even though his fellow military men had lost interest in the conversation.

"We're going to find out who caused all of this," he said. "I don't know that it'll do any good, or that we'll even survive this, but we need answers before we piece society back together. We might not be able to save the ones already lost, but we might find a way to make certain anyone bit doesn't die from it."

"We get it," Weir said, "but that doesn't make it a rational idea."

"Look, I'm sorry we aren't here to help with rebuilding things," Bryce said. "The fact is everyone is on their own for a while. I know that isn't reassuring, but getting things up and running will take years, and it'll be a town-by-town endeavor. The government managed to save some of our best minds, so maybe we'll get things right this time instead of catering to the almighty dollar."

"Good luck with *that*," Mullins said with a doubtful edge to his voice.

Bryce saw the same structure in place currently that remained in power when the world fell apart. He wondered if there truly was any escape from a society where people who held power and influence dictated everyday lives. Even though currency had changed, the same people still held all of the items people wanted and *needed* to survive. He couldn't disagree with the two cops, although they were free to be with their families and move forward as they saw fit.

Exhaling heavily through his nose, he decided to weigh his future once he returned to Norfolk. For now, he needed to focus on making it in and out of Buffalo alive.

***

Dan Metzger walked down one of the aisles inside the warehouse, finding the interior much more immense than he imagined. After more than a month of sitting vacant, the building smelled musty, though a heavy scent of gunpowder lingered in the air from all of the fireworks sealed inside.

While larger crates and boxes remained atop the stronger shelving that reached close to the ceiling, a moderate inventory of unopened fireworks remained atop the counters below for perusing by customers. Metzger knelt down beside one of the counters, pulling a small flashlight from his pocket to examine the inventory. Skipping past the traditional noise makers that sat on the ground, he quickly found several gift baskets full of items that fired into the air, producing both loud booms and a brief light show.

"That'll do," he said, scooping up the basket.

"How many do you need?" Nestler asked, as he and the other two Marines stood guard over Metzger while he conducted his search.

"Two more to be safe," Metzger answered. "We're already cramped in the Humvees."

Nestler grunted in agreement, grabbing one of the baskets and handing it to Stanley before scooping up another, which he personally carried outside.

No one bothered to secure the door, though Metzger stopped to close it as best he could. He didn't want to be responsible for zombies randomly walking inside and attacking anyone who chose the building for shelter. He found his brother talking to the two police officers, which surprised him, because he figured everyone would give the outsiders the cold shoulder.

"Everything good?" he asked Bryce when he approached, still carrying the fireworks gift basket.

"For me?" his brother asked, feigning surprise.

"They're more of a party favor," Metzger replied before nodding toward the two police officers. "You guys tagging along?"

"We'll probably let the professionals handle this one," Mullins said cautiously. "We aren't exactly equipped to walk into contaminated areas."

"Are *we*?" Metzger asked his brother.

"Yes. Everything we need is loaded in the Humvees."

"We were grabbing a few things and heading south later today," Mullins said. "Is there anything we can do for you guys before we take off?"

"Just tell me if we're doing the right thing by going through town instead of using the interstate," Bryce requested.

"For sure," Weir said immediately. "You'll see more undead in town, but the streets are basically vacant otherwise."

Nestler walked over to the group, having dropped his basket of fireworks into the first Humvee.

"We don't have time for this," he stated. "Either these fuckers come with, or they don't."

"We don't," Mullins answered for both. "But we wish you luck."

Bryce reached into one of his pockets, plucking out a business card before handing it to Mullins.

"I know it's a longshot, but if your travels take you near the base and you need anything, a fellow New Yorker might be of assistance."

"Thanks," both officers said simultaneously before collecting their guns and walking to the squad car.

"Did you have a reason for doing that?" Metzger asked his brother as they returned to their Humvee.

"I have the same question," Nestler said before Bryce could answer. "Those two could lead us straight into a trap."

"Doubtful," Bryce replied. "They don't want a thing to do with that place."

"And after two minutes of deep conversation you know that for a fact?"

"I'm damn certain they wouldn't attack us by themselves, and they don't have time to gather a small army before we reach the plant," Bryce said, adding some steel to his tone. "They were more than willing to help us before they knew we were heading to ground zero."

"And naturally you laid out our entire plan to complete strangers."

"I did no such thing," Bryce rebuked. "Now we can stand here arguing about this, or we can get down to the business of finding out who murdered most of the world."

Nestler grunted once again, making his way around the Humvee to assume the driver's seat.

"Are you sure those two were for real?" Metzger asked his older brother.

"Yes. And I have little doubt we're about to walk into something far worse than any of us envisioned. Those two would be suicidal for following us anywhere close to that place, and they know it."

As Metzger crammed into the back of the Humvee, between two Marines, his brother assumed the front seat, looking back to him with concern in his eyes. He wondered for the first time if the fireworks might help, or if the group of ten was destined to be afternoon lunch for the ravenous horde awaiting them at the factory.

Five

Sutton received two swift punches to the gut before the soldiers forcefully dragged him away from the bus toward the incoming convoy. Still injured from the skirmish at the abandoned diner just a few days prior, Sutton couldn't put up much of a fight if he wanted to. At the moment he simply needed to buy his group time, and hope to find some means of escape, which looked highly unlikely.

When several vehicles stopped in the middle of the road, audible brake noises filled the air from a few of them. With his arms secured by soldiers on either side, held straight outward, his midsection was left completely exposed for Lieutenant Keppler to saunter up to him before unleashing a swift right fist into his gut.

Reeling, Sutton gasped for air momentarily as Keppler ordered the soldiers to drop him to the ground. They complied, and Sutton hit the concrete hard, still trying to catch his breath while he looked for any opening. His eyes came to rest on Keppler, who knelt down before him, wearing a mixed expression of disappointment and arrogance. He simply shook his head momentarily before speaking.

"You could've simply left," he said, staring at the ground and fidgeting with his hands momentarily. "What you did was unspeakable."

"Taking back my property?" Sutton asked, wondering why Keppler made such a fuss about a box truck full of supplies.

He noticed about twenty pairs of eyes glaring angrily at him, which indicated the lieutenant riled them up with a fictional account of what went down.

"We were just keeping watch over it for you," Keppler outright lied. "But you had to kill Jones when you took it back, and that was your mistake."

"Jones?" Sutton questioned, slowly realizing the name of the man who accompanied the lieutenant and allowed Sutton to sneak up on the pair. "I didn't kill him. I didn't kill anyone."

Ignoring him, Keppler motioned for the soldiers to stand Sutton up, and he launched another fist into his captive's abdomen, flooring him once again. Letting go of the dead weight, the soldiers allowed Sutton to drop once again. Keppler kicked him in the gut three times in a row, and Sutton strategically placed his arms across his body to keep from receiving broken ribs.

"What I ought to do is let every man here take a swing at you," Keppler said, faking fury over the dead soldier only he could have killed. "We have more pressing issues, however, like hunting down your friends."

"No," Sutton said defiantly, lurching forward only to have his arms caught by the soldiers who held him back.

"They're guilty by association," Keppler said with a sneer.

"There's only one guilty party here. What did you do to your man?"

Several sets of eyes looked to Keppler with inquisitive stares, as though they believed the lieutenant capable of excessive violence.

"I made the mistake of bringing only him with me," Keppler replied. "And I wasn't able to stop you from shooting him in cold blood."

"Funny I don't remember that."

"Stand him up!" Keppler shouted, not wishing to give Sutton the opportunity to state his case.

Once Sutton was forced to his feet, and held in check by the two soldiers, Keppler grew theatrical with his next speech, as though inspiring his men before charging into battle.

"The man before you shot and murdered one of your fellow soldiers," he declared. "We've been forsaken by a military that no longer functions and doesn't care about the life of one man. If we want justice for Jones, we need to take it for ourselves."

Sutton squirmed each time Keppler amplified his falsehoods, but he couldn't break free from the soldiers. Even if he did, he couldn't get far before they tackled him or shot him in the back. His body possessed few reserves, and he decided not to use them up before an opportunity to escape or fight back presented itself.

"We could simply shoot him," Keppler pondered aloud. "We could crucify him, but that would make him too much like Jesus. Hell, we could stone him, but that's too close to the stories we used to hear on Sundays, too. What do you boys think?"

A number of suggestions rang through the air, causing Keppler to smirk because he didn't expect such a rousing response. They were sold on his lies, and no matter what Sutton said, his words would ring hollow to their ears. His eyes darted cautiously, looking for weaknesses he might exploit if he needed to break away suddenly. Having delayed putting up much of a fight, he suspected he could assault or snap free from the two hands clasping his arms. Most of the group focused their attention on Keppler, and they stood in a circle that didn't encompass Sutton.

"I've got it," Keppler proclaimed, holding his arms above his head. "Firing squad."

He strolled around the area momentarily, satisfied he'd righted the wrongs of the world.

"It's a two for one," he added airily. "We get revenge on the man who killed one of ours, and we draw the infected to us so we can thin their numbers with some target practice."

Sutton decided he needed to make a move momentarily or feel dozens of bullets piercing his skin and internal organs mere seconds before dying.

"We won't shoot you in the head," Keppler said, addressing Sutton directly. "No, we want you to turn and wander the earth like the piece of shit you are. Eventually, someone will put you down after you've started deteriorating and you've been wandering in search of human victims. That way you'll just be another nameless dead body in the middle of the street who pissed and shit himself and wandered around that way for days on end."

Sutton said nothing, because he needed to study his surroundings and plan for one last escape attempt.

"Tie him up," Keppler said before he found time to make a dash for the nearest opening, and as Sutton tried, they anticipated the move, throwing him to the ground.

Before he knew it, the soldiers used plastic ties to secure his wrists to various vehicle components. Sutton felt his heart begin to race, because the idea of dying suddenly became a reality in his mind. Previously, he envisioned a bite in the arm or the shoulder causing the sickness that would inevitably force him to take his own life. He always wanted to go out on his own terms, and now a lying, murdering lieutenant was about to get exactly what he wanted.

Sutton watched helplessly with secured wrists as Keppler lined up his soldiers in a straight formation to aim their rifles at their intended victim. If ever Sutton would welcome a horde of zombies, this moment was that perfect time, but only a few undead stragglers remained in the distance, slowly ambling toward the noise the military men created.

Most of the soldiers simply carried out their orders, their duty, following instructions given by Keppler, but Sutton noticed a spring in the man's step, as though power and murder provided him a certain fulfillment unattainable through ordinary means. As the last of the men fell in line, and Sutton fought to keep cool and collected, refusing to give Keppler any satisfaction, the lieutenant walked over and leaned in so only Sutton could hear his words.

"I win, asshole," he said just above a whisper.

"You'll get yours," Sutton said confidently, mirroring the tone and volume the lieutenant used. "There'll be piss and shit in your pants, too."

Sutton smirked.

"And that's before you die."

His words irritated Keppler, who desperately wanted the upper hand until the very end.

When the lieutenant turned around, Sutton noticed something in the distance, behind the small convoy, heading straight for the group.

"Prepare to fire," Keppler said as the soldiers raised their rifles.

Sutton didn't dare say anything, because he might provoke Keppler to have his men fire immediately, instead stretching his neck upward in defiance, noticing four vehicles closing on their position. Some of the soldiers turned and took notice, then a few more, finding their National Guard brethren had come looking for them, and located a most disturbing scenario.

Closing his eyes, Sutton wished with all of his might the lieutenant wouldn't fib his way out of the justice potentially coming his way. He couldn't imagine

Keppler received permission to go on a witch hunt for anyone when the National Guard's primary function was to keep Naval Station Norfolk safe from living and undead alike.

Five military vehicles came to a stop just short of the three armored Stryker transports Keppler used for his purposes. A man stepped out with purpose, flanked by four armed soldiers as the rest of the military men and women stepped out of the five vehicles, remaining still, but holding their own firearms. Sutton immediately knew this man ranked higher than Keppler, though he couldn't see the insignias on the officer's collar.

"What have we here?" the officer asked Keppler directly.

"This man shot Jones at our base, Colonel," the lieutenant replied immediately, as though the words justified his actions entirely.

"Is that so?" the colonel asked, raising an eyebrow as he shrewdly glanced in Sutton's direction.

Closing his eyes momentarily, Sutton could only think he was fucked, regardless of what he said or did.

"So, you abandoned your post to be judge, jury, and executioner of this civilian without so much as a trial?" the colonel pressed.

"Sir, the trail would've grown cold."

"Indeed it would," the colonel said, motioning with his head for Keppler to follow him over to Sutton, who remained helplessly strapped to a vehicle on either side of him.

"Colonel," Sutton started to say, but the officer held up a foreboding hand immediately.

"I don't need to hear from you, son," the man said, and Sutton finally saw the man's name on his uniform, which provided a surname of Rawlings.

Likely in his mid-forties like Sutton, his choice of the word 'son' threw the captive man slightly. The words drew a thin grin from Keppler, which disappeared immediately when the colonel snapped his head in the direction of the lieutenant.

"I know exactly what happened at your post, Gabe," he growled, addressing the lieutenant personally. "You tried to steal this man's property, and when you got called on it, you shot your own man in the skull."

"I did no such-" Keppler stammered, trying to defend his honor.

"Stop right there," Rawlings ordered, keeping his voice hushed so even his security detail, some ten paces away, couldn't hear what he said. "I have a witness who came forward and informed me of everything. We even recovered the gun you tossed aside after the deed."

"You're going to believe the word of an enlisted man over me?" Keppler asked, raising his voice enough to draw attention from the others.

"Yes, I am, Gabe."

Now Rawlings turned to Sutton. Keppler began to shrink away, barely able to stand, knowing his position, possibly his life, were now forfeit.

"Sir, I'm so very sorry you went through all of this. As I'm sure you can understand, I don't need the headache of a trial, much less sinking the morale of the people I oversee. Still, Lieutenant Keppler must receive ample punishment for his misconduct."

Pulling a knife from his pocket, Rawlings cut Sutton free from his restraints, immediately returning full blood flow to Sutton's wrists and fingers. Sutton set to working them, trying to get rid of the pins and needles tingling that accompanied the lack of circulation.

"Where are this man's weapons?" Rawlings barked, prompting two of the enlisted men to scurry, grab them, and place them at Sutton's feet.

"Thank you," Sutton said with as much gratitude as he could muster for the inconvenience of nearly losing his life.

"You're welcome," Rawlings replied. "Now I need to ask you a favor."

Sutton stared at him skeptically.

"I want you to take possession of Lieutenant Keppler and do with him as you see fit. The last thing I need is a scandal and more unrest at our base. He's not welcome back at our outfit, and for that matter, you probably shouldn't return after shooting down a drone worth half a million dollars."

Sutton smirked.

"Sorry."

"Don't be sorry. Just help me with my problem."

Sutton reached down, scooping up his weapons, including an M&P .40 he planned to use to keep Keppler at bay.

"Just so I have this straight," Sutton said, "he's mine to do with as I please and I shouldn't get anywhere near your base again?"

"That's the gist."

Sutton offered his hand, and Rawlings shook it. Rawlings handed him several zip ties after snatching them from a nearby soldier, providing Sutton with the means to keep Keppler at least partly subdued. Without another word, the colonel turned, raising his forefinger in the air and spinning it, indicating everyone in his vicinity needed to follow him and not ask one single question.

"Just shoot me now," Keppler said with a scowl when the two men finally locked eyes.

"I'm not going to make it that easy for you."

"I'll *make* you shoot me."

Sutton glanced to see all of the soldiers climbing into their respective vehicles, with only a few bothering to turn for a look at Keppler and his new situation.

"We need a vehicle," Sutton said, aiming the Smith & Wesson at the lieutenant.

"You're really not going to shoot me?" Keppler asked with surprise.

"Time will tell."

For reasons he couldn't explain, Sutton wanted answers from the man, though he'd already termed him a sociopath incapable of caring about others. Anyone who shot his own people certainly couldn't be trusted, so Sutton needed to remain vigilant. He dared not take Keppler to South Hill, meaning he needed to decide the man's fate before they traveled too far west.

Without fanfare, the soldiers departed the area, making little noise as they did so. Sutton glanced their way, and as he returned his gaze to Keppler, he knew the man wanted to make a run for it. He trained the pistol on the disgraced military man, providing a stone-cold stare to keep the man from carrying out his inclination.

Providing no warning, Sutton rammed his forehead into Keppler's, knocking the man back a few steps. Before the lieutenant could recover, Sutton pinned him against a nearby vehicle. The move bought him enough time to wrap a plastic tie around the lieutenant's wrists, subduing him enough that the man would be hard-pressed to attack him or flee.

"That's for kicking me when I was down," Sutton spat. "Try anything and there'll be a lot more where that came from."

Shaking his bloodied forehead, the military man appeared deflated, if not defeated, with his hands bound before him. He simply stood there as Sutton trained the pistol on him with his right hand, slinging the sniper rifle's strap around his shoulder, using his free hand.

"Why did you do all that?" Sutton asked, getting directly to the point as he nudged the officer in the direction of several vehicles that might start.

"You want to hear that I had a bad upbringing, or some sorry shit like that?" Keppler answered with a question. "Truth be told, I was meant to be a leader of men."

Figuring what Sutton wanted, he walked in the direction of an SUV and a smaller car that might prove gas efficient if the engine turned over.

"In my experience, better leaders are the people who don't really want the power."

"Don't be a sucker," Keppler said in a straightforward manner. "People who fall into those positions either can't handle the pressure, or they can't make a decision when the pressure's on."

"They also don't murder their own people. Would you have killed me if the chance presented itself?"

"Of course I would. Still plan to if the opportunity comes along."

"I'll give you points for honesty."

Sutton couldn't picture a future where he cut Keppler loose, but he wasn't willing to simply commit murder. He'd killed people already in the apocalypse, but those situations were self-defense in his eyes. Putting a gun to a defenseless person's head and pulling the trigger wasn't the same thing.

Wanting nothing more than to catch up to his group, hug his dog, and retrieve his box truck that ensured his survival for months, Sutton looked at the SUV first, finding it useless. One peek inside revealed wiring from beneath the dashboard that indicated someone did a messy hotwiring job, or a zombie pawed at the panels until the wires came falling out. Seeing no keys in the ignition, Sutton suspected the worst and moved to the red Chevy Cruze parked several yards away.

Feeling certain he was dreaming, Sutton found the doors unlocked, keys in the ignition, and an interior free of blood and stains. He opened the front passenger side door, turning the key just enough to reveal the electronic dashboard, which crushed his perfect scenario. Abandoned because the vehicle ran out of gas, it presented the best chance of running smoothly based on the nearby selections. Sutton kept a watchful eye on Keppler, and the man seemed to know what he found, and what he required.

"There's a motorcycle on its side over there," the lieutenant said, pointing to a ditch beside the road. "Easy syphoning if you have a hose."

"I don't," Sutton grumbled.

He didn't particularly want to take the time to dig around for something to use as a makeshift hose, and the chances of a garden hose or gas can lying around appeared minimal. Finding a different vehicle sounded like a smarter alternative, but most of the nicer cars and trucks were already taken.

Unable to search the area and keep a steady eye on Keppler, he ushered the military man to the school bus. There, he used a zip tie to secure Keppler to the steering wheel beside the dead driver and closed the door partially as he departed the vehicle.

"Oh, come on!" Keppler protested. "You can't just leave me like this!"

"I'm not going far," Sutton commented without turning around.

Most of the vehicles had been picked over for supplies, including food and everyday items, but Sutton found a shortened utility hose that someone likely discarded after syphoning fuel from one vehicle to another after nearly fifteen minutes of searching. Every so often he looked around, and when he spotted a single straggler zombie or two, he used his knife to stab them in the skull without making a ruckus. He grew thirsty expending so much energy, and no water, or even a warm soda pop, presented itself during his search.

He periodically glanced over to ensure Keppler remained in the bus, attached to the steering wheel, and often his eyes were met with a penetrating glare.

Knowing full well the lieutenant spent every unobserved moment trying to free himself from the bus, Sutton dared not stray too far, or grow careless. He used gas from the motorcycle to add more than a gallon of gas to the Cruze, and he found a Volkswagen Beetle too damaged to run. Before attempting to move it, he verified it took regular gas, rather than diesel, because many German vehicles were manufactured both ways.

After a lengthy struggle pushing the Beetle, and creating a vacuum within the hose, Sutton managed to add several additional gallons to the Cruze, ensuring his trip to South Hill was minutes from its inception. He walked over to the bus, finding Keppler sitting in the bus driver's seat after having tossed the body aside. The angle at which he was bound to the steering wheel didn't allow for him to sit naturally in the seat, so he faced the door instead, his eyes affixed on his captor.

"I'm leaving," Sutton said flatly through the half-open bus door.

"You're leaving me like this?" Keppler questioned as though his personal rights were somehow being violated.

"You've got the means to escape all around you," Sutton replied.

"I know."

Sutton shook his head, confused by the man's motivations and consequences.

"What the fuck is your problem?"

"It's the rest of the world that has the problem," Keppler answered. "You were either built for what's around us, or you weren't."

"You never told me why you killed your own man," Sutton noted while Keppler appeared a bit more revealing than usual.

"He was the means to an end," Keppler responded. "Jones was weak and inferior. I asked him to carry out one simple task and the motherfucker failed. Do you keep the meek and mild in your company?"

Sutton looked to the ground, deflecting the question.

"You may think you're the shepherd looking after his flock, but the world takes those sheep eventually, my friend."

"We *aren't* friends," Sutton said assuredly while shaking his head.

"But we aren't that much different, either."

Sutton saw the man's eyes look beyond him, and as he turned, Sutton noticed a handful of undead drawing dangerously close. He turned, finding Keppler looking at him for an answer, not afraid of the undead, or what the future held. The lieutenant seemed almost insanely fixated on Sutton's next choice, as though the move would tell him everything he ever needed to know about his captor.

He disliked the lieutenant, which forced him to take a long, hard look at himself. Sutton hadn't been kind to other people since the apocalypse. He blamed self-preservation for part of his shortcomings, but he simply hadn't allowed himself to get close to others. His sons might be dead, and the possibility of finding them kept him going. He wasn't corrupt, or on the same level of evil as the sociopathic officer, and he didn't want to lose that much of his humanity.

Taking a deep breath and exhaling, Sutton made a decision that wouldn't haunt him forever.

Pressing the door shut to the bus, Sutton couldn't help himself as he glanced back one last time, finding the lieutenant giving him a knowing smirk that indicated Sutton had been measured by the military man in full. Without saying a word, Keppler called him a fraud, either to himself, or the group he wanted to get back to. Sutton portrayed himself as a capable badass, and though he'd prepared all his life for an event that reshaped the world, not every action he took benefitted only him.

He wanted to flip off the lieutenant, or show some other act of defiance, but instead he pounded the bus with his fist a few times to draw the undead closer and ducked around the side of the large vehicle. Most of the undead noticed Keppler inside the bus and began clawing at the door, which the officer could easily brace with his feet if he stretched his body out far enough. More than likely, however, Keppler would find something nearby to free his hands from the steering wheel and exit out the back of the bus at some point.

Sneaking his way around several vehicles to the Cruze, Sutton slid into the driver's seat, gathered his bearings, and finally took off in a westward direction. He made better time the further he traveled from the military base, paying attention to the green informational signs along the highway. Although he'd traveled extensively through Virginia, he didn't know every town, and he couldn't afford to waste time missing exits and backtracking.

Highway 58 would lead him straight into South Hill, but as he passed Suffolk, the check engine light appeared on the dashboard of the Cruze. Knowing he couldn't do much about checking the engine, much less fixing any issues, Sutton continued down the interstate, occasionally checking the rearview mirror. He almost expected Keppler to catch up with him and mess with his mind again. Part of him wished he'd put a bullet in the lieutenant, but Sutton knew that would make him the same sociopathic person. Although he'd prepared himself long ago to take a human life in certain instances, Sutton didn't want such an act to come easily.

He didn't share the same optimism about the future as some people he'd encountered. Mankind could certainly rebuild, but it wasn't going to happen overnight, and life for any survivors was going to get far worse before it took an upswing.

Almost half an hour west of Suffolk, Sutton had nearly forgotten about the check engine light when the car began to sputter. His eyes immediately went down to the fuel gauge, which indicated the car remained nearly half-full. Any number of problems could have plagued the car as it began to lose speed, dying completely as Sutton guided it to the edge of the state highway.

"No," he muttered, contemplating his next move because no travel options were visible half a mile in either direction.

He gathered what little gear he possessed and began walking down the highway to look for the next available ride. Sutton didn't bother looking under the hood, because he didn't have the means to fix any issues with the car. A lack of tools, antifreeze, and parts left him at a disadvantage, and he didn't know what the last driver did to the car to make it cut out suddenly. For all he knew the gas he added was contaminated and seized the engine.

With a dry throat, Sutton walked half a mile, finding little of interest along the road. He dealt with three separate zombies rather easily, but knew he needed to find water or transportation soon. Passing up several houses because they were distant from the highway, he finally spied a house with some acreage and a pickup truck parked nearby. Not trusting that the residence wasn't occupied, Sutton approached cautiously, having a look at the truck first. Looking as though it would run, the truck presented no visible keys. He looked around, seeing and hearing nothing nearby, so he tried the door, finding it unlocked. The Ford pickup appeared to be over ten years old, meaning it contained several hiding places for keys.

He searched the glovebox, the door slots, and the center console, finding no keys. When he tried both sun visors, nothing dropped down, leaving him empty-handed. Thoughts of trying the old house crossed his mind, at least to get a drink of well water, but a noise reached his ears before he could exit the truck. Voices came from behind the house, and he ducked down to avoid being seen, although a sinking feeling told him the two men he heard were heading straight for the vehicle he unwittingly tried to steal from them.

Several seconds passed, and when he raised his head for a peek, he found four men and their firearms pointed directly at him.

"We're going to ask you one question, and if you answer it right, we might not kill you," the leader of the pack said with a gravelly voice.

Six

When the group entered the streets of Buffalo, Metzger felt certain his fears were unjustified because only a smattering of the undead roamed the streets. No one dared say a word, for fear some jinx would descend a plague of zombies upon them. Passing a handful of older businesses that included machine shops, used car dealerships, and strip malls, they saw a slight increase in the undead population.

Metzger knew they were easily within a few miles of the factory, located about a mile away from the lakefront. He began to think they might slip past a few undead, get into the factory, and carry out their search with minimal contact, but as they drew within a dozen city blocks of the mammoth, vintage building, Metzger felt certain he was late to a local rock concert.

Closer to the Humvees, the undead appeared spread out, but even with the naked eye, Metzger saw them standing wall to wall further ahead. No one said a word within the vehicle, as though even Nestler hadn't expected such a massive gathering of the sole threat to their mission. Gazing out the windshield as though in shock, the second-lieutenant absently licked his bottom lip in thought.

"We can't go through that," Bryce spoke first.

"The hell we can't!" Wheeler said with borderline defiance in his voice.

Metzger knew better.

"If we try plowing through them and their body parts gum up the engine, we'll be trapped with hundreds of those things around us."

"You're the expert," Nestler said, deferring to Metzger. "I'm open to suggestions."

Spending a few seconds looking out each of the windows, Metzger saw open space with fewer buildings to the left. If the undead could be herded in that direction, they might also make their way to the lake and the old industrial zone, which might declutter the area ahead. Off to the right, more buildings stood in defiance of the skyline, which made any attempt to move the zombies that way incredibly difficult.

"We need to lead them to the left," Metzger finally said. "The best strategy is to use one of these vehicles and the fireworks to lead them away from the target."

"That could take hours," Nestler noted. "And we need these vehicles to load any evidence we find. It wouldn't be secure in anything else."

"Can you hotwire a vehicle?" Bryce suggested.

"*I* can't, but we have two mechanics behind us," Nestler said. "I say we get out and secure a vehicle before the infected take notice of us."

Still hundreds of yards away, the undead wouldn't pose a threat for another five to ten minutes. Only a handful had noticed the Humvees and started stumbling in their direction.

Nestler jumped out first, signaling for everyone behind them to join the search for transportation as each of the ten spread out, attempting to locate a useable vehicle. Not nearly as plentiful in the city as they were on interstates or highways, several vehicles lined the streets, and a few appeared to be in top running condition. Bad luck followed the group, because none of the better prospects had keys in the ignition. The Marines began breaking windows to search the vehicles for keys hidden inside, but nothing turned up in the first five attempts.

"Can either of you hotwire one of these cars?" Nestler asked two of the Marines who'd been riding in the second Humvee.

"Possibly, but it takes some time," an enlisted man named Ortega answered.

"Pick one of these and get started," Nestler ordered. "Stay with him and provide cover," he added, nodding toward one of the other Marines. "Everyone else keep searching for a vehicle that's already prepped."

Metzger darted down another street, mindful of which turns he'd already taken. His brother wasn't far behind, and the two found another vehicle that appeared in rough shape and didn't appear to have keys available anyway. Metzger walked to the end of the block, which presented left and right turns, in addition to the possibility of continuing straight. No vehicles were visible ahead, so he looked left, seeing a car a block down the street, and turned right, locking eyes with dozens of the undead. They couldn't have planned to spring a better trap, and as Metzger started to back away, a few took notice, and soon the entire cluster of the undead began stalking him.

"Run!" Metzger yelled to his brother, just above a hushed whisper, and Bryce saw the issue immediately as Metzger ran back to him.

Faced with the decision to lead the undead back to the group and deal with them, or take another direction, the brothers decided to let the zombies follow them back to the Humvees. Finishing off the zombies wouldn't be difficult for a group of ten, but the hundreds, possibly thousands, of undead half a mile down the road would certainly follow the sound of gunfire.

When they arrived, however, the brothers were pleasantly surprised that Ortega had the best car of the bunch up and running.

"We found the keys after all," he announced.

"That's great," Bryce said, "but we have a group of infected about a city block behind us."

Nestler wore an expression of neutrality. He required only a few seconds to make a decision and give the orders.

"Ortega," he said. "You drive and have Fuller shoot of the fireworks as you head back the way we came, towards the water. Take a radio with you."

He looked to everyone else as the undead rounded the corner, spying even more lunchtime possibilities.

"Everyone else, gather into the Humvees. We're going to stage away from this clusterfuck and wait it out."

Now provided with orders, each of the military men and Metzger jumped into their respective vehicles. Less than a minute later, as the Humvees went in the opposite direction of the car, Metzger heard fireworks in the distance, and the few visible undead stared blankly in the direction of the noise, following the clouds that suddenly appeared in the sky. Because of the daylight, the sky was invaded by clouds of either black or yellow smoke that lasted mere seconds instead of intense, bright sparkles.

Fortunately, the effect worked the same on the undead that blindly followed the noise and temporary colorful clouds in the intended direction. Metzger hoped the two Marines in the civilian vehicle remained vigilant and safe because the car provided no true defense, and their firearms couldn't hold off a large group. Most of the zombies that pursued the Metzger brothers broke off and followed the herd behind Ortega and Fuller.

Nearly an hour passed as everyone inside the Humvees grew sweaty, smelly, and impatient. A steady stream of the undead walked passed them without hesitation, simply following the herd for no particularly good reason. Zombies from every walk of life staggered past the Humvees, including factory workers, business people, and first responders that included firefighters, medics, and police officers. Men and women who responded to the explosion that fateful day died from bites, or the residue they inhaled, forever doomed to wander aimlessly wearing their work gear.

The military vehicles parked a safe distance away, and without the engines running, the zombies found no reason to deviate from their current path. No one talked, and fortunately no colds or allergies prompted anyone to sneeze. Metzger wasn't certain the undead would hear anything through the thick armor anyway, but no one felt like testing fate.

Ortega and Fuller hadn't called on the radio, which didn't necessarily mean something terrible occurred. Metzger figured the Marines simply maintained radio silence to keep their fellow soldiers safe. He considered it entirely possible the two men remained far too busy to check in with their assigned leader.

"We should get moving," Nestler said once the number of undead began thinning out.

"Wait," Bryce said firmly, asserting his rank in one of the few situations he deemed necessary to do so.

Metzger, much like the two men crammed in the back with him, regretted the decision not to send one person from their vehicle to the other Humvee when Ortega and Fuller left in the car. As much as he wanted to stretch his legs and breathe open air, he considered the risk of moving too great until more of the undead left the area.

"As miserable as this is, my brother is right," he said. "If we move now, we'll just draw a few hundred back to us."

Nestler groaned, but he didn't argue the point.

A few lingering zombies pawed at the Humvees, but the people inside paid them no mind. Barely any sound penetrated the vehicles, and the group lasted only another fifteen minutes before they were ready to step out and mow down zombies instead of enduring the conditions inside. Now a walking trickle, the undead didn't pose nearly the threat they originally did when the two Marines drew them away.

"Bryant, get in the second Humvee and tell those three we're heading for the target," Nestler ordered one of the two men crowding Metzger in the rear seat.

Opening the door on the passenger side, Bryant closed it quietly before approaching the other vehicle, avoiding the three zombies lingering outside altogether. Seeing his movements, the other Marines opened the door, helping him scramble inside before closing the door behind him. Nestler waited until Bryant was safely tucked away before starting the Humvee and following Bryce's directions.

Few threats remained during the first half of the journey, but as they neared the factory, undead traffic picked up once more. Metzger estimated a few hundred zombies lingered within a block of the factory, and he suspected the Marines wanted some target practice, which wasn't the wisest course of action.

"Let's look for the safest entrance to the building," Nestler said almost to himself since he was doing the driving.

Three stories of window frames were visible across the front and sides of the old building, but only two windows actually remained intact. Dozens of old windows occupied the factory when it functioned, but the explosion blew out the old glass, likely compromising other entrances and much of the equipment inside. Metzger recalled the news reports about workers being killed instantly from the blasts in each factory, and those less fortunate suffered greatly before passing away hours or days later.

None of the doors appeared closed, and several huge cracks showed in various parts of the brick building, making it look as though it barely survived a shelling during wartime. Long since painted beige in color, the bricks now put forth a dingy charcoal tone, covered by soot and elements years before an explosion rocked the interior.

Nestler drove around the entire building, including the loading docks, which appeared intact, but closed off by sealed doors or trailers backed up against their frames. No part of the building could be deemed completely safe, and the areas less inhabited by zombies didn't have open entrances.

"Too bad we couldn't get to the second story," Metzger surmised aloud. "They don't climb very well."

"I didn't see any ladders," Nestler stated. "We need to get our masks on before we exit this vehicle, so I suggest we formulate a plan while we can still understand one another clearly."

"I could climb that semi parked back there," Metzger offered, speaking of the truck still attached to one of the two trailers parked in the loading dock. "Lead them away and I could find the safest way in from the inside."

"Not a good idea," Bryce said immediately. "Our best bet is to find the safest entrance, stay in formation, and mow down any threats before we start searching for evidence."

"Agreed," Nestler said before looking to Metzger. "But I appreciate your spunk."

Metzger wanted to contribute, though he wasn't certain his brother shot down his idea because a formation was truly better, or he simply wanted to avoid harm coming to one of his few remaining blood relatives. He watched as Nestler pulled up to the front of the building where two large bay doors showed signs of damage from within. Perhaps the factory took in raw materials in the back and shipped them out the front once they were completed and loaded, but Metzger questioned exactly where the explosion took place.

"If the back is secure, and these doors are closed, where the hell did the explosion happen?" he asked, instead of dwelling on the question.

"We think a truck was staged inside, waiting for loading or unloading," Nestler answered. "Whoever did this probably had a device onboard that let them know the best time to unload the payload, because none of the devices went off at the same time."

"We find that truck," Bryce said, "and we start figuring out who's behind this."

"Time to gear up, gentlemen," Nestler said, prompting Bryant to reach behind his seat and grab four masks, distributing them accordingly.

Metzger quickly got his mask sealed on his face but struggled to secure the straps on the side that helped maintain its contact with his skin. Bryce started to reach back, but Bryant tugged the straps to a snug fit first, saving Metzger the feeling of inadequacy that younger siblings sometimes experience.

Before securing his own mask, Nestler radioed back to the four men in the other Humvee that they were about to make entry. He reminded them to don masks, grab what supplies and weapons they required, and step out of their vehicle in exactly thirty seconds. Not very patient at all, the undead began circling the vehicles from their various positions around the factory, and Metzger wondered if any amount of time was quick enough for them to exit and make a stand.

His pack was already secured to his back, and his right hand gripped the sidearm he brought from Virginia, so he took a deep breath, closed his eyes a few seconds, and waited for the door to open.

When all four doors opened, the Marines were immediately making efficient headshots against the zombies. Metzger was impressed, though he knew the danger of making so much noise, and he did his part to shoot a few undead squarely in their foreheads when they drew close enough for him to feel confident doing so. All eight men formed a circle of sorts, occasionally bent but not broken by the surrounding debris and everyday objects. No zombie could penetrate their mobile perimeter, and as they drew closer to the front door, Metzger couldn't afford to look, because he needed to shoot occasionally.

He heard Nestler give one of his Marines an order to breach the door, but no show of force proved necessary because the door wasn't secured. Metzger knew daylight could penetrate the broken windows throughout the old building, but he wasn't certain the group would be able to see around every corner inside. He assumed they were attempting to enter a typical employee entrance based on the downed fence surrounding it, meaning they needed to enter single file.

Tucked safely between two of the Marines, Metzger wasn't close to Bryce or Nestler, meaning he needed to wait his turn before entering the building. Once inside, the Marine behind him closed the door, and the group faced a new horror because dozens of the undead lingered inside. Metzger heard a scream to his left as one of the men was surrounded and taken down by four undead. He prayed his brother was safe, and the lighting inside proved difficult because a lot of shadows were occasionally broken up by the streams of light from above.

Fighting to keep from panicking, Metzger heard some of the military men yelling, and it sounded as though they were trying to establish their positions and find areas of safety. Personally, he always preferred making noise and drawing the undead outside before entering a building, but the circumstances in this case appeared dangerous either way.

Pulling his flashlight from his pocket, he was able to navigate to some nearby stairs where he shone its beam downward once he reached a landing above the ground floor. Half a dozen zombies continued to feed on the intestines, arms, and legs of the downed Marine, and fortunately for him, he died almost immediately after the initial or second bite. Looking around, he saw that Bryce and the six remaining Marines had also reached forms of safety, their eyes indicating they hadn't expected such horror when the undead discovered victims.

Knowing the gunfire would attract more of the undead, and resources wouldn't hold out long enough for them to hole up inside the factory, Metzger decided to carefully deal with the situation the best way he knew. Drawing the shorter of his two swords from his pack, he held his light with his right hand and slowly descended the stairs where zombies already attempted to climb up to intercept him.

He promptly sliced through the skulls of the first two, uncertain if dozens, or hundreds remained inside the confines of the dimly-lit factory.

"I'm sorry about your man," Metzger called over to Nestler, his voice muffled by the gas mask, "but we need to deal with this now because more will be heading our way."

Nestler gave a nod before aiming down from the top of the large press he'd scrambled atop for safety from the incoming dead. He was able to shoot them in the skulls like fish in a barrel from his position, because they couldn't grasp the small, sometimes slick, metal components to pull themselves up to him.

Everyone joined in, opening fire on the undead before the collective could surround them and ensure certain doom. The group made good progress, thinning the zombies in their immediate vicinity, but Wheeler failed to notice a zombie already lurking in the shadows along his landing. By the time the others took notice and attempted to yell warnings, the zombie had gotten behind the Marine and chomped into his shoulder blade, causing an agonized scream from the man. It somehow missed the portions of his body armor that covered his shoulder areas, and bit hard enough to pierce his fatigues. Within a few seconds, he drew his knife and thrust it behind him, into the zombie's skull.

Wheeler groaned in pain a few seconds as the reality of what the bite meant entered his mind. Everyone ceased shooting, speaking, and breathing for a few emotional seconds, feeling as though part of them shared his impending doom. Wheeler reached up, clutching the shoulder with a wince and a groan before glancing at the faces around him.

"Flesh wound," he said, trying to lighten the mood, possibly smiling behind the gas mask.

No one else could muster so much as a smirk, knowing their comrade wouldn't be making the return trip with the group. For his part, Metzger felt his heart sink, having experienced the heartache of seeing someone fade away and die before his eyes.

Not wasting any time, Wheeler looked directly to Nestler, removing his mask before speaking.

"Permission to lead these fuckers away from you and take as many of them with me as I can," he stated more than asked.

"Granted," Nestler replied solemnly.

Wheeler started down the stairs from his respective landing, shooting several zombies on the way, and taking a clear path toward the back of the factory, drawing many of the undead away from the others. He occasionally turned to shoot a few more of them, but his ammunition wouldn't hold out forever, and his injury might prevent him from reloading his rifle correctly. Metzger imagined the man would go down swinging, stabbing a few of them in their skulls, serving his country to the last.

"Let's clear this place out," Nestler said, putting forth a stoic front, leading the charge as he jumped down from his perch to shoot a few lingering zombies through their brains.

Everyone else followed suit, but Metzger headed for the front door, deciding to deal with the zombies devouring the downed Marine before they grew bored and looked for a fresh meal. He cut through the skulls of the first two, forced to shoot the other two before he stabbed the cranium of the fallen soldier through the side of his skull. Recent dead maintained solid skulls for a few days, and the side, particularly the temple, provided an easier kill that didn't damage his swords.

Outside the front door, Metzger heard the undead moaning and clawing at the building's exterior. He questioned how the group would survive the day after drawing more undead to their location. Flicking the blood off his sword, Metzger carefully navigated the dark aisles of the factory, catching up to the group who'd banded together to ensure no one else was surprised by the undead.

At this point, everyone held a firearm, and several used their free hands to aim flashlights in various directions. The factory felt like a labyrinth with no end in sight because machines and work stations blocked their view every way they turned. The experience felt akin to haunted houses around Halloween, though Metzger couldn't openly shoot the people who leapt out to scare him back then.

Every so often, the group heard gunfire further into the large building as Wheeler continued to battle the undead. Metzger couldn't imagine the other reconnaissance missions went much more smoothly, and he now questioned the risk of human life to discover who detonated multiple chemical agents across the world. There wasn't a cure for reanimated death, and though they might save a few lives by manufacturing a cure for those bitten by the undead, the military risked good lives simply attempting to reach that point.

"Look for remains of the truck itself," Nestler said. "We can also use shipping invoices from the office, or their computers."

"Computers?" Metzger questioned, staying in formation with the group.

"We can power them up at the base and search through their hard drives," Nestler answered, though sounding a bit annoyed about being asked questions at such a risky moment.

Carefully moving through the ground floor, the group managed to take out most of the zombies in their vicinity. As his eyes adjusted to the low lighting, Metzger began to see details that included char along the walls and the structural beams that supported the upper floors. The damage appeared superficial, as though the explosion itself didn't rip through the factory, incinerating people instantly. By no means an expert in fires or explosives, Metzger wondered if the bomb simply served to release the chemical agent.

Considering he currently wore a mask to protect his lungs from chemicals, he felt reasonably certain he knew the answer.

Within a few minutes, the group made their way to several offices, closing doors behind them, even though the doors didn't necessarily latch correctly. Nestler ordered Stanley to keep an eye on the access points the undead might use to bombard them, and everyone else began looking for useful intelligence.

Metzger rummaged through a nearby desk, finding nothing of use, so he moved to another desk while the others went through filing cabinets and began unhooking computers in case answers didn't come in a form that weighed less. Familiar with waybill papers from his father's work on the railroad, Metzger remembered that other forms of transportation were required to provide paperwork when carrying hazardous materials. Trains, planes, boats, and land vehicles all carried paperwork and warning labels while transporting chemicals, so he looked for a binder that contained information about ordered or received chemical products.

With paperwork scattered everywhere throughout the room, he didn't find any binders hanging along the wall where they might normally be for immediate retrieval. He searched along the floor and furniture, locating a thick, white binder a moment later. Upon inspection, it revealed scheduling and personal day requests, which failed to help at all.

He continued searching, but like everyone else in the group, he didn't turn up anything useful once they ransacked the office. Nestler and one of the other soldiers set the two computers near the door, obviously planning to retrieve them as a last resort once they cleared the remainder of the factory.

"I don't know about any of you, but I don't plan on spending the night here," the second-lieutenant commented as he nodded for Stanley to open the door and take point to their next location.

Spilling into the hallway, the group took turns shooting several zombies in their skulls as they moved forward. Only a few seconds on their way to the next set of offices, they heard an agonized scream further into the factory. Metzger could only assume Wheeler met a horrific end after running out of ammunition, or getting ambushed by another zombie, because no one uttered a single word. They stood perfectly still only a few seconds before collecting themselves, not wanting to share his fate.

Two offices that shared a common divider wall came into view within a minute, and the group cautiously stepped inside, clearing the area with a flashlight before delving into any potential answers. Like everyone, Metzger carried out the same kind of search as before, but this time he found a file organizer hanging on the back of the office door. He scooped out two binders, finding shipping information inside both of them.

"These might help," he said, handing them to Nestler.

"This might be the jackpot," Nestler said as he thumbed through the pages quickly.

A few minutes later, the group set another two computers from the offices in proximity to the door, daring to step outside once again. An incredibly eerie silence filled the factory, and even birds fluttering and cawing along the upper floors could be heard like surround sound in a home theater. Now at the heart of the factory, its absolute center, the group followed the char markings as they grew darker and more intense. Whatever blast initiated the onset of the apocalypse in Buffalo occurred near the loading dock, and as the group passed several machines that blocked their view, they came upon the source directly.

Each of their eyes widened at the sight before them, and for Metzger, the image seared into his mind, due to return in his nightmares, because it reminded him of apocalyptic images he'd seen in movies and magazines over the years.

"Holy fuck," he muttered, ready to examine the wreckage and leave the factory behind forever.

Seven

From the front passenger's seat, Jillian navigated Vazquez through the state highway until they reached the outskirts of South Hill, which caused butterflies to churn in her stomach. She understood the anxiety Metzger talked about when searching for his parents, because not knowing the fate of a loved one left a glimmer of hope inside one's mind.

Not finding them beat finding them already dead.

Highway 58 became Atlantic Street within the town limits, and basically comprised the business district of South Hill. Unlit signs of Cracker Barrel, McDonald's, Best Western, and a dozen or so other businesses lined the road where a few vehicles remained frozen in time. Several undead wandered around the area, but what little tourism South Hill received throughout the year likely dried up when the apocalypse struck. Less than five-thousand residents occupied the entire town, and a majority likely left, or died on their own property.

A large water tower painted a powder blue proclaimed the town's name in large black lettering, looming above the businesses and their signs. Jillian remembered times when returning home for college breaks, or the holidays, meant something special to her. Part of her put off returning home because she needed to find her sister when the maniacs at the converted school abducted her. After that, she wasn't sure her parents could withstand the news of Deena's death if they'd survived the first month of the world's end.

"Where are we heading?" Vazquez asked.

"There," Jillian answered, pointing to State Road 47, which would take the van through the primary residential area of South Hill.

Quaint, familiar houses looked much the same to Jillian as they passed through the neighborhood. Lawns were untended, several driveways displayed red, bloody streaks, and an eerie quiet overtook the area. Strangely, she noticed only one zombie as they passed by residences and a variety of roads, as though the town was evacuated. The occasional reddish stain indicated South Hill wasn't exempt from the violence that swept through the world during the first week of the outbreak.

"It's about half a mile up the road," she informed Vazquez, looking behind her to see most of the group getting some needed rest.

Her folks lived on the fringe of town, just short of being considered rural residents. Their house was addressed off Arrow Wood Lane, a single road slightly northwest of the main town. Not attached to any other streets, except for the highway, it would provide isolation for them during the onset of the apocalypse. Although her father wasn't a prepper by any means, he believed in staying prepared for common issues, such as inclement weather, intruders, or some form of local terrorist attack.

When Vazquez passed the last true street on the right before Arrow Wood Lane, Jillian began to feel physically ill from anxiety. She didn't want to appear weak in front of her travel companions, but she wasn't certain she wanted to face *any* of the impending events alone. Having Metzger or Sutton around wouldn't change her feelings on the subject, and she wouldn't want them to scout the area for her. She knew she needed to face the familiar homestead alone and see the details for herself. While she didn't consider her own saga particularly important in the history she penned, Jillian wanted the chapter concluded so she could move forward with her life.

Arrow Wood Lane contained nearly a dozen nice houses, and with each passing residence Jillian saw nothing unusual, leaving her with hope that her parents, and some of their neighbors, might have survived. No undead staggered around the yards, the grass actually appeared tidy compared to some areas she'd witnessed, and no evidence of looting or chaos was visible.

"This is so weird," Vazquez commented.

"I know, right?"

"Which house?"

"Second to the last on the right side," Jillian answered.

A two-story house painted a beige bordering on yellow, the house and its garage of the same color appeared undisturbed. Her father hired a company that painted the exterior with some sort of resin and ceramic mix so he wouldn't have to paint for at least a few decades. He preferred doing most things himself, so Jillian was surprised to hear he used any contractors.

When the van pulled into the driveway, no one came rushing through the front door to meet them, and no curtains floated or whisked from the living room to indicate anyone even peeked outside. A maroon, four-door car she didn't recognize was parked at a strange angle in the yard, rather than the driveway, indicating someone either didn't care how it was parked, or hurried to get out of it.

"Let me check it out," Jillian insisted, opening her door as the others began to stir in the seats behind her.

Vazquez nodded affirmatively, though he reached for a pistol tucked to the side of his seat, prepared for the worst. Gracine pulled up with the box truck, parking at the end of the driveway.

When she opened the door, Jillian felt a cool breeze as clouds grew darker overhead. A storm approached from the west, and she wanted to step inside before any heavy rain pelted the town, bringing its darkening effects with it. Exploring any building was challenging, but the inability to see clearly around corners, and behind doors, sometimes proved lethal to those unprepared.

Jillian approached the front door, trying to look through the windows, but with curtains or blinds drawn behind the glass everywhere, she couldn't see inside. Opening the storm door, she tried the front doorknob, finding it unlocked, much to her surprise. Not considering the sign a good omen, she slowly stepped inside, rapping her knuckles against the door frame several times to either draw any undead, or let her parents know someone was visiting.

She refused to fool herself into thinking they couldn't be dead, though she wasn't mentally prepared to see them as walking corpses.

"Hello?" she called out. "Mom? Dad?"

Her heart immediately sank because she wanted to hear *something*, even if it wasn't the positive response she'd dreamed about the past month.

As she began walking through the house, she heard the van doors close outside as her companions stretched their legs and kept lookout for trouble. Everything appeared in order, as though she were returning home from college for a weekend and her folks expected her. Jillian saw nothing out of place in the living room or the adjoining kitchen, so she made her way to the two guest bedrooms where she and her sister slept when they returned home, finding them much the same after opening the doors.

Saving the bedroom where her parents slept for last, Jillian felt a sense of dread as she reached for the doorknob.

"Everything okay?" Vazquez asked from behind, startling her enough that she jumped a few inches off the floor. "Sorry," he immediately apologized.

"I don't think it's going to be," she replied, turning the doorknob to confirm her worst fears. "Oh, God," she said, turning away from the room as Vazquez gave her a hug, shielding her from the single corpse lying atop the king-size bed.

Jillian didn't want to know the details, at least not yet. The image of a bed made up as well as any hotel chain left beds for guests and a body atop the sleeping surface etched its way into her mind. A massive blood stain covered the wall behind the bed, and a gun remained loosely clasped by the person's right hand, near the head, indicating the deceased pulled the trigger to end her life.

"I think that's my mother," Jillian said softly to Vazquez.

"Let me," he said, softly gripping her arms before stepping into the room to look for clues about the person's identity or why she claimed her own life.

Able to look into the room only while she focused on Vazquez's movements, she saw him look at the body a few seconds before turning to find something on the dresser. Jillian took in a few deep breaths, trying to remain calm, even as she felt numbness and shock begin to cloud her mind.

He scooped up a sheet of paper and brought it out with him, shutting the door behind him as Jillian moved aside. Vazquez slowly handed the paper to her, and her eyes immediately went to the bottom, causing her to see that her mother indeed took her own life. A lengthy letter likely gave an explanation, but Jillian wasn't certain she wanted to process another death in her life quite yet.

"Would you like me to read it?" Vazquez volunteered.

"No, thank you," Jillian said as she made her way to the couch, slumping heavily into it as her mind felt foggy and numb, despite her best efforts to prepare herself for the inevitable tragic scenario.

"I'll be outside with the others," Vazquez said slowly, turning twice to ensure she was okay as he made his way to the front door.

Jillian said nothing to him, and for the next few minutes she avoided looking at the letter's contents, afraid even more bad news awaited her.

Finally, curiosity got the best of her when she questioned where her father, a man that other men looked up to, ended up in this mostly picturesque setting. She wiped a tear away from one eye and looked down to the letter, prepared to find out.

> *To My Dearest Daughters,*
>
> *I'm so sorry all of this happened to you, and I hope this letter finds you in good health. I'm afraid I have some bad news regarding this past month, but it shouldn't end here for you as it has for us.*
>
> *We held our own for several weeks, staying close to home and getting supplies from around town. Most of our neighbors didn't make it, so we took it upon ourselves to grant their wishes and put them down when they grew sick. It wasn't easy for either of us, losing our friends and neighbors, worrying about you girls, so we busied ourselves around the street, and later the town. Your father went to the local store and gathered what supplies he could bring back on a daily basis, clearing any dead he encountered each morning.*
>
> *It kept us going while we prayed and waited for you girls to come home safe. The phones and radios went down so quickly, we lost touch with the outside world.*
>
> *About three weeks in, your father went into town and didn't come back by lunch. He always returned by early afternoon, and I grew worried. Stupid me, I took one of the neighbor cars, which were readily available by this time, and drove into town. I brought a gun with me, thinking it was enough to defend myself, but I wasn't prepared for the things your father saw. He never told me details, and it wasn't in my nature to ask, so I was ill-prepared for what awaited me in town.*

*I looked for your father, and never found him, but I did en-
counter some of the dead. There were several of them, and instead
of running, I wanted to do right by people I knew. My aim never
was very good, especially under pressure. One of them got me and
bit my arm, and after watching the news at the beginning of all
this, I understood what that meant. I made it home that night,
but your father never did, and by the next morning I was running
a fever while my body felt like it was being covered in ice and hot
pokers at the same time. There was no chance I'd ever let either of
you girls find me like that or put you at risk by turning into one of
those things, so I took the only obvious course of action.*

*Just know that I love you always, and I hope to see you again
one day.*

*Love,
Mom*

"Damn it, Mom," Jillian muttered after finishing the letter.

She didn't begrudge her mother for taking her own life after becoming infected, but rather for going into town needlessly. If her father could have made it
home any humanly way possible, he certainly would have, so rushing into town
wasn't a reasonable move. Jillian felt robbed of finding at least one of her parents
alive, even though she knew from the onset what a longshot she faced by returning home.

Her parents attended church, fully believing in the teachings and sermons
each Sunday. Jillian found herself agnostic, wanting to believe, but finding little
to cling to both in life and evidence of an afterlife. She carefully placed the letter
on the coffee table in the living room where she sat, thinking it was the last link
to her parents, because her sister would never lay eyes on it.

No longer did she want to stay in the house, in part because of her mother's
body, but also because reminders of her former life surrounded her like ghosts,
threatening to haunt her memories forever. Her father's work boots, her mother's
half-knitted afghan, and even the paintings on the walls served only to remind
her of happier days that she'd never experience again. For a fleeting moment she

considered going into the bedroom and using the same firearm her mother used to end her life for a duplicate purpose. Jillian cupped her face in her hands, knowing she didn't want her death to burden her companions, but not knowing how to continue forward.

"You okay?" Gracine asked, stepping through the front door, standing there momentarily as though unsure of what to say or do. "Of course you're not."

Sitting beside Jillian, Gracine placed a comforting arm around her shoulder, pulling her into a side hug. Jillian wanted to cry, scream, or throw items across the room, but she felt trapped inside her own body as a spectator. Violently dismantling the home her parents created wasn't going to bring them back, and Jillian doubted she'd feel better afterwards.

"We need to find somewhere else to stay," Jillian said after a few seconds.

"Naturally," Gracine replied sympathetically.

"But first," Jillian added, feeling her resolve return, "we need to pack up every canned good and weapon we can from this house."

"We've got a day or two before Colby catches up," Gracine noted. "We have plenty of time."

"I know. But I don't plan on coming back here."

"We can handle this," Gracine said as Jillian stood. "Why don't you take a few minutes to gather yourself?"

Jillian wasn't exactly sure what she meant by the last statement, but Jillian doubted Gracine spoke the words with any kind of ill intent. She walked out of the house, noticing how everyone watched her cross the threshold before deflecting their eyes to the ground. No one knew how to handle grieving friends and family, even in the apocalypse. Only Buster approached her, and she scratched him on the head briefly, understanding what Sutton's pet was enduring. He wore a sad expression, and his body language indicated he didn't like being separated from his master, but he didn't run off blindly to find Sutton, either.

Based on the glimpse of her mother's corpse, and the information provided in the note, Jillian guessed her mother died the previous week. If her father survived the trip into town that fateful day and returned home, he most assuredly would have buried his wife and carried on, hoping to see his daughters again.

He raised both of them to handle themselves, learning how to fish, shoot firearms, and throw a ball before sending them off to college. From her mother,

Jillian learned how to cook, sew, and use various devices around the house. It wasn't until she spent a few weeks at college that Jillian realized her parents lived in a rather traditional marriage considered outdated by many. By no means did her mother consider herself inferior, or lost in a man's world, but she enjoyed keeping house and raising daughters.

A feeling of unfinished business nagged at Jillian, knowing her sister and her mother couldn't complete the task of keeping her father from wandering the paved streets of South Hill as a zombie. The group had enough to keep them busy for a while, and she didn't want them accompanying her on this particular quest. Jillian needed to know definitively what happened, so she walked to the front door, beating everyone else inside before drawing Gracine's attention in the living room.

"What is it, girl?" Gracine asked, turning from the pantry where she'd started to look for any dry or canned goods.

"Car keys," Jillian replied, standing at the door, preventing anyone else from stepping past her.

"Keys?" Gracine questioned. "To the van?"

"No. The car out front. Have you seen them?"

Both women conducted a visual search of the area until Gracine located some keys and tossed them to Jillian.

"Thanks."

"Wait. Where are you going?" Gracine asked as Jillian headed for the front door.

"I'll be in town. There's something I need to take care of before we find a place to stay."

"You need help?" Gracine inquired, though her expression indicated she already knew the answer.

"No. Take your time, and look for the maroon car when you come back to town."

Gracine nodded, though her expression failed to mask her concern.

"You be careful. Take some weapons with you."

"Thanks."

Jillian glided past everyone at the door, taking a pistol and a hammer from the van before getting into the car and backing out of the yard. Less than five minutes later she reached the town limits, traveling along the main drag while looking for any undead in front of the stores and restaurants. Her father obviously kept the population in check, because she didn't see any action until she reached the local general store where her father indicated he was heading before he disappeared.

Parking along the outskirts of the parking lot to leave the car visible, Jillian stepped out, immediately approached by three zombies who didn't have her best interests at heart. Tucking the semi-automatic pistol along her back, she walked a fast pace up to the male zombie in the lead, striking him in the side of the head with the clawed portion of the hammer. He fell before she could retract the common tool, nearly taking her shoulder out of socket as she tried wrenching the hammer from its skull. A female zombie that looked almost sun bleached groped at her, but Jillian kicked her away, finally yanking the hammer free with blood and skull fragments falling away from the deadly blow.

Swinging hard, Jillian struck the side of the zombie's head with the blunt end of the hammer, doing enough damage to down the attacker for good. She turned her attention to the last of the trio, seeing a male zombie wearing a green T-shirt with white lettering that read 'Dragons' across the chest. The young man died with a proud display of their high school colors and mascot on his torso. A gaping neck wound indicated how he perished.

Jillian hesitated, realizing she basically *was* this person just a few years prior, before she left for college. Thus far, she hadn't recognized any of the undead, but having to permanently down her own townsfolk felt foreign and unreal to her. She couldn't fathom the emotional pain her father experienced while cleansing the town of people he attended church and school functions with, like they were suddenly vermin threatening to infest his hometown.

Cutting loose with the hammer, Jillian struck his skull with the blunt side of the tool, staggering the young man, but not finishing him. Sticking his arms forward, he went to grab at her, but Jillian sidestepped his advance, striking him in the head once more. This time he fell to the ground and ceased moving, but Jillian hammered down upon his skull once more, and again, and again, until his hair, skull, and brains became one mushy pile of rotting tissue.

"Bastard," she said under her breath, though her issues didn't stem from her fellow South Hill resident.

Looking to the store, Jillian walked toward the front entrance, seeing several of the undead pawing at the glass, wanting their freedom and a chance to gnaw on her flesh. She wondered if her father joined their masses, somehow getting tripped up or overconfident during his cleansing efforts. Someone locked the undead behind the thick doors, without harming them, and Jillian decided she needed to know for certain what happened to her town, her father, and the undead mysteriously locked away.

She pulled the gun from behind her, knowing it served as a last resort if she ran into trouble. Taking a deep breath, Jillian aimed it at the front door, thinking she had enough ammunition to deal with at least a dozen of them after she freed them from their confines. She was about to squeeze the trigger when a footstep sounded behind her.

"Punkin?" a voice asked, calling her by her childhood nickname.

She whirled, instinctively lowering the gun as she heard a familiar voice, finding her last remaining relative standing before her, against all odds.

"Daddy?"

Eight

Metzger circled the lengthy box truck, or what remained of it, along with the military men, finding virtually the entire cargo hold split open with metal curled and clinging to the remains of the frame. He only knew the truck's original length because of the thick undercarriage that remained mostly intact. Behind it, any paint along the walls was replaced with black char, and several bodies that were incinerated beyond the point of reanimating lay still on the ground or slumped against pillars and walls.

The lucky ones, Metzger figured, because they didn't suffer or feel a thing.

Now near the loading dock, the group discovered more undead in the area, and a glimpse to the left revealed several of them knelt down, feasting on a fresh kill. Metzger started forward, feeling incensed toward the mindless creatures, but a hand clasped his arm.

"We got this," Nestler said as he and the remaining Marines trudged down the hall, angrily making short work of every zombie that crossed paths with them.

Using knifes, the Marines didn't draw attention to their actions, swiftly dispatching the undead before the small group knelt beside their fallen comrade, snatching his dog tags before gently inserting a blade into his brain from the side.

Metzger stood beside his brother, surveying the area for danger, surprised the original blast hadn't crumbled walls or brought down the roof. He questioned what horrific odors awaited him if he were daring enough to remove the gas mask. A great deal of heat initially struck the workers and facility that fateful day, but no significant gouges or damage showed in the walls. It confirmed his theory that the explosion was designed to dispense a chemical agent rather than simply murder a few hundred people in its proximity. It continued to spread, possibly in unanticipated ways, reaching most of the population within the first few days of the event.

Taking a look in the truck's cab, Metzger found several sheets of paperwork inside a thin, cardboard folder. With the blast aimed out the rear, much of the cab remained intact, and the papers appeared legible. When Nestler returned, Metzger handed them to the second-lieutenant, who peered inside the cab for his own peace of mind.

"Thanks," Nestler said. "It's time we gather our shit and blow this popsicle stand."

"It's going to be safer out the side or the loading dock," Metzger noted.

"We're in for a fight either way," Nestler replied, not disagreeing with the assessment. "We start with two shooters while everyone else carries the intel, and if things get hairy, we drop the computers and we all open fire."

Metzger didn't want to drop anything if possible. He'd risked life and limb to return to Buffalo, and he certainly didn't want the guilty party escaping justice because they left evidence behind. Following the group, he assisted with picking up the binders while two of the Marines grabbed the computers. Everyone followed Nestler to the front where the second-lieutenant used his flashlight to survey the area, dealing with a few lingering undead before gathering the dog tags from his other fallen colleague. He slid a blade into the base of the dead man's skull to avoid going through the hard bone above, unaware that Metzger had already pierced the brain.

Darting up a nearby landing, Metzger was able to look through an opening where a window once resided. It appeared the zombies that followed the group to the factory drew more undead their way, because a sea of undead surrounded the two Humvees. He hung his head momentarily, trying to deduce a way out of the factory that didn't end with them being downed like gazelles and eaten alive.

"How bad?" Nestler inquired.

"Bad," Metzger replied from above, slowly making his way down the stairs. "They're surrounding our rides."

"We've cleared out the interior, right?" Bryce asked the others. "If the back is halfway clear, I might have an idea."

"And what's that?" Nestler asked, sounding drained almost to the point of defeat.

"We lead them in here."

Everyone's eyes widened, including Metzger's, but he quickly realized what his brother implied with the statement.

"They travel in herds," Metzger said, quickly defending his brother. "We could make noise, leading them in here single file, and slip out the back once we have this place filled to capacity."

"That's assuming the back is safe," Nestler noted.

"If we can't get out the back, we're fucked anyway," Bryce said. "Unless your boys do another sweep with the fireworks, we're on our own."

Metzger knew the undead outside weren't going to move along unless something attracted them. They tended to linger in one spot or move in a pack once something drew their attention. Leading them inside the factory wouldn't be a quick solution, but his instincts told him it was the safe play.

"We can't wait here forever," he stated. "Our choices are lead them in here and make our way around to the Humvees, or we can flee on foot and take our chances that we find a ride somewhere down the road. Carrying the equipment is going to slow us down and tire us out faster, though."

"It'll take forever to get them all in here," Nestler said, his face registering that he hadn't decided which course to follow.

"We don't need them *all* in here. Just enough to safely make our way to the vehicles."

Nestler pointed to Metzger and Bryce.

"Make us an exit in the back and clear out any infected. We'll get the front doors open and lead them back through the factory."

Nestler nodded for the three other Marines to hand over the computers and binders because they needed every ounce of agility possible to escape the horde of undead about to file through the front. Bryce and Metzger managed to carry everything back to the loading dock where they set the items beside an employee entrance door and popped it open just a crack for a look outside.

A handful of undead wandered around the fenced in area, unable to get inside or leave the area due to the mesh wire fencing. It looked similar to a prison yard, except the zombies weren't looking for exercise or friendly conversation.

The brothers looked back to the front, finding no signs of their companions before Metzger looked to his older brother, reaching back for his shorter sword.

"Stay here. I can handle this."

Bryce gave him a strange look in return.

"What?"

"It feels like yesterday that I was protecting you from bullies and the neighbor kids."

Metzger smirked.

"I never needed protecting. Keep that door open."

Stepping outside, Metzger immediately drew the attention of the nearby undead, waiting until they drew closer to cut through their skulls with practiced precision. He remained aggressive, attacking them before they could form any kind of perimeter around him. After a few minutes he heard yelling from inside, followed by banging sounds, and he knew the military men had begun drawing the undead through the front door.

He dared look around the closest side of the building, finding a few undead walking aimlessly or standing around. Not ready to make a move just yet, Metzger didn't want to lure them his way and risk drawing more from the front when they needed to be filing in through certain doors. Returning to the employee entrance, Metzger found his brother keeping vigil over the Marines who made their way toward the back as the men continued to make noise.

"Will this work?" Bryce asked while scooping up a few of the binders from the concrete floor.

"It should," Metzger answered quietly, "unless there are more than we figured, or they get distracted by something else."

Despite the losses suffered thus far, Metzger felt reasonably certain the remainder of the group would escape with their lives and the necessary evidence. He didn't know what the future held, but he wanted to feel safe again, either with a group of people, or at the base.

"The guy who killed Mom and Dad," Bryce said while they waited for the Marines to slowly make their way back to them. "Do you think he escaped that airport?"

Metzger hesitated, suspecting he knew where his brother's line of conversation might be heading.

"It's a distinct possibility," Metzger answered evenly nonetheless.

"Where would he go?"

Metzger provided his brother with a perplexed look.

"How the fuck would I know where a deranged psychopath would go after being booted from his stronghold?"

"Do you really think someone like that who fortifies a schoolyard, kidnaps people, and murders them if they don't comply is about to let that place go?"

Metzger hesitated, having avoided thinking about the school since leaving it behind.

"And you don't think there's any way he doesn't still have friends out there?" Bryce pressed, drawing within a few inches of his brother's face. The binders Bryce held dropped to the ground. "You don't think he wants that school back at any cost?"

Panic alarms filled Metzger's mind because he always assumed the school would be safe once Molly and her defenders took it from Xavier and his Wardens. It crossed his mind that Bryce wanted him to lead the way to the school so they could search for Xavier along the way. Metzger hadn't exactly made peace with how his parents were brutally murdered by the man, but he wasn't looking to start any wars.

"Damn it, Bryce," he said sternly, "we can't go rogue on this. You've got a wife and kid at the base."

"They're safe," Bryce noted.

"Even so, we can't go on some witch hunt. What are we going to do? Track his cell phone? See where his credit cards were used? Unless he goes straight back to that school, we could be years trying to find him. If he's *even* alive."

"He's alive," Bryce said assuredly. "Assholes like that always find a way to survive the things that claim the best of us."

"This is hardly the time to plan your defection," Metzger said. "You'd make us fugitives, and outcast your kin from the base."

Bryce barely skipped a beat before his next suggestion.

"What if I got taken down by a herd of infected and you couldn't save me?"

Taking a deep breath, Metzger couldn't believe what his brother proposed.

"You're all about God and country until this very moment?"

"You don't want to get back at the son-of-a-bitch who murdered our parents?"

"Of course I want to, Bryce. I shot the man for Christ's sake. He's in no condition to overtake anything at the moment."

"What better time to track him down?"

By now the Marines neared the halfway mark across the factory, and the sounds of dozens of undead filled the air with hisses and unearthly growls. Metzger required more time to talk his brother down from this figurative ledge that helped no one in the long term.

"If you're saying this shit to impress me, it's not necessary."

"When am I ever going to have a realistic shot at finding this guy again?"

"You haven't found him *now*, Bryce. This is a needle in a haystack! You're talking about betraying your country and risking your own family for petty revenge that isn't going to bring Mom and Dad back."

Bryce looked at his brother as though he'd been caught off-guard and stabbed in the guts.

"You're telling me you don't want a piece of this guy?"

"I'm telling you the risk far exceeds the reward, big brother. I know you're probably never going to receive a paycheck again, but free room and board with three square meals for us doesn't sound too bad."

"We could miss the plane, Dan. We'd grab one of those planes at the hangar later and get back to the base."

Metzger couldn't believe how stubborn his brother suddenly became over the issue of Xavier and the school.

"I'm no pilot," Metzger insisted. "You're no pilot. We're getting this gear back to your plane, we're heading back to Virginia, and you'll enlist in whatever new mission they have waiting for you. If you're going to insist on going rogue, at least leave me with Izzy and Nate so I can watch over them."

"We aren't going to get any closer than this," Bryce said with his final attempt to sway his brother.

"No," Metzger insisted as the sounds of Marines and the undead grew much closer.

Part of him wondered if Bryce suddenly wanted to shirk responsibilities altogether, but his brother constantly remained in control of his emotions. Intelligent, driven, and dedicated, Bryce aspired to reach goals and move on to the next challenge. Tracking down and murdering a man who might not even be alive felt like an unnecessary risk to Metzger, and he knew his brother felt the same deep down.

"There's going to come a day when we get a chance to come back here," Metzger said. "I'm sure of that in my heart. We can find this guy when there's less to lose on our end."

Bryce said nothing, which worried Metzger all the more. He saw the wheels churning within his brother's mind, causing him to wonder if Bryce might break away from the group at some point. His brother didn't know the location of the school, meaning he needed Metzger's assistance to save valuable time. A few tense seconds passed while Bryce looked down at the ground, contemplating his immediate or distant future. Danger drew closer as footsteps joined the myriad of noises reaching Metzger's ears.

He reached down to grab one of the computers, and Bryce joined him, scooping up the binders as the Marines joined them. Slowed by the machinery within the factory, the undead made their way around the metal presses and storage cages, less than fifty paces from the group who'd risked their lives on a gamble they could reach the Humvees before the zombies intercepted them.

"We've got this," Nestler said, having one of the Marines relieve Metzger of any computer hauling duties. "Can you use that sword and clear us a path to the front?"

Treating Metzger as an equal, Nestler said the words without hesitation or worry. Now it was Metzger who harbored concerns about his brother that caused him to balk a few seconds. He eventually gave a nod, knowing he couldn't communicate with Bryce until the entire group was safe.

He stepped outside, leading the charge as everyone else carried items behind him. He heard the employee entrance door close behind him, trapping the zombies inside and leaving the armed men alternative hiding or escape routes if they got outnumbered around the front side. One of the Marines took his side, assisting with the growing number of undead by stabbing them with a large knife. The duo made good headway until they reached the front where a few dozen undead remained lingering near the front of the building.

Nestler gave the order for one of the other Marines to seal the front entrances while everyone set down their computers and binders to assist with clearing the threat. The doors were barely closed before shots rang out, though Metzger continued cutting down the undead with his sword. He'd run dangerously close to being out of ammunition during his solo travels and hated using a firearm unless absolutely necessary for that reason.

"We need to look for Ortega and Fuller," Nestler said once he jumped into the driver's seat of the first Humvee.

Once safely seated inside, Nestler pulled his gas mask off, and the others quickly followed suit. They found their faces drenched with sweat from the rubber seal and the lack of airflow.

He didn't address Bryce or Metzger specifically, but both of them knew where to look unless the duo deviated incredibly far from Buffalo's streets that led toward the lake. Metzger waited a few seconds to see if Bryce would take the initiative and give directions, but his brother appeared to be contemplating something else.

"We need to stay to the left to avoid the undead seeing us," Metzger said, pointing to streets somewhat removed from the lake area.

"Ortega, Fuller, we're leaving the factory," Nestler said over his radio. "What's your twenty?"

Nestler used the 10-20 code, often used by first responders and military to ask their current location. Metzger had watched enough cop procedurals to understand that much of their lingo.

Several seconds passed with no response. Nestler repeated his message, continuing to drive parallel to where the two Marines should have led the danger.

"You can circle around up here without us being completely visible," Bryce said, finally contributing to the discussion.

Metzger looked to his brother, but Bryce wouldn't even acknowledge him, as though ashamed of his earlier thoughts, or genuinely pissed off at his brother for not entertaining them.

He fully understood his brother's anger, having gone through a similar phase once he learned about his parents, but in the middle of an important mission where trained fighters had already died was not the time to ponder revenge.

Nestler radioed the other Humvee, ordering the driver to stay back as he slowly pressed forward, looking for signs of the car the two Marines commandeered to carry out their mission. Instead, he found a wall of undead between their location and the waterfront. Some of the undead took notice of their vehicle, either hearing the noise of the engine, or simply turning from boredom and spying the Humvee.

"If we ram through them, we risk their body parts getting into the engine compartment," Metzger stated, having experienced such vehicle failure during the journey to Buffalo. "We might be able to get around the thinner population over there."

He pointed to the left where fewer undead stood, feeling a bit concerned that the herd wasn't moving in formation.

Nestler drove toward the lake, striking a few zombies along the way. Metzger could tell the man wasn't optimistic, but Marines weren't the type of people who left their own behind. Two more attempts to reach the men on the radio went unanswered, which only caused Nestler to push down on the gas pedal. More undead went flying to the side, and Metzger genuinely worried if the armored vehicle could withstand blood and intestines wrapping around its motorized parts much longer.

Because the path to the lake consisted of city streets, their route began to narrow as more undead occupied the pavement closer to the water. Nestler attempted to push toward the front of the pack to see if he could locate the car. A particular group of zombies could be seen surrounding an object ahead of them in an intersection, and as Metzger craned his neck he saw the car the Marines took with blood stains on the driver's side door when zombies moved out of the way.

"Shit," he muttered, echoing the same word Nestler spoke.

Nestler turned left, prepared to leave the hopeless situation behind, but as he made the next left turn, he spotted something ahead that drew his attention.

"No way," he muttered, causing the brothers to look upward where the trio found the two Marines waving them down from a low rooftop.

Despite the building being surrounded by about a dozen undead, Metzger felt a sense of hope in the situation until he saw Fuller clasping his right arm. Nestler noticed the injury as well, but still pulled up to the building as more undead clamored in their direction. He pointed to his radio, showing it to Ortega through the windshield. In response, the man pointed toward the abandoned car, indicating he dropped it somehow between the car and the building.

"We need you up here, Gray," he addressed one of the Marines in the other Humvee over the radio. "We're going to have to extract these two from a rooftop."

Nestler motioned to Ortega that he would have to jump down onto the Humvee's top, which wasn't particularly accommodating with a mounted gun occupying the rear half of the vehicle. Ortega stared only a moment before nodding affirmatively that he understood. Engaging the increasing number of undead meant certain suicide for the group once they ran out of ammunition or grew fatigued from dodging so many of the attackers.

He held up a finger to indicate for the two stranded men to hold on momentarily before driving the Humvee away from the building, leading some of the undead in another direction. One of the Marines from the other vehicle radioed back to indicate they were about a block away. Nestler ordered for them to stage within visual distance of the building and watch what he did before replicating the same rescue attempt.

Metzger figured he knew what the second-lieutenant had in mind, but highly-trained stunt people jumped off buildings in the movies. Any mistake in the jump or the landing would surely result in the two Marines being dragged off the Humvee and devoured within a matter of seconds. He watched with trepidation as Nestler swung the vehicle around for a straight shot at the side of the building, plowing into any undead between them and the objective. When Nestler slammed the Humvee to a stop within inches of the building, he pinned a zombie between the front bumper and the adjoining business, causing the zombie to reach forward at the windshield fiercely, because it couldn't act on its instincts.

Ortega jumped down first, landing hard, but assuming the gunner position before any hands could grab his body parts or bite into his ankles.

"Tell Fuller to wait for the next Humvee!" Nestler yelled back to Ortega, who quickly relayed the message.

Not wasting any time, Nestler pulled away from the building so Gray could attempt the same maneuver. He circled the area, trying to draw undead away from the others, while obviously remaining close enough to act as backup if necessary.

When Gray drew close to the building, Fuller either jumped half a second too early, or didn't center his landing very well, because the side of his body impacted against the driver's side of the Humvee, bouncing him to the ground. Everyone watched in horror as he scurried beneath the vehicle for cover, but several undead had already trained their eyes on the Marine, dropping to their knees to pursue him. Nestler reached for the door handle, ready to step out and defend his fellow Marine.

"Tell him to drive away slowly," Metzger said to Nestler, noticing the imminent danger grasping for Fuller.

"We should-"

"There's no time!" Metzger said firmly. "Dragging him out of there is the only chance he has."

Nestler spoke the order over the radio, and Gray pulled away slowly, hesitating a few times to give Fuller ample opportunity to grab something beneath the Humvee. When he finally did pull away at a steady speed, Fuller couldn't be seen through the swarm of undead, meaning he acted just in time.

Following the other vehicle until they reached an open area free of the undead, Nestler breathed a sigh of relief, though he didn't thank Metzger for the quick thinking. A few minutes later, the group stood outside the vehicles, minus the two members they lost inside the old factory. Only time would tell if their sacrifice proved worthwhile, and Metzger still wasn't certain what the military hoped to accomplish if and when they found the person or group responsible for the deaths of millions.

A few tense seconds passed before the military men, including Bryce, broke out in laughter after surviving such a close call. Metzger couldn't share in their fleeting joy, and thankfully they all recalled the gravity of the situation and returned to their normal emotional states a moment later.

"Are you bit?" Nestler asked Fuller, suddenly turning deathly serious as he stared down the man's wound.

Metzger hadn't noticed blood along the area where Fuller clasped his right arm, and the man didn't waste one second stripping off his gear to show the group his skin was free of bite marks.

"Smashed it trying to climb up that building," Fuller stated firmly. "No, I wasn't bitten."

A few minutes later the eight men divided into the two Humvees, and barely a word was said the entire trip back to the military plane. Metzger sat beside his brother in the rear of the lead vehicle, and Bryce avoided eye contact, much less addressing the talk they had at the factory. Metzger felt certain whatever notion plagued his brother came and went, and any chance of them leaving the group proved virtually impossible as the two Humvees drove straight into the open cargo hatch of the plane when they arrived at the small airport.

Metzger couldn't talk to his brother during the return flight, because their headsets were likely on the same channel as everyone else's. He didn't know what life held going forward, because he wasn't in the military, or a spouse, so he questioned his acceptance level on the base. As he watched the Marines sort the items they found, he hoped it led them to the party responsible for the apocalypse, but didn't expect the search to prove easy. The military devoted a lot of manpower and resources to the investigation, because no longer could they use a few keystrokes to narrow down the suspect pool.

At one point the same soldier came over to them, requesting a blood draw for comparison to the original sample. Metzger and his brother complied, and for his part, Metzger figured the military wanted to study reactions in the blood after the men were exposed to air outside of the safe zone known as Naval Station Norfolk. Metzger noticed particles floating around in the factory's sunbeams, though they looked no different than the dust he saw routinely before the apocalypse.

He wasn't going to live his life in paranoia, but recklessly navigating any of the explosion epicenters wasn't wise, either. As he laid his head back to shut his eyes, Metzger wondered how his friends were faring in a land not too far from where he was heading.

Nine

Sutton quickly sized up the four men taking aim at him, finding two with shaved heads, one with a fohawk haircut cropped close all around, and one with more piercings than he could count. He quickly assumed he'd encountered some kind of modern Nazi group who banded together after the world fell apart.

"We should just shoot him," the one with the piercings said flatly.

"No," the larger of the two men with shaved heads replied, still holding a pistol on Sutton. "He's one of us, or at least he'd better be."

Sutton dared not say a word. He felt certain the men didn't require much of a reason to pull the triggers on their firearms. As though he'd been pulled over by the police, he kept his hands on the steering wheel and tried to avoid provoking his captors.

"What's the greatest race on earth?" the same man asked of Sutton. "And I don't mean racecars or the Tour de France, neither."

"The white man, of course," Sutton answered without hesitation, having contemplated what they would ask him during the past minute.

"Step out slowly," the same man said as none of them removed the barrels of their guns from his general direction.

Sutton complied, and the men quickly retrieved his few belongings from the truck and his clothing.

"Where you headed?" the same man inquired.

"Away from the Navy base," Sutton answered.

"They turn you away?"

"The benevolent government is no longer so kind and giving," Sutton answered, adding a pinch of disgust to his words that didn't ring far from his true thoughts.

"What were you doing with our truck?" the man with the fohawk inquired, drawing a penetrating stare from the leader.

"Didn't know the truck was spoken for," Sutton answered on the verge of sheepishness to let them think he was entirely compliant. "Was just looking for transportation."

For a moment the four men looked to one another without saying a word. Sutton wasn't sure if he would be executed without warning or embraced into their fold. Before the apocalypse, such groups thrived on loyal, capable members, and he didn't suspect much changed after society collapsed.

"You got anyplace to be?"

"Not particularly," Sutton lied, knowing he'd rather reunite with his group, or go search for his sons at his cabin off the lake.

"Any family left to speak of?"

"No."

Sutton wasn't about to give out personal details about his past, or his family, to complete strangers. No longer could people simply locate others via the internet, but he didn't want to place any of his friends or family in danger by mentioning them, or their possible whereabouts.

"Can you handle yourself in a fight?"

Sutton looked at him quizzically before answering, sensing he wasn't being asked a trick question.

"I can shoot, and I can use my fists, if that's what you mean."

Another silent pause gave Sutton reason to worry, because he couldn't get a read on what the men thought of him.

"You're with us," the leader said, handing Sutton his firearms, as though Sutton had no say in the matter. "Try anything before we trust you, and the four of us shoot you dead like a dog. We're just wasting time standing here and debating about what to do."

Sutton remembered the dog he left in the care of others, hoping they remained safe during their journey to South Hill. He wanted to join them, but couldn't afford to make one wrong move in the presence of four men who just put him on notice.

Holstering his sidearm, Sutton waited for direction about what the group planned next. Although they spoke their distrust of him, he *really* wasn't trusting of men who accepted him so easily.

"Let's get our stuff," the leader said. "Hawk, take the new guy with you and grab the boxes from the house."

Despite all of his questions, Sutton remained quiet, simply surveying his surroundings as they walked around the side of the house. A glance indicated the three men behind him were tinkering with the truck, as though it wasn't running properly, or they weren't the proper owners and needed it to start.

"If you're thinking about trying anything, don't," Hawk said as they entered the rear door of the old farmhouse. "They aren't hard to get along with, but I've seen what they do to people who break their trust."

After a small mudroom, the two men entered a kitchen where two boxes sat atop the long kitchen table, stained a dark mahogany. Sutton picked up one of the boxes, noticing something from the corner of one eye. Behind the table, placed side by side, two bodies were almost certainly the house's older occupants based on their attire. The man wore overalls and a flannel shirt that appeared stained in numerous spots, and the woman was dressed in blue jeans and a similar shirt. Sutton suspected the couple died and turned before the four men entered their humble farmhouse, but he wasn't positive.

Hawk followed his gaze, grunted, and offered no explanation, which caused Sutton to further question the company he currently kept.

Both of them loaded the boxes into the back of the truck, and within five minutes the group was on its way out of the driveway and heading in the direction Sutton wanted to travel. He rode in the back with the younger man who helped carry the boxes and appeared to be new to the group as well. Sutton asked no questions, and Hawk offered no elaboration on the group or their intentions.

He didn't know a thing about this group except that he didn't want to be near them any longer than necessary. If an opportunity arose for him to strike out on his own, or make his way to South Hill without being followed, Sutton planned on taking it.

In the meantime, he studied his new colleagues while the wind from the high rate of speed cut through his clothes and chilled him slightly.

*****

Jillian barely spoke a word to her father the first half hour they spent together in the parking lot of the old general store. In part, they felt completely stunned to find one another alive, and the undead refused to let them make up for lost time. Whenever either started to speak, a zombie would come from the rear of the building and head directly for them. Jillian let her father deal with the first two, but when the third straggler emerged, she motioned for him to stay put as she stood and put a blade through its skull.

"You look good," Jillian finally said when they sat atop concrete median in front of the car she drove to the store.

Her father, John Michael Varitek, displayed the beginnings of a beard that likely started the day he discovered his wife's departure from the living world. She saw the hurt in his blue eyes, but also a spark that emanated from the discovery of his youngest daughter being alive. He possessed a full head of hair, often cut short by his local barber when barbers still existed, but his appearance indicated he didn't much care how he looked at the moment.

He sported a gun at his side, tucked safely within a holster. Occasionally, he carried a concealed weapon before the apocalypse, but with the laws of man no longer enforced, Varitek decided to carry in the open.

"I thought you were gone," her father admitted, a tear forming in the corner of his right eye. "Some hooligans delayed me from getting home one day, and your mother got worried about me."

He hesitated, stifling back tears and emotions.

"She never should've come to town. I didn't even know until I got home and found her like that. I left the note for you or Deena, but I just couldn't bear to stay at the house. I planned to bury her, but eventually I lost hope that you girls would come home, so I just left everything inside the house the way it was and didn't go back."

Jillian pulled him into a hug, surprised she needed to support the man who raised her, guided her, and began putting her through college. She understood his loss, because she shared in it, not knowing what her future held with so many familiar people dead and gone.

"I've done the same thing practically every day," Varitek said. "I can't imagine the hell you went through to get here."

"I'm with friends," Jillian confessed. "They're getting supplies, but they'll be here shortly."

She intentionally neglected to mention *where* the group was loading supplies.

"What made you come here?" her father asked.

"If you'd become one of them, I was going to take care of it."

Her father required a moment to register what she meant, and the implications of him turning into a mindless zombie.

"I'm sorry to have put you through any of this," he said.

"It's not your fault, Dad," Jillian replied with an understanding smile. "I'm the one who stayed behind to find Deena."

"Did you have any luck?" her father asked with hope in his eyes that Jillian would crush no matter how she put the ordeal into words.

"She was abducted by a group near Buffalo, Dad. They put people to work at some school, basically turning it into a prison camp. Deena didn't make it."

Her father said nothing as his head drooped and he sobbed openly. Jillian felt the pain of her sister's death all over again, and though she'd put on a brave face for the others, she now wept with her father.

It felt like an eternity before either one spoke again, because they simply shared in their grief.

"Where have you been staying?" Jillian finally asked.

"I've had my pick of houses," her father answered with a chuckle, though his smirk quickly ran away. "I only stayed because of you girls. Cleaning up the town became a job that kept me busy, but now I see strangers walking around. They're usually dead, but sometimes the living pass through, and I never know whether to trust them or not."

Jillian understood such a dilemma. The incident at the school scarred her, and a few close calls on the road with her group informed her that not everyone they met could be trusted. What frightened her most were the people who could put on a front and gain trust before mercilessly stealing or killing.

A member of the undead deviated from the road, crossing the ditch and falling over as its eyes focused on the father and daughter. Jillian had seen it for some time, choosing to avoid approaching it because it would obviously come to them. Standing, she marched over to it before the zombie could regain its footing and thrust her knife into the top of its skull.

"What do you do with the bodies?" she asked her father when she returned.

"You're pretty good at that," he commented before answering. "I take them to the old cemetery on the outskirts of town. Seems fitting, even if I can't bury them."

He nodded toward a late model red Ford pickup across the parking lot.

"I got that from one of the neighbors after I had to take him and his wife to the cemetery one day. Never did figure out how they got sick. One week they're in Tampa on vacation, and the day after they got back they both got real sick."

"Why are there still undead in the store?" Jillian inquired, seeing a few of them still pawing at the front door.

"The door out back came off the hinges. A few things inside make noises that attract them, so they go inside and get trapped like flies on the wrong side of a window."

He suddenly looked a bit more serious before addressing his daughter again.

"Punkin, I know you've got friends with you, and they're welcome to stay a while, but I'm hoping maybe you'll stick around here."

"There's nothing here, Dad," Jillian answered. "Eventually you're going to run out of supplies, then you'll end up like we are, hitting the road and looking for stuff every day."

"I'm too old to be moving from place to place."

"You just turned forty-six," Jillian said, forcing a grin. "You're not too old for anything. And you can't stay here with Mom's ghost forever."

"The road is no life, punkin."

"*Here* is no life, Dad. I didn't come back here to watch you shrivel up and waste away. We're staying until our other friend catches up with us, and when he gets here, I expect you to be packed and ready to go."

"What happened to the little girl I watched drive away for college?"

"She died at that college, Dad."

Jillian hesitated, hearing a vehicle in the distance. Sensing no danger, she returned her attention to her father.

"That girl has seen and done more in the past month than she ever did in her life before that." She looked her father in the eyes. "And it hasn't all been terrible."

Jillian watched as the box truck and the van headed her way, holding up her arms so they could see her more easily from the road. She wasn't sure if her father meeting them would strengthen her case for him traveling with them or annihilate it.

***

Less than an hour into their trip, the truck ran out of gas, stranding Sutton with the four men who took him in, rather than murdering him on the farm. For some reason vehicles seemed cursed for Sutton that day, but the group walked several miles until they came upon a small, isolated house near some untended cornfields. The other four men included Sutton when it came to sweeping through the house for threats. Finding none, they set to searching for food and supplies, and he immediately felt like part of their faction. Some of their beliefs seemed extreme, even to an isolationist like him, so he continued to exercise caution.

Instead of staying inside the house, however, the group decided to use a firepit in the backyard to cook some of the canned goods they found inside. Before Sutton could question why they opted to stay outside as dusk surrounded them, he received an answer that the men wanted to see any threats coming their way. The growing darkness gave the cornfields an ominous appearance, like a thousand undead scarecrows reaching out for unwelcome visitors.

Sutton was informed that everyone in the group would take an overnight watch shift except for him, because he was still on probation in their eyes. The younger man known as Hawk took the first shift, and once everyone was asleep, and Sutton couldn't drift off, he decided to converse quietly with the sentry to avoid waking the others.

"So, what kind of name is Hawk?" he began.

"It's a nickname," the man answered with a bit of a slow drawl. "We don't use real names. They named me after my haircut."

Sutton questioned what nickname they might plant on him in the morning. Part of him wanted to break away from the group, but under the cover of darkness they could still hunt him down, especially without transportation to whisk him away.

"Is this what you guys do?"

"What do you mean?" Hawk asked with a furrowed eyebrow.

"Go from place to place and forage what you can before moving on?"

"What else is there?"

"I guess I'm asking if anyone gets hurt during these supply raids."

Hawk nodded in understanding.

"No one who doesn't deserve it. Usually they're all dead by the time we get somewhere."

"Usually?"

Hawk shrugged.

"I just joined these guys a few days ago. It's just a matter of survival at this point."

Sutton didn't picture the younger man as one to throw up his arm in solidarity with the white power movement. He likely looked close enough to the part that the other three men invited him to join their faction. Of course, he could also be saying just the right things to lure Sutton into admitting compromising information.

"Two months ago, I was carrying two cell phones just to keep up with all of my business contacts," Hawk stated. "One for buyers, one for salesmen. I'm kinda glad the hustle and bustle is behind me."

"What kind of business, if you don't mind me asking?"

"I sold guns," Hawk said with a crooked smile.

"How the hell are you not holed up somewhere defending your stash?"

"I had to trade the guns to get a stash to begin with," Hawk admitted. "Gave most of the food and supplies to my family, and they got overrun within a week by the dead, then the living. I'd gone scouting, and by the time I got back, it was too late. No family, no food, nothing left to call a home."

He hung his head momentarily, shaking it.

"There was a minute there where I thought about putting a gun to my head, but my daddy was a fire and brimstone kinda preacher. I'm not going to take a chance on eternal damnation, and I figure there's a reason the big man above left me here on this wretched planet."

"Did you have kids?" Sutton inquired.

"No. The wife and I were going to try over the winter, but that plan obviously went to shit. You?"

"I had two boys," Sutton decided to confess without providing details. "I don't know where they are, but they know how to survive, so I just keep looking in every town, around every corner."

Sutton put a spin on the truth, leaving out his other traveling companions and Buster, the dog he currently missed dearly. He stared at the fire momentarily, listening to the crackle of the burning logs and sticks, realizing he hadn't camped in several years preceding the apocalypse.

He wondered if his friends in South Hill anxiously awaited him or planned to leave without him. After working so hard to stock the box truck, Sutton worried about someone stealing it, which created the issue between him and Keppler. He didn't imagine Keppler was going to be catching up to him anytime soon, and the officer was incredibly fortunate if he escaped the bus with his life.

"Did you ever catch up with the people who killed your family?" Sutton inquired.

"Yes," Hawk said in a way that indicated he wasn't going to elaborate.

He nodded to the shotgun lying at his feet, implying he dealt the murderers swift justice.

"You should probably get some sleep," Hawk suggested, pulling out a pouch of leaf tobacco, popping a wad between his gums and cheek with practiced ease, leaving a bulge on the right side of his cheek. "This stuff will be gone in a matter of months. It's already tough to find when I raid stores and shops."

"Maybe we'll plant tobacco beside the vegetables someday," Sutton replied.

"Maybe," Hawk said with a smile, holding out the pouch.

Sutton refused politely, having left behind most of his bad habits before the world went crazy. He rested his head against the old pillow the group found inside a closet within the old house. Sutton figured if they planned on killing him in his sleep, there wasn't much he could do about it anyway. They would have been justified for killing him when he tried to take the truck, so he figured their offer was genuine, but wondered if it came with strings attached.

Closing his eyes before rolling to one side, he decided to wait and see what the morning brought his way.

Ten

Jillian couldn't determine why, but her overnight sleep felt like the best she'd experienced in weeks. Perhaps the safety blanket of having her father back in her life left her feeling secure, or maybe exhaustion simply caught up with her, forcing her body to sleep through the night without outside cares and worries.

Introductions between her friends and her father went well, though everyone looked as surprised as she originally felt about her father being alive. He cooked them supper that night, and everyone exchanged stories with him about their journeys and the horrors they saw. Even Samantha, who barely spoke a word around so many adults, appeared brighter and more talkative than usual.

Varitek put them up in the largest area house to keep the group together. A large, two-story building just short of mansion status, the house appeared virtually immaculate and offered enough rooms for them to sleep individually, or in pairs if they chose. Having a bathroom and a kitchen felt completely foreign to Jillian, and she was surprised at the pleasant aroma of breakfast being cooked when she awoke just after dawn.

Stepping outside the back door, she found her father using a large cast iron skillet over a firepit he obviously built that morning. The skillet rested atop a sturdy screen, and the choices of corned beef hash and pork and beans awaited anyone ready to eat. Jillian knew the three staple meals went to the wayside when food selections came from cans or prepackaged food boxes, but she noticed a few eggs within a container beside the fire. No longer did survivors differentiate between breakfast, lunch, and dinner, because cooked food was a delicacy they seldom experienced.

"Where did you find eggs, Dad?" she asked.

"I managed to rescue a few chickens," he answered. "They stay a few houses down from here, tucked in a pen."

"I would've thought some town ordinance would forbid that."

"It did, but I found the chickens in the store and built them a home. It's reasonably safe from the sick ones."

"That's the first time I've heard them called that," Jillian admitted, seeing a member of the undead lying at the edge of the yard with a blood spot in its skull.

"He came visiting this morning," Varitek stated neutrally. "It's getting to the point where I don't recognize them anymore. Some of the town's people left when it started, and the others who stayed didn't make it. I've seen them during my trips to town, and I knew them when I put them down, but the ones who come now are new faces."

"They just walk and walk," Jillian said with a deflated tone. "And they outnumber us so badly, there's no thinning the herd."

"I remember watching the news," her father said, stirring the food inside the skillet. "Our best minds couldn't figure it out, so I wondered what chance did we have?"

"Don't give up just yet, Dad. It sounds like the government is looking into what happened."

Her father didn't look impressed, or convinced.

"Even if they find out who did this, there's no reversing it," he said. "How can we expect to return to any sense of normalcy when we have millions of these things wandering around? Hell, there probably aren't enough bullets to deal with all of them."

"That's what knives are for."

Her father smiled at the comment.

"You've come so far."

"I had a good teacher."

Now Varitek turned a bit more serious.

"Have you given any thought to making a go of it here?"

"I have," Jillian admitted. "I'm not sure how long we can last before we need food and supplies, but I'm not leaving you after everything I've gone through to get here."

"Your friends seem nice," Varitek noted, openly prodding for his daughter's thoughts on her travel companions.

"They've been good to me."

"You mentioned some losses?"

"One of our people was bitten, and he died after our plane crashed in Virginia."

"I still can't believe you got a plane."

"And to think we lucked into finding a pilot," Jillian said with a smile, feeling at ease around her father. "We also lost Dan, but only because he found his family at the Navy base."

"You seem fond of him."

Varitek possessed a knack for noticing details.

"He was one of the good guys," Jillian replied, trying to suppress any outward signs of the kinship she shared with him. "Dan teamed with us to rescue people he barely knew."

"Sounds like he's one of the good guys."

Footsteps interrupted their conversation as Luke stepped out the door, followed by Samantha, who gleefully sniffed the air, drawing the pleasant odor of cooked food into her nostrils. Varitek fixed each of them a plate and added some additional cans of food to the already warm pan. A moment later he handed Jillian a plate with a little bit of everything, including scrambled eggs, before taking a smaller portion for himself.

Everyone ate silently for a few minutes before Luke finished first and addressed his host.

"Thank you so much for putting us up," he said.

"You're quite welcome," Varitek replied. "Any friends of Jillian's are friends of mine."

"What do you say?" Luke coaxed Samantha, who continued to eat at a feverish pace.

"Thank you," she said almost sheepishly at Varitek.

"You're welcome, sweetheart," he replied with a warm smile. "And you're all welcome to stay as long as you want."

Jillian decided to speak up.

"We're waiting a day or two for our last person to make it here."

"Why exactly did he stay behind?" Varitek questioned.

"He angered a military unit, and volunteered to stay behind and deal with them," Luke said before Jillian could provide a less forward answer.

"That doesn't sound like the kind of thing a person walks away from," Varitek said with a concerned expression.

A momentary awkward silence overtook the small group.

"If he's not here by tomorrow we planned on moving on without him," Luke said. "He's been a disruptive force for us the entire time, so maybe it's for the best."

"This true, punkin?" Varitek asked, looking to his daughter.

"Colby isn't so bad. He's good with firearms, and he's prepared. The man simply wanted to look for his sons."

"And make trouble with the National Guard," Luke added.

Jillian looked to Samantha, who didn't need to be present for adult discussions about the people around her. Luke's comments weren't unwarranted, but he didn't need to speak negatively about any group members while the girl was within earshot.

"A few of the National Guard guys rummaged through his truck, presumably to steal items for themselves, and Colby didn't let that happen," Jillian explained for the sake of her father. "He tied them up, but he didn't hurt them, and it wasn't long before we noticed a drone following us from above."

"That's when he finally manned up and did the right thing," Luke said, unable to hide his bitterness.

"If he hasn't made it by now, that doesn't bode well," Varitek noted. "He might have gotten himself into some trouble."

"That man *is* trouble," Luke said.

Jillian didn't want to imagine anything terrible happening to Sutton, but there weren't many realistic reasons why he wouldn't have reached the small town already. Thankful to have her own reunion out of the way, she hoped to see Sutton alive and well soon.

***

When the group stopped in Lawrenceville to pick the small town clean, Sutton questioned whether or not he wanted to attempt a parting with his new companions. His back felt sore from a lack of sleep, combined with a bumpy ride in the back of the pickup truck. After his talk with Hawk, he didn't sleep particularly well because his mind conjured up strange nightmares about the undead, his current company, and even his sons returning to him only to reveal they'd been bitten by the undead.

Downtown Lawrenceville appeared to be constructed entirely of brick, like some kind of large LEGO town. More than likely, some bylaw forced businesses and government buildings to keep the aesthetic much the same regarding local architecture. Some of the brick was traditional red, some rustic, and less of it beige or lighter in color. Highways 58 and 1 shared the same road, running through the small town, indicated by signage down the main drag.

Stopping the truck in the center of town, the leader, whom Sutton came to know as Clean, stepped from the driver's seat to the intersection in which he'd parked. Sutton could only assume the nickname came from the old Mr. Clean commercials since the man kept his head shaved and didn't sport any facial hair. Given a nickname of his own, due to his own facial hair, Sutton became known as Goatee to the group, which suited him fine, because he didn't want to divulge personal information, and the collective didn't ask.

A few zombies staggered around the streets, but none of them close enough to pose a threat against the five men. Sutton stood and stretched momentarily before climbing down from the truck bed. All five men gathered their firearms and surveyed the area until Clean spoke.

"Scruff, take Goatee and check out the buildings that way," Clean said, pointing in the direction of a few government buildings, followed by several businesses beyond those. "We're going to check the square for any stores or stashes."

Sutton felt as though he'd been assigned a babysitter to ensure he didn't run, but he didn't much care. Scruff was the other man with a shaved head, but he kept a five o'clock shadow that appeared too spotty to turn into a presentable beard. In the apocalypse, people weren't incredibly judgmental about how others appeared.

Except for several bodies lying in the streets that hadn't returned to life, and the occasional blood stain atop the sidewalks, the town looked as though it had simply been abandoned. Sutton didn't say a word, following Scruff to their designated area where they easily gained access to the first building that looked like a courthouse to Sutton. A quick look inside revealed that no one hid any secret cache of food or weapons, so the two men moved to the next structure.

Each of the government buildings proved worthless for their purposes, so the two men moved down the street, into the business district.

"You don't say much, do you?" Scruff asked when they approached a hardware store with two zombies clawing at the large front window.

"I don't have much to say."

"Or you have something to hide. You're not some serial killer, are you?"

"No. I had kids."

"Serial killers are often married, leading normal lives, you know."

Scruff turned the knob on the front door as both men reached for their knives.

"I'm aware. You seem highly in tune with how serial killers work."

Each of them took down a zombie as the attackers quickly closed on their location once the men stepped inside. Scruff barely wasted a second looking at the two corpses before banging his hand against some tools lining the wall. The variety of clanging noises failed to draw additional undead, so the two men set to looking for perishable goods.

"I just watched a lot of true crime stuff," Scruff said. "It was always interesting to see what made those guys tick."

"Did you save your violence for ethnic folks?" Sutton asked as he scooped a box of random candy bars into a knapsack he'd brought from the truck.

Most of the snacks were the ones people originally didn't want, left behind, but now anyone coveted compared to other food options.

Scruff shot him a suspicious, mildly angered look.

"I'm beginning to think you're not a believer in what we stand for."

"Simply making conversation," Sutton replied evenly, not afraid of the man if it came to an exchange of blows.

Or gunfire.

"I'm not opposed to reimplementing slavery," Scruff said with a hint of fire in his tone. "It's survival of the fittest and the white man is back on top again."

Sutton didn't immediately respond to the statement. He didn't want to seem too anxious to jump on the bandwagon, but he didn't want to risk appearing completely opposed to the notion he actually considered ridiculous.

"Are you in favor of a class system?" he asked instead.

"I don't know about *that*," Scruff said, searching through several drawers and cabinets for additional food or ammunition. "Most of my life I felt fucked by the system, stuck behind rich folks who hired Mexicans and screwed Americans. But if I were at the top of that system, I might be inclined to see it return."

Sutton didn't see anyone in his current group being near the top echelon of a class system, but he accomplished his goal of getting Scruff off his back about racism and slavery.

Or so he thought.

"You ever punch any niggers or burn some crosses?" Scruff asked in a manner that indicated he considered Sutton a sympathizer rather than a member of the brotherhood.

"I was more covert," Sutton lied. "Slashed tires, painted messages on their garage doors, and shit like that. You're no good to the cause if you get caught and tossed in the clink."

Scruff didn't appear convinced, but his opinion didn't matter when several gunshots rang through the air, indicating trouble down the road.

Both men dashed outside, leaving their loot behind for the moment, finding their comrades dealing with just over a dozen undead closing in on their location. They quickly took their sides, shooting the remaining zombies in their skulls because the noise would already attract more assailants to their location.

"What happened?" Scruff asked once the shooting ended and the corpses of zombies lined the streets.

"Hawk got a little spooked and started shooting," Clean replied, drawing a shake of the head from Hawk, who didn't agree with Clean's version.

"I was surrounded, and couldn't knife them without getting bitten," he said in his defense.

Sutton noticed a nearby open door where someone had likely gone inside and drawn too many of the dead to his location. After experiencing a few close calls in close proximity to the undead, Sutton knew all too well blades weren't always an option. He wasn't sure if the group picked on Hawk because he was new, or because he was the youngest, but he certainly didn't deserve a hard time for defending himself.

"We found some stuff," Scruff reported to Clean, getting them off the subject of gunfire in the streets.

"Us, too," Clean stated. "We'll get what we can here, and move west. There's a little town called South Hill that has a general store. That'll be a treasure trove if the locals didn't get to everything first."

Sutton didn't want his group heading to South Hill where he hoped the others were staying, but he dared not dissuade them. They already harbored suspicions about his loyalties and beliefs. Holding his tongue, he decided to follow the group's lead until that method no longer proved possible.

"Let's finish up here, load the stuff into the truck, and see if we can find a second vehicle," Clean suggested. "With luck, we'll make it to South Hill in plenty of time to set up camp and spend the night."

As Sutton prepared to return to the last building he'd been searching, he noticed Scruff sizing him up as though he might take action at some point. Either way, Sutton knew a conflict was in his future, and he needed to decide his best course of action.

"Let the kid go with Goatee," Scruff said to Clean. "I need to talk to you about something."

Sutton didn't trust the man, but he wanted the opportunity to speak with Hawk a bit more privately, so he welcomed the pairing for the moment. Their fifth group member wandered off to explore a different nearby street, so Sutton walked with Hawk back to the building he'd already gone through once.

"That was weird," Hawk noted as they entered the front door.

"You're telling me," Sutton replied with a sigh. "Your buddy Scruff doesn't trust me very much."

"He doesn't trust anyone, but in particular he doesn't think you share the group's values."

"And you share in their beliefs one-hundred percent?"

Hawk held the door open for Sutton, not answering immediately.

"I firmly believe in doing whatever it takes to survive."

Sutton considered the answer a bit too vague, causing him to wonder if he was being tested by the group. He needed to frame additional questions carefully to avoid raising suspicions and putting his own well-being in jeopardy.

"The less you say around these guys, the better," Hawk stated once they began picking up boxes and packing loose items into whatever containers they could find nearby.

"They seem like bullies," Sutton noted.

Hawk shrugged.

"It's their nature. It's the nature of the world now. Eat or be eaten."

A few minutes later, each of them picked up as many boxes and containers as they could handle. Sutton led the way toward the door when a brief crash, followed by a rattle, reached the ears of both men. It sounded like a dropped metal lid to a frying pan wobbling atop the floor in the storage area above them before it suddenly ceased. Hawk looked to Sutton as though questioning whether or not they wanted to investigate the noise. Sutton didn't particularly care if someone was hiding in the attic above the main floor, figuring such a move indicated they didn't want trouble, but Hawk set his items down.

Knowing the etiquette for exploring a building silently, Sutton didn't say a word as he reached for the semi-automatic pistol at his side. Fortunately, the attic space wasn't reached by some pulldown ladder, or a hole in the ceiling that required a ladder to reach. A door behind the main portion of the store led to a narrow hallway with another door at the end. There, a staircase ascended to a closed door, and presumably the attic. Sutton wasn't certain if he would have gone through the trouble of looking behind every door or not, because the group's time was precious at the moment. They simply wanted enough supplies to carry them through the next few days to a week at most.

Hawk silently led the way because he fit through the narrow doors and hallways better than Sutton. Moving up the stairway silently proved impossible, because their footwear clopped against the uncovered stairs, no matter how silently they attempted to trod. Hawk gave a virtually silent sigh as he reached the door, looking upward as though in prayer because neither of them knew what lie behind the closed door.

For all Sutton knew, the store owner might be huddled against a wall, aiming a shotgun in their direction, waiting for backlight to silhouette them before blowing them away. Hawk pulled out a flashlight, turning it on before reaching for the doorknob and crouching down to make his profile a smaller target.

When the door creaked open, however, they found a black woman huddled in a corner, holding a young black boy in her arms for dear life, as though exiting a sinking ship on a lifeboat and fearing him falling out. Numerous boxes occupied the room, storing various decorations and seasonal items, but they weren't sufficiently large enough to conceal two human beings. Several toys, pots and pans, and dirty plates were visible along the floor, making it readily apparent the woman and child lived in the attic at least part of the time.

Sutton immediately saw that neither of them posed a threat, and his eyes shifted to Hawk, who returned his gaze. Both of them tested one another, and before either made a regrettable move, Sutton tapped Hawk on the shoulder, indicating they needed to back out. In his right hand he held the pistol, prepared to use it on his companion if Hawk proved his beliefs mirrored those of the other three men.

Both the woman and the child shivered in fear for their lives, and Sutton didn't know what brought them to the building, or the town for that matter, but he wasn't about to shoot anyone in cold blood. Several agonizing seconds passed with everyone breathing heavily and no one uttering a word. Finally, Hawk holstered his gun and showed the woman his hands to indicate he meant no harm. Sutton began to holster his firearm, but his eyes didn't leave Hawk for one second in case the man attempted some kind of trickery.

Sutton let Hawk slide past him so he could be a human shield between the younger man and the two terrified people huddled within a storage attic. Both of them navigated the stairs downward, and Sutton wondered if Hawk intended to inform Clean so the men could murder or enslave the duo. He didn't like thinking the world had reverted back a century in one month's time, but he knew people often clung to the past.

As they picked up the boxes near the front door, Sutton was about to speak when Hawk beat him to it.

"I'm no murderer," the younger man confessed. "My way of thinking certainly isn't perfect, but I'm not killing people for the color of their skin. If you're going to say something to Clean, give me a head start, or just shoot me, but I can't be *that* kind of extremist."

"I don't know what you're talking about," Sutton said, pushing the door open. "We're just two guys carrying boxes back to their group who didn't find anything else."

Hawk gave an uneasy smirk, knowing his choice wouldn't have been so easy if one of the other three men had accompanied him inside. As Hawk brushed past him, Sutton worried just as much about where they were heading as he did about the scene upstairs. With so many unknown variables in play, he dared not say a word to Hawk, even if he trusted the man more than the others. Sutton hoped Clean changed his mind about their destination, or the members of Sutton's other group had moved on, but he sensed trouble in his near future.

Eleven

Jillian sat beside the fire her father relit for cooking dinner just outside their chosen residence. None of the group had gone very far all day, and they seemed to be rather cozy staying inside a house that wasn't trashed, having cooked meals prepared for them. Jillian knew the situation might last for her, but her friends would have to move on in the near future.

Vazquez and Gracine joined her outside, sitting on the ground near the fire as Luke kept Samantha occupied inside. Buster walked off to relieve himself in one of the nearby yards before returning to the group and sitting dejectedly between Jillian and Gracine. He missed Sutton, and hadn't eaten much, despite being showered with affection and physical contact from everyone around him.

"We can't wait much longer for Colby," Vazquez said apprehensively. "At some point we have to keep moving, and looking for the rest of our families."

"He should be here by now," Gracine said with a concerned tone. "I'm afraid he did something stupid with those military types and got his ass killed."

"Do we go back and check?" Jillian questioned in general, hoping someone would search for her if she got lost and found trouble.

"Look where?" Vazquez asked, raising his voice slightly. "He's either a corpse with a bullet in his skull, or he's a corpse looking to eat us when we go back there."

Jillian stared into the fire momentarily.

"Maybe he couldn't get a ride. We've gone through stretches where it isn't easy to find a car."

"He knew what he was doing when he stayed behind," Vazquez said, his tone easing a little. "It was a sacrifice on his part for fucking up."

"Those military types were assholes," Gracine commented. "They're supposed to be protecting what's left of our country's infrastructure, *not* pillaging off citizens."

Luke walked outside, and when all eyes fell upon him, he looked taken aback slightly.

"Samantha's asleep," he reported. "A full day of scouring the neighborhood wore her down."

"We were just discussing whether to callously abandon Sutton, or make an effort to locate him," Gracine said.

"Isn't it a little early to decide anything?" Luke said, sitting on a log Jillian's father had placed in the yard for the group to use.

Jillian wondered if Luke worried about losing the group's best protector when push came to shove, because he personally wasn't adept at using firearms and bladed weapons. He worked with weapons sometimes, showing Samantha little tricks he'd learned from his partner, Albert, before the man was bitten. It showed that Luke still wasn't confident about his aim, or his ability to put a knife through undead skulls.

Without electricity, mornings and nighttime were spent near the fire for cooking and warmth, giving the yard a summer camp feel. If not for the weight of their conversation, their gathering might have felt like many a night during her childhood in the town she grew to miss.

"This is pretty much the end of day two, and Colby could've made it on foot unless something happened to him," Vazquez said.

"Do we take this to a vote?" Gracine inquired, attempting to be diplomatic with so many opinions in their group circle.

"Guys, I'm staying with my dad," Jillian revealed. "I just wanted you to know, because I won't be tagging along. He's the last family I have."

"What about you?" Luke asked Gracine.

"I don't really have much family," she answered. "The reason I drove a truck was to get away from my hometown."

"I'm not sure where my sister is," Vazquez said. "She could be anywhere between Washington and the Navy base. And those assholes wouldn't let us through the front door."

"Why didn't you ask them about her?" Jillian inquired.

"She's a civilian, and I don't know if her politician connections would've gotten her safe passage or left her to fend for herself. Maybe it's best I never know."

He spoke the last words rather dejectedly, as though he'd already written her off in his mind.

"I'm not sure three of us can care for a child and a dog," Luke said, realizing the group's current predicament. "Why doesn't your dad want to come with us?"

"His roots are here," Jillian answered. "I thought maybe he'd want to leave after what happened to Mom, but he seems determined to make a go of it here."

"Someone will loot this place," Vazquez said. "Someone always does."

"I'll talk to him," Jillian promised, "but I doubt I can change his mind."

As though summoned, Varitek walked out from the house, and Buster immediately ran to him. Jillian didn't know if the dog thought her father resembled Sutton, or perhaps he found a human to identify with, but Buster stayed by her father's side as he settled in with the rest of the group around the fire.

"All of you discussing how to fix the world out here?" he asked no one in particular.

Everyone chuckled awkwardly a moment.

"Worried about your friend?" Varitek inquired.

"It's a mixed bag," Luke replied.

"It sounds like he helped you out of some tight jams."

"He did," Luke added, "but he came with some baggage."

Varitek sat silently a moment, scratching Buster on the head, which the canine greatly appreciated.

"If he was that much of an asshole, I feel like you all would've gone your separate ways, or kicked him to the curb. Believe me, I've seen some assholes come and go through this town the past month, and it doesn't sound like he holds a candle to them."

Jillian missed her father's sagely words of wisdom, and she appreciated him sticking up for a man he'd never met. Whether they wanted to admit it, or not, the group needed someone with Sutton's skills around. He could fix most anything, knew firearms better than any of the others, and he possessed a sense for detecting people's intentions almost immediately. True, he put his own needs above others much of the time, but in the end, he always took care of those around him.

She felt rather certain if they decided to check on Sutton, and she chose to accompany them, her father would tag along to protect her. Glancing over, she caught him staring her way with a smirk, at least as thrilled to have found her as she felt about learning he was alive.

"What are you kids planning on doing about your friend?" Varitek asked, his gaze wandering between each of their faces.

"We were about to take it to a vote when you walked outside," Luke admitted.

"It seems to me the four of you are rather split on the issue," Varitek said. "Not to sound callous, but you've got a child, a dog, and one another to worry about. It sounds like your friend was more than capable of getting himself here if he were able."

"We also run the risk of passing one another if he's taking a different route here," Gracine noted. She looked to Varitek. "What would you recommend?"

"Maybe one or two of you could head to that area to see what happened. A quick recon trip of sorts."

Everyone looked around with uncertainty, as though expecting others to take up the figurative torch and run with it.

"I'll do it," Jillian said, pushing the issue. "We all owe our lives to him several times over, so it's the least any of us could do."

Her father looked at her with a mix of pride and concern, about to speak when the sound of multiple vehicles down the road reached their ears. Jillian looked, seeing a pair of headlights briefly when a truck traversed a hill down the road from them.

"The fire," Varitek said, bolting to his feet and grabbing a nearby shovel to scoop dirt on the campfire, smothering it rather quickly. "Everyone, get inside and find a weapon," he ordered while tossing the last scoop of dirt over the dying embers.

Jillian looked to the horizon, seeing the last bit of daylight and the sun struggling to stay afloat over the sea of dry land. She wondered if the vehicles had spotted the fire, or detected other forms of local habitation. Running for the closest door, she chose to be prepared for the worst, but hope for the best.

Experience, however, taught her to trust no stranger if she couldn't point a gun at them.

***

"Did you see that?" Hawk asked from the bed of the pickup truck where he and Sutton rode.

Despite the group finding another vehicle on a side street, the two of them were relegated to the same spot while Clean drove the car they discovered alone. Sutton grew concerned that Scruff had the man's ear, and voiced some suspicions about their newest member. Knowing each of the men were nearly his equal in firearms, he dared not make trouble, choosing to follow their lead in silence until he reached a real or figurative impasse.

Hawk referred to the glow of a fire in the distance when the two vehicles entered the town of South Hill. Sutton had indeed spotted the orange shimmer, feeling helpless to keep his new allies from heading straight for it if they chose to. He hadn't experienced their interactions with strangers, so he wasn't sure of what to expect if his two most recent groups of allies came face to face.

Within a minute the two vehicles were parked beside one another, and Clean stepped out just long enough to address Scruff, who remained in the driver's seat of the truck.

"Shall we see who's camping out?" he asked rhetorically, since he made all of the decisions.

Sutton considered the idea terrible, even if they were approaching people he didn't personally know. As dusk overtook the town, they could easily be shot by people who knew the lay of the land while approaching the campfire. It dawned on him that Clean didn't seek any new friendships, and he likely figured the quickest way to locating goods was through the people who already searched for them, or scoured the town ahead of time.

One look to Hawk revealed the younger man shared his concerns about disturbing a camp. While Sutton suspected a small group awaited them, Clean and his crew couldn't know if they were about to impede upon a single person or a small army. Sutton questioned how the group survived so long while carrying out such impulsive acts. He couldn't count on Hawk as an ally if guns were drawn, and shooting commenced, but the man appeared to share his reservations.

"We going to do this quiet like, or go marching in there?" Scruff asked his leader.

"We're going to let these people know who we are," Clean said with an almost sinister grin.

Sutton couldn't understand why they would bother confronting other people when they'd already located supplies enough to last them at least a week. He fought to suppress his displeasure, ensuring he kept their trust if he ever truly possessed it. With Scruff working against him, Sutton didn't trust anyone, but he didn't have the jump on four men. He knew a pistol, a knife, and a sniper rifle weren't means enough to deal with them by himself, so he simply watched events around him unfold for the time being.

"You up for this?" Scruff asked, his elbow resting along the driver's side open window, looking back to Sutton.

"I'm up for whatever," Sutton lied. "Is this a take no prisoners kind of thing?"

"Nah," Clean answered almost casually. "We're like pirates. We take what we want, but we ain't murderers."

Sutton noticed the man in the passenger's seat eyeing him intently, as though looking for a reaction. He hadn't learned the man's nickname, but based on the man's shaved head, he considered the possibility the man was related to Clean somehow.

"Is there some kind of plan to this?" Sutton asked, not wanting to look *too* willing to take such a huge risk by invading an existing camp.

"We'll take the lead," Clean assured him. "This isn't our first rodeo. Just look intimidating and have our backs."

Sutton felt as though he was being tested, and part of him wanted to make certain his firearms and magazines still contained live ammunition. He'd never heard of a group simply accepting members the way they had with him, and being brazen enough to steal from other camps while they were still occupied.

Within a moment both vehicles began traveling in the direction of the campfire, and he couldn't picture any scenario where this encounter would end well for both sides. Part of him hoped they weren't heading for Gracine and the others, but he feared he might not be able to act if it wasn't his own people in danger. A nagging feeling told him his current group somehow knew about his other group, heading there purposefully to test his loyalty and eliminate him if he balked at assisting them.

Riding in the back of the truck, Sutton noticed the man in the passenger's seat looking back at him several times, causing him to ponder his immediate future, and the decisions he'd be forced to make.

Without the sun, the air suddenly felt cold, smacking him in the face as the truck drove in the direction of the camp. The fire went out rather quickly, because Clean and Scruff didn't understand the meaning of the word discretion. They hadn't exactly entered town in quiet fashion, and with no undead staggering along the streets, and industry long since gone from the area, any vehicle would be heard for miles.

"Have you done this before?" Sutton asked Hawk, feeling reasonably certain the sounds from the wind and the truck motor drowned out his words to the two men in the cab.

"No," Hawk answered. "I've gone scavenging with them in a few towns and some houses, but we've never messed with the living."

Hawk didn't appear very enthusiastic about rushing headfirst into unnecessary danger, but as they neared the area of the campfire, he began scouring the area for people, or the undead, just the same as Sutton. Both vehicles slowed as the collective drew closer to the source of the campfire, and the odor of burned wood penetrated Sutton's nostrils, letting him know they weren't far from the shy campers.

When Sutton spotted a lingering puff of smoke from the side of a house, he said nothing, but he knew the others spied the same image when the vehicles abruptly came to a stop. Hawk jumped out first, and Sutton eyed the truck bed for any extra weaponry. He spotted a shotgun, but didn't have time to seriously consider snatching it before Scruff and the other man stepped from the cab. His sidearm held enough rounds to deal with a dozen people, but Sutton suspected the second he drew it, a figurative target would be planted on his torso.

"Fan out," Clean said in a hushed voice as all five men approached the yard in question from different directions.

Standing several paces apart, the men all froze in their tracks when the clicks and clacks of firearms being readied and aimed in their direction came from the yard. Sutton found himself confronted by his old group, and he knew so despite daylight fading away. He wasn't certain they'd noticed him specifically because he stood to one end, though it was possible they knew better than to call out to him for everyone's safety.

"You're trespassing," a man whose voice Sutton didn't recognize said gruffly.

Holding a pistol up in the general direction of the group, he appeared very capable, and extremely serious. Sutton wondered if Jillian had found a relative in her old town, or some family friend put them up for a few nights. No one in his current group attempted to reach for their own firearms, so Sutton didn't either, but he slowly moved toward Hawk with good reason.

"What do you want?" the man asked, not wasting words as Clean took half a step forward before the man fired a shot into the ground near his toes.

Clean took a step back, providing Sutton time enough to see Gracine, Jillian, Luke, and Vazquez standing near the stranger, all holding firearms. Samantha wasn't in sight, which he considered a blessing, and he hadn't spotted Buster yet. If Buster saw or heard him, the dog would likely bring about a course of action Sutton wasn't certain he could avoid anyway. Although he wanted to survive the impending outcome, Sutton didn't want to see anyone in his original group harmed if possible.

Gracine finally looked his way, and he provided an extremely subtle nod, which she reciprocated without being noticed. A few embers breathed their last beside the fire as their orange glow faded to black. Features were lost as darkness overtook South Hill, and the ten people standing in the yard could make out little more than shapes.

"We just want a safe place to hole up for the night," Clean said, holding up his hands defensively.

"There's five of you, and you're armed," the stranger said. "You're more than capable of handling yourselves. This town is clear of the dead, so you can stay anywhere you like. Just *not* here."

"Here seems like such a good location though," Clean pressed his luck. "And you've been *so* hospitable."

Sutton noticed no one truly had their firearms aimed at him or the four men he accompanied. He wished they would put forth a more threatening front, but he couldn't say a word. If Hawk had told the truth, there wasn't some codeword or signal Clean would give for them to draw their firearms, and the five men were at a disadvantage from the start. He considered the possibility the three original members of the group possessed their own signals, possibly hoping the two recruits would follow their lead. At this point, Sutton didn't know what to think, but his heartbeat accelerated as an inevitable skirmish drew closer.

"We didn't mean no harm," Clean said evenly. "We saw the fire and thought maybe we could see if there were supplies left around here."

"Meaning you wanted to bully us and take our supplies?" the stranger asked sharply. "Why don't you just get your ass to steppin' before we use some of these supplies on you and your crew."

When he spoke the words, he waved a hand at the firearms loosely pointed at Clean and the others.

Sutton could tell Clean was itching for a fight, as though he needed to provoke people to somehow justify a shooting match in his mind as legitimate. Recalling stories about how the shootout at the O. K. Corral went down from different perspectives, he knew if bullets flew, it was simply because Clean couldn't let the matter go. His pride, and his need to push other people to their limits, was about to ensure someone received serious injuries, or died.

Closing his eyes a few seconds, Sutton opened them as his right hand slowly went for his sidearm. He hoped no one in his original group noticed the motion, or if they did, understood that he meant them no harm.

Before his right hand clasped the firearm, however, Clean took another step back from the group. He held up his hands again as though asking for peace.

"My bad," he said. "We'll leave you folks alone."

Sutton knew as soon as the words were spoken, Clean didn't mean them. Sutton and Hawk took a few steps back from both groups as Clean and the others virtually marked off the steps, giving themselves a safe distance from being struck by people with less accurate aims. While Clean assessed the temperament and abilities of others well, he didn't necessarily pay attention to those around him.

When Clean and the others turned to draw their weapons and shoot, Sutton was already prepared, drawing his sidearm with practiced speed, taking down the unnamed man with a headshot. Knowing he couldn't fully trust Hawk to follow his lead, Sutton rammed his shoulder into the man standing beside him, flooring him before he could draw a firearm or decide which side to take. Firing commenced between both groups, and Sutton ducked, even though he heard Gracine informing the others not to shoot in his direction before the gunfire drowned out her voice.

Any distance between the two factions appeared nullified to Sutton because everyone stood in the open, without the benefit of cover, so he acted quickly. Scruff and Clean were occupied, firing at the stranger and anyone around him, and he saw Scruff take a bullet somewhere in the leg that staggered him momentarily. Sutton took a step forward, firing at Scruff's skull, attempting to finish the man. Scruff moved at the last second, causing the bullet to strike him in the shoulder instead. He whirled, facing Sutton with a scorned look on his face from the betrayal, before taking aim at the man he never trusted. A second shot from Sutton's firearm struck its intended mark, dropping Scruff as a female scream pierced the calm night air.

Sutton would guess the entire shootout lasted less than twenty seconds, and as Clean turned his attention to the betrayer of his group, Sutton took aim at the man. He didn't have the time to accurately place a headshot if he wanted to avoid being shot in the process, so he fired immediately, striking Clean in the thigh. The man barely flinched, his fiery eyes staring through Sutton as he strategically aimed at Sutton's most vital body parts, not caring if he lived or died at this point.

Lining up his own shot, Sutton was about to put an end to his current nemesis when he was blindsided, struck by a tackle of sorts that sent him to the ground like a downed tree. A shot rang out, and as Sutton looked up, he saw that Hawk had tried to keep him from harm, now taking the bullet meant for Sutton. Knowing only one chance remained to end the encounter, Sutton took aim at a stunned Clean, squeezing the trigger and delivering a headshot that downed the man immediately.

"Please tell me you did that to save me, and not to get me back," Sutton said as he walked on his knees over to Hawk, who was already clutching his right side.

"A little of both," Hawk answered with a pained chuckle.

He removed his hand, revealing that he'd been clipped slightly beneath his right armpit where no vital organs could be struck.

"That's a flesh wound," Sutton commented sourly.

"Still hurts like a bitch," Hawk said with a pained expressed as Sutton helped him to his feet.

Sutton quickly evaluated the situation surrounding him, seeing the three men he laid to waste nearby, and Jillian and Luke knelt down beside the stranger. Vazquez and Gracine kept watch over the yard, and as he approached her, Gracine addressed him. He noticed both of them wore concerned expressions, indicating the other nearby situation appeared grave in nature.

"Is that everyone?"

"Yes," he answered, looking back to Hawk. "He's okay."

Sutton said the words with a nod, indicating Hawk didn't pose a threat to the group. He couldn't be entirely certain his words rang true, but he could sort out allies and enemies later.

Walking over to the other half of his group, he saw the stranger lying on his back, struggling to breathe. Blood dribbled from his mouth, and Sutton's heart immediately sank, because he didn't want for anyone to get hurt, much less die. Spying a seeping hole at the top end of the man's abdomen, near the heart, Sutton knew nothing could be done to save him. Jillian held his hand, talking to him, saying all of the things people said to dying loved ones, knowing nothing could be done. She appeared despondent, and the gravity of the situation struck Sutton like an anvil because this man was no random stranger helping the group.

Shock had likely set in, because the man's eyes didn't focus on one particular person or object. His mouth continued to open and shut as blood interfered with his airway, and he struggled to draw oxygen into his lungs. Inadvertently, he made pained noises that came from the wound and his inability to inhale. Requiring all of his remaining strength, the man squeezed Jillian's hand, looking her in the eyes with the last of his focus, knowing nothing else could be done for him.

"I love you, punkin," he said before struggling to take a few more breaths, sputtering blood as he spoke.

"No," Jillian said, tears streaming down her face. "I just found you. You can't die on me."

He drew a few more labored breaths before his body went limp, his face falling to one side with the eyes wide open. Sutton knew death never looked pleasant, but he hated when people died with open eyes, as though they didn't know the last breath they drew was exactly that. He wanted to die in his sleep, not caught off-guard and bitten by a zombie, or shot while in the middle of a conversation. Such sights haunted him, though he wouldn't tell the rest of the group such a thing.

Jillian slowly let go of her father's hand, looking at him lovingly a moment before turning her attention to Sutton with fury he'd never seen in her before.

"You!" she stammered, pointing a finger at him. "You led them here! You did this!"

"I'm sorry," he said more sheepishly than he intended. "I was stuck with them."

"How *could* you?" Jillian demanded. "I just found him, and now you've taken him away forever!"

She leapt at him and pounded his chest with fists and his face with open slaps, and Sutton allowed it to happen. Jillian needed to grieve, to process such a profound loss, and he couldn't help but feel somewhat responsible for what happened. He could have dealt with Clean and the others earlier, but he didn't know the extent of their depravity. Buster came running from the house after hearing his master's voice, trying to take Sutton's side, but Sutton couldn't acknowledge his pet, even after Jillian broke away, sobbing as she knelt beside her father's body.

Everyone stood momentarily, unsure of what to think about the last few minutes. For his part, Sutton couldn't believe he judged Clean and the others so poorly, blaming himself for not acting sooner. Although he portrayed a hard case to the group, he didn't like taking human lives unless absolutely necessary. He looked back to Hawk, who appeared both perplexed and stunned about what went down in the yard. Sutton wanted to take him aside and talk to him, just to make sure the man didn't pose one last threat to the others, but the timing wasn't right.

Gracine approached Jillian, being as delicate as possible considering the young woman had just lost her last remaining relative. She spoke gently, touching her on the right arm with both hands.

"Jillian, we have to-"

"I know what we have to do," Jillian replied quietly.

Most everyone started to step forward, ready to volunteer for the obligation of putting a blade into the man's skull.

"I'll do it," Jillian said, reaching for her waistline.

Instead of pulling out a knife, however, she drew a pistol and immediately aimed it at Sutton, surprising everyone with fire and hatred in her eyes.

"Jillian, you don't want to do this," Luke said, trying to step partway between her and Sutton.

For his part, Sutton said nothing, figuring Jillian didn't truly want to shoot him, or she would have already.

"I stuck up for you!" Jillian screamed at Sutton, her hand unsteady with the firearm as she aimed it at his face. "They were ready to write you off, because you're so much trouble, but I took your side. I saw the good in you, and then you turn around and bring death to my doorstep? You took away the last thing that meant anything to me, and naturally you're going to walk away without a scratch because you're Colby, and Colby just does whatever Colby wants, whenever he wants, and no one says a *fucking* thing to him."

"I'm sorry," Sutton said, genuinely remorseful for any part he played in the death of her father.

"You're sorry?" Jillian demanded, not lowering the gun. "Fair would be me taking something you love, like your dog, but your dog is more loyal and caring than you'll *ever* be. Get the fuck away from me, and take your piece of shit friend with you, before I shoot you both."

Sutton called for Buster to take his side, slowly walking away with his dog and Hawk before the situation escalated any further. He looked back, seeing Jillian lower her firearm and draw her blade, prepared to put her father down for good. Uncertain of his future, Sutton decided time and some distance might be the best thing for him and the others. Hoping he hadn't misjudged Hawk, Sutton wasn't certain he cared if the man betrayed him and put a bullet in his skull.

He wasn't sure he cared about much of anything at the moment except making amends with his group, if that was even possible.

Twelve

Just over a week at the base nearly drove Metzger crazy. He'd been settled in with other civilians in an area away from the ships and large weaponry, but he couldn't truly relate to them. Most of them were sheltered in the town, or the base, right from the start, and hadn't truly experienced the hardships of dealing with the undead.

Or other survivors.

Most of the civilians worked in some capacity to earn their keep. Metzger fell into a teaching position, but felt that instructing children on the value of math and history didn't benefit them nearly as much as training with firearms and defense techniques. Part of him longed to leave the base and find his old group, which felt foolish when outsiders clamored to locate safe lodgings, food, and security.

In part, he felt rejected because he and Bryce had barely spoken since the incident in Buffalo. He wondered if embarrassment kept his brother from bringing up the subject, or Bryce still wanted revenge on the phantom known as Xavier. Metzger's thoughts often strayed to the mysterious man as well, but for different reasons. He wanted to know why the man set up the prison schoolyard so quickly, because although people stooped to carrying out evil on one another, the school situation was a whole other level. It seemed to Metzger the man almost knew what he needed to do ahead of time, because the conversion of the property appeared to start almost immediately after the apocalypse.

Currently done with teaching and studies for the day, Metzger opted to walk outside around the base. Civilians were encouraged to leave any weapons in their bunk areas, so he left his swords and two sidearms secured in his footlocker at all times. He felt a bit naked without weaponry as the breeze picked up on the partly cloudy day. The perpetual winds that accompanied life on the waterfront wore him down, because simply existing among such elements wasn't normal for most Americans. He questioned what the winter months would be like with icy water, piercing winds, and a mix of hail and snow pelting the base.

Not far from the airfield portion of the base, Metzger strolled in that direction, wondering if his new acquaintance had returned from whatever mission they sent the pilots on regularly. After he thanked their pilot in person for getting them back safely from Buffalo, a friendship began to blossom.

"Dan!" someone called to him.

Isabella spied him in the distance, and he changed direction to walk over to her. Because of his brother's odd behavior on the Buffalo mission, Metzger hadn't really spoken much to any of his family over the past week.

"What's up?" he asked when they drew near.

"Not much," she answered. "Just finished work for the day."

"I see the dead have been thinning out," he said, nodding toward the fence area where the dead often congregated when they reached the base.

"They're talking about making a push to reclaim the city and give everyone their own quarters," Isabella stated. "It's bad enough we're going to start running out of food and supplies, but you couple that with us living on top of one another, it'll be unbearable."

"No doubt," Metzger commented.

"Look," Isabella said with concern in her eyes, "I've noticed you and Bryce haven't spoken much this past week. What's going on?"

"That's probably best discussed with him."

"You know he doesn't tell me the manly stuff," Isabella said bitterly. "He thinks shielding me from the bullshit makes my life easier, but it just makes things worse."

Metzger's gaze traveled from the fence to the soldiers, sailors, and civilians crossing the base. He hoped his sister-in-law was right about living arrangements improving, because he hated sharing a building with four dozen other people. While the building provided a few common areas, much of it was simply rows of cots, old mattresses, or inflatable mattresses that didn't always stay inflated through the night.

He'd noticed the National Guard moving their posts closer to the base, which indicated a change in military directives.

"What does Bryce say?" he asked, returning his attention to Isabella.

"He doesn't say *anything* about the mission." She paused. "Something happened between you two out there, didn't it?"

"Bryce had a crazy idea, and I talked him out of it," Metzger answered, leaving his words as vague as possible. "We made it home safe, and that's the important thing."

Isabella didn't appear convinced.

"He's been up nights," she said. "There's something he wants to do out there, and he won't be contented until he finishes whatever it is."

"Are you saying I should go along with his plan if the opportunity presents itself?"

"Anything is better than having him restless like this. I can tell this isn't the Navy, and it's not about the undead. There's something personal gnawing away at him."

Metzger wasn't providing additional information, and Isabella sensed his reluctance to speak about the trip to Buffalo.

"Look, I've got to go pick up Nathan. Don't be a stranger."

"I won't," he promised.

Metzger gave her a quick hug before they parted ways. He walked in the direction of the hangar, finding a few Army enlisted men guarding the main entrance to the airstrip. They recognized him from previous visits and one produced a thin smile.

"The captain got in about an hour ago."

"I thought I heard a plane land," Metzger said. "Is he free?"

"I'll check," the second soldier said, ducking inside the gateway momentarily.

Metzger wasn't entirely certain what led to him and Captain Scott Timmons speaking on a regular basis. It seemed Timmons wanted ways to pass the time on the base, and conversing with Metzger helped. When the younger man expressed an interest in learning more about flying, the pilot took to coaching him about some piloting basics. He explained from the beginning that each aircraft was different, and military aircraft couldn't be flown without extensive training, so they stuck to terminology, general flying tips, and maintenance.

Whether he meant to or not, Metzger looked at the older pilot as a father figure of sorts, and Timmons taught him a lesson or two with each visit about flying. Military aircraft required hundreds of hours of class time for pilots, so the captain provided Metzger with general concepts about piloting that applied more to civilian aircraft. Even if they wanted to, the military couldn't enforce a complete lockdown on the base that kept civilians from engaging with the military men and women, so Metzger reaped the benefits.

"He's free," the soldier reported, holding the gate open for Metzger, who nodded thanks before heading inside.

He walked around the corner, finding Timmons already heading his way, as though he didn't necessarily want the civilian walking back to the area where most of the pilots congregated. Metzger understood the men often had missions and orders to discuss, so he wasn't about to push his luck in any regard with the captain.

"Good to see you," Timmons said, extending his hand, which Metzger shook vigorously.

"Likewise, sir."

"Cut the 'sir' bullshit, son," Timmons said, leading him toward any number of planes on the apron. "Call me Scott, or even Captain if you have to, but not sir."

Metzger respected the man, so he didn't want to address him inappropriately, but he also didn't want Timmons upset with him.

"How have things been going?" the captain asked him as they walked past a helicopter and one of the two fighter jets currently housed at the base.

"Can't complain," Metzger replied. "The teaching thing isn't too bad, but it's a little mundane compared to surviving outside the walls."

"I got a little taste of the infected in Buffalo," Timmons said. "I wasn't a big fan."

"You apparently took care of business just fine."

Timmons scoffed.

"My aim is a little rusty, so I had to let them come a little closer than I care to admit."

Metzger knew the captain spent most of his younger years in the Knoxville, Tennessee area, only moving once he joined the Navy. He admitted what little instruction he received from his uncle, who flew planes to spray pesticides over farms, didn't help a great deal when he entered flight school.

He proved to be a good instructor in his own right, spoon feeding Metzger a little information each time, often pointing out parts on nearby aircraft for illustration.

"What are we working with today?" Metzger inquired.

"This," Timmons said, pointing to the mammoth plane they stood beneath.

Metzger recalled it as the same transport plane the group took to and from Buffalo for the reconnaissance mission.

"Seems a little above my skill level," Metzger said, staring up at the gray coloration that seemed to run forever, taking up a quarter of the landing strip.

"It's a lot above your skill level. But a plane is a plane, son," Timmons said, leading him back to the open hatch in the rear. "There are major differences between every model, and we spend weeks or months training on each one. If my bosses didn't get too upset, I might be able to work with you on one of these noncombat planes."

"Really?"

"I wouldn't shit you," Timmons stated with a serious expression before leading the way up the ramp. "You're my favorite turd."

***

Bryce Metzger wasn't entirely certain why he got an invitation to join the joint military brass inside the largest convention room on the base until he met up with his ship's captain. While men in uniform filed into the large room, Bryce stood with Dascher just a few steps from the door, conversing about the topic at hand.

"They have some answers about who's responsible for the explosions," Dascher said after Bryce asked why he was invited to such an exclusive meeting. "You're responsible for a lot of those answers, so I insisted you be allowed to attend because you're entitled to this information."

"I don't know about that, sir," Bryce said, knowing only a handful of executive officers would be allowed to attend such an important meeting.

Typically, only the men and women in charge of making decisions received invitations to such major events.

"You belong here," Dascher assured him. "We lost good men doing these recon assignments, so you deserve to see the fruits of your labor."

Bryce nodded, and the two men walked inside, standing along one wall because every seat was occupied by someone with equal or higher ranks. Within a few minutes everyone had settled in, waiting for the presentation to begin, murmuring and whispering amongst themselves. A general named James McCall with the Army led the discussion, introducing himself and some of the officers flanking him. His hat sat on the conference table before him, and his gray hair remained closely cropped to his scalp. The general's face appeared wrinkled, not from age, but from a life spent outdoors in both the field, and possibly leisure activities during his vacation time.

A computerized slideshow remained at its initial screen, projected on a blank, white wall where everyone could see clearly.

Because of the power shortage throughout the nation, meetings that easily could have taken place over a computer, or even a phone during better times, now required people to meet in person.

"We now know several facts about both the infection, both in how to combat it, and who caused the explosions that decimated major cities across the globe," McCall began, calling up a flat image of the world with red dots occupying much more of the region than Bryce expected to see. "Thanks to no less than a dozen expeditions across the nation, and some cooperation with our neighbors to the north, we've carried out an investigation that delivered both names and possible locations for where we might find these folks."

McCall nodded to an officer who pressed a button atop a remote control to forward the computer to the next slide. Basically a screen with equations, cellular diagrams, and a variety of atoms in different colors, the image made little sense to Bryce or most of the personnel occupying the room.

Chuckling, McCall thumbed toward the image projected on the wall.

"Doesn't make any sense to me either," the general admitted. "What matters, is our scientists are making headway with the formula. There's no cure for death, so we can't fix the pale stalker types out there, but our people feel confident they can create a formula that will stall, or stop, the infection from killing those who are bitten, or breathe any remnants of the chemical residue near these factories."

Everyone nodded with satisfaction at the good news including Bryce and Dascher.

By now most everyone on the base understood the leader of the free world was indeed staying at the base with the combined military force. Only a few people reported sightings of the man, and from what Bryce understood, they frequently moved him from ship to ship to keep his location a secret for his safety.

Looking around, Bryce didn't see him present, feeling as though the man who ultimately called the shots, that the military *still* protected, could at least make a token appearance at such an important meeting. For all they knew, the man might be dead and the higher ups in the military gave orders in the name of a specter to fulfil their own agendas.

"I know you all came here for the main event," McCall stated, pushing the slideshow forward to a blank outline of the United States and Canada, smattered with more than two dozen red dots. "We've learned the identity of the man responsible for causing the shit storm around us. It took our people cross-referencing data from all of these different sites, but we now know who placed the trucks, and their cargo, in the right places at just the right time. He's a French-Canadian named Jean Pierre Nadeau, eccentric millionaire, distributer of goods across the world, and extreme environmentalist."

Everyone exchanged perplexed glances as an image of a head and shoulders professionally photographed image of a handsome man wearing a pure black shirt looked casually at the camera with a thin smile. He hardly looked like the type to execute a plan that incurred genocide across the globe with his sea blue eyes and full head of light brown hair.

Bryce felt like a racist after expecting a man wearing a turban who owned a chain of convenience stores to be the culprit. Even a disgruntled prepper seemed more plausible than a French-Canadian. He remembered a few of the *South Park* episodes in syndication where they depicted French-Canadians as evil beings, finding the joke now held true in this particular case.

"Don't let this fool you," McCall said, pointing forcefully to the projected image. "The man in this picture said many a time he thought people were killing the planet without regard for overpopulation, pollution, and the demise of thousands of species, both known and unknown to mankind. He worked as a chemist first and foremost, developing eco-friendly cleaners that he delivered across the world, sometimes for free in the name of charity to lesser developed nations. All of us were guilty for letting him slip past our defenses, and considering his resources, the man could literally be almost anywhere at the moment."

McCall switched the slide back to the last image of North America, dotted with red in several areas between the United States and Canada.

"These are the areas where Nadeau could be hiding. They include his businesses, his residences, and places where his known associates lived or vacationed. We're still looking into his projects prior to the apocalypse, thinking he might have built a secret bunker, or some chalet in the mountains, but without computers, the search will take time."

A list of names and locations appeared on the wall with the next slide, and Bryce studied it, not expecting to find any useful information. He finished about half of the list when McCall spoke once more, turning his attention away from the list.

"We're still combing through computers and journals we've found on his properties, and on those of his closest friends and business partners," McCall stated for everyone's benefit. "We don't know if this was some grand conspiracy, or Nadeau acted alone. Unfortunately, he covered his tracks well, and our manpower is spread thin. I don't have to tell you that communication is sketchy, because you've all experienced the woes of talking a town's distance away, much less reaching our other bases."

Bryce thought about satellite phones, but such devices were in short supply, and wouldn't hold out indefinitely. The military was about to be set back two centuries regarding their communications, possibly requiring telegraphs and the Pony Express to reach other installations. Much of the world faced the same dilemma, able to communicate only in person or through notes, because they didn't have technology better than a police radio.

"This effort is going to require some time," McCall added. "We intend to find Nadeau, not only with the intention of bringing him to justice, but also for some answers. We want to know how he manufactured a chemical that brought about this result, and if this was actually his intention."

"This seems like a lot of risk for answers we'll probably receive from our scientists anyway," one seated admiral said. "With our technology handicapped, isn't this search a needle in a haystack?"

"I know what you're all thinking," McCall responded. "We're wasting resources and risking lives, and for what? History is going to demand that we get justice for this tragic event, and our children and grandchildren will want to know that we did everything in our power to find a cure. This isn't nearly as insurmountable as it sounds."

Bryce listened, but his eyes returned to the image projected on the wall of the known friends and associates of the terrorist known as Nadeau. His eyes scanned the names and locations of each person until they froze on something he could not write off as coincidence.

Xavier Fournier, Buffalo, New York.

"No," Bryce muttered, finding coincidence more difficult to believe in the apocalypse.

"What is it?" Dascher asked, giving him a quizzical look.

"I think one of those names is the guy my brother dealt with in New York."

"When?"

"The prison school I told you about."

Dascher nodded, and both men noticed more eyes shifting their way because no one else had spoken out of turn during the briefing.

"Can I help you gentlemen with something?" McCall asked directly, rather than waiting for one of his subordinates to speak up.

"Actually, sir," Bryce said after clearing his throat, "I think I might be able to help you."

***

Metzger learned that flying didn't vary quite as much as he thought between various aircraft. Mastery of learning what each button and switch did for the pilot seemed to be much of the battle, and Timmons was exceptionally patient with him as he tried figuring out the aircraft components.

"You're a quick learner," the captain noted as Metzger produced three consecutive correct answers.

"When every day is a matter of life and death, you tend to bring your A game."

A few minutes later, both men exited the back of the plane, and Metzger took notice that Timmons donned a flight suit on this particular day. Sometimes the man wore varying degrees of uniforms, and when he wasn't due to fly somewhere, he often wore blue jeans and cowboy boots. As though they knew they were indispensable, pilots were given more leeway than most soldiers, and certainly took advantage of it.

"Heading somewhere today?" Metzger inquired once their feet touched pavement again.

"They've got me on standby," Timmons grunted, as though they placed him on standby too often, or for ridiculous reasons.

Several other pilots milled around the area, most dressed more casually than Timmons, as though their day off was assured. Metzger envied them slightly for having a larger portion of the base to themselves while everyone else crammed into buildings like they were prisoners of war. Even his brother possessed better accommodations aboard the *Ross* while many of his fellow sailors made do in the various converted buildings.

"You've never mentioned it, but do you have any family left?" Metzger decided to ask now that he'd gotten to know the captain a little better.

"Well, I was divorced, and my son who lived in Nevada wasn't on speaking terms with me," Timmons answered. "Duty called, and by the time I tried reaching out to my sister, there was no answer. We were all scattered across the country, so there's no real way of me finding them, and so little hope that I just keep them alive in my mind."

"Sometimes knowing the truth is worse," Metzger admitted.

"You and your brother fairly close?" Timmons inquired as they strolled back to the guarded entrance of the airfield.

"We've always been fairly tight, yeah."

"But not this week," Timmons noted, giving away his keen observations.

Metzger smirked.

"We had a bit of a dispute in Buffalo."

"Don't be too hard on him," Timmons said. "Despite everything that's happened, they still expect the world from us military types. He's got a lot on his plate."

Metzger wished the answer proved that simple. He couldn't believe his brother wanted to toss responsibility aside for revenge, knowing the risks to his mission, his country, and his own family.

"No offense," he said to Timmons, "but you're obviously past military retirement age. Why did you stick around so long? Isn't there money in the private sector?"

"First off, I'm barely old enough to be your dad," Timmons said, making the point that he wasn't quite as old as Metzger assumed.

"Sorry," Metzger apologized with a grin.

"I made money in the private sector during my time off," Timmons admitted. "Daniel, there's nothing like being in the thick of it with these guys and knowing you're the only thing keeping them from being stranded, pinned down, or outright killed by artillery. They're waiting for you to swoop in and save the day, and by God, there's no better feeling than pulling them from the jaws of death. You're going to think I'm an arrogant asshole, but there aren't many men who can pull off the things I do, and that alone keeps me in this line of work."

"I don't think you're arrogant. Sounds like you're driven to make a difference. That's something we didn't see a lot in the old world, and we certainly can't expect it nowadays."

"Part of me was lonely, too," Timmons said, a sullen look crossing his face. "When you throw yourself into your work, you don't worry about failed marriages, and kids who don't talk to you. Retirement concerned me, because I wasn't sure what I'd do with myself, and I wasn't ready to face the demons in my past. The dating pool gets scary after a certain age, and I didn't want to sit home and drink beer all day when I wasn't flying. I guess civilian life was scarier for me than doing the crazy shit I do here."

"There has to be more than this," Metzger said, his eyes scanning the entire base.

"More than what?"

"More than getting by, hoping the dead don't bite us. I know this was the furthest thing from anyone's imagination, but you'd think our leaders would've had some kind of plan in place for a major disaster."

"They're working on things," Timmons said, taking a seat on one of the chairs placed outside the nearest hangar. "They want to clear the town and get folks living there again."

"And after that?"

"They work their way north, or south, and make the land habitable again. It's not going to be an overnight thing, Dan. We lost a lot of good workers, and good minds, when this thing went down."

"It concerns me that the mind behind this whole thing is still out there. He may not be planning anything else, but I hate to think that asshole won."

Timmons fidgeted with his fingernails momentarily, finally biting one that proved peskier than the rest.

"You really think it was a win or lose kind of thing?" he asked. "Who benefits from murdering ninety-nine percent of the world?"

"Is that the number they figure perished?"

Timmons shrugged.

"No one really knows. No one's left to calculate that kind of thing."

Standing, the pilot stretched momentarily.

"I'm going to tell you something you've got to keep to yourself, Dan."

"What's that?"

"You may think we've been thrown back to the Stone Age, but the government managed to save a lot of brilliant minds before migrating this way."

"So we can save our class system where the rest of us work in factories and build things to make the world work again?"

Timmons chuckled.

"I'm not sure how all that'll pan out, but I do know the big man was saved, and he's still calling the shots."

"Not much of a shock there, but how do you know he's here?"

"Who do you think brought him?"

Timmons gave a cagy wink when Metzger looked his way.

Metzger was about to ask for details regarding that particular flight when an enlisted Army man came running up to the pair, stopping to catch his breath a few seconds before speaking. Both men figured Timmons had been summoned for some kind of important mission, requiring his attention, but the soldier basically ignored the captain, addressing Metzger directly.

"Mr. Metzger, your presence is requested in the main conference room."

"*My* presence?" Metzger asked, looking to Timmons as though the captain set him up for some kind of joke.

Timmons simply shook his head, equally surprised.

"We have a vehicle waiting for you, sir," the soldier said, leading Metzger out of the airfield, through the gate.

Metzger felt certain he'd broken some rule, or some parent complained about his teaching style, having no idea why the military took any interest in him at all. A few minutes later he was escorted into the building where the conference room held at least a few dozen high-ranking military men. For a second, he felt like a lamb led to the slaughter, but the enlisted man took him to a side room where Bryce, a general, and a Navy captain awaited him with a laptop computer opened and running atop a desk.

"Dan, this is General McCall, and my commanding officer, Mark Dascher," Bryce said, making introductions as Metzger shook hands with both men.

"Son, your brother says you may be familiar with a man we're looking for in the Buffalo area."

Metzger felt confused, wondering if Bryce was playing out some kind of scheme to return to their hometown for revenge.

Instead of providing him with additional details, the general clicked a button on the laptop, bringing up a digital dossier, complete with a surveillance photo. Metzger bent down, studying the photo momentarily, focusing on the details, realizing he'd seen this man only once before in his life. Ignoring the text beside the image completely, his eyes narrowed from recognition of the man.

"Xavier," he muttered angrily.

"So, you know him?" McCall asked with a furrowed eyebrow.

"He transformed a schoolground into a reinforced prison facility in record time," Metzger answered. "I wouldn't say we've been formally introduced, but during our one and only encounter, I shot the man."

Now McCall looked slightly alarmed.

"Fatally?"

"No. He crawled under his car, and as far as I know, he escaped the area."

Metzger suddenly wondered why the military showed any interest in the man who killed at least a few dozen innocent people for his own benefit.

"What the hell is this about? And don't give me some classified bullshit, because I'm part of this apocalypse family."

"This man is associated with the person who caused the explosions worldwide that brought about the infection," McCall answered. "It's possible he could lead us to that man if we were able to locate him."

Metzger thought momentarily.

"Based on his previous actions, I'd imagine he'd make a play to get his property back. If he's not already there, he's likely monitoring the area and creating a plan to take it back. To put it bluntly, he's kind of a dick."

"Your brother kindly explained your experience up there to us," McCall stated. "I know this is a lot to ask, but would you be willing to take us to the place where you last encountered Xavier Fournier?"

Metzger exhaled through his nose.

"The *last* place was the Lancaster airport, and he was gone when we last visited Buffalo," he said, giving a stern glance at his brother in case Bryce harbored other ideas about this potential operation. "But if you want me to take your people to the school, I can do that."

McCall looked to Bryce.

"I'll have a team together within two hours to escort you both to that school, because I know you aren't letting him head there alone." The general looked to both brothers in turn. "Boys, you're going home again."

Thirteen

Sutton knew how in-laws, or friends who weren't on the inner friend circle, felt when tagging along as a fifth wheel. Life changed significantly for everyone in the group when Jillian's father was shot by Clean, or one of his followers, and only Sutton was left to bear the brunt of the group's anger.

Hawk remained with Sutton, which only seemed to agitate the group even more, as though the man represented something evil and heartless that Sutton led straight to them. By now Sutton knew the man's true name to be Steve Driscoll, and the man wasn't ruthless or evil like those he ran with before, but he possessed some of their flaws.

Although he once again possessed his box truck, and his faithful dog remained by his side virtually every minute, Sutton felt an emptiness from living in a friendless world.

Strangely, the group hadn't even left the area, basically living off the remains of the town's general store, raiding houses during the daylight hours. Sutton was condemned to a street on the opposite side of town from the others, but he occasionally saw them when he went into South Hill to grab supplies or check in with Gracine. Today, he stood on the front yard of the house he kept to himself while Driscoll occupied the neighboring residence.

Fall weather set in, bringing cooler temperatures and dew that lingered on the untended grass blades longer than usual. Sutton considered leaving the group numerous times, heading back to the camp to check on his sons, but he didn't especially like leaving with Jillian harboring so much hostility. Buster took his side, and Sutton scratched him between the ears, causing the pit bull to give a gratuitous moan.

"Is today the day?" Driscoll asked, stepping out from his current residence.

"The day for what?" Sutton replied, already knowing what the younger man was asking, but wanting to make Driscoll work for the answer.

"The day we leave this town and your former friends behind?"

"You're awfully anxious for the two of us to strike out on our own and test the waters," Sutton noted after hearing the same words for a week straight.

"The three of us," Driscoll said, nodding in Buster's direction.

Sutton frowned at the statement, knowing his dog ranked higher than Driscoll in both companionship and usefulness against the undead.

"They aren't taking you back," Driscoll pressed, taking a few steps from his yard into the property Sutton occupied.

"Where do you want to go so badly?"

"I'm just ready to keep moving. Staying in one place isn't my thing these days."

"So, food, a roof over your head, and a plethora of supplies doesn't work for you?"

"We're not even two months into the end of the world. Supplies aren't going to be tough to find for a while."

"I'm not stopping you from going," Sutton said, pointing out the obvious.

"Yeah, but you're the one who stuck me in this situation when you shot three people in the back."

Sutton realized he hadn't spoken with Driscoll much during the past week, and suddenly their talk took a very harsh, truthful turn.

"I did my damnedest to keep them from coming here, because my loyalties were always to this group. I've fucked up and left them in some hairy situations twice now, so yes, I did what I had to do to keep them safe. For the record, I didn't shoot them all in the back, and I could've easily made you a casualty before taking aim at them."

"Why didn't you?"

"I was hoping you weren't as bad as they were."

Now Driscoll simply grunted instead of continuing to run his mouth. Sutton had begun to realize his new neighbor talked a good game, and possessed some survival skills, but the man didn't like being on his own. He understood why Driscoll needed to stay with gruff, likeminded people, because they were the only ones willing to put up with his incessant talking.

"I know you come from a place like me, where you were your own boss," Sutton stated. "We made the rules, and made some money along the way, but in this world you need people. It ain't easy putting up with their shit all the time, like their emotions and the dumb decisions they make, but in the end, you can't last long on your own."

"I'm not real fond of the company you keep," Driscoll said, having met the others in passing a few times over the past ten days.

"We're all pink on the inside," Sutton replied. "I've seen *that* firsthand. You need to get right with what I'm trying to do, or you might as well head down the road."

"Did you tap that?" Driscoll persisted, inquiring if Sutton and Gracine had physical relations.

Their conversation halted when the sound of a vehicle approaching caught the attention of both men. When Sutton saw Gracine alone, behind the wheel of a compact car, he smiled on the inside, but a glance to Driscoll showed indifference on the man's face. He remained in the yard as Gracine stepped out, a look of concern crossing her countenance.

"What's wrong?" Sutton asked.

"It's Juan. We haven't seen him since last night."

"Maybe he went out scavenging."

"We do everything in pairs. No one goes off solo except when they relieve themselves. And even then it's not recommended."

"Have you looked for him?"

"No. Jillian thought maybe the problem was bigger than we could handle."

Sutton felt both flattered and insulted at the same time. He didn't like being the hired help when it suited the group's needs, but he wanted to rejoin the fold at some point, so he'd assist them if possible.

One glance to Driscoll indicated the man wasn't interested in tagging along.

"If you two are hunting down the Mexican, you can do it without me. He probably met up with some of his own kind and headed south."

"He's charming," Gracine noted sarcastically.

"You don't know the half of it."

"Shall we?" Gracine asked as Driscoll turned his back to both of them to return inside his current residence.

"Let's go."

Buster whimpered a bit when his owner stepped toward the car with Gracine, so Sutton turned to address him.

"Stay."

Wiggling his hind end, and lowering his head and front shoulders to the ground, Buster uttered a protest with several whimpers and groans.

"No," Sutton insisted firmly. "Stay."

"Let him come," Gracine said. "There aren't any zombies left in town, and your buddy's racism might rub off on Buster if he stays."

Sutton needed only wave a few fingers to indicate Buster could tag along, and the canine immediately ran over to them. Gracine assumed the driver's seat while Sutton opened the opposite door and pulled the seat forward to let Buster jump in the back. Once he slid inside, it occurred to him that he wasn't armed with anything except a small knife and a semi-automatic sidearm.

He considered asking for a moment to fetch a rifle, but given the quiet nature of the town the past week, Sutton decided to settle for what he possessed already.

"What happened last night?" Sutton asked once the car rolled halfway down the block.

"We think Juan stepped outside to piss, or get something, and we lost track of him."

"Lost track?"

"Look, early bedtimes, operating by candlelight, and the fact that we're walking on eggshells around Jillian all contribute to the fact that we don't exactly hang out like a slumber party."

"He disappeared after dark last night and no one's seen him since?"

Gracine nodded without a word.

"No vehicles missing?"

"He didn't duck out if that's what you're asking. The cars were there, and I didn't see any evidence he was attacked."

"Juan was shot recently. Could there have been some complication related to that?"

"He was healthy. No fever, no sweating, nothing like that."

Sutton sighed. Vazquez didn't strike him as irresponsible, or likely to depart without saying something to the others.

"Where do we start?" he asked.

"I've already checked our neighborhood over there, and Jillian doesn't particularly want to see you, so we're going to start downtown, and branch out to the houses if that doesn't work."

A few minutes later, the pair exited the car and Sutton let Buster join them as they walked toward the front entrance of the general store. Both of them had seen the inside numerous times as they plucked goods from the shelves on a daily basis. Unfortunately, most of the useful items ran low in the inventory as the group took from an already depleted supply when the townsfolks ate food and used medical supplies as they survived, grew sick, and died in that order.

Struck with a feeling that something wasn't right about Vazquez's disappearance and his surroundings, Sutton stopped short of the front door, noticing Buster sniffed the air, obviously sharing the sentiment. He entered the store with a little more caution than usual, followed by Gracine and Buster as their footsteps echoed throughout the general store's interior.

A true throwback to such stores, the building sported a wooden floor along the front half, and concrete in the back where bulk goods and building materials were stored. Even a barefooted visitor would assuredly cause the floor to emit clops and creaks, so their entrance wouldn't go unheard if anyone else occupied the building.

Although he'd seen the store several times during his time in South Hill, Sutton harkened it to the Christmas section in a retail store where all of the good items were picked over before, or soon after, clearance prices were applied. Less desirable items during the apocalypse remained on the shelves, like toys, pet items, decorations, and virtually anything that required electricity to operate. A number of Halloween items sat atop endcap shelves near the front of the store, and one of the front display windows contained a string of orange lights wrapped around it along the inside. Halloween displays remained frozen in time within many a store since the world's end began around Labor Day.

"This is weird," Sutton noted, seeing empty spots where candles and incense lined the shelves just days earlier.

"That's not all," Gracine said, motioning for Sutton to join her at the end of the aisle.

She led him one aisle over, standing near an endcap of wicker baskets and picnic essentials where an odor struck Sutton's nostrils before he spied a pile of human waste on the floor.

"So, someone pissed and shit right here rather than using the restroom?" he questioned.

"Apparently so. And none of us are in the habit of dropping our britches right here."

Like Gracine, Sutton suspected the town of South Hill had more visitors, but if the group hadn't seen new people, he wondered where they chose to make camp.

"You think Juan met up with some people?" she asked.

"I think he unwittingly found some unfriendly people. The fact that he just disappeared doesn't bode well for the rest of us. We need to find him, or circle the wagons with everyone we have left."

"I'm not giving up on Juan," Gracine said sternly. "He's the only one who can fly us wherever we want to go once Jillian moves on."

"*If* she moves on. She can't stay handcuffed to her dad's grave forever."

"You're one to talk, considering we were doing just fine, about to go look for your sorry ass, until you brought the Klan to our doorstep."

"Look, I was surviving and trying to get back to all of you. I can't state this enough."

"We would've been just fine with the dog and your box truck."

"Thanks," Sutton replied, turning to walk to the front of the store.

He'd seen what he needed to inside, so he wanted to take the search elsewhere.

"You've got everything you came for, so why aren't you out looking for your boys?" Gracine pressed, walking behind him. "Why exactly are you sticking around with your project?"

"My project?"

"The sole survivor of your last posse. You didn't shoot him, and now you two are thick as thieves. What gives?"

"I fight and claw my way back to you, and because Jillian's pissed at me, and my roommate choices are slim, you're criticizing me?"

"Something tells me you were along for the ride with those boys," Gracine chided. "You're all about Colby Sutton when it comes down to it."

Sutton stepped outside before turning to address Gracine directly.

"I stopped for you, didn't I?"

"Oh, you stopped alright. But we both know it didn't go down the way you tell everyone."

Sutton could have thanked her for allowing him to spin the tale his way, but he didn't. In truth, he didn't appreciate her badgering him for his recent choices, and the pair didn't have enough history for him to take jokes very well.

"My hero," Gracine said sarcastically.

Even as she spoke the words, her eyes noticed something in the distance that Sutton had already spied. His eyes immediately focused on a plume of gray smoke in an area other than where the group made camp at the large house.

Sutton knew the difference between a campfire and the darker smoke billowing from a burning structure. During his travels he'd seen destruction and disasters of all kinds, already possessing far more life knowledge than most people he encountered along the way.

"Someone set up camp," Gracine uttered the same words Sutton thought.

He looked to her, and she nodded, indicating she wanted to check out whatever campfire was burning down the road in a neighborhood less than a mile from where the main group stayed. Sutton considered the close proximity dangerous, and either someone moved in, oblivious to nearby occupants, or they brought malicious intentions with them.

Sutton wished Jillian had come along, because her knowledge of the town might prove invaluable when approaching the area in question. She wasn't ready to forgive him, and might never reach that point. Had Sutton found his sons, only to have them ripped away from him in an instant, he surely would have felt the same rage as Jillian.

"Come on," he called to Buster, who sniffed something near the front door, which his owner guessed might be some kind of odor related to food.

Buster jumped into the backseat, and Gracine drove them in the direction of the smoke, turning onto a road that took their car into a comparatively nice residential area. No words were spoken and he and Gracine scanned the yards and buildings for any unusual activity. Not one member of the undead was visible, and Sutton only recalled seeing two enter South Hill during the past week.

Jillian's father had done a remarkable job of clearing the town, but now it seemed strangers chose to make themselves at home.

Sutton smelled the wood fire from several blocks away, and Gracine slowed the car, not wanting to ruin any element of surprise the pair held over the strangers. When they pulled within a few blocks of the smoke, he questioned why she wasn't pulling over, because he felt they were dangerously close. He decided to say something when Gracine pulled the car into a driveway behind a van, and for a split-second, Sutton wondered if the owners would mind. He snapped out of his old-world thinking, attributing his thoughts to how tidy the town remained compared to other settlements.

Houses on the street were lined up parallel with residences the next street over, usually divided by wooden privacy fences of natural or white coloration.

"We should get over there and sneak a peek at whatever they're doing," he suggested, receiving a nod from Gracine.

As they exited the car, Sutton addressed Buster.

"You stay put, and don't destroy anything," he said, making certain the window was rolled down slightly in case he was gone longer than planned.

Both of them crossed a lower mesh wire fence nearby, staying on the pavement of the other street to avoid making noise. Several driveways held cars, trucks, and vans, as though the owners might be inside, or skipping work for the day. Sutton knew from experience that everyone reacted in different ways that fateful day the apocalypse undeniably took hold of the world.

Some sheltered at home, others fled for a safe haven, or to meet family, and many simply died before they understood the danger surrounding them.

Sutton believed himself organized and prepared for the worst, but the necessary travel to find his sons threw his plans to the wayside. Never much of a people person, Sutton avoided survivors for the longest time until he found it necessary to merge with a group. He always played off the fact that he stuck with a group as a means to survive, but Sutton secretly required some interaction with others, or his mind traveled to some dark places. He'd already done things in a world of the dead that he never envisioned during his previous life.

He smelled the smoke more intensely as they drew closer to the yard, and the crackle of wood entered his ears, meaning the mysterious residents made no secret of their arrival. If Vazquez hadn't gone missing, the others might not have noticed the smoke, or the fact that someone else arrived in South Hill, but Sutton wasn't going to leave without knowing if these people were tied to his disappearance.

Now two houses away from the yard in question, Sutton heard a throaty growl, which concerned him. A look to Gracine, only a few paces to his right, indicated she heard the noise as well. He knew the undead didn't start fires, and this certainly sounded like a zombie, rather than any kind of animal. Sutton chose a yard adjacent to the backyard where the fire and smoke originated, standing on his tiptoes for a look over the wooden privacy fence. Unable to see much from the angle, because this house's fence extended to the front corner of the house, Sutton decided to try a different angle.

He walked along the front of the house, remaining quiet in case someone living occupied any of the houses or yards. Gracine remained close behind, and as they reached the other side, the pair discovered a weakened area of the fence that Sutton was able to push down silently. They stepped into the yard, crossing the space with crouched walks, hearing the crackle of an outdoor fire and at least one throaty growl.

Gracine found a plastic outdoor chair, pulling it to the fence for use as a substitute ladder to allow her a view into the next yard. Sutton found one of the wooden slats broken near the top, so he put his face up to it, shocked at the view next door.

As though cued by his presence, a male zombie on the other side turned to sneer and growl at Sutton. Slightly unnerved by the zombie staring back at him from two feet away, Sutton noticed the member of the undead was chained to something heavy in the yard, stuck in place like a guard dog on a chain. A collar secured around its neck ensured it didn't stray more than a few feet, and in order to break free, the zombie would literally need to break its head free from the neck.

What disturbed Sutton to the core, however, was the zombie across the yard with a steel post through its abdomen and left shoulder, securing it in different fashion. Like a moving statue, it flailed its arms and tried turning its head, and eventually its flesh might deteriorate enough for it to pull free from the rod, but for now it acted as a display piece only. Several vehicles and wagons painted like carnival movers sat beyond the cryptic scene, and Sutton wondered if a band of traveling carnies had settled into the area.

He glanced at Gracine, who appeared equally unnerved by the scene in the yard. The fire pit, little more than a circle of stacked bricks, contained a small fire where sticks and a chunk of wood continued to burn. Although the rear entrance to the house next door appeared open, no one emerged, and no voices or sounds came from within the recently occupied residence.

Gracine turned to him, pointing to the zombie across the yard from the pair, mouthing words that Sutton couldn't understand. He sidestepped her way, monitoring his surroundings because he didn't trust the bizarre scene separated by a weakened wooden fence.

"That's Juan," she whispered when he drew close enough to hear the words, and as Sutton stood on his toes to have a look, he saw the eyes of the zombie turn to meet his with a lifeless glossy gaze.

Sutton agreed immediately with Gracine, standing frozen in shock momentarily because someone he saw alive the previous day now failed to recognize him. Up to this moment, the undead were always something impersonal to Sutton, simply an obstacle that required permanent removal. Vazquez stared at him, not as a man, but a creature seeking to devour him if fate dictated it. One look at the man's chest indicated he was stabbed or shot, ensuring he became the trophy placed inside the yard by at least one deranged individual. Someone murdered Vazquez, and Sutton felt his blood boil because the man didn't deserve to die, much less given such an undignified afterlife. Unless the man was bitten or contracted the disease in another way, Vazquez shouldn't have become a zombie, and Sutton couldn't explain what he witnessed.

Seeing Gracine turn from the corner of his eye, Sutton heard her scream for the first time ever as he spied something behind them. He turned, too late, seeing a mammoth blur already upon him, driving him into, and through the fence, knocking the wind from his lungs. Gracine started to run to assist him, but her eyes locked with something frightening, and she turned to retreat instead as Sutton's large assailant hovered over him. The man clutched him by his shirt collar, yanking him to his feet.

Uttering grunts and groans, the man attacking Sutton seemed like something out of a horror movie, possibly part of some cult, following orders to appease friends or family. Sutton didn't get a good look at the man, but a glimpse indicated the man possessed hideous features and a simple, yet angered, look in his eyes.

Nearly three-hundred pounds, Sutton considered himself a physically capable individual, but the man attacking him possessed animal-like strength, outweighing him by at least fifty pounds. Sutton was scooped off his feet with ease by his larger adversary, tossed like a ragdoll before he could react.

As he hit the ground, Sutton heard Gracine shriek once again, and he knew she was being pursued by a different adversary. Hearing a growl overhead, he looked up, seeing Vazquez in undead form staring down at him with ravenous eyes, unable to attack because the rod held him in check. Instead, his former friend snapped his teeth repeatedly, staring at him with unblinking, glazed eyes that viewed him simply as food.

Still disoriented, with his surroundings beginning to spin, Sutton quickly regained his footing but his attacker slugged him across the jaw with a fist, sending him to the ground. Sutton wanted to rise up again, but his body refused to cooperate as his attacker stood over him, waiting for orders, or for Sutton to make a move.

"Put him out," he heard a woman's voice say from the rear entrance, prompting his attacker to bend over and ram a large fist into Sutton's right cheek, throwing his head back against a concrete landing and rendering him unconscious.

Fourteen

As though attempting to spite Metzger personally, the military leadership didn't give Timmons the assignment to fly the small group back to Buffalo. Even so, the trip went smoothly, and Metzger barely spoke a word to his brother the entire way. Because their headset was wired in with the four Marines traveling with them, he wouldn't have brought up the topic of Bryce's lapse in judgement during the last mission.

Unlike the last time, it appeared Bryce was placed in charge of this particular assignment, and the Marines accompanying them were protective brawn. The four men spoke little, and seemed mildly annoyed that they were the unlucky ones assigned to a reconnaissance mission.

Like the last time, both the pilot and his copilot stayed with the cargo plane while the group traveled in two armored vehicles. Since Bryce didn't know the location of the school, Metzger instructed the driver of his Humvee on which roads to take until they reached familiar territory that he didn't particularly care to see again. While he felt satisfaction that he'd helped good people escape the tyranny of Xavier Fournier, the school served as a cold reminder that his parents died from unnatural circumstances.

"What should we expect?" the Marine driving the Humvee asked Metzger through his headset.

Everyone on the mission had been briefed, but none of them viewed earlier events like Metzger.

"If we're lucky, we'll find friendly people at the school, and that'll serve as a starting point. Xavier and his cronies were pissed when they lost the school, so hopefully he hasn't gone too far."

"Careful what you wish for," Bryce commented. "This guy obviously has resources, especially if he knew all of this was coming."

Metzger feared he only helped kick a hornet's nest if Fournier possessed additional people and resources outside of the schoolyard. For all he knew, he and the former prisoners at the school took out one small faction of evildoers while the others were away gathering resources or people to imprison.

"I'm hoping Molly and the others found additional clues after I left," he said. "Fournier must've had paperwork of some kind connecting him to Nadeau if they planned all of this ahead of time."

"He wouldn't keep that around," Bryce scoffed.

"Why do you say that?"

"Once he set up shop, there wasn't any need to leave a paper trail. Hell, I doubt he ever planned on communicating with the man again."

"Where the hell is this Nadeau dude at?" the Marine driving the Humvee asked without removing his eyes from the road. "He's probably holed up in some bunker somewhere, living off dry rations the rest of his life."

"I just hope he's miserable as fuck," Bryce muttered.

"I hope he's already dead," Metzger added.

Most Canadians Metzger met during his lifetime proved to be good-natured people who liked basic liberties and hated their free healthcare system. Stereotypes indicated they all enjoyed beer, hockey, and maple syrup, and Metzger learned most Canadians liked any given two of those staples in their lives. He supposed terrorism could come from any country if a person possessed means and bad intentions, but Metzger wondered if Nadeau truly planned on murdering millions, or creating the undead legion that now walked the earth.

Both Humvees managed to avoid the occasional zombie, and no survivors were spotted during the trek. When they pulled up to the familiar fences, Metzger immediately felt alarmed because the back gate remained wide-open, and several undead wandered the grounds both inside and outside the mesh wire fence. He didn't see any open doors along any side of the building, which possibly indicated survivors huddled inside to wait out some form of danger. Metzger said nothing, but he feared something terrible occurred at the school during the past three weeks since he'd assisted a few dozen people.

Parking the vehicles in a manner that blocked the one remaining entrance to the interior of the fencing, the Marines jumped out with firearms in a ready position. Metzger stepped out without hesitation, using his short sword, the only one he brought this time, to cut down two consecutive zombies. He stared at the bodies momentarily, finding the tone of their skin different, even unnerving, because they hadn't decayed very much. No stab wounds, or holes from gunfire, appeared on their skin, or the clothes still covering their bodies.

"What's wrong?" Bryce asked, taking his side.

"These folks died recently. It's almost as if they lived and died right here."

Bryce understood the implication as a grim look crossed his face. He led the way to the nearest set of double doors, finding them secured when he tugged on them. The next set, which Metzger considered the main entrance, gave with a simple tug when his brother pulled them open. Immediately, the group found sheer darkness inside, and the Marines switched on their flashlights before leading the way into the first hallway.

Metzger immediately sensed danger, because no one met them, and no talking or sounds of work echoed through the halls. He instinctively rapped on walls when he entered buildings to draw out the dead, but this time he decided not to because he didn't want to startle the military men, or draw a group of zombies in such a tight space.

"Something's wrong," he said in a low voice to his brother.

"You think?" Bryce asked sarcastically.

While the Marines weren't willing to let Metzger take the lead, possibly not wanting their pride wounded, they let him point out the direction he felt best to find answers. Although he wasn't entirely sure what spaces the residents chose for lodging, cooking, and socializing, he decided to start with the area that formerly served as the cafeteria in the old school. When they rounded the first corner, the two Marines leading the way nearly jumped out of their skins when a growling zombie appeared in the beam of a flashlight. Both immediately opened fire on it, which caused Metzger to shake his head.

Their first few shots struck it in the torso due to their initial surprise, but one of the two men quickly managed a headshot and put it down. Metzger walked over to it, studying it for wounds other than the three bullet holes.

He saw none.

"What are you looking for?" one of the men asked gruffly.

"These people don't have any wounds," Metzger answered as he patted down the body, finding a small flashlight in one of the pants pockets.

"So?"

"So, if they weren't stabbed or shot, how did they die? It doesn't stand to reason all of them inhaled or ingested the toxin that caused all of this."

"We aren't here to solve a fuckin' mystery."

Metzger inhaled through his nose, his eyes locking with the Marine's.

"Actually, we are. I don't know about you, but I want to know who the fuck I'm up against before we meet the son-of-a-bitch. I also want to know if there's a chance we're breathing something toxic."

Turning on the flashlight, Metzger started down the hallway, using his sword to stab two other zombies in the skulls, seeing no wounds on their bodies. He couldn't explain what happened at the facility, but he knew the chances of finding any survivors were practically zero. Pressing forward, he got halfway down a long hallway when he spotted a male zombie lurking near some lockers. When it turned, Metzger didn't recognize the pale eyes, but he knew the young man as someone he assisted when he helped people take back the school.

"Ryan," he muttered the young man's name, shaking his head as he turned away from the staggering zombie, letting the Marines deal with him instead.

"You knew him?" Bryce asked with more sympathy than normal.

"He was a prisoner here when we took back the school. I know that asshole Fournier is behind all of this. If he couldn't have this place, no one could."

"That's a lot of work on his end to simply throw it away," Bryce surmised. "You sure this wasn't some kind of accident?"

"Doubtful. These people weren't stupid. They were just put in a bad position by Fournier and his people."

"Maybe our Canadian friend left behind a present that went off and killed your friends here."

Metzger wasn't certain he'd ever find answers. With Ryan out of the way, lying at the foot of some lockers, he followed the Marines down the hallway, finding natural light entering the school from a few different classrooms off to either side.

He felt a strange combination of anger and regret because he'd risked life and limb to help the people at the school, only to see his efforts wasted due to someone's callous actions. Knowing his parents met their demise at the school weighed on his mind, and he kept looking to Bryce to see if his brother showed any emotion about their surroundings.

As usual, Bryce registered a poker face, giving no indication about the thoughts running through his mind.

Much of the school looked clean and overhauled, as though the survivors who stayed behind made a go of living there. Gone were the blood trails, horrible stenches, and closed off areas where bodies and waste were stored.

When the group encountered two more zombies that looked recently deceased, Metzger lost all hope that anyone survived whatever wave of death crashed over the converted school. The Marines dealt with them swiftly, using bayonets attached to the ends of their rifles before walking confidently toward the cafeteria. He noticed Bryce taking in the surroundings, trying to act businesslike, as though scouting the area, but his eyes lingered at several rooms and hallways a little too long.

Less than a minute later, the group reached the cafeteria doors, which were strangely closed and secured. Metzger felt an initial surge of hope that survivors might have barricaded themselves inside. Pessimistic thoughts immediately followed, causing him to wonder if scores of the undead lingered behind the doors instead.

Even the Marines looked to one another hesitantly before one of them slowly reached forward and grasped the doorknobs while everyone held their various weapons in ready positions. Metzger actually sheathed his sword and drew a sidearm because he worried the group could get overrun if zombies came pouring out of the large cafeteria area. He swallowed hard as the armed man turned the knobs, pulling the doors back to reveal a mostly dark area.

A single, thick stream of daylight poured from a side window, striking the center of the cafeteria like a spotlight during a stage performance. The rest of the windows were covered in thick paper materials of some kind, which wasn't the case during Metzger's last visit to the school. Chairs and tables were moved to the sides, as though placed there so the eyes drew toward the centerpiece. Metzger required a moment for his eyes to adjust to the dark once he knew a horde of undead weren't coming at him. In fact, not a single member of the dead legion occupied the room, so he stepped cautiously inside, studying the manmade structure that stood taller than two men and encompassed a radius of nearly twenty feet.

Four large wooden branches that acted as beams intersected one another in a central location, bound together with thick ropes, forming a three-dimensional double 'X' that supported itself with four appendages. His nostrils detected the odor of freshly cut wood, remembering times when his father downed trees with a chainsaw during his youth.

Metzger suspected the bizarre artwork was placed there for someone's benefit, not likely his own, because Xavier couldn't have expected him to return. As he stepped closer, he discovered a body tied to the center of the wood where all four logs intersected, and had it been a zombie, it would have assuredly hissed and growled at the group the minute the doors opened.

Metzger virtually needed to step beneath the structure to see the face of the person bound by arms and wrists to the wood. With so little light entering the room, he used the flashlight, aiming it carefully upward, because he wasn't certain he could handle more familiar deaths just yet.

As though sensing the moment belonged to Metzger, Bryce and the Marines remained a few steps behind, curiously looking, but not interfering. He couldn't imagine why Nadeau and his people would return to slaughter the entire compound, but leave one person alive, though it appeared they did exactly that.

"Molly?" Metzger asked just above a whisper, causing the person above him to stir.

For the briefest moment he wasn't sure if the eyes would flutter open and stare at him with ravenous pale irises, or he might find life after the emotional distress of seeing familiar faces deceased in the hallways.

"Dan?" she questioned, as her eyes fluttered open a few times before she went completely limp against her restraints.

"We need to get her down," Metzger said, finding strength and energy that just moments earlier felt completely sapped.

When the Marines momentarily hesitated, Bryce took his brother's side and began cutting the ropes binding Molly.

"Some help would be nice, guys," he said. "She may be our only link to Nadeau at this point."

Once Molly was freed, the military men assisted with lowering her to the ground. Being practical, Metzger checked her for wounds, particularly bites, without being indecent.

"She seems clean," he reported. "We need to get her hydrated and fed so we can figure out what the hell happened here."

"We don't have a lot of time," Bryce noted. "If Nadeau and his people retaliated, they've already got a head start on us."

"This wasn't done today," Metzger stated. "The undead roaming the halls have been that way a day or two. Short of some kind of thermal imaging from the air, I'm not sure how you'd expect to find them."

"And you think they laid out their entire diabolical plan to your friend?" one of the Marines asked skeptically.

"I've seen stranger things," Metzger replied, standing to see if the nearby faucet functioned well enough to get Molly a glass of water.

Well water couldn't be trusted in certain locations, but Metzger felt reasonably certain the school tapped into the township's water supply. He found a glass, and the water from the faucet wasn't discolored or full of particles when he poured it, so he walked it over to the group. Molly seemed to be coming to, shaking her head, not particularly fazed by six men standing around her.

"What happened?" Metzger asked, handing her the glass, which she readily accepted.

After downing nearly half the glass, Molly looked to the only familiar face, addressing him directly.

"After you left, they managed to poison our food supply with whatever agent killed people in the explosions," she said. "By the time I figured it out, it was too late, and everyone was sick."

"Why didn't you get sick?" Bryce asked, openly trying to conceal his doubts.

"Because the kindly, trusted member of my group who brought my meals to me was the mole for Xavier and his people. They made sure I didn't get sick and die because they wanted to make an example of me. By the time I figured out their scheme, everyone else was too sick to put up a fight."

"Why didn't they stay?" Metzger asked. "Why kill everyone and bug out?"

"I never saw Xavier personally, but they said he was making some migration to see his boss. They were going to follow him in a few days once they had things finished here."

"But why come back here at all?" Bryce asked.

"They'd left documents behind, and they were ordered to retrieve them and leave no survivors. I guess they expected me to starve in due time, so they left me as an example to anyone who tried to take back the school."

"This whole thing sounds weird," one of the Marines commented.

"These guys are assholes," Metzger said. "They have no regard for anyone outside of their group. They made this place their fort because Nadeau gave them a heads up about the results of his chemical bombs."

"Who's Nadeau?" Molly questioned.

"Long story," Metzger said, offering her a hand to help her to her feet.

She accepted, finishing the water before standing in place momentarily, as though uncertain her legs could carry her very far.

"Did they get all of the papers they came for?" Bryce asked.

"They got most of them," Molly answered, but her face didn't express regret, anger, or shame.

Metzger spotted a gleam in her eye, and he knew her fighting spirit and instincts had discovered something that might help the group and get their mission on track again.

"What they didn't know, was that I read their papers in full and replaced them just in case I was being watched."

"Not everyone here was trustworthy?" Metzger inquired.

"I didn't know most of these people," Molly answered, a bitter tone entering her voice. "From the start I knew there could be at least one spy in this camp, and I was right to think so."

"Did the papers hold anything useful?" Bryce asked, openly considering the situation hurried.

"Molly, meet my impatient brother, Bryce," Metzger said, introducing them as Molly provided a weak, but genuine smile.

"You found him."

"I found him," Metzger said warmly, not worried about macho pretense despite the rugged military men behind him. "And we came back here because we have some answers. We're hoping maybe you can help us fill in some of the gaps."

"These people knew this was coming," Molly said angrily, speaking of the heartless thugs who took over the school and murdered Donald and Connie Metzger.

"I know," Metzger said. "The guy who did this was connected. And rich."

"The assholes who left me for dead are heading to meet him," Molly stated. "I got the impression from the paperwork that there are hoops for them to jump through, but they're going to ask him for refuge."

"I wonder how benevolent he'll be if his location could be compromised," Bryce questioned aloud.

"If you want answers to any of your questions, we need to get to St. Catharines before they meet the middleman," Molly suggested.

"In Canada," Metzger said, familiar with the Canadian city just across the border directly west from Buffalo.

"We can't go trudging into Canada," one of the Marines stated.

"What's going to stop us?" Metzger questioned. "There aren't exactly enforced borders, or people guarding them."

"Our mission was to come *here* and dig up answers. This could be a wild goose chase, or a trap, and if we cross into Canada, unguarded or not, there's no one coming to bail our asses out of trouble."

"*Our* mission is to find the man responsible for the end of the world," Bryce argued. "If we don't intercept them at this rendezvous point, it could take years to find another clue about their whereabouts. I'm not letting this slip away, and your job is to keep me safe while I conduct this investigation."

"Your investigation doesn't mean a thing if none of us survive to tell the tale."

"Boys," Molly interjected, getting her second wind after a moment's rest and the glass of water, "they already have a head start, and may very well already be in St. Catharines by now. If we're lucky, they're spending the night there, and we may catch up with them, but I can promise you this is a one-time chance."

None of the Marines spoke as their eyes glanced back and forth between one another. They seemed undecided about which orders to follow, regarding their general orders to check the school, or new orders to proceed into Canadian territory. Military tradition indicated the decision fell upon the senior officer present, in this case the lieutenant commander, but the Marines didn't appear to interpret the orders the same as Bryce.

"How many family members do you have left?" Molly asked the Marine who verbally objected.

"None that I'm aware of," he answered, a perplexed look crossing his face. "Why?"

"So, you're willing to let the man who basically murdered your loved ones get away with it because you refuse to interpret your original orders differently?"

Licking his lips in thought, the Marine didn't know exactly how to answer.

"This is on me," Bryce said before any of them could answer. "I interpret our orders as find this son-of-a-bitch and get some answers. If you're willing to risk your lives a little farther, we can find these assholes and bring answers back to Virginia. In the scheme of how things stand, I'd say we'll be heroes if we help find Nadeau. He's the biggest at-large bad guy since bin Laden."

Everyone knew bin Laden didn't wipe out more than ninety percent of the world population.

"We have guns, and we have armored vehicles," Metzger added, prompting his brother to hold him back with one arm so he didn't speak out of turn excessively.

"Fine," the lead Marine agreed. "We get to the border and take a look. If it's too risky, we don't cross over. Like us, they still have a military presence, and they may not believe one of their hometown heroes murdered millions of people."

Gathering up their gear, the group headed toward the cafeteria door, ready to get to the vehicles and continue their mission.

"Got your passport?" Metzger asked Molly with a cagy grin.

"I think it's at home," she replied with a smirk. "Thank you, by the way."

"I have to admit this isn't what I expected to find."

Molly turned grim once again.

"We underestimated these people. They were ahead of us the entire time."

"Now we know why," Metzger said as they turned into the main hallway where Ryan's body drew his attention, along with Molly's. "None of this was an accident, and while he prepared for the apocalypse, we lived oblivious to what was coming."

Molly requested the group stop momentarily when they passed a certain room. She ducked inside, returning with a paper that held handwritten instructions she'd obviously copied from the original documents the Wardens left at the school. For some perverse reason, the group that took over the school, turning it into a prison of sorts, decided to name their faction.

She didn't offer to hand over the paper, and no one asked her to, yet, so the group continued walking down the hallway. As the others walked ahead, Metzger stopped with Molly short of the main entrance.

"Did you see him?" he inquired.

"Their leader? Xavier?" she asked with a furrowed eyebrow. "Oh, yes, he made certain to make his presence known to me before addressing me with his stupid French accent. He's such an arrogant asshole that I'd love to stick a spike up his ass and let him think about it as he dies a slow, painful death."

"That's not very ladylike," Metzger kidded.

"What he did to me wasn't gentlemanly, either."

"I left him a present before my group departed for Virginia."

"Oh?" Molly asked as they followed the others out the double doors.

"I managed to skim his skull when I exchanged gunfire with him at the airport."

"Center mass would've been preferable."

"I know, but in the heat of the moment I felt lucky to make any contact."

Vigilantly, the Marines led the way to the Humvees while monitoring the area around them.

"Sounds like he had a few weeks to heal, and he wasn't bandaged up," Molly reported. "Too bad infection didn't set in."

"Yeah."

Daylight stung Metzger's eyes momentarily when he returned to nature from the dark hallways of the school. Taking a glance behind him, he didn't want to lay eyes on the school ever again, because it held only painful memories for him. Twice, the people who wanted the property to themselves murdered innocent people for no good reason. Nadeau and his terrorist ways trickled down to his associates, and Metzger didn't care if any of them survived another day. The government wanted answers, but he wanted each and every one of them to pay for their sins, whether by his hand or the monsters they created devouring them.

"What was that?" Molly asked while Metzger watched where he was walking and the Marines vigilantly stared in various directions.

Metzger looked up, seeing she was looking ahead to the right, where the path led around the school. Several bushes occupied the area on the other side of the fence, where Molly's gaze was fixed, and he saw nothing by the time his eyes locked onto the area.

"What was it?"

"I could swear someone was behind that bush," Molly said adamantly, but quietly enough that no one else heard the words.

Based on her tone, Metzger didn't think she sounded entirely positive she saw something for real, and after her experience the past few days, it wasn't inconceivable that her mind played a trick on her.

Both of them continued to stare in that direction until the group reached the two vehicles, and by that time their vantage point allowed them a clearer look to see no one lurking behind either bush. Metzger considered it possible someone could have run from the bush to the far end of the fence, but such a sprint didn't seem plausible to him.

"You've been through a lot," Metzger said, trying to provide her with a reasonable excuse for her eyes playing tricks on her.

"I'm aware," she replied evenly. "I'm ready to see this prick get what's coming to him though."

No one objected to Molly coming with them, possibly because Metzger was already a civilian riding with them, and leaving her behind would be an inhumane move.

Only after he packed into the back of the lead Humvee with Molly did Metzger look past the Marine driver and his brother up front to see a few undead staggering toward the school. Metzger wondered if Molly somehow spotted one of them, or if the group they now tracked sent someone to make certain their work was finished. He didn't like the idea of their extended mission parameters being compromised, so Metzger hoped his brother put a rush on reaching the Canadian border.

If he didn't, the entire group might be ambushed and killed within the next two hours.

Fifteen

Jillian waited as long as she dared before packing a few items around the house for travel, hoping to locate Gracine. She'd spent the past few hours recording history by hand, the only realistic way to organize her notes until she came across a typewriter and a bulk supply of ink ribbons. She tried to find time each day to put recent events to paper, but since the death of her father Jillian hadn't found much motivation to write.

Given the choice between worrying about Vazquez, or finally confronting the events that took her father from her life, she decided to dive into her journal. Jillian usually wrote without any bias, trying to act like a journalist or historian, keeping a neutral view, but Sutton's actions bordered on criminal, and she found it difficult not to blame him in words that mirrored her thoughts.

Eventually she finished the piece, feeling mentally and physically worn down. Only then did she realize how much time had passed since Gracine left, so she began packing some items for light travel. She put two handguns in the small satchel she decided to bring along, wishing Metzger was still with the group. He brought a sense of calm and levelheadedness to the collective, keeping them safe, and away from terrible decisions. She slept with him during their travels, and even in bed he proved a tender, caring lover. Jillian appreciated that time, and the tricks he showed her to survival in the new world.

She finished packing the satchel with a few snacks, and a knife, wishing the group had radios or some way to communicate. The house looked messy compared to when they first occupied it, possibly indicating they needed to clean up, or move to a new destination.

"Where are you going?" Luke inquired, Samantha by his side in the living room of the house the group still occupied.

"I need to find Gracine, to see if she's found any clues about where Juan got to."

"We should come along."

Jillian questioned why Luke would volunteer to bring Samantha into town with potential danger around, but she quickly realized the alternative was them remaining at the house unprotected. After the death of his partner, Luke took up the mantle when he started teaching Samantha the need to keep quiet around the undead and strangers. He continued her training when it came to shooting and hiding a blade in her clothing.

Before the apocalypse, teaching an eight-year-old such things would be considered a form of child abuse. At the very least, it would flash warning signs on the moral compasses of anyone who witnessed such a thing. At the moment, Jillian considered such teachings a must, and she felt bad that Samantha was robbed of her childhood, though the alternative was joining her parents in the afterworld sooner than expected.

"We should start at Colby's place," Luke said, automatically making them a trio in whatever endeavor they were about to attempt. "We need to know if him and his new friend went along with Gracine, or if they're somehow involved with why Juan disappeared."

"What makes you think Gracine went over there first?"

Luke made a face, pursing his lips, indicating Jillian should have known better than to ask such a question.

"Fine," Jillian conceded. "We'll start there."

She didn't begrudge Gracine for continuing to visit Sutton, though she didn't understand why everyone in her group wasn't furious with the man. He brought some incredible survival techniques and firepower to the group, but he regularly endangered them and wasn't very good about sharing.

Within a few minutes, Jillian selected a four-door Chevy Malibu from a few houses down the street. Her father chose to leave keys to every car in the ignition, or in the visor, making it easier on himself during his treks to town. With so many vehicles in South Hill, a massive heist would be required to make them all disappear suddenly. Luke and Samantha walked with her to pick up the blue car, and

Samantha appeared liberated and happy without the oppressive shackles known as car seats from days gone by.

"How much longer can we stay in this area?" Luke inquired as Jillian drove in the direction of the houses where Sutton and Driscoll stayed.

She took the question as a roundabout way of asking how much longer Jillian planned on clinging to the memory of her parents.

"The resources won't hold out forever," she answered. "We'll probably have to start thinking about our next destination as soon as next week."

"Will that include our *entire* group?"

"I don't trust the man with Colby," Jillian responded. "I'm not sure I trust Colby, either, after what he pulled."

Jillian pulled out to the main road that ran through town, seeing a thin plume of gray smoke to the right. Finding the sight odd, she decided to delay heading there, wanting to check at Sutton's residence before heading the other way. She figured if Gracine had located Vazquez, they certainly would have returned, or at least dropped in to say something. His disappearance struck everyone as uncharacteristic because the entire group stayed close to home, or said something before departing, even if they were just heading to the general store.

When Jillian neared the neighboring houses, she found no one around, but pulled into one of the driveways anyway. She waited half a minute, about to back out, when Driscoll emerged from the house he occupied.

"Great," Luke muttered sarcastically, knowing the man's views on anyone who wasn't Caucasian, male, and straight.

Jillian shared the sentiment, but said nothing as she stepped out of the car to speak with Driscoll, hoping for a brief encounter.

"What brings you out this way?" he asked.

"I'm looking for Gracine."

"She stopped by and picked up your boy earlier."

"He's *not* my boy," Jillian said testily. "How much earlier?"

"A few hours ago," he answered as his eyes narrowed. "They aren't back?"

"Obviously not. Did they say where they were going?"

Driscoll shrugged.

"I got the impression they were going to search the town until they found the Mexican."

"We saw smoke on the other end of town," Jillian reported. "I'm going to start there."

She really didn't want to ask for his help, because he ran with the men who killed her father. Any wildcards endangered her and the others, assuming they weren't already in trouble.

"I can help search," Driscoll offered. "The only thing to do around here is read books or work on the cars. I'm bored out of my skull."

"Suit yourself," Jillian replied. "We can check out the smoke, if you want to try the other neighborhoods."

Driscoll gave a knowing smirk, taking notice that Jillian didn't want him tagging along with her group. Even so, he nodded.

"Alright," he said. "I'll take one of the trucks and see what I find."

Jillian didn't say a word as she walked a few feet to the car and slid inside the driver's seat. She hoped to find Vazquez and the others safe, possibly distracted by something they found on the other end of town, but a nagging feeling told her they would've checked in if they possessed good news.

Backing out of the driveway, she hoped to know something soon.

***

When Sutton came to, he felt an incredible headache, and a ringing inside his skull as the odor of the fire within the yard reached his nostrils. He tried keeping his eyes open, but light hurt them, and he wondered if his earlier skirmish caused a concussion. Even so, he fought to take in his surroundings, spying Gracine lying next to him, hands and feet bound by rope as she lay prone atop the concrete landing. This area was separate from the house, likely an outdoor gathering area with chairs and some form of table.

Hands bound behind him, Sutton felt his back against the fence that divided this property with the backyard he and Gracine used to spy on the newcomers. His feet were also secured, and one glance toward the house revealed an older woman, two large men, and one skinnier man who kept watch over the pair.

He immediately recognized the man who attacked him and rendered him unconscious. The man appeared simple, as though he followed orders without question. The other large man was also familiar, but not from recent events.

When the group was all together, traveling along highways to the Navy base, they spotted a man standing across the road from them, cut off by stalled cars and other objects. He wore various animal hides and skins all along his body, even across his face, like a mask, and Sutton wondered if the man used them to mask his presence from the undead, or he also possessed mental issues.

Coverings on the man's body included a deer pelt, either cow or horse hide, and even fur resembling that of a dog. His mask was mostly pieces of skin sewn together, with no hair of any kind. His pale blue eyes were visible through eyelets, and appeared to be the only genuine portion of him visible in his getup.

Because he ducked in and out of the house, the skinny man wasn't available for Sutton to study. Despite the fall temperatures, he wandered around shirtless, and appeared as though he might be on drugs, or psychologically disturbed based on his nervous behavior. He never stood still for more than a second or two, but Sutton got just enough of a look at him to guess the man was in his early forties.

Sutton noticed both the unknown zombie and Vazquez remained planted in their spots, unable to attack the living, despite their best efforts. Only now, noticing him conscious, did the woman approach him, holding a pistol in her right hand. Dressed in faded clothes, complete with a beige twist front beanie, the woman looked the part of a gypsy. Likely in her sixties, she either served as a maternal figure to the three men, or indeed shared a bloodline with them.

Her skirt possessed a printed pattern of black and red with flecks of yellow, and her bohemia top was a blood red that regular wear and sunlight had reduced to a reddish orange. Instead of heels, or traditional footwear, she wore a form of leather sandals that allowed her to easily navigate the grassy yard.

By this time, Gracine began to stir, and managed to roll her body over to a position where she could see. She wriggled her way to the fence, propping herself up as the older woman walked over to them with a rather neutral expression. Sutton didn't know if she planned on conversing with them, or shooting them and adding to the undead ornaments in her new yard.

"What were you two doing, snooping around my new place?" she asked somewhat gruffly.

"Looking for our friend," Gracine answered quickly, as though not trusting Sutton to give an appropriate answer.

"Did you find him?"

Neither said a word, but their eyes shifted towards Vazquez, who continued to battle his restraints and hold his arms outward, in case one of them proved stupid enough to walk into his grasp.

"He got a little too curious," the woman said. "The boys picked him, the way a dog finds a critter in the wild to play with until it dies. The other one we picked up a few days back in South Boston. He wanted some help until he got a better look at us."

"It does appear you murder people indiscriminately," Gracine commented. "Most people have concerns about that kind of thing."

Sutton shot Gracine a look that indicated she needed to choose her words more carefully.

"I didn't realize a group of you were staying here," the mysterious woman said. "We used to travel around, back in the day, but we weren't welcome around here in the end."

"Kidnapping and murder is frowned upon in most places," Gracine noted.

"We didn't do such things back then. This world changed things for us, and now the people who held us down aren't around. My name is Velvet, by the way. My stage name was Dark Lady, like the Cher song, and not the color of this young one's skin."

"Oh, so now you be Racist Lady," Gracine said, letting her Ebonics talk for her with a sideways shake of her head.

"Hardly, my dear. I like you already. You're spunky."

"What is it you want?" Sutton asked, struggling to keep his anger and irritation in check.

He should have felt fear, but this group kept them alive for a reason, and they hadn't given him an indication they planned to make him a yard ornament.

Yet.

"I want this town for starters," Dark Lady answered.

"What does that even mean?" Gracine asked testily.

"It means there isn't anyone around to kick us out of this place," Dark Lady said with an eerie calm as she drew closer to Gracine, speaking with their faces only inches apart. "For you, it probably won't end well either way, but I need to know if you have friends coming. Based on what the boys indicated, you all were living in a rather large home."

Sutton and Gracine remained silent on the subject, and for Sutton's part, he didn't consider himself a good liar, so he wasn't going to bluff. Giving out any information put the remainder of their group in danger, and he wanted to give Luke, Jillian, and even Driscoll a fighting chance.

Dark Lady walked over to Sutton, who looked up defiantly, not feeling as confident as he acted, because his bindings weren't loosening one bit on his hands or feet. She ran her forefinger slowly along the bottom of his chin, almost as if he were a pet dog, or she planned on making him part of her collection soon.

"It won't be long before you join your friend," she said. "I know you weren't one of the townsfolk who wronged us, but you're *all* the same. You all look down on us as freaks. You judge us for things we haven't even done, and you think you're better than us because of the way we make our living. Well, you aren't."

With her last words, she gave Sutton a bit of a push, and he cut the bottom of his right hand on a jagged piece of concrete embedded within the landing. Feeling blood ooze from the injury, he immediately attempted to position his hands to a spot where he could cut the rope. As Dark Lady walked away casually, Sutton learned that he couldn't even begin to cut the binding unless he laid flat with his hands against the ground. Short of pretending to fall unconscious, he wasn't sure how he could convincingly pull off such a feat.

"We have to get out of here," Sutton said just above a whisper to Gracine because the group members holding them stood across the yard.

"No shit, Sherlock," she retorted. "How do you propose we pull it off with the moron squad watching over us?"

"I might be able to cut these ropes, but if they're watching me, they're going to get suspicious."

"So, you need a diversion," Gracine reasoned with a sigh.

She turned from him, scooting across the landing away from him, drawing the attention of the simple men standing across the yard. Sutton slowly rubbed the rope against the jagged portion of the concrete, not satisfied with the protracted results. He glanced, seeing all eyes focused on Gracine, so he laid down flat, trying to expedite the process. In order to make any significant progress, he would need to slide his wrists up and down along the sharp edge, which required his elbows. Sutton quickly realized it might require more than a few minutes to get anywhere significant with the weakening of the ropes, and his actions would certainly be noticed. He cleared his throat, and when she looked his way, Sutton indicated she could stop wriggling with a negative shake of his head.

If either of them got stabbed or shot ahead of their scheduled execution times, their allies would suffer. Sutton often saved the group with his firearms training and ability to scout bad situations ahead of time. He didn't like the chances of the remainder of the group saving themselves, much less him, if he didn't find a way to get free.

Both Sutton and Gracine observed their surrounds to find something, *anything*, useful in getting them free of their predicament, but the former tenants kept the yard cleared of toys, gardening tools, and other debris. Despite his lingering headache, Sutton knew the circus folks had taken even the smallest knives from his pants. He studied them momentarily, noticing only the skinny man spoke. The man covered in animal pelts, the largest of the three, only grunted or nodded, as though incapable of speech. To Sutton, the scene before him reminded him of some apocalyptic movie where humanoids born of holocaust survivors lived and acted like cavemen.

Such men weren't incredibly intelligent, but they presented a different sort of danger.

He questioned why the nomads hadn't taken a more proactive approach to seeing if other people occupied the town, but they appeared capable of handling virtually anything that came their way. Strangely, they didn't seem to recognize their own shortcomings and weaknesses, and Sutton itched for a do-over where he visited this property armed to the teeth.

Dark Lady had ducked into the house, and the skinny man spoke to the two enforcers, saying something that caused them to also disappear inside.

"What was that about?" Gracine questioned.

"I don't know, but it can't be good."

"It might not be as bad as you think," an unseen voice said from behind the fence, quiet enough that their abductors couldn't hear.

"Jillian?" Gracine asked, purposely not turning her head.

"It's me. What the hell did you two get yourselves into?"

"We found Juan," Sutton answered.

A momentary silence followed, and Sutton imagined Jillian peered through one of the numerous natural holes in the wooden fence. He and Gracine hadn't found proper time to process Vazquez's death, or mourn the man, and Jillian re-acted much the same.

"We need to get you the fuck out of there."

"Barney Fife is keeping watch over there," Gracine noted.

Sutton heard a thump behind him once the skinny man glanced to one side momentarily. His hands felt around the soft ground until they came upon a knife blade that nearly sliced into one of his fingers. Using the tool, he freed himself in a matter of seconds and flipped it to Gracine, who quickly did the same with her hands. Severing the rope at her feet would certainly be noticed by the posted guard, so she hesitated.

"How do we play this?" she asked.

"Where are the others, Jillian?" Sutton asked.

"Luke and Samantha are with me. Your buddy was checking the other end of town."

Sutton wondered if the two larger men went after Driscoll, possibly hearing a vehicle, or seeing a sign of life. South Hill wasn't a very large town, but it covered considerable acreage with a highway running through it. Perhaps Dark Lady grew impatient and sent them ahead on a scouting mission.

"Do you have a gun?" Sutton asked Jillian without turning to the fence.

"I have several."

"Then I say Gracine cuts that last rope and we get the fuck out of here."

Gracine swung the knife around, sawing through the rope binding her feet with only a few strokes as the man keeping watch over them took a few steps their way before realizing Sutton was unarmed and he didn't possess any weapons.

"Mama!" the man cried, drawing Dark Lady from the house as Jillian stepped through the opening in the fence created by the largest man tackling Sutton through it earlier.

Dark Lady stepped out from the house, causing an unusual standoff, particularly between Dark Lady and Jillian, who appeared to know one another as though they were lifelong mortal enemies. Their eyes narrowed, and their icy stares were figurative daggers flying through the air.

"You *bitch*," Jillian said emphatically.

"You *whore*," Dark Lady spat in return, causing everyone else present to stare with wide eyes at the bizarre standoff.

Sixteen

Metzger wasn't certain of what to expect when he drew near the Canadian border, because he hadn't visited the country since his teenage years. Little had changed since then, as a row of small booths and articulating crossing arms remained visible from a distance. Both Humvees drew to a stop as every passenger within them spied the same dilemma. On both sides of the border, vehicles clogged the area for almost a hundred yards each way where people had desperately tried to get to loved ones, or escape to safer areas, only to fail in their quests.

"Well, this looks dangerous as fuck," one of the Marines commented as everyone stepped from the military vehicles.

"Agreed," Bryce said. "But if we have to hoof it across there, that means they did as well. We can grab a vehicle or two on the other side."

Every lane of the border appeared to have nearly twenty vehicles blocking the path to the booth, meaning the Humvees could not pass, because even the service areas on the side were clogged with trucks and debris. With fifteen booths, and so many stalled vehicles, the United States side of the border looked like an overcrowded bumper car ride. Just beyond the booths, the lanes merged, leaving only two functioning lanes because construction had begun to create a pedestrian lane, along with three paths for vehicles.

Construction hadn't finished before the apocalypse, leaving Peace Bridge littered with cars, orange construction cones, and a number of undead that hadn't yet fallen off the precarious edges of the international crossing. Metzger could barely make out the details ahead of the booths, but he knew the journey was about to intensify in danger.

"They can't be far ahead of us," he said to his brother. "That bridge is almost a mile long, and there are cars lined up all the way across."

"Agreed. We need to get moving."

Bryce turned to the leader of the Marines.

"One of you needs to stay with these Humvees."

"We may need all hands on deck, sailor," the man replied, getting in a dig as he tried to usurp Bryce's authority, or at least test it.

Bryce didn't back down.

"That's lieutenant commander to you," he said, drawing closer to the man instead of backing down, "and the last thing I want is someone with a little bit of knowledge stealing our only means of getting back to the plane."

Metzger had learned that the Humvees didn't have keys, per se, but rather switches that military people knew how to operate, and civilians might figure out with a little bit of tinkering. No solid means of locking them up, or keeping them safe from marauders, came to mind except for leaving a stationed guard with them. From simple observation, Metzger knew how to turn on the batteries and the ignition, so it wouldn't be difficult for someone else to figure out the system.

"I know we need the numbers," Bryce said to everyone present, "but all of this is for nothing if we don't make it back to the plane. The pilots are already on edge after I told them we were taking a detour, and they'd shit their pants if I told them we were crossing the border, so we need to keep this short and sweet."

Molly stepped forward.

"I'll do whatever I can to make up for leaving someone behind. I've gotten good with firearms through all of this."

Bryce nodded his appreciation.

"Choose a man," he told the Marine leader.

"Coffey, that's you," the man said to an obviously disappointed Marine.

Shooting zombies and exploring uncharted territory was always preferable to babysitting military hardware.

"Stay right here, and stay frosty," the Marine leader warned the man, giving direct orders after being cut down by Bryce in front of his squad mates.

Bryce began weaving through the vehicles toward the booths, and everyone followed his lead, keeping weapons drawn. Metzger kept his sidearm holstered for the moment, opting to carry the short sword instead. Only a few zombies staggered aimlessly before them until they heard the noise of the approaching group. When the two dead lurkers locked eyes with members of the group, Metzger looked to his brother for permission to silently deal with the threat.

Bryce nodded, and Metzger stepped forward, slicing each of them through the skull with precision before they got close enough to bite at him.

Not even to the booths yet, the group proceeded tensely, carefully panning for zombies behind cars, and even at their feet, because the undead sometimes lurked beneath vehicles until something caught their attention. Metzger felt the wind slap his face, and he knew he couldn't hear anyone from his group speak unless they yelled, because the wind off the lake created a chilly, noisy environment.

Molly stayed close to Metzger, possibly because he was the only familiar face to her. As the group drew closer to the small booths, he saw the damage done to the area as none of the crossing arms remained intact. He could almost feel the panic as civilization broke down and frenzied people tried their damnedest to find their loved ones. Metzger envisioned people trapped in cars, or pursued by ravenous undead, many dying tragically on a bridge of all places.

Metzger had to squeeze between a black car and a booth once he neared the bridge itself, startled when a zombie trapped inside the booth smacked the glass from inside. His heart skipped a beat, and one look at Molly indicated she was caught off-guard as well. Ordinarily, Metzger might have opened the door and dealt with the member of the undead, but he didn't have a second to spare. He glared at the zombie, which seemed to sneer at him for not opening the door as it pawed at the glass. Although faded and dirty, the man wore a blue shirt to indicate he worked in the booth, and Metzger imagined he was bitten early on and barricaded himself in his workplace until the grim reaper came for him.

"We can deal with him later," Molly said, literally giving Metzger a light push to urge him forward.

Except for Metzger and Molly, the group fanned out, each passing through a different booth to ensure the path ahead looked clear. They couldn't convene on the other side due to the sheer number of stalled vehicles continuing to block the roads. On a few different occasions, Metzger witnessed zombies appear from behind the cars, vans, and trucks, but the military men dealt with them silently, careful to avoid drawing attention to their group.

He wondered if Fournier and his people walked into danger, or if they simply skirted past it, hurried to reach their safe haven in Canada.

"These instructions," Metzger said to Molly. "Do you think they apply to more than just Fournier and his group?"

"You mean multiple groups?" she questioned. "I think so, but it seems they had a network in place, which means they probably have multiple rendezvous points. I doubt anyone is simply going to walk up to one of these and find the mastermind behind all of this."

"Nadeau," Metzger reminded her of the name.

"Right."

Pressing forward, the group spotted a zombie ahead of them along the left side where construction suddenly stopped and only the initial groundwork of the road was visible. Without any barriers along the side, and only portions of the foundation completed with solid materials, a person not paying attention might fall off the side of the bridge altogether. As this zombie took notice of the group coming her way, she focused her gaze at them and began walking without once looking to the ground. One instant she was walking at them with slacks and a tattered blouse, and the next she disappeared from sight as the ground vanished from beneath her feet.

Metzger didn't see how until he stepped closer, but she walked off solid concrete to a portion of the bridge where only guide wires and rebar formed a skeletal version of what the bridge was meant to become. He peered off the bridge, finding the Niagara River flowing below, meaning a fall that would almost certainly kill someone when they impacted with the water where the river met Lake Erie. At best, the victim would break enough bones that they drowned shortly thereafter from an inability to swim.

A thought occurred to Metzger that Fournier and anyone with him might spot them and take shots with a sniper rifle, or lay some kind of trap. More than likely, however, they were moving as quickly as humanly possible to the rendezvous point to escape their due punishment. The trip to Canada wasn't extremely far, and Metzger assumed they located a vehicle at some point, so they were likely two days behind Fournier, but this was their *only* realistic chance at finding some answers.

Crossing the bridge didn't take as much time as Metzger initially figured. It felt like a one-mile hike with a few murderous obstacles along the way. Several cars dangled precariously over the side of the bridge, and more than once they encountered undead trapped inside vehicles for eternity unless someone put them out of their misery. On the other end of the bridge they found the booths in much the same condition as the others, with vehicles lined up in all varying degrees for a quarter mile.

During the trek across Peace Bridge, Metzger saw a few zombies floating in the Niagara River between Lake Erie and Lake Ontario. Short of bottled water he occasionally discovered on the road, Metzger didn't chance drinking water from any natural source after seeing the undead contaminate virtually every stream, river, pond, and lake he'd seen during his travels. Even a rural well might present a hazard if a zombie randomly fell into it, and though Metzger couldn't scientifically determine whether the undead contaminated water through extended contact, he didn't want to take the chance.

Fighting their way past a few more random undead, the group finally saw some clear patches off the side of the road where vehicles once slowed for the border crossing. Metzger consciously began looking for a vehicle or two that might transport the group to their destination, still at least an hour away by car if they didn't encounter any issues.

"See anything enticing?" Bryce asked as the group came back together, divided by the occasional vehicle as they neared the end of the congestion.

"There," Metzger said, pointing to an older van that might hold all of them.

Bryce allowed the Marines to scope out the vehicle first, perhaps giving their leader a chance to look good in front of his men and regain some dignity after creating an unnecessary argument. They surrounded it, guns in a ready position, and one of the subordinates slid the side door open. No zombies emerged, and after half a minute or so the leader walked over to Bryce, Metzger, and Molly.

"It's clear, but we couldn't locate any keys."

"Let's spread out and look around," Bryce ordered no one in particular. "Every passing second puts us that much closer to losing this lead."

Metzger and Molly fanned out toward a group of cars near a crew cab truck, finding one car occupied by a zombie and another with two flat tires. The truck, however, posed no threat, and after a brief search, Molly came up with keys from the glove compartment. She dangled them in front of Metzger with a thankful smile.

"Let's just hope it has gas," she said, putting them in the ignition and getting the truck to turn over.

Two of the Marines found a small green car that functioned, so those two took the car, leaving Metzger, his brother, Molly, and the Marine leader in the truck.

Navigating the roads and highways proved a cinch once they were away from the border crossing, and Molly read and reread the instructions about how to meet the liaison once they reached St. Catharines. She expressed concerns that they might not fit the bill regarding what this person expected, so Metzger and Molly volunteered to pose as a couple, leaving the military men a safe distance behind them until the trap was sprung.

Oddly enough, the instructions ordered them to drive through a number of residential areas along mostly urban roads on their way to the rendezvous point. Molly pointed to an area of the map the Marines had found with a concerned look on her face.

"General Motors of Canada Company," Metzger read aloud. "Hell, that's probably where they would've detonated one of those trucks."

"It is," Bryce confirmed. "We'd better hope that shit isn't lingering in the air, or we'll all be breathing it."

"Why have us meet someone so close to a target site?" Molly questioned.

"Could your instructions be a trick?" the Marine leader inquired.

"I doubt it. They weren't easy to find, and they would've just hidden them instead of putting dummy copies in their place."

"This is dangerous, sending them in without backup," the Marine warned.

"They volunteered," Bryce reminded him. "We won't be far behind."

Molly continued to study the instructions.

"Unfortunately, you may not be able to get too close without giving away your position," she stated. "This place has two buildings several blocks removed from any other structures."

Metzger stole a glance at the magnified, more detailed map attached to the instructions. They were heading to a dead-end street near a canal, and at the edge of a business district. He wasn't sure what purpose the two buildings served before the apocalypse, but it stood to reason that Nadeau's people planned ahead and repurposed them before that fateful day. They stood in isolation, surrounded by lots of green that might have been a cornfield, a golf course, or some kind of large park, tucked away from the hubbub of the rest of the city.

When the vehicles turned onto Glendale Avenue, Metzger knew they were drawing close to their destination. He leaned forward from the backseat, holding the map for his brother and the Marine to view.

"Once we cross the bridge over the canal, they'll probably hear us coming. Might I suggest Molly and I take the car the rest of the way and you guys go on foot to cover us?"

Bryce contemplated the plan momentarily, and the Marine remained silent, deferring to the designated leader of their mission.

"It's our best chance," Bryce decided, but you'll have to give us reasonable time to find cover and watch your backs."

Strangely enough, their turn was an unnamed road off Glendale Avenue, and until they drew closer and spotted a row of trees along the back of the property, no one spoke. They'd followed the instructions perfectly, and the wording even spoke of an unnamed road. The undead were present throughout the area leading to the road, but in the immediate vicinity, no zombies were visible.

"They've kept this area clear," Metzger reasoned aloud. "They *are* expecting guests."

"The question is whether you're going to be the first guests they see, or are they going to shoot you on sight?" Bryce countered.

"Only one way to find out," Molly said, reaching for her door handle.

She and Metzger exited the truck, fully prepared to swap vehicles. Metzger felt somewhat amazed that odors of death didn't linger in the air like they often did in urban areas. Urine and fecal release accompanied death in any mammal, so in a concentrated area the smells became overwhelming, sometimes worse than standing in a landfill.

At the moment, the group remained a few city blocks from the two buildings in question, but they had no idea of knowing whether they were detected, and if their plan might work.

"The instructions say there's a tree in the front yard with a bell on it," Molly stated, still clutching the sheet of paper. "We ring it three times, and someone is supposed to greet us. No random person is going to know this, so I think we can pull it off."

"We don't have much choice," Bryce reasoned. "Take the car, miss the unmarked road on purpose, and turn around and go back. That should give us enough time to get in position and cover you while we scout the property."

When Metzger and Molly started to turn to leave, Bryce stopped them.

"I want you to give me a signal if you see trouble right away and need us to come running," he said.

"I'll hold two fingers out near my hip," Metzger said, demonstrating what he meant until he received affirmative nods from everyone around him.

Metzger had read the instructions with Molly several times through, but he still harbored a feeling of doubt about the plan working. He wasn't sure if one set of people possessed the instructions, or several hundred different factions knew about the backup plan from various locations. Curiosity ate at him, and he wanted to get to the bottom of their plan, and understand how so many people appeared to know about the end of civilization, and not one of them found the courage to speak out.

Perhaps the information wasn't disseminated any further than a handful of lieutenants, because Metzger couldn't imagine all of them who knew would be onboard with seeing their loved ones and much of the world murdered. Another possibility occurred to him that the intended consequences never meant to turn people into zombies without heartbeats.

"You drive," Molly said, nodding towards the car.

Metzger complied, and once they were inside, he started the car and drove it slowly in the direction of the unmarked road. He tried keeping their actions realistic, like a couple searching for the road listed on their tattered, vague map.

A few different times he glanced in the rearview mirror, failing to find his brother or the Marines. Hiding spots near the two buildings were fairly easy to come by because trees and shrubs formed a line behind the property and along the side closest to Glendale Avenue. Metzger worried more about the closing distance between the vegetation and the buildings if he and Molly were ushered inside. If the buildings were modified before the dawn of the apocalypse, the military men would be blind to the interior, possibly walking into a trap if they needed to enter.

For his part, Metzger planned on acting harmless, hoping his new hosts didn't shoot him on sight or believe he threatened their plans.

He turned around just down the road, finding an unusual number of vehicles around, indicating someone carried out routine sweeps of the area to clear vehicles and staggering dead. When he pulled into the short driveway that made a curve in front of both buildings on the property, he parked in the middle, eyeing the tree with the bell on it. He looked to Molly, who tried providing reassurance with a grin, but they both knew the danger they faced, even if they weren't certain the risk was worth the reward.

Metzger glanced in the rearview mirror, unable to see the military men, wondering if they hadn't yet reached their positions, or simply remained well-hidden.

"Ready?" he asked Molly.

"As ever," she replied.

When Metzger stepped from the car, he noticed the one building appeared more like a garage, or outbuilding of some sort, and on the side facing the house, not one window existed. Built like a metal pole barn, the building appeared to exist for storage, rather than living quarters. He pictured a lawn mower, perhaps a tractor, and other large equipment being housed beneath its metal roof.

Strangely, the house appeared fortified, its windows boarded up with wood coverings as though hurricane season were expected to hit at any moment. Metzger had seen similar houses, and such décor was usually a dead giveaway that the living still occupied them, or *had* occupied them, expecting to ride out the storm of the undead plaguing the world.

In this case, however, the people inside likely found good reason to keep themselves holed up as they waited for visitors in the days following the apocalypse.

Molly walked over to the tree, and looked to Metzger before reaching up to grab the small rope attached to the bell that hung from a branch at eye level. He provided a nod, and she rang the bell slowly, and distinctly, three times, so anyone inside knew the ringing was not the wind, or random passersby fooling around.

Daring to glance at the tree line surrounding the property along the back and the side closest to Glendale Avenue, Metzger still didn't see a soul. He worried that the Marines had been pissed off by Bryce and taken the opportunity to revoke their orders and harm him, but they were professionals. Chain-of-command seemed a bit lax with government employees not being paid in the traditional sense, and a lot of ego appeared to accompany some of the more dangerous missions, at least from his perspective.

From the corner of his eye, he caught a glimpse of a rifle barrel, barely emerging from the side of one tree, and he knew someone had his back. He turned to the front door, wondering why their reception took so long. He pictured a small gathering inside, and Fournier being extremely paranoid after his close call with death and the grave misdeeds carried out at the former school. Clenching his right fist at his side, Metzger contemplated the kinds of punishments he wanted to inflict upon Fournier, but the door opened to a young man dressed in black jeans and a black long-sleeve shirt who studied them briefly before speaking.

"Can I help you?" he asked.

Molly held up the sheet of paper with the instructions.

"We're here for refuge," she replied.

Giving a crooked grin, the man didn't immediately move from the doorway.

"That's odd. You're the second set of people in the last day to come here. Where'd you come from?"

"The greater Buffalo area," Metzger answered, trying to avoid being specific.

He suspected Fournier and any associates were holed up inside, and Metzger couldn't state he was part of their group, or the door would be slammed in their faces.

Still not moving, the younger man looked between them suspiciously. Metzger knew he and Molly would be outnumbered once they stepped inside, and these people would likely ask for their weapons in exchange for protection.

"We didn't think anyone else survived," Metzger said, quickly thinking of a way to neutralize the man's distrust.

"Survived what?"

"We got back to the school, and this group of assholes had taken it over. We've been on the road a few weeks, trying to find our people, but I didn't think anyone else survived the attack."

"What group were you with?" the young man asked, obviously intrigued by the story, likely because Fournier told him a slightly altered version.

"We were with Xavier Fournier, but we left on an errand that day, and when we got back, everything had gone to hell."

Metzger's wording registered a barely detectable hint of recognition in the man's eyes, and he knew his arch nemesis was either hiding within the walls of this house, or had been as recently as a day ago. Whether this man let them inside, or not, no longer mattered to him. He needed answers immediately, and he wasn't going to put Molly at risk by getting them locked inside a modified homestead.

"Is he here?" Metzger asked, feigning interest enough to bestow him an acting award if such things still existed.

Now the man appeared on the fence about letting them inside, or screaming for help, so Metzger attempted the last move in his arsenal.

"If he survived, then everything isn't lost," he said, holding out two fingers near his hip area.

Seventeen

Jillian felt her blood boil as she confronted the woman who caused so many problems in her town for several years.

"How dare you step foot in South Hill again," Jillian stammered as Gracine, Sutton, Luke, and Samantha took her side.

"You uppity people always thought you were too good for us," Dark Lady spat her reply. "We brought our goods to your little town festival, so you could chew us up and spit us out."

"Because you overstayed your welcome, bitch."

Gracine tapped Jillian on the arm that held a firearm loosely pointed at Dark Lady and the three men who now took her side.

"Girl, what the fuck is going on here?"

"This bitch and her band of simpletons waged war against our town after they tried to make South Hill their personal storage facility and the town council took action."

"Your precious council ripped us off," Dark Lady said. "As restitution, we're taking the town for ourselves."

Jillian didn't want to give in to demands, but she had three adults and a child to worry about. For the moment, she wasn't going to address the worst of the crimes the people before her committed against her formerly quaint town.

"Where the hell is Buster?" Jillian quietly asked Sutton to the side.

"He's in a car a few blocks from here."

"Lot of good that does *us*."

"Sorry," Sutton replied with a slight rolling of his eyes.

"My cards told me about you," Dark Lady stated, her eyes burning daggers into Jillian. "They revealed a virgin would degrade herself by fornicating out of wedlock."

Everyone looked from Dark Lady to Jillian and back with surprised stares. Jillian recalled Dark Lady proclaiming herself a fortune teller within her tent every year at their hometown festival. Jillian considered her words bullshit back in the day, and nothing had changed regarding her feelings about the woman's occupation and behavior.

"Did they tell you that you might die today?" she asked, pointing the gun directly at Dark Lady.

"No, they did not."

"Shoot the lot of them and be done with it," Sutton said with a hint of concern in his tone.

He typically remained stoic, regardless of what odds the group faced, but something about the carnies got to his psyche.

"You need to get off our property," Dark Lady demanded, which seemed rather bold considering no one in her party held a firearm.

"Start shooting," Gracine said, nodding toward the animated corpse of the man who flew part of their group to Virginia when they otherwise wouldn't have made it.

"I can't," Jillian replied, drawing quizzical stares from her group. "There might be more of them."

"Look at it as thinning the herd," Sutton prodded.

"Starting a war with them right here and now isn't what we need," Jillian insisted. "We need to regroup before we do anything."

Dark Lady took a step forward before speaking, looking like a cross between a witch and the crazy townsperson who uttered ominous warnings to passersby.

"My cards foretold of bloodshed," she announced with a deepening to her voice. "If you and your friends don't leave, it's inevitable."

"You killing our friend made conflict inevitable," Jillian countered. "We want him back."

"You can't have him back, you tramp," Dark Lady sneered. "Shoot me if you want, but it won't save you."

Jillian fought to make a decision while leaving the emotional element behind. Any move based on rage, or made in the heat of the moment, might create a situation too large for her friends to handle, especially with one of them already deceased.

Instead of shooting anyone, Jillian walked over to Vazquez, who saw her only as food at this point, while she slid the gun into her back pocket. He groped at her, completely unaware in his primal state that she reached for a pocket knife in her front pocket, quickly unfolding it because she didn't want the goons occupying the property to charge her. Vazquez growled at her, and as she risked getting close to him, his fingers began to clasp her clothing, but Jillian ended the conflict before any damage was done, stabbing him in the side of the skull with the knife forcefully.

He slumped over, but couldn't fall to the ground because of the rod stuck through various parts of his body to keep him standing as an animated display piece. Jillian wanted to remove him from the post and give him an appropriate burial, but time didn't permit. She didn't want to endanger the others.

She simply needed to make a statement, and she'd accomplished that much. Playing a human chess game against Dark Lady and her assembled family required patience and strategy. Jillian wasn't about to leave her hometown to such mentally unstable people, though she personally found little reason to stay.

"Where are the rest of you?" Jillian demanded, wiping the knife blade clean along some of Vazquez's clothes before pocketing it and drawing the sidearm.

Dark Lady simply provided a smirk that turned into a sneer after a few seconds.

"Wouldn't you like to know?"

"Bitch, I will murder you right now and hunt them down if I have to."

"It's not in you, honey," Dark Lady said confidently. "My cards said so."

Jillian looked to Samantha, who huddled by Luke's side, confused by all of the adult conversation and negativity. At that moment, Jillian knew the gypsy woman spoke the truth, but she wasn't going to let her and the dangerous, deranged people who accompanied her win in the end. She couldn't bring herself to murder, particularly in front of her group members.

"Let's go," Jillian said to her friends, storming toward the opening in the fence.

Everyone followed, but once they were a few houses away from the dangerous clan, Sutton spoke.

"Give me that gun so I can eliminate them right here and now," he said sternly.

"You're in no position to make demands," Jillian told him, stopping to point her finger directly at his face. "And you don't understand the situation. There aren't just four of them. We'll be lucky if their whole lot didn't survive the apocalypse, then you can count on a caravan driving circus trailers and fucking clown cars through my hometown."

"So, we run?" Luke asked with a shrug.

"No," Jillian said firmly. "They don't get off that easy."

"We can't just leave Juan with them," Gracine said. "I know he's no longer, you know, but he deserves better than being stuck with those crazies."

"I don't plan on leaving anyone behind," Jillian said. "They overstayed their welcome before, and we got rid of them then."

"Because you had cops and state troopers," Luke stated the obvious. "What are we going to do against a small army of oversized morons?"

"We don't need brawn," Jillian said, "when brains will work just fine."

She looked in the direction of their four new enemies, but no one followed them, and as the group made their way to the road, Jillian still saw no signs of threats.

"We need to get our stuff from the house and load up," Jillian stated.

"So, we *are* leaving?" Luke asked, his face depicting his confusion.

"No, but we're going to let them think they've won," Jillian answered.

"This is insane," Sutton argued. "We should either count ourselves lucky and move on to our next destination, or we should go back and shoot all of them right now."

Jillian felt a growing anger, because her group didn't understand how Dark Lady and her people worked. She faulted herself for not giving the more detailed story, but she decided to rectify the situation immediately.

"You guys have to understand these people, and what they're about. They're an infestation that will take over my hometown, and then they'll move on, like nomads, and suck up any resources they find anywhere they go. We won't be done dealing with them until we're dead, or they are."

Jillian emphasized her final point by swinging her right arm wildly at the camp they just departed.

"How do you propose we deal with them?" Luke asked.

"We poison the well," Jillian answered, drawing some confused looks. "The remaining items in the general store are things we aren't dying to take with us. We tamper with the food and any bottled items, and let them come and get it."

"That's dark," Sutton admitted.

"It's necessary," Jillian said emphatically. "These people aren't going away, and they're dangerous as hell."

Sutton tapped his chin momentarily.

"Okay," he agreed. "But we need to come up with a plan, and all of us need to be on board."

Jillian wondered if his words were an attempt to make up for his past discretions, but she needed someone on her side, regardless of who stepped forward.

As though on cue, Driscoll pulled up beside the group and stepped from the car he'd used. Standing silently momentarily, he waited for someone to say something because he knew within a matter of minutes, he'd missed quite a bit of backstory.

Within a few minutes the group caught him up on their ordeal, and he appeared to take their side without even meeting the cause of their latest problem. In the meantime, he'd driven them to the car where Sutton kept Buster safe, and the canine appeared thrilled to experience open air momentarily before immediately being confined in another vehicle with barely enough room for humans, much less him.

"Sounds like we need to get every gun we have," Driscoll said. "Can I offer you fine folks a ride?"

His statement broke the tension, drawing grins and smirks as the group piled into the car, despite the crowded conditions.

Once they reached what would be considered the highway portion of the road that connected much of the town, Driscoll stopped as though waiting to see if traffic approached in either direction.

"What are you waiting for?" Sutton asked. "I think we have the right of way these days."

"Look at that," Driscoll said, staring to the left.

"Look at what?" Jillian asked before a dust cloud grew in the distance, as though they were parked in the desert and strong winds swirled dirt and blasted it their way.

Jillian immediately knew what it meant, and for a moment, she and her group shared uncertainty of what action to take next.

Forced to be spectators, because there wasn't really anywhere to go, the group watched as two large trucks pulling painted trailers behind them rolled past, and the people inside the vehicles looked much like Dark Lady and her other three followers. Both vehicles barreled through without incident, though Jillian suspected her group was carefully observed by the newcomers.

"The circus has come to town," she muttered once both vehicles turned, heading toward the still present plume of smoke in the distance.

Her chances of recovering Vazquez and giving him a proper burial with so many enemies encamped in her old town felt minimal. Squeezed between Gracine and Luke in the backseat, with Samantha seated atop Luke's lap, she began to lose hope of battling the trespassers and chasing them to the next town.

"What the hell do we do about that?" Driscoll inquired, his voice cracking a bit from the intimidation they all felt.

"I've still got a sniper rifle," Sutton said. "And she has a damn good scope."

"We need to get our asses back to the house and get our shit together," Gracine said. "These freaks aren't going to sit around after the show Jillian just gave them. You and that woman got beef, girlfriend."

"I know," Jillian said. "And that's why I can't let this go."

"They now double us in number," Sutton noted.

"I know, but they aren't armed like us," Jillian replied, "and they aren't as smart as us. I can get us around the town so they'll have no idea we're still here."

"You seriously want to go to war with these nuts?" Luke asked incredulously. "I can't let you throw a little girl in the middle of this vendetta."

Driscoll started driving toward the house where most of the group stayed. One glance around indicated to Jillian that they weren't being observed or followed by Dark Lady and her adopted children.

"They're a threat," Sutton said firmly, but in a tone that didn't indicate he'd picked a side in this debate.

"We can't go charging into that camp of theirs," Gracine said. "They're going to fortify that place and lock it down."

"There's no need," Jillian said, still confident they could deal with their adversaries in more covert ways.

A few minutes later, the group arrived at the house, finding the setting a bit different as the front door remained wide open, and several items were strewn across the yard.

"What the hell?" Luke stammered, stepping from the car as he surveyed the damage.

"They were here," Jillian answered slowly. "They must be using some kind of short-range radios."

Gracine gave her a look that registered somewhere between desperation and anger.

"What?" Jillian asked.

"The guns."

Everyone dashed inside, finding the house decimated with their clothes lying across the floor, and atop furniture, and virtually anything of value missing.

"Fuck," Gracine muttered. "They got almost everything."

"There wasn't time to grab everything," Jillian said, upending some furniture, finding a few smaller pistols and handheld weapons still in their hiding places. "They made a quick sweep while we were distracted."

Sutton stepped inside, surveying the chaos within the house. Buster walked in behind him, taking his master's side, but his tail remained down because he sensed the human tension.

"We have a stockpile where we were staying," Sutton said. "We need to get over there and decide what our next step will be."

Before anyone could utter another word, the sound of a large truck roaring from down the road reached their ears, and everyone knew their situation was about to get much worse.

Virtually defenseless, and being pursued by their adversaries, the group scrambled outdoors to find their worst fears realized.

"Get in the car," Sutton said with an eerie calm. "We're getting the guns and dealing with these fucks."

"I'm scared!" Samantha shouted, looking to Luke for guidance and protection.

Luke looked helplessly to the group for reassurance or ideas. Jillian knew she couldn't place the child in danger, and she didn't want Sutton to bark something that put them in further peril.

"Go and hide," she instructed Luke. "Both of you. And don't come out until this is finished and we come find you."

"What if it doesn't go well?" Luke asked with a tone that indicated guilt because he didn't want the others getting hurt due to him.

"Then you get out of here and make your own way."

Luke nodded his thanks, took Samantha by the hand, and headed into the house to grab a few items, or stay out of sight.

"We need to move," Jillian said, looking to Sutton, who nodded affirmatively, giving a slight indication of happiness they were on the same side again.

Driscoll jumped into the driver's seat while everyone else, including Buster, occupied the remaining spaces within. Driscoll wasted no time getting the car out of the neighborhood and up to speed on the main road where the larger vehicle bore down on them with intent to maim.

"Well, this is going to suck," he commented, making a sharp left turn ahead of the vehicle, and another tight turn to the right, sending the larger custom painted vehicle flying past them on the highway.

"This isn't the best way," Jillian commented, forgetting that everyone else had spent a week or more in her town, which provided plenty of time to memorize the layout of the streets and explore South Hill.

"It is if we want to lose them," Driscoll responded, continuing to weave in and out of streets before the men in the pursuing truck ever caught sight of them.

"Just get us back to the house so we can grab those guns," Sutton said, his voice lacking its self-assured confidence.

Jillian couldn't believe how quickly tensions escalated between her group and the faction led by Dark Lady. One simple mistake, or lapse in judgment by Vazquez, allowed the carnival people, who went completely feral in the apocalypse, to swoop in and take over her hometown. Even worse, she felt stupid for not believing in her own people, allowing them to get captured, without ever sensing the true danger around her.

When Driscoll finally turned onto the correct street leading to where he and Sutton had stayed the past week, Sutton tensed, looking forward, muttering some words Jillian could barely understand.

"Fuck, fuck, fuck. Where is it?"

"Where is what?" Gracine questioned, looking nervously between Sutton and the houses ahead of them.

"His box truck," Jillian answered, not seeing the mammoth large object anywhere in the distance.

"Please tell me your guns weren't in that truck," Gracine said more than asked.

"No," Sutton said blankly, as though shock were setting in, his despondence clearly evident.

By now the larger circus vehicle had located them, and made its presence felt as it turned behind them on their current street.

"You *do* have guns, right?" Gracine asked, turning to Driscoll.

"Well, fuck, I hope so, but if they got the truck, God only knows what else they got."

Suddenly the four of them possessed a common goal of survival, despite past feuds, the color of their skin, or their individual and collective losses. Jillian worried about Sutton because the man appeared transfixed on the loss of his box truck, and not the immediate threat to their very lives.

"Colby, snap out of it," Jillian said lightly tapping him on the face. "If they have your truck, we're *going* to get it back."

"And how do you propose we do that?" he asked, still not completely snapping out of his trance.

"We'll kill every last one of them if we need to."

"Girl, you got an unhealthy obsession with these freaks," Gracine commented.

"You would, too, if you saw how they were before the world fell apart," Jillian replied. "They were built for this, and believe me, it's them or us. Or did you already forget they were going to make lawn ornaments out of the two of you?"

"I haven't forgotten."

Driscoll pulled into the driveway, finding the front doors of the two residences he and Sutton occupied wide-open.

"This doesn't look good," the man commented, parking in the lawn between the two houses so the group could split up and look for firearms inside either house.

Driscoll and Gracine immediately exited the vehicle, but Sutton remained seated, still blankly looking for his lost truck, which was long gone in Jillian's estimation. Even Buster exited, taking Jillian's side, figuring his owner would join him momentarily.

"There's no way they could've gotten it that fast," Sutton mumbled, his eyes in a trance as he looked at the vacated parking spot.

"Come on," Jillian said, tugging at his arm.

She glanced up, finding the much larger circus vehicle barreling at them, and not slowing down. Continuing to pull on Sutton's arm, Jillian knew she was either about to get Sutton to move, or they were both going to be roadkill. Personally, she didn't want to give Dark Lady any free kills, because she wanted their group wiped off the face of the planet.

"Come on!" she yelled more emphatically, tugging at Sutton with all of her might, seeing the noisy truck drawing dangerously close.

Jillian knew Gracine and Driscoll would be on their own in another five seconds if she couldn't get Sutton to budge, and by the time his eyes locked on to hers, Jillian wondered if he'd come to his senses too late.

Eighteen

An awkward moment passed as Metzger, Molly, and the stranger at the door all exchanged glances, and Molly held up the document to enforce their right to gain entry into the sanctuary. In reality, she bought them a few precious moments as indecision crossed the sentry's mind of their legitimacy, because Fournier obviously hadn't mentioned any other survivors from his party. They either died in the skirmish against Molly's people, or he left them behind.

In a sudden move he tried to slam the door on them, but Metzger threw his right palm against the door before the latch caught, keeping precious inches between them and the answers they sought. By now the military men had reached their position, and everyone threw their combined weight into the door as much as a cluster of six people reasonably could at one time.

Metzger felt the brunt of the door against his chest and right cheek as he was slammed inward by the military men behind him, including his brother. He fell to the floor momentarily, watching feet run past him as Molly knelt by his side.

"You okay?" she asked, shaking her head as though she'd been a casualty of the door thrashing as well.

"I will be," Metzger answered, scrambling to his feet, hearing noise in virtually every direction.

Patting himself down for injuries, and to ensure his weapons remained with him, Metzger heard the sounds of yelling and footsteps growing distant. He looked around, seeing a reasonably normal living room, kitchen, and small sleeping area off to one side, but the noise came from farther down the hall.

Much farther.

"What the hell?" he questioned, tapping Molly on the arm before heading in the direction of the noise.

They quickly left the light and safety of the main living area to a darkened hallway until Metzger ran into a wall.

"Where are they?" he questioned, reaching his arms out in each direction, feeling nothing except a wall on either side.

Stuffing his hand into his right pocket, Metzger produced the miniature flashlight he often carried, turning it on to find two doors on either side of the hallway. He shined the light inside the first one on the right, finding a bedroom with a square about two feet by two feet cut in the center of the room.

"What the fuck is that?" he questioned aloud.

"They built some kind of bugout tunnel," Molly answered. "Let's check the other rooms."

Metzger went with her to each of the rooms, shining the light, and finding similar squares cut into the floors, but in various locations. By no means concealed, they were meant for a very quick escape if danger burst through the front door.

"Which one?" he questioned aloud, wondering which of the squares the greeted jumped down, and if their actual target had taken another.

"They went to that side," Molly pointed across the hall. "Maybe the tunnels on this side meet up somewhere."

"Better to cover our bases," Metzger said, shining the light into the closest hatch, finding a ladder that led directly into the ground.

He scurried down, with Molly behind him, realizing immediately that such a network of vast tunnels wasn't created in a month's time. One aim of his light down the hallway revealed that the tunnel before them went on as far as the beam reached.

"Let's go," he said, realizing the echoes of voices and footsteps ceased the moment they went underground.

Instinctively taking Molly by the hand, because he held the light, he started down the hall, which proved just wide enough to allow a single person passage at one time. Like a mine shaft, it possessed wooden beams for support in regular intervals, but the job hardly looked professional to Metzger. At the end of the tunnel, he was presented with a right turn, which he took, realizing the tunnel didn't necessarily meet up with any other passages.

"Have your gun ready," he instructed Molly just above a whisper, knowing he couldn't light the way and draw weapons at a moment's notice.

"Already do," she answered.

Metzger made three more turns before he discovered the tunnel met up with another opening, which he assumed was the other bedroom's tunnel from the same side of the house. Not once had he heard a peep from the military men, and he began questioning his decision to take a separate route. Safety concerns didn't weigh on his mind, but rather the notion that chose incorrectly, or worse, picked a dead-end the workers hadn't finished.

Although the journey felt like half a mile, Metzger didn't imagine they were incredibly far from the original house, and once the two tunnels merged, he saw a hatch or door at the end of the path.

"There's an exit ahead," he informed Molly, still tugging lightly on her arm so she didn't get disoriented in the dark behind him.

He reached what looked like a half door, and Metzger needed to crouch just to get to its level. With no handle to pull, he gave it a push and quickly surmised the door pushed outward only. Likely a security measure to keep the undead or animals from entering, the hatch appeared spring-loaded to snap shut once he and Molly passed through it to a small room with a ladder leading about six feet upward. Metzger shut off the tiny flashlight and pocketed it for safekeeping. Above them, daylight pierced a heavy screen that once covered a square opening, but now looked tossed hurriedly to one side. Metzger's heart raced as he realized someone had used the tunnel just before them and escaped to the vast outdoors.

Molly noticed it, too, and urged him to ascend the ladder with a nod when he looked to her.

"Kick his ass."

Metzger adeptly climbed the ladder, shoved the screen aside, and felt his feet hit solid ground as he surveyed each direction around him, seeing no sign of his brother or the Marines. In the distance, however, he spotted a man running as hard as a person could toward the nearby bridge, and beyond it, the city.

"Shit," Metzger muttered, before turning to Molly, who climbed the ladder behind him. "I'm going to follow him into the city. Send help when you find the others."

"You got it," Molly replied, not volunteering to come with him, because the pace already appeared grueling and she hadn't recovered from her ordeal at the school.

With a gun at his side, and a short sword strapped to the pack on his back, Metzger took off in a dead sprint behind the man, who had nearly a quarter mile lead on him along open ground. Beyond the bridge he saw the safety that the small Canadian city offered the man he assumed was Xavier Fournier. He figured Fournier didn't know the layout of the city, despite being Canadian, but hundreds of buildings offering sanctuary to *anyone* willing to brave the undead masses that likely lingered along the streets.

If Metzger lost sight of him beyond the city limits, Fournier was as good as free, for what little good it did the man without aid, manpower, or a place to call his base of operations.

Picking up his pace, he could only hope something slowed Fournier before the man reached the heart of St. Catharines.

***

Bryce felt terrible about helping slam his brother to the ground, but he maintained his grouping with the Marines, who possessed firearms and their attached flashlights. Only his familiarity with the house and the property allowed the gatekeeper who answered the door a head start down a tunnel in the first right side bedroom of the house.

One of the Marines caught the man, pinned him to the ground, and subdued him within seconds of his boots hitting the dirt floor below the bedroom. Bryce carried on behind the remaining Marines, who continued the search without having many facts. They had seen that Fournier didn't answer the door, and Bryce's brother wouldn't have signaled for assistance if only one man opposed him.

Following the men single file further into the underground lair, Bryce couldn't see very well because he didn't have a flashlight attached to his rifle, and the beams ahead of him kept bouncing up and down as the Marines raced down the narrow passageway. It looked exactly like the television shows and movies where the camera followed the action, never capturing much detail because it bobbed up and down so often. He fought to surge ahead too quickly, worried he might bump into one of the men ahead of him and cause a chain reaction of them tumbling to the ground.

Keeping his rifle pointed safely to his side, Bryce decided to maintain contact with the man ahead of him by pressing his left palm against the man's back. When the Marines made several turns he followed them, eventually taking note that their tunnel met up with another underground system. Seeing what he thought might be daylight ahead of them, he heard the Marines shout orders and dash down the tunnel. Almost left behind, Bryce managed to keep pace, stopping short of the room where the three men pulled a man off the ladder, hurling him to the ground before one of the Marines scrambled upward to check for any additional escapees.

"Stay down!" one of the Marines ordered the man plucked from the ladder.

"Not our target," Bryce said after one look at the man's face. "But he's still got information we need."

Clamoring up the ladder, Bryce found the Marine who went before him chasing down another man into the woods behind the house. He took a moment to look for any other activity, but the house itself blocked his view of the front yard. Unable to spot additional activity, or his brother, Bryce followed the Marine who chased the man through the lightly wooded area behind the house. Eventually the young Marine, in peak physical condition, caught up with the last known suspect, tackling him to the ground.

Although this man wasn't in excellent cardiovascular condition, he proved to be a larger man than any of the military men pursuing him. He immediately turned around, punching the Marine across the jaw before Bryce noticed the impending scuffle, stopping it before it truly began by jumping on the man's chest and pinning him to the ground so the Marine could draw a plastic tie from his gun belt.

"Let me go!" the larger man protested from beneath Bryce's weight. "I ain't got nothin' in this!"

He sounded distinctly American, almost from a southern state based on Bryce's experience in the Navy, working with men and women from every region of the United States.

"Where are you from?" he asked the man without giving the notion much thought.

"None of ur fuckin' business."

Bryce delivered a swift elbow to the man's jaw, partially as retaliation for being so difficult, but also to subdue him long enough for the Marine to secure his wrists with the plastic tie. The man groaned, still not being cooperative as he struggled against the two of them, despite lacking functional use of his hands.

One of the other Marines joined them, looking directly to Bryce.

"The woman says she and your brother chased another man through another set of tunnels and your brother is chasing that man into the downtown district on foot."

"Fuck," Bryce muttered. "That *has* to be our guy."

"Want us to load up and pursue him?"

"No," Bryce said, thinking aloud. "We have three prisoners already. I'll take Molly with me and we'll find him. If you're able to load these sons-of-bitches into the vehicles, feel free to back us up."

"The woman is up front," the Marine said, refusing to call her by name for some reason.

"Thanks."

Bryce ran around the house, rather than returning to the tunnels without the benefit of a flashlight. He entered through the front, finding a concerned Molly standing in the main room.

"We took another set of tunnels but the guy had a head start on us," she said.

"That's fine," Bryce said. "Are you well enough to come with me?"

"I can tough it out. We need to find this guy."

"Agreed."

Bryce walked outside first, still holding his rifle, making room for Molly to step past him and lead the way. She gave a nod and pointed to an area across the bridge where neither the man, nor Bryce's younger brother, were visible.

Running into the heart of a city, even a smaller city by comparison, brought about challenges, which included navigation, the undead, and worse, survivors.

***

Metzger reached the edge of the city where he'd maintained visual contact with Fournier the entire time, but when the man found an opportunity to change direction, he turned left at a city block. Metzger followed, less than a block's distance behind the man now, finding him running along some restaurants and banks that looked worse than abandoned buildings in the world before the apocalypse.

What he termed 'zombie dust' covered everything from vehicles to buildings and signs as dead skin flakes floated freely through the air from the undead. Virtually everything walking upright was dead, meaning any breeze carried the skin cells through the air until they found somewhere to land, and no shortage of flakes existed.

Immediately spying the danger of running into the city, Metzger noticed several zombies milling around the streets, taking notice of two men darting past them. They growled and hissed at Fournier, but most of them turned their attention to Metzger before he reached them. Barely slowing his run, he drew his sword by reaching his hand over his shoulder, and sliced both of them through the skulls without slowing down. He consciously made the decision not to use his bladed weapon on Fournier. The man held answers the group so desperately needed, and murdering the man by slicing him open, or poisoning his bloodstream with contaminated zombie innards, would certainly thwart any future plans of interrogating him.

Both Fournier and Metzger began to tire, and both knew they needed a little reserve in their stamina to deal with undead adversaries. At the next intersection, Fournier nearly got taken down by a zombie, but the lifeless adversary stumbled and fell down atop the concrete instead. Landing on its face, an injury that would stun or bloody a live person, the zombie simply rolled over and took a swipe at Metzger's foot as he ran past.

Drawing closer to Fournier, Metzger almost didn't have time to react when the man stopped, whirled around, and pointed a pistol at him. Metzger ducked into a doorway with matching white pillars as several bullets struck the nearest pillar, splintering it in several places. Daring to peek out, he saw Fournier had already taken off again, but there was only one direction for him to go, so Metzger followed.

His instincts kicked in, and Metzger knew the gunfire would draw the attention of surrounding zombies. Fournier had put more distance between them, but Metzger hadn't lost sight of him yet. He watched as the man attempted to bust into an old Burger King, but failed because the doors were secured. Fournier didn't give up, however, and when he pulled on the doors of a business building across the street, they offered him sanctuary. Metzger watched helplessly as the man slipped inside where three stories and dozens of rooms provided areas in which to hide.

"Damn," Metzger muttered, reaching the doors, but not yanking them open.

He knew pulling the doors would leave him perfectly silhouetted for Fournier to open fire and down him in a heartbeat. Thinking quickly, he found some supplies lying nearby that included a collapsed tent, some blankets, and a backpack. He scooped the backpack off the ground, prepared to use its straps to bind the doors together. Unzipping it, he located some rope among other handy items like bottled water and a satellite phone.

He tied the two handles of the double doors together with the rope to keep them from opening. Admiring his knot for less than a second, Metzger darted around the right side of the building, which took up half a city block, searching for other exits. Carrying the backpack with him, he remembered that he also possessed a few zip ties gifted to him from the Marines during the flight to New York. A single door fire exit with no exterior knob or handle presented itself along the side of the building. Along the next side, Metzger found more double doors serving as a second entrance to the various businesses inside, teeming with huge windows between metal supports. Suspecting the last side of the building possessed another exit only door, he decided to take action before Fournier discovered an escape route.

Letting himself inside, Metzger used the ties to create loops along each door handle before binding them together with another tie. With the two main entrances sealed to anyone who didn't readily have a knife, or sword, to cut them, only two exits remained. Fournier likely possessed a blade, but Metzger was counting on precious seconds it would require to create an escape for an opportunity to pounce.

He sheathed the sword, and drew his pistol, prepared to subdue Fournier with the means at his disposal. Standing perfectly still a moment, trying in vain to slow his breathing from the long sprint into the city, Metzger held his breath a few seconds, listening intently for any sounds.

A noise that sounded like furniture being kicked reached his ears, and Metzger couldn't tell if Fournier lost his way inside the darkened, unpowered building, or if the undead roamed the halls, searching for a warm meal. Some light entered through the main windows, letting Metzger know the building was segmented into separate businesses on each side of the building, and presumably each level. The noise he heard came from his right, which appeared to be some kind of accounting business when money still mattered to people.

Metzger set the backpack down in a corner so it wasn't readily visible. He wanted the sat phone from it more than anything, because he wanted to contact his former group if the opportunity arose. Although it didn't appear to have a charger, he pocketed the phone for safe keeping, knowing some spots where he might find accessories for it later.

Due to the closed doors, the building appeared mostly unaffected by dust and decay, as though it had simply closed for the weekend. Metzger calmed himself and slowed his breathing, stepping quietly toward the door to the business. He wondered where the two side exit doors were found within the building, hoping Fournier hadn't already discovered them and fled into the streets. Some relief washed over Metzger, knowing the man wasn't going to meet up with his hero anytime soon.

Every few steps, Metzger stopped, listening for additional noise, but nothing reached his ears in the game of cat and mouse. It occurred to him that Fournier might be lying in wait, ready to put a bullet in him for retaliation from the events at the airport. Metzger certainly hadn't asked for a fight, but he did well when he and his group took down their pursuers. At the time, Metzger thought he landed a headshot on Fournier, but the bullet must have simply grazed the man's skull.

Hearing noises from the outside due to the eerily quiet interior, Metzger realized the undead were beginning to scour the area, drawn by the gunfire. Unsure if help was coming his way, or if they could locate him, Metzger stepped forward, warily looking between the businesses located on either side of the wide hallway.

Made completely of glass, with writing on the doors, each of the businesses provided a clear view inside without Metzger needing to open a door. At each end of the hallway he spotted stairwell access doors and elevators that clearly weren't going to transport anyone. Avoiding those momentarily, Metzger peered into the business on the left, seeing no activity before he focused his attention on the accounting business where he'd heard the noise less than a minute prior.

He opened the door carefully, but the hydraulic door spring announced his arrival, much to his dismay. Crouching, he tried reducing his profile while searching the area, but several desks and chairs occupied the space. It looked as though people had started moving furniture with the intention of barricading the business, or the building, but their work came to a sudden halt.

Ducked behind the desk, Metzger waited patiently for another noise. The undead weren't adept at stealth, and no sounds of objects being bumped or knocked over reached his ears. Instinct told him Fournier was trapped inside this business with him, but the accounting firm consisted of multiple rooms that grew darker the further one got from the main lobby. Metzger couldn't use his flashlight without giving away his position, and he dared not move until he discovered a clue about Fournier's whereabouts.

Concealed by the limited lighting inside the office space, Metzger breathed carefully, waiting until he heard footsteps coming his way before sidestepping from the desk and taking aim at the figure coming his way. He immediately realized his mistake when the adversary hissed at him lurching forward with the intention of taking a bite from whatever piece of his body it could reach.

Still holding the sidearm, Metzger didn't want to fire and give away his position to Fournier if the man didn't already know. He kicked the zombie in the stomach, sending it back where it fell awkwardly to the floor, wasting little time in regaining its footing to pursue him. Metzger began reaching for his sword, but he saw a shadow move too quickly to his right to be a zombie. Fournier was running from him, but trapped within the confines of the accounting firm unless he discovered a side exit.

Figuring Fournier knew his location, and possibly directed the zombie wearing a tattered suit his way, Metzger raised his right arm, shot the zombie in the head, and walked in the direction where Fournier had run. Darkness followed him the further he walked from the light of the main lobby, and Metzger dared not draw his flashlight. He turned corners and crossed hallways carefully, trying to reduce his profile so Fournier couldn't simply gun him down. Figuring the man wasn't a phenomenal shot, because a gunman would have stood his ground and taken careful aim earlier in the pursuit, Metzger still played it safe.

His decision came easy when he heard the sound of a metal door opening because the noise of someone using the push bar reached his ears and he knew Fournier had located a fire exit. As he rounded the corner, however, he spotted a silhouette in front of the already closing door, realizing the man had tricked him into revealing his location.

Metzger dove into the hallway behind him as bullets fired in his direction, none striking him as Fournier likely couldn't see very well in the darkness as his body blocked much of the exterior lighting. Hearing the door open a second time, Metzger stayed low, sticking his head around the corner to find Fournier darting outside. Caught between immediately pursuing the man and risking his life to do so, Metzger dashed for the door, still holding his firearm, and bursting through the metal barricade where he kept running in case he was targeted.

No one fired at him, and Metzger quickly gained his bearings, seeing the man hadn't yet reached the corner of the building. He darted in Fournier's direction, seeing zombies entering the alley around him, but Metzger was able to dodge them without them laying a finger on him because they focused on, and turned to Fournier once he sped past them. Unsure of how much longer his stamina could hold out, he followed the man into the main streets once more, trying to keep pace.

He got to the end of the block, realizing Fournier was nearly a block ahead of him now, and he began to think the leader of evil men might escape once again. As Fournier reached the next block, however, about to turn to the right in another attempt to lose Metzger, a fist appeared from behind the building at the corner and clocked Fournier squarely in the jaw, dropping him to the ground like a sack of potatoes.

Finishing his sprint at that exact spot, Metzger found his brother and Molly standing over the unconscious Fournier, smirking at him.

"You two suck," he commented.

"Thanks for flushing him out of hiding," Bryce replied. "We didn't know where you two got to."

"We played a little hide-and-seek inside a large business office."

"Well, he belongs to us now," Bryce said, openly happy at the prospect of a successful mission. "I think we caught a few of his buddies, too."

Several zombies staggered in their direction, attracted by the noise of footsteps and multiple gunshots. Metzger holstered his firearm, instinctively drawing the sword to deal with the threat silently, rather than attract more danger.

"Get him back to the vehicles," Metzger said, turning around just long enough to utter the words. "I'll deal with this."

He went to work, slicing through several skulls, all the while thinking that he couldn't wait to get answers from the men they captured at the compound. With the element of surprise, any number of maps, plans, and weaponry might await them inside the converted building.

Hopefully the answers would lead to the man responsible for the apocalypse.

Nineteen

One Month Earlier

As though Velvet Markle didn't have enough worries after losing most of her business contacts, the apocalypse transformed her into a caregiver. Her sister, Harriet, a few years younger than Velvet, barely took care of herself before the world fell apart. A diabetic since her teens, she constantly allowed her blood sugar to bottom out, and seeing a fire truck or ambulance at her house wasn't an unusual sight for her neighbors.

Sitting on the edge of her sister's bed, Velvet felt the pressure of caring for her sister, both in food supply and managing her diabetes. When Harriet remained conscious, making her something to eat, or giving her something sugary to keep her blood sugar elevated wasn't difficult, but when she bottomed out, the task felt nearly impossible. Dangerously close to unconsciousness during these times, Harriet struggled to eat or drink because her body began to shut down, meaning rudimentary tasks might become monumental.

Whenever the medics came by, they checked her blood sugar, and when it proved too low for her to recover on her own, they put a needle in her arm. Attached to a tube that provided fluids and liquid sugar, the needle gave her body a temporary boost in glucose levels. A few minutes later, Harriet came to, sometimes thanking them, and sometimes questioning how she fell into such a state. Today she remained conscious and alert, but too weak to get herself out of bed due to other health concerns.

Although Velvet knew the procedure well, and she'd dabbled with the needle personally, the means to provide her sister artificial sugar ran low in the world outside of their simple home.

"You need to leave this place," Harriet told her sister as Velvet dabbed her forehead with a damp cloth. "Your other family needs you."

She spoke of Velvet's other life, her business, and her lifeblood that recently took a downturn, even before the apocalypse.

"You're my blood," Velvet answered softly. "I'm not going to leave you."

"Dear sister, you've practically handcuffed yourself to my bed this past week. I see what's going on out there, and it isn't getting any better."

One look outside the window revealed anywhere from three to a dozen zombies depending on the time of day. Velvet knew from the early news reports how to deal with them, but even the media outlets left her in her time of need, much like the rest of her biological family.

"I'm sixty-years-old," Harriet said tenderly, barely above a whisper. "I've lived a good life."

"It's not your time," Velvet replied with genuine compassion. "We can get through this."

Harriet appeared disappointed, not because of her condition, or any self-pity, but because she knew her older sister wouldn't abandon her.

"Where are your people?" she finally asked, referring to Velvet's employees in her transient line of work. They went from town to town, setting up rides, booths, and tents for a week before moving to the next location.

When their father passed away, he willed his business to both daughters, and Velvet bought her sister's half because she didn't want the employees being displaced. Harriet showed no real interest in travel, and her condition made it difficult to leave the house some days. She kept the house, which included land enough to store the rides, booths, and other items for the traveling carnival during the colder months. Velvet already possessed her own small house just down the road, and they worked out an agreement to leave the rides on her father's old property.

In truth, Velvet supposed her sister wanted visitors, and to be checked on regularly, because she sometimes slipped, forgetting to take her insulin when needed, or check her blood sugar before bedtime.

"They're safe," Velvet said of her employees. "I found most of them and got them to a storage facility. We found enough food and supplies to keep them going for a while."

"Go to them. I'll be okay."

Velvet gave a soft smile, and both of them knew her sister's statement wasn't true.

"At least go and get yourself something to eat. Check on your other family. I'll be just fine for a few hours."

"Can I get you any soup, or something to drink before I go?" Velvet asked, conceding that she needed a break from the humdrum life at the house.

Her duties grew more difficult when the house lost power after a few days, meaning everything in the refrigerator either spoiled or reached room temperature. Heating and cooling weren't an issue in early September, but Velvet questioned how to keep her sister safe with only two firearms in the house and limited ammunition.

A .22 pistol and a shotgun belonged to her father, who passed away nearly five years earlier. Harriet kept most of the handed down belongings at her house, since Velvet worked on the road so often. Any hope of the overall situation getting better faded with each passing day as more undead roamed the fields near their rural Virginia home.

"What are you going to do about Audie?" Harriet inquired from her bed. "He doesn't belong in that jail."

"Those people in South Hill accused him of touching that girl," Velvet said angrily. "That poor boy don't know no better."

"If things are as bad as they seem, the people in charge might let everyone in that jail starve in their cells. Whether he did something or not, that poor child is lost among those killers and thieves."

"He didn't do nothin'," Velvet spat emphatically. "Those simple townsfolk made something up so they could kick us out of town."

Intense media coverage over a statement Velvet felt certain a little girl made up in the first place took a toll on her business. Towns began canceling their services when they found other carnival ride operators and food vendors. Financially, Velvet got by just fine, but she worried about her workers who didn't exactly have other job skills or education to land other work. Audie Frost lived a difficult life from childhood, possessing large facial birthmarks that most people mistook for scars or severe burns due to their deep redness when compared to his pale white skin and icy blue eyes.

He often concealed his facial features as best he could with makeup, baseball caps, or masks when Velvet found parts he could play in haunted houses or other attractions. Although capable of speaking, Frost typically remained silent with his self-esteem at rock bottom. Everyone who worked with him protected him and took him in, even after the accusations of him inappropriately touching a child.

"You need to see them," Harriet insisted. "It's been two days now, and you need a break from me."

"Let me fix you a peanut butter sandwich first."

"No," Harriet said, waving off the notion. "You've already made lunch and checked my sugar. I'm not going to crash while you're gone."

"What about those things outside?" Velvet questioned. "Or worse, intruders. People are doing whatever it takes to eat and take shelter."

"Then load the guns and leave them beside me," Harriet suggested. "I know how to use them, and I'll know if someone other than you comes through that door."

Velvet leaned over, kissing her sister on the forehead.

"Fine. You win, but I won't be long. I'm going to start looking for insulin and your testing strips when it's safe to enter the clinics and pharmacies."

"I doubt there's anything left out there. People like me aren't built to survive in this kind of world."

"Nonsense. You're going to be fine."

Harriet provided a knowing, sad smirk that indicated they both knew such a statement was entirely false.

"You go and enjoy your other family, Dark Lady. I'll see you soon."

Harriet called her by her work alias, which she used when reading tarot cards or acting in one of the spook house attractions. Her sister brushed her cheek gently with the back of her hand, indicating she appreciated Velvet's dedication and sacrifice. Each passing year reminded Velvet that her profession waned as families sought other forms of entertainment, including theme parks, time shares, and their phones, which they often appeared glued to.

Her cards often spoke the truth when turned, and Velvet possessed a sense she considered beyond earthly realms. Some part of her sixth sense placed foreboding within her, as though someone she cared about might be in mortal danger.

When Velvet went to talk to her employees, who remained loyal to her despite the rest of the world fending for themselves in all sorts of selfish manners, she asked a few of them to scout the jail where Frost was being held by authorities. Tending to her sister and her employees kept Velvet too busy to check on Frost's status, and she hoped any remaining jailers and deputies might have realized the futility of continuing to work, and abandoned their posts. If Frost were suddenly freed, he most assuredly would have made his way back to their home base, had a feeling of being left and forgotten didn't overwhelm him.

Seeing they were all in good health and still had enough to eat, she assured them her next visit wouldn't take as long, and took a detour on her way home to see about supplies at the two nearby pharmacies. In both places, she needed only take a few steps inside to see undead corpses lining the floor, indicating other desperate people had already raided the stores. All of the canned or packaged goods were gone from the food aisles, and even the bagged items like potato chips and pork rinds appeared all but gone.

Back in the pharmacy area, several packages of random drugs were lying around, mostly in pill form. No insulin remained in the refrigerated areas, and even the varied forms like cartridges and pens weren't anywhere Velvet looked in either store. She didn't expect fruitful results, and she had personally gone through several stores earlier in the apocalypse, scoring her sister some supplies to tide her over.

Disappointed, she drove to her sister's house, turning into the driveway to find a disturbing scene in the front yard. Several undead staggered around, some covered in blood, and behind them, half a dozen bodies were lying completely still along the grass and dirt. Fearing an attack on the house, Velvet jumped from her old truck, drawing a knife from her side, stabbing each zombie furiously in the skull, downing them one at a time without much consideration of her own safety.

Seeing the front door to the house swung inward, Velvet felt her heart sink, knowing her sister wouldn't be able to defend herself very well, if at all.

She began running to the front door for a look inside when movement from the corner of her right eye caused her to freeze in her tracks.

"No," Velvet muttered, seeing a reanimating corpse sit up from the bloodied grass, staring straight ahead momentarily until her head turned to the left.

Blood covered Harriet's body, and her entrails dripped from her lower torso where other undead had feasted on her body after undoubtedly taking her down like lions hunting a gazelle. Unable to clearly think momentarily, she thought back to her sister's state of mind, feeling reasonably certain Harriet grabbed the guns and went on a kamikaze mission, taking down as many as she could, knowing full well she wouldn't survive the ordeal.

Time stood still a moment as their eyes locked, and Harriet's had turned a pale, lifeless blueish color because her body stopped producing pigment for their natural hazel color. Velvet knew no human portion of her sister remained, but thoughts of stabbing a loved one in the head haunted her before she even took one step forward. Harriet's eyes didn't blink, and her walk appeared like more of a stagger because her intestines continued to fall out and trip her up with each arduous step. As her body reeled and returned, somewhat like a serpent coiling to find an attack position, Harriet revealed more damage to her body in the form of random bite marks and chunks of her flesh and tissue missing. Only the sound of rustling leaves broke the silence in the yard as the two sisters shared a parting moment on their property.

"Oh, no," Velvet said, a tear forming in one eye as her sister opened her mouth and gave a throaty hiss in return.

Backing away, she couldn't bring herself to stab her sister in the skull like the other zombies lying at her feet. Part of her wanted to lead her sister into the house to lock her inside, but she quickly dismissed the thought as irrational. Finishing her sister off made the land safer for anyone else crossing the yard, but Velvet wasn't sure she cared about other people at the moment. She simply got into the truck, closed the door, and rolled up the window as Harriet placed bloody hands on the glass, pawing like a hamster wanting out of its clear habitat.

Instead, she wanted in.

Safe from the horrors of the outdoors, both in sight and sound because she lowered her head to sob, Velvet ultimately cried herself dry until her chest hurt and her nose ran. Instinct finally kicked in, and she began to weigh her options.

Her frugal nature, and the fact that her other family needed assistance spoke to her, saying she needed to get inside the house and grab any remaining food, weapons, and supplies. The bond with her sister, formed over six decades, told her to leave the property and never look back if possible. Harriet would be someone else's problem, and if she needed to return to the house again, her undead sister would likely be miles down the road.

Refusing to look at her sister as she backed out of the driveway, Velvet knew she needed to gather her other family and begin to make a stand in the apocalypse. Harriet sacrificed her own life to free Velvet, and Velvet knew in the new order she would cut ties with her old life, becoming her stage persona full-time to bury her feelings, and the past.

***

Her first order of business was to free Frost from the satellite jail location in Mecklenburg County. While the main location held nearly seven-hundred prisoners, the satellite location housed under one-hundred. Ironically, the so-called satellite location was located adjacent to the sheriff's office, while the main jail sat halfway across the county. Very contemporary, with bricks lining the lower half, and red painted upper portions, the smaller jail looked more like a youth detention center than a jail.

She last saw him when the apocalypse set in, granted visitation when everyone thought the initial crisis might end in a few days. Even then, a certain tension ran through the building, and she noticed fewer staff than usual, as though a blue flu might have struck the jailers, because something pressing kept them away from work.

Her extended family now consisted of seven men, not including Frost. Some of the men who originally traveled with her, and the four women who helped sell tickets or operate booths, left her operation to return to their families or find shelter when the world fell apart. Her loyal followers accompanied her to the Meherrin River Regional Jail where, after little more than a week of chaos throughout the world, the property appeared in shambles.

Two overturned patrol cars, white with gold and red trim, adorned the front of the building. One remained teetering on one side, while the other rested on its lightbar, the roof crushed slightly inward. A few unanimated bodies lay nearby, and a half dozen zombies staggered around the front of the facility, which didn't possess guard towers or even tall fences to keep people out. Velvet knew the layout from previous visits, and she came prepared with her crew of seven, bringing a tow truck and a van they sometimes used for transportation of their crew.

Her boys, as she affectionately referred to them, jumped out of the van and dealt with any zombies before hooking up some chains to the front doors of the facility to yank them off the hinges. She planned on dealing with each layer of the facility individually, knowing security would either be light, or nonexistent, and walls of any kind could eventually be breached with a little knowhow and some heavy equipment.

Sauntering up to the door as though on a stroll after Sunday service, Velvet tried the doors, finding them secured despite the lack of power keeping the magnetic locks active. She noticed manual locks on each door, figuring it wouldn't be as simple as opening a door and walking inside, even in the apocalypse.

"Use the chains, boys," she said, referring to the chains on the back of the tow truck.

With practiced precision, her workers set to securing the chains and their hooks on the door handles. As one of them walked back to the truck, however, one of the doors produced a noise that sounded like a key turning, and a man dressed in a uniform slowly stepped outside with his hands halfway up to ensure he wasn't attacked immediately.

"Just who are you?" Velvet asked the man, who appeared to be in his middle twenties, wearing the standard uniform jailors wore in Mecklenburg County.

"My name is Randy," he said, standing so the door wouldn't close, either for fear of his life, or the lack of a way inside if it locked behind him. The chains awkwardly blocked his path anyway. "I stayed behind to feed the inmates when everyone else bugged out."

"That's very noble of you, Randy," Velvet replied, seeing his surname Morrison printed on the uniform he still wore. "I'm not interested in hurting you, or freeing everyone inside. I just came to retrieve one person who's like a son to me."

Now the young man appeared confused, as though wondering which particular inmate she had in mind.

"I need Audie Frost remanded to my custody," she said plainly.

Morrison took a few seconds to think before putting the name and face together.

"Oh, Audie. He's never given me an ounce of grief, unlike everyone else in there."

"May I come and get him?"

"Yeah," the guard said hesitantly. "But just you."

He held the door open for Velvet as she approached the entrance, motioning for her former employees to wait for her. She knew if freeing Frost took too long, they would make their way inside by carrying out the original plan.

Following the man, she made her way past the front desk, now devoid of employees who once fielded calls and acted as a barrier between the public and the prisoners. A large square hub, the interior held several chairs, phones, and paperwork, but the once tidy area now appeared unkempt.

"You run this entire place by yourself?" she inquired, knowing the shape and size of the building mimicked some high schools.

"I do," the man confessed. "Everyone else had families, or escape plans, but my job was kind of my life."

She heard the jingle of several keys along the man's belt, realizing he, and he alone, stood between seventy-nine hardened criminals and freedom. To her, Frost wasn't a criminal at all, and the people who accused him of wrongdoing simply hated people who made an honest living on the road.

"Why not just let them go?" she asked.

"Ma'am, a lot of them are thieves and killers. Wouldn't do nobody no good if I let them loose on society."

Both of them passed through a door held open by a brick at its base to prevent it from shutting. Velvet suspected keeping doors open allowed the man to freely pass through the various areas with ease, not requiring keys whenever he needed a door opened.

"I would've let Audie go free," Morrison said, "but he never asked. I doubt he liked it in here, but he never showed any interest in leaving."

"He knew we'd come," Velvet said conversationally, trying to keep her emotions in check. "And he knew if we didn't, we were dead, and that's what he'd want to be."

Morrison cleared his throat but said nothing as they passed through another door into the general population where the sealed doors kept the prisoners at bay. The moment they saw someone new enter the room, they shouted any number of requests at Velvet, asking her to free them, kill Morrison, or fuck them all night long. She ignored them all, focused on finding Frost and leaving without delay.

She'd never seen so many bars, and so much concrete in her life, and the prisoners lived up to the picture Morrison painted, not one of them remaining quiet, or acting like a decent human being. In a way she envied them, still shielded from the horrors outside, being fed three square meals a day, but she didn't envy the guard and the inevitable decision he needed to make. Letting them starve once the food ran out wasn't humane, but neither was setting them loose on society. Velvet didn't want hardened criminals sharing potential camps with her, and once free, these men could disguise their true nature with a cold shower followed by a change of clothes.

When they came to Frost's cell, Morrison didn't hesitate to place the key in the lock and manually turn it, opening the door for Velvet, who stepped inside, not worried the guard would dare close the door behind her. Sufficient backup awaited her outside, and gut instinct told her Morrison wasn't the kind of man to go back on his word.

"You okay, baby?" she asked as she knelt beside the large man, placing her arms gently around his neck.

He didn't react immediately, as though the gravity of the situation overwhelmed him. After a few seconds Frost returned her embrace by gently wrapping his arms around her shoulders, pulling her a bit closer. When she finally looked into his steely blue eyes, Velvet saw a tear forming in one of them, and she knew she'd done the right thing coming to free him from a hell within a hell.

"You need to come with me, baby," she said, taking his hand. "Everyone's waiting outside for you, and we'll keep you safe."

Frost required being kept safe from himself more than anything. Although he didn't mean to, he sometimes gawked at people too long and made them uncomfortable, or wanted to touch objects that didn't belong to him. People mistook him for some kind of weirdo or pervert, but Velvet saw nothing except an innocent child trapped in a man's body. She blamed some of his social awkwardness on his self-conscious nature regarding his appearance, but her group helped him come out of his shell, at least within their clan.

Holding his hand, she led him out of the cell, past Morrison, and neither man said a word, or made a move toward the other. Some understanding had been reached between them, and Frost wasn't naturally violent in the first place. He hung on Velvet's every word, willing to carry out any task she asked of him, which would certainly include harming someone, even to the point of murder if necessary.

Velvet allowed Morrison to take the lead because she didn't want to spend one unnecessary extra minute inside the facility as the inmates yelled obscenities and unsavory offers in her direction. Some of them took to booing her, some of them throwing objects or spitting through the small openings in their cell doors.

Any sympathy she might have initially felt for them dissipated during her visit, and she felt even more horrified that Frost spent one second around such degenerates who likely showed no sympathy or respect for him. Only his size kept him from being picked on in the outside world, and she hoped the same held true within the concrete confines.

Behind her, the thick walls eventually drowned out the yelling, and their voices completely diminished by the time she reached the lobby where no one remained to greet them. She saw her companions waiting outside, ready to be reunited with Frost. Before exiting, however, she turned to Morrison, prepared to ask one last question.

"What are you going to do with them?" she inquired, nodding behind him where the rowdy prisoners remained safely tucked behind bars.

"I'm not sure," he answered slowly. "I've thought about letting them out one at a time at gunpoint so they can't gang up and do anything terrible. Maybe one or two of them each day, or something like that. It would solve my rations problem, and give them a chance at survival."

"Do any of them deserve a second chance?"

"A few," he answered honestly. "I was going to let them go first."

"And what about you?"

"Ma'am?"

"What are you going to do when everything runs out and you don't have anyone to tend to?"

"I guess I'll make my way out there and see what happens. There's no way I'll let those things be the end of me, so I'll keep a gun around in case I have to take matters into my own hands."

"Let's hope it doesn't come to that," Velvet said as sweetly as she could, contemplating her own struggle with putting the dead down.

She opened the door, letting Frost outside first, finding the chains remained secured to the door handles. Removing them, she let them drop to the ground, freeing herself from the building though the voices of inmates continued to run through her mind. Everyone embraced their comrade as he jogged jovially their way, happy to be with friends again, rather than unruly strangers.

About to give an order for everyone to load into the trucks, so they could return to their makeshift camp and plan their next move, Velvet heard a vehicle approaching before the words emerged. Of all things, she saw a patrol car racing toward the front lot, and one glance back at Morrison indicated he felt as surprised as anyone to see a cop car speeding onto the property. Having seen no indication of radios, or communication, she doubted the guard could have called for help, even if he wanted to.

Morrison stood at the doors, one of them partly ajar, witnessing the events about to unfold, but able to withdraw inside, like a turtle into its shell, if necessary.

When the car finally came to a stop, a reasonably safe distance from the group, the driver's side door opened, and a man dressed in a dingy uniform stepped out, placing his right hand atop his firearm. After a week on his own, the man sported an infant beard just beyond the stubble phase. His eyes examined everyone in Velvet's group, and she knew he was a lawman of some sort, and not just someone playing the part who came across an abandoned squad car.

"What is this?" he asked, not removing his hand from his sidearm, despite seeing none of them brandishing firearms.

Velvet looked back to Morrison, who wanted no part of the discussion, remaining safely behind thick glass doors. She wondered if the deputy before them deserted his post, returning at last because he'd run out of supplies, or needed something from the jail or the nearby sheriff's office.

"What's your business here?" Velvet asked, prepared to leave because she possessed what she came to retrieve.

"I could ask you the same, lady."

"We were just leaving."

"Not with that freak, you're not," the man said, locking his eyes directly on Frost. "That piece of shit touched a little girl, and that's why he's supposed to be locked away."

"He did no such thing," Velvet replied. "We don't want no trouble. Just step aside, and we'll be on our way."

"I don't see any of you carrying weapons," the man replied. "Maybe I should put the whole lot of you in there."

"We clearly outnumber you," Velvet said, adding more firmness to her voice. "Step aside, and we'll all pretend this little encounter never happened."

Now the deputy, or former deputy, drew his weapon, and Velvet heard the door shut and lock behind her as Morrison severed any connection he had with the argument and its participants. Taking aim directly at Frost, the deputy appeared extremely concerned with law and order after obviously putting himself first during the initial week of the apocalypse.

"Why are you even here?" Velvet asked, trying to diffuse the situation before it escalated.

"I figured those dirtbag prisoners don't need food and supplies as much as me and my family, so it seemed they were ripe for the taking."

Stepping away from his patrol car, the man kept his gun trained on Frost, which concerned Velvet gravely. She didn't like that the former lawman put his own needs ahead of prisoners, but she supposed he had his own family to support in the unforgiving world.

"If you want your supplies so badly, step on past us and go get them," Velvet offered, still trying to resolve the situation peacefully as her companions grew restless, prepared to pounce on the man, despite being unarmed.

"I'm not letting that freak back on the streets," the deputy responded sourly. "I've seen people who still have their kids with them. He'll find them and do God knows what to them. I'm sorry, lady, but he needs to go."

"Down!" Velvet shouted to Frost, who moved just enough that the shot didn't strike his head, but clipped him somewhere as blood droplets flew through the air when the deputy fired.

Without waiting for her order, everyone else charged the man, and though he went to fire again, his gun jammed and he was pancaked to the ground by at least four of her companions. Velvet remained perfectly still, taking deep, furious breaths, looking to Frost, who cupped his injured shoulder with one hand. He finally looked in the other direction at what could only be described as a gridiron sort of tackle.

Although the situation ended without a casualty, the deputy clearly intended to kill Frost in cold blood before opening fire on the remainder of the group until they died or fled. She couldn't stand for anyone else in her family being placed in jeopardy, or lost to her like Harriet. Taking a deep breath, she stepped forward, ushering her first command.

"Stand him up," she said to the four men holding down the deputy, who continued to struggle.

Forced to his feet, the man continued to fight and kick, even spitting on Velvet as she neared him.

"You're no better than the men inside those walls," she told him in a hostile growl.

"And you're assisting and abiding a child molester, bitch," the deputy replied, as though sensing he wouldn't come out of their interaction unscathed.

She looked to his nameplate, seeing his surname Barton across the silver tab.

"You should've spent more time cleaning your gun," Velvet said, and as the deputy looked to his firearm lying just feet away from him, he didn't see her draw the knife from her side and stick it into his abdomen, just below the sternum.

His face registered utter shock and he groaned from the pain, and the deputy immediately knew his life was measured in seconds, or minutes at best.

"And you can call me Dark Lady, Deputy Barton," she said staring into the man's eyes, even as the life faded from them.

Withdrawing the blade, Velvet turned away as her colleagues dropped the man like a sack of potatoes to the ground. She walked away, knowing she wouldn't let anyone threaten her clan again. Feeling responsible for losing her sister, Velvet vowed to keep everyone around her safe, even if it meant their group took on the entire apocalyptic world.

Dropping to one knee beside Frost, she began tending to his wound. One glance at the front doors of the facility showed Morrison cautiously looking outside, knowing what just transpired.

Good, she thought. Let the word spread that we aren't taking shit from anyone.

Twenty

Luke Johnson never imagined his life changing once he found the love of his life and bought a house with the man. They occupied themselves with updating the old house, creating a colorful garden, and gaining acceptance from the people living on their block. Fortunately, they weren't the only gay couple living in the area, and modern beliefs had caught up with their Buffalo suburb.

When the apocalypse began, they treated their house like a fortress of sorts, letting no one come inside while living off their packed and canned goods. Albert McConnell, his lover, knew firsthand what the sickness meant after narrowly escaping the hospital where he worked as a nurse, abandoning his duties when he saw the dead returning to life. The two decided to stay inside and observe the neighborhood from their second story level where they were safe from being spotted.

Over the course of a few days the neighborhood thinned out, either from people catching the mysterious illness, being ravaged by the undead, or simply leaving to find loved ones elsewhere in the country. Luke became a quick study in how the undead functioned, and how to kill them, but Albert did all of the dirty work, often stepping outside to put them down, or searching vacant nearby houses for food and supplies. Even simple items like toilet paper and deodorant became luxury items when they couldn't be grabbed from a store shelf and paid for with a credit card.

Saying he was comfortable during this time would've been a gross exaggeration, but Luke felt as though he and Albert were capable of toughing out anything together. He personally wanted to contribute more, but Albert insisted on dealing with the issues outdoors. In the back of his mind, Luke knew he needed to learn how to use blades and guns out of necessity. The couple didn't exactly have support, because their families didn't approve of their relationship, and their neighbors were literally dropping like flies.

Not long into the apocalypse, a knock came at their front door that changed everything. Cautiously examining what stranger dared interrupt their usual peace and quiet in their Victorian home oasis, they discovered the person wasn't a stranger at all. Covered in blood that wasn't her own, little Samantha Robinson stood there with a blank stare, in shock, for what felt like an eternity. The two men brought her inside, carefully checked her for bites or other injuries, and let her lie down in one of their spare beds until she put the trauma behind her enough to speak.

Albert insisted on checking her house, not far down the street, suspecting something terrible happened to both of her parents, who opted to remain in the neighborhood like a handful of families. Leaving the area without a destination in mind proved a recipe for disaster for dozens of families, and the Robinsons understood this truth.

When he returned from his short walk, Albert stated he believed something visited the unsuspecting family in the form of an injured neighbor or church member. He found three bodies inside the residence, and never really cared to speak much about what he saw. When pressed, he revealed two of the bodies were animated when he arrived, and all three were no longer a threat to anyone by the time he left.

Neither man ever anticipated becoming a father, and the topic of adoption never truly came up during their years together because their lives already felt complete. They understood the laws in New York allowed for them to legally wed, which they hadn't, and even if they made their love official, two men adopting a child wasn't a typical scenario unless one of them was the natural father. Despite their lack of experience with children, or the lack of desire to raise a child before Samantha knocked on their door, both felt like papa bears almost immediately when she became their responsibility.

Obligated by no law, the men could have tried giving her to a family with children, or acted without morals and let the child fend for herself in the open. Neither ever suggested such a notion, because both knew they had atoning to do after shutting themselves away from the world when disaster struck. Albert felt especially terrible after abandoning his nursing duties at the hospital, despite almost certain death being his reward if he'd stayed.

Now on his own, missing his former lover, located in a strange place with only a child to keep him company, Luke missed his old life more than ever.

"What's wrong?" Samantha asked at his side as he searched the living room of the house where they'd been staying for any remaining weapons or useful items.

"Some bad people robbed us," he answered, seeing the place overturned, and not by his hand.

"What did they take?"

"Our guns," he said, looking at her with dismay in his eyes. "Can you help me search for any guns or knives left inside the house?"

"Yes."

"*Carefully*," he emphasized before leading the way to the back of the house.

Samantha didn't come out of her shell easily after the shocking deaths of her parents, and often when she answered Luke and Albert, her words weren't full sentences. Only recently had she begun to speak more often, and usually only when the others weren't around. Luke wasn't sure he'd call his relationship with Samantha as bonded, but he didn't know what else to call it.

Feeling almost certain the second vehicle of carnival hoodlums reached town and raided their residence, Luke believed Dark Lady had some form of communication with them, or they wouldn't have known where to search.

He hadn't liked the idea of bringing Samantha so close to the property where the woman and her followers made camp. Although he saw Vazquez's undead corpse in the yard, he didn't think his adopted daughter had made the connection, and he wasn't about to discuss such a morbid topic with her. Losing a friend, a valuable member of their group who could pilot an aircraft, hit Luke hard. He dared not dwell on the loss because he and Samantha remained in danger until they left, the carnival people left, or a dispute between the two factions left only one standing.

Worried about the others, now pursued by the second vehicle full of dangerous survivors, he began looking in every kitchen drawer or cabinet, wondering if his group members hid some of the firearms exceptionally well. He found a pocket knife on the floor beside the depowered refrigerator, scooping it up as a first and last resort until he located something more suitable. Continuing his search, he monitored Samantha as she mimicked his actions, looking beneath clothing, and pulling out every drawer the various furniture offered.

"Find anything?" he called out.

"Not yet," she answered.

Once the girl grew accustomed to being around Luke and Albert, the latter decided to show her how to use a firearm. Although not vehemently opposed to the idea, Luke wasn't thrilled about the idea of an eight-year-old child waving a gun around like a toy. He eventually learned he was wrong on two counts. One, no child was allowed to act youthful in the apocalypse, because childish behavior wasn't an afforded amenity. Two, Samantha understood the dangers around her. She didn't always express her thoughts and feelings perfectly, but Luke was beginning to understand her distinct way of communicating. Dealing with a child was new to him, but he strived to make their relationship work now that Albert was no longer around to assume half of the responsibility.

Luke didn't exactly keep a calendar around, but he knew they were under two months into the world's major change. Samantha had bounced back well, considering she witnessed both of her parents being ripped apart.

He couldn't fathom how four marauders went through the house so quickly and efficiently, taking every decent weapon from the group. It occurred to him that Dark Lady and her minions knew about the others the moment they arrived, keeping tabs on them and waiting for one of them to slip up. Vazquez likely took a casual stroll, as he sometimes did to clear his mind, getting swiped up by the thugs before he sensed any danger. Perhaps he spotted them, and the gypsies couldn't afford to let him live to tell the tale.

Deciding to check further into the house, Luke opened bathroom cabinets and checked under everything, hoping one of his roommates hid a weapon he didn't know about. Unfortunately, they kept the weapons mainly in one area except for the guns and knives they personally carried. In his hurry to join the others halfway across town, Luke hadn't grabbed any firearms, feeling certain his companions had firepower enough to cover them.

Live and learn, he thought as he looked back, seeing Samantha standing like a frozen statue between the front and rear doors of the house, near the living room.

Her eyes focused on something at the door they had entered, and he didn't dare speak a word in case a living person or the undead mesmerized her.

Carefully, he stepped over to her, trying to avoid making a sound because he didn't want to lose the element of surprise, regardless of who or what distracted Samantha.

When he carefully looked around the corner, Luke saw a figure standing in the doorway, somewhat silhouetted by the daylight behind him. The stranger and Samantha had locked eyes, but for entirely different reasons as she shivered in terror, and he made animalistic breathing noises with his face obscured by various skins from creatures or deceased human beings. Recognizing the man from afar a few weeks prior, and more recently with Dark Lady, his unmistakable appearance tended to burn itself into one's memory.

Covered virtually head to toe in fur and various sewn together skin patches, the man sounded simple as he stood there examining Samantha like an object to be taken. He made a few groaning noises that sounded orgasmic in nature, as though he couldn't control himself, and Luke finally stepped in front of his adopted child, carefully ushering her behind him.

His heart pounded from nervousness, because he'd never been much for confrontation. After dealing with bullies and hateful people his entirely life, Luke preferred to avoid conflict, but now his papa bear instincts took over. For possibly the first time in his life, he decided to risk life and limb to protect the child beside him.

"Go hide," he instructed her, and she wasted no time dashing into the other half of the house.

Following her every move, the man at the door attempted to follow her by cutting through the alternate hallway, but Luke ran forward, intercepting him and tackling him into a chair that fell sideways as both men toppled into it clumsily, hurling them to the floor. Luke considered that the man might possess a weapon, so he stood to distance himself from harm, but the man shoved him into a wall, denting the drywall before Luke fell to the floor, momentarily stunned.

Shaking his head, Luke regained his footing as a shriek emanated from a bedroom down the hall. He navigated the hallway quickly, finding the odd man standing in the doorway, blocking Samantha's exit. Terrified, she stood behind the bed where she'd chosen to hide, horrified by the stranger who made no attempt to hide his infatuation with her.

With Samantha safely far enough away, Luke threw his shoulder into the odd man's back, knocking them both into the bedroom.

"Run!" he shouted to Samantha. "Get outside and run!"

Out of patience, the man turned and struck Luke along the jaw, overpowering him immediately before wrapping his large hands around Luke's throat and squeezing. Gasping for air, Luke reached out for any useful nearby object, but before his fingers located anything, the man stood and threw Luke against yet another wall, but this time the back of Luke's skull took the brunt of the impact, leaving him on the verge of unconsciousness for at least a few seconds.

Collecting his wits, Luke got to his feet again, and when he stumbled outside through the door he'd used to enter with Samantha, he found several familiar vehicles in the driveway, but he didn't see Samantha or the man who pursued her. Horrific thoughts ran through his mind as he envisioned her being scooped up and carried off for to be violated, or raised in the murderous image of the carnies.

Luke whipped his head in every direction as he walked forward, searching desperately for Samantha. He couldn't imagine how they could have gotten away from the property so quickly, feeling certain he hadn't blanked out for more than a few seconds. About to weave between a few of the vehicles, Luke spied something out of the corner of his eye that caused him to duck down momentarily.

Now the strange man stared into one of the cars, and Luke surmised Samantha had jumped into the vehicle as a new hiding place, knowing she couldn't outrun him. Making strange noises once again, the man stared intently into the glass, touching it with his hands as though carrying out some ritual before he touched or grabbed the girl. Only a car door separated them, and Luke wasn't confident Samantha found time enough to lock the car doors once she jumped inside.

Taking action, he snuck around the car, assuming a strategic attack position before getting a running start and tackling the man from one side, knocking him to the ground.

Changing his tactics this time, Luke managed to maintain his footing, backing away from the man, hoping to be pursued, allowing Samantha time enough to escape the area. Now highly annoyed, the animalistic man gave Luke his wish, quickly rising from the ground before rushing his attacker, who ran down to the street, constantly looking behind him to make certain the strange man didn't break off the pursuit.

Narrowly avoiding a diving tackle, Luke realized his escape only served to raise the ire of the man, who regained his footing and began the pursuit anew. Doubling back to the cars, because he now understood this man was faster and stronger, Luke weaved between the vehicles, discovering that Samantha hadn't taken the opportunity to run at all. Seeing a shadow, she looked up from her spot in the back of the car, where she'd either been ducking down, or searching for something.

Noticing the man passing the vehicle was Luke, and not the man covered in recycled animal skins and fur, she glanced only a few seconds before ducking down again. With no time to spare, Luke ran around the few cars until the man caught up with him and brought him down near the road, pinning him face down in the dewy grass. Luke immediately attempted to wrest his body from the grip of the man, like a robin pinned by a bird of prey, but his struggles simply sent blades of grass flying into the air.

In no mood to have his observations of Samantha interrupted again, the man slugged Luke across the face twice with a closed fist after turning him over like Luke was a toddler. The two blows brought Luke to the brink of unconsciousness as he felt only pain and disorientation. Next, the man wrapped his large hands around Luke's throat, squeezing immediately. Luke bucked a few times, and brought his knees up to strike the man in the back, but neither caused the stranger to flinch, because his blue eyes bored into Luke with hatred and utter contempt for interrupting his plans.

Already compromised from the last barrage, Luke felt his eyes begin to roll back in his skull, wondering what the afterlife might bring, who would take care of Samantha if she survived, and if his group might return to save him at the last second. What seemed like a thousand thoughts crossed his mind at once, and he wondered if this sensation was what people meant by their lives flashing before them.

Just before reaching unconsciousness for what would assuredly be the last time, Luke heard a gunshot. He didn't know if the sound was real, or something his mind experienced in some out-of-body experience. The ringing in his ears indicated the gunfire was legitimate, and his eyes noticed the bloody hole in the center of his attacker's chest before the man gave a light groan. The man's eyes focused on nothing in particular, appearing dazed until they froze in a half-open position when he slumped to one side. Behind him, Samantha stood still, her eyes in disbelief, her hands still grasping the revolver she used to shoot the odd man.

Light smoke rose from the barrel of the gun, and Samantha appeared incapable of movement as Luke pushed his assailant the rest of the way off, standing quickly to take Samantha's side and secure the gun in his hands. He stuffed the firearm behind him, quickly scooping her up into a hug as he carried her toward the house, trying to avoid having her look at the body behind them by angling his walk a particular direction.

He brought her inside, flipping a cushioned chair right side up, before placing her in it. Feeling sympathy for her, having to endure such a bizarre ordeal, he knew he needed to deal with the body in the yard for her sake. Luke knelt down beside her, seeing her still in shock, not saying a word as her eyes vacantly stared at the wall ahead of her.

"Baby, I have to go outside and move his body," he said as gently and kindly as possible, uncertain if she heard the words he spoke. He pulled her into a light hug. "I'm so sorry you had to go through this."

"It's okay, Daddy," she replied, and Luke wasn't certain if Samantha said the words, or her condition spoke for her, reverting back to a better time in her life.

Clasping both of her shoulders with a gentle squeeze, he looked into her eyes as he drew back slightly, realizing she meant the words in the present, cognizant in mind.

"I'm so sorry," he said, hugging her again, and not letting go so easily this time. "I'm going to make sure the bad man can't hurt us."

"I'll be okay."

Luke reached back, pulling the gun from behind him and setting it on the chair's arm beside her. He understood why Albert wanted to instruct her on how to protect herself, because people in the new world didn't adhere to boundaries and laws. People with moral compasses were the most susceptible, and children had few protections than ever.

"I'll be right back," he promised. "You've got protection right here if you need it."

Samantha nodded, though she seemed reluctant to touch the gun again. She understood the consequences of her actions, which Luke considered a good thing. He felt thankful for her intervention, but he couldn't really discuss the ramifications with her, at least not yet. He hoped she never needed to use a firearm for real ever again.

He doubted he needed to puncture the brain of the dead man, but Luke wanted to be certain the man didn't return to life. The science on the topic of reanimation seemed sketchy at best, and he wasn't taking chances. Truthfully, Luke wanted to stab the man as retribution for nearly killing him, even if the man wasn't alive to experience pain and agony.

Stepping outside, Luke spied the body immediately, portions of skin and fur blowing in the breeze. It reminded Luke of his childhood, when his Golden Retriever, Dusty, was struck by a car and killed early one morning. Much to his horror, Luke made the discovery when he awoke one Saturday, expecting a day of frolic and play, instead finding his dog lying beside the road in a heap. He remembered watching his parents bury his best childhood friend through tear-filled eyes as the clouds let loose with a cold, miserable drizzle that added to the already somber mood.

Moisture formed in the corner of his right eye currently, because he'd just survived almost certain death. Feeling almost certain Samantha watched his every move, he discreetly wiped the tear away before running a hand through his hair.

He walked over to the body, observing it only a moment before reaching into his pocket and drawing the pocket knife. Folding out the blade, he knelt down, half expecting the man to jump to life like some kind of horror movie antagonist, but nothing happened as he surgically slid the knife into the side of the man's head, bringing closure to the ordeal.

Looking back to the house, he found Samantha standing at the door, watching his every move, and he knew from that moment forward he was her role model in virtually every aspect of life. A month before, he wouldn't have found the courage to save anyone except himself and his partner, but now his blood coursed with parental instincts. He would die for the girl, and she'd saved his life, cementing a bond already in motion before necessary actions on both of their parts.

Wiping the knife on the man's clothing and fur combination, Luke closed the blade, careful not to slice his skin. He walked over to Samantha, still feeling woozy from the man clubbing him with bare fists and nearly strangling him.

"Where should we go?" he asked, since Samantha appeared fully aware of her surroundings now.

"We need to help the others," she replied, warming his heart with the spirit only a child could provide.

"You're right. We do."

Twenty-one

"We have a problem," Metzger noted as they walked Fournier across the bridge to the area where the isolated house stood on the other side.

Fournier had regained consciousness shortly after Bryce rendered him unconscious, saying nothing as he scowled constantly at his three captors.

"What's that?" Bryce asked.

"How the hell are we going to fit all of us and three or four prisoners in those Humvees once we cross the border?"

"We won't need *all* of the prisoners," Bryce replied, which sounded ominous to his brother.

Metzger couldn't imagine the Marines asking them a few simple questions before discarding them with bullets to the forehead. He wasn't sure Nadeau's supporters would act as benevolent captors if the roles were reversed, but he wanted to hear what the lot of them had to say before decisions were made about their future.

"They won't talk," Fournier spouted coldly with his French accent.

"Oh, he speaks," Metzger said, taking a verbal jab at the man. "And you can attest to their tight lips because you know each of them personally?"

Fournier said nothing, choosing to walk across the bridge in silence.

"I wish you would've died at the airport," Metzger said so only the Canadian would hear his words. "You cost me a good friend with that little stunt you pulled."

"You've cost me more than you'll ever know. Twice."

No one spoke another word during the walk across the bridge, and when the group reached the converted house, they found the Marines waiting beside the two vehicles with three prisoners and two boxes of paperwork and items confiscated from the stronghold. One of them spoke on a satellite phone to a higher authority, and Metzger questioned why anyone back in Norfolk wouldn't call his brother instead. He thought of the sat phone he acquired in town, thankful he stuffed it in a pocket because he hadn't found time to retrieve the backpack or the remainder of its contents.

"I understand, sir," the leader of the Marines said, spying the approaching group from the corner of his eye. "New secondary objective."

Metzger wasn't certain if his brother heard the words or not, because his brother's face displayed neutrality when he stole a glance. The Marine abruptly severed the call, turning his attention to the four people returning to the compound.

"Target acquired," he said, a broad smile crossing his face before he shook hands with Bryce. "We have some people *very* interested in meeting this son-of-a-bitch."

"Did you get anything from these three?" Bryce inquired, looking to the three men seated on the ground with their hands restrained behind them with zip ties.

"Negative. They're staying tightlipped."

"It's going to be crowded in those vehicles if we take them all back."

"Don't see where we have much choice," the Marine replied. "We can't leave any of them around to warn their people further up the chain."

"Agreed."

"We can secure another car," Molly suggested.

"We'll have to," the Marine said, looking behind the returning group. "Looks like you brought some company with you."

Nearly a dozen zombies staggered in their direction across the bridge, slowly catching up after spying human activity in the city.

Metzger supposed the Marines had their hands full securing the three prisoners, but he questioned why none of the men crossed the bridge afterwards, because Fournier was certainly the primary target and the reason they returned to Buffalo. He supposed they considered Bryce reinforcement enough, so they monitored the prisoners instead.

He didn't particularly like the lack of organization from the military end, but he knew they originally planned on extracting Fournier and dealing with possibly one gatekeeper. He didn't expect two additional people to be staying there, though he felt glad the men weren't simply expendable, meant to be shot and disposed of like cattle.

"Let's load up," Bryce ordered, more than suggested. "We'll keep Fournier in one of the vehicles and a few of us can walk with the other dickheads until we find additional transportation."

Bryce and one of the Marines guarded Fournier in the green car, while another Marine guarded another prisoner in the truck they already possessed, forcing the man to drive. Molly, Metzger, the lead Marine, and the remaining two prisoners walked behind the small convoy, heading east to the United States and their transportation awaiting them at the airport. Two of the prisoners walked alongside, knowing escape was impractical with their hands bound and nowhere in particular to go. Metzger continued to glance at the Marine walking just a few paces to his right, wondering who the man conversed with on the sat phone, and what the conversation entailed.

In his mind, he couldn't shake the words "new secondary objective" because he wondered what else in their current location could be even remotely important by comparison. Thus far, the man hadn't given any new orders to his men, and he certainly hadn't spoken about the conversation to Bryce, or the civilians assisting them.

Before long they reached city streets, knowing they needed to cross a dangerous portion of the city before reaching the border. Metzger pulled away from the group several times to try a few suitable vehicles parked alongside city streets or sidewalks, as though hastily left when their owners ran for their lives. One indicated no fuel was left in the tank, while another refused to turn over at all. Metzger couldn't determine if the battery died, or something else caused the problem, but he wasn't going to waste time peering under the hood.

Much to his surprise, Metzger found a 1979 Chevy pickup truck that turned over immediately, and registered a tank more than half full. He looked to Molly when she opened the passenger door to see his progress.

"It's a stick," he said, unable to recall the last time he drove a manual transmission vehicle other than a motorcycle.

"Allow me," she said with a smile. "I used to drive these all the time at my uncle's farm."

Molly drove, and the Marine chose to remain in the truck bed to guard the two prisoners, which provided Metzger and Molly an opportunity to talk. Even with open windows, anyone in the back wouldn't hear their conversation due to the gusting wind.

"Did you hear what that guy said on the sat phone?" he inquired.

"I did," she answered without removing her eyes from the road ahead. "What do you make of it?"

"It sounds like we have something else going on before we fly back to the base, but he's not coming off the details."

"Think someone cut a deal?"

Metzger gave a sideways smile.

"What?" Molly asked as though she'd said something grievously wrong.

"You're always so suspicious of everyone."

"Considering my recent track record, I have reason to be."

"I'll admit I didn't like the way he hung up so quickly," Metzger said. "Whatever he was talking about, he didn't want anyone knowing it, including my brother."

"Isn't your brother leading this expedition?"

"In rank, yes, but some of these Marines answer to different bosses. I don't entirely trust the powers that be to do right by us. Or him."

"What are you saying, exactly?"

"I don't see some kind of double-cross coming, but we need to stay vigilant. I'm ready to get back to Norfolk and sleep for days, but I won't relax until we board that plane."

"We haven't really discussed this, but am I welcome to come back with your group?"

"I figured that was a foregone conclusion," Metzger replied. "They're picky about who gets to stay at the base, but they've been taking back the city so families can spread out."

"Or the military can have privacy to do what they will."

"There is that," Metzger thought aloud.

Metzger felt trapped with his thoughts the remainder of the journey until they reached the United States border and he called upon his heightened senses and instincts to keep him safe. He expected something to happen, either in the form of an ambush, or some new twist brought about by the phone call the Marine received. The fact that the Marine didn't speak a single word about the conversation to Bryce concerned him even more.

"Cross this bridge and we're home free," Molly stated as she drew the truck to a stop. "In theory."

"That's for sure," Metzger said as he opened his door and stepped out from their borrowed vehicle.

All three vehicles had drawn as close as they could to the border on the Canadian side due to the blockage. In his travels, Metzger experienced such congestion on bridges, along highways and interstates leaving urban areas, and within the cities themselves. Outward appearances indicated no one ever truly wanted to *enter* a city when certain death awaited them.

"Time to walk," Bryce announced as the prisoners were harshly prodded from the vehicles, forced to cross the bridge at gunpoint.

None of them attempted to run, or worse, leap off the bridge at any point. Either they trusted the remnants of the government to treat them decently, or they anticipated a rescue attempt. Metzger didn't foresee the latter because he doubted anyone knew the men were holed up in the isolated Canadian building. He also doubted they made contact with people at the next destination that led to Nadeau, suspecting multiple stops and checkpoints stood between them and the man who ended the populated world.

A few undead blocked their paths along the bridge, but Metzger silently dealt with them using his sword. Before long, the group stood at the booths marking entry to the United States, met with no resistance as they weaved through the various booths and the vehicles clogging the paths. On the other side, Metzger looked around, seeing no danger in any direction, though he knew with another couple hundred vehicles in front of them, hazards might lurk in any direction.

"What's the matter with you?" Bryce asked once he met up with his brother between stalled vehicles.

"Did you hear the conversation your Marine was having on the phone when we returned from the city?"

"Of course I did. I'm not deaf."

"What the hell does 'secondary objective' mean?"

"Who knows?" Bryce answered with a shrug. "The jarheads like to feel important."

"It was more than that," Metzger insisted, ignoring his brother's slang for the Marines. "He cut off that call awfully quick when he saw us coming."

Bryce said nothing, choosing to observe one of the prisoners walking ahead of him.

"You're supposed to be in charge of this operation," Metzger said. "Why wouldn't that come through you? And why does that guy have his own sat phone anyway?"

"Look, this unified military thing isn't exactly catching on with our superiors. They talk shop together in their conference rooms, then they give orders, but that doesn't mean they like each other, or their ideas. Hell, for all I know that guy was just updating his superior about what we'd found."

"It didn't sound that way to me," Metzger said assuredly before leaving his brother's side to join Molly, even though he didn't feel like conversing with her either.

Metzger loved his brother, and perhaps out of obligation to stay with his last remaining family member, he left his friends and opted for life on a military installation, but he regretted the choice more often than not. So long as Bryce felt his government was doing right by its few remaining citizens, he wouldn't abandon his post, and while Metzger hoped those who enforced laws and fought for civil liberties continued their work, he sensed something more ominous afoot.

When the group emerged from the sea of abandoned vehicles, they found the Marine sentry Coffey standing diligently between the two Humvees, unscathed, though a bit more reddened by the sun. He said nothing, but he smirked at the results of the collaborative search. Much like before, the group quickly discovered that two vehicles would not sufficiently hold the Marines, Bryce, Metzger, Molly, and four prisoners.

"Lucky for all of you I tested a few nearby vehicles and found a Dodge truck in working order," Coffey stated, taking notice of their dilemma.

Seating arrangements remained nearly the same, but Metzger and Molly were asked to occupy the Dodge while one of the Marines and the stout prisoner sat in the bed. While Metzger wanted to desperately grab some of the family items and heirlooms he left locked inside a car at the airport when he first departed Buffalo, he wasn't about to compromise his brother's assignment. Although his knowledge as an amateur pilot continued to expand, he didn't foresee a return flight to New York soon, but he wouldn't rule out a future trip.

"I'm glad you found your brother," Molly finally said from the passenger's seat as Metzger followed the second Humvee along a highway.

"I'm sorry things went so badly at the school," he said. "We should've known these assholes weren't done."

"We thought we were prepared," Molly said as she stared out her passenger window. "We weren't."

"Choosing my brother over my group was one of the hardest decisions I've ever made," Metzger admitted. "And what's weird is I barely got to know those people."

"It doesn't take long to bond in this kind of environment. You learn who to trust quickly, or you don't make it."

"Living with the government isn't all it's cracked up to be."

"What's left of our government these days?" she inquired.

"That's a tricky question," Metzger admitted. "They claim the President and many key members of Congress and the House are safe, but I've never laid eyes on a single one of them so far as I can tell."

"I can't imagine they'd put everyone in Virginia, though. In fact, they probably have fortified bunkers like our good friend Nadeau."

"Maybe. And they have other bases and locations secured."

"I'm curious how well they can communicate, if that's the case."

"Surely they have satellite communications up and running, but I'm not privy to the inner workings of our military. I know they put a limit on use of their resources."

"If there's infrastructure, then we might have a chance of rebuilding."

"They've got some smart people at the base," Metzger said. "They've been sending soldiers and civilians into the town to wipe out any lingering dead. One of those aircraft carriers can power a small city for about twenty years, and if we haven't figured out how to get things working by then, shame on *us*."

"We're screwed either way," Molly said without any passion in her voice. "We're going to run out of stable fuel for our vehicles, the dead heads are going to wipe out the animal population, and we can't trust half the living. Not exactly a strong foundation, if you get my drift."

"I know," Metzger said, comprehending the reality. "Part of me wanted to join the cause and help the military begin to rebuild, but I'm not sure that's their primary goal at this point. Maybe they're multitasking, and I'm not seeing nearly half of what they're doing, but we keep chasing after this Nadeau character like getting him to fess up is going to solve our problems. I remember when the government finally tracked down bin Laden after 9/11, and knowing he was dead didn't exactly heal old wounds."

"You seem to be a good judge of character, Dan. If they don't deliver on their promises, I suspect you'll make your own way, or straighten them out."

Metzger chuckled.

"Well, if they hold elections in the future, maybe I'll run for something."

"If you're not seeing leadership in there now, maybe there isn't any," Molly suggested.

"Meaning they're hidden away?"

"Meaning they might be lying to you, and none of these career politicians are alive like the military types would have you believe."

"Were you this skeptical before the apocalypse?"

Molly grinned.

"I'm a survivor. So are you. I know you don't take everything they spoon feed you at face value. Otherwise you wouldn't have been so concerned about that phone call back there."

Metzger couldn't argue her point. Living in the base made him feel claustrophobic sometimes, because military people and their civilian families shared the space, except for the areas closed off to civilians. He couldn't readily recall seeing any familiar faces from the political or celebrity realms wandering around the base, and he didn't imagine even those folks wanted to remain cooped up aboard a ship every hour of every day.

"Do you think this guy will provide answers about how to find Nadeau?" Molly asked.

"I bet one of them squawks," Metzger replied. "The paperwork we found might be more help."

"I'm a little surprised they let you come along on this little expedition."

"I can take care of myself. They know that."

"I meant I figured they'd be more secretive, not wanting a civilian to learn any important secrets before their brass found out."

"I think my brother had a lot to do with talking them into letting me come along. They would've been forever trying to find that school without me."

"Thank God you tagged along, then."

"I'm just sorry Fournier and his people put their future above human lives. They killed all those people, even my folks, for what? A few sheets of paper that might lead to salvation in Canada?"

"We can't assume he's in Canada," Molly said. "He was one of the richest people in the world, and he might very well be holed up in our country to rub it in our noses. Hell, he might have jumped on his private jet and gone to Europe or some exotic island where he'd be safe."

"That would make his magic instruction sheet a complete fabrication, though."

Molly gave a knowing look.

"Would you expect anything less? We don't even know what his motivation was. He might have become unhinged."

"I doubt someone insane is going to create a fake paper trail. Maybe he knew a fight was inevitable and he's trying to build an army."

Metzger grunted, curious about the man's motivations. He wondered if the military, or anyone, would ever discover why he decided to spread a fatal disease across the world.

Within the hour they approached the airport, and a horrifying sight awaited the group as they spotted the cargo plane beyond the downed fences, surrounded by the undead. Metzger wondered if the zombies spotted the plane's descent, knowing they'd been gone long enough for their natural adversaries to make their way to the airport. He saw the cargo hatch of the plane sealed, which caused him to wonder why the undead lingered in the area.

"Not good," he muttered, not deviating from his course as the Humvees slowed, but continued toward the plane.

Metzger wondered if the Marines shared his thoughts, caught between securing the prisoners and safely boarding the plane for the return flight to Virginia. When the first Humvee stopped, and the second one pulled beside it, Metzger followed suit. Immediately, the undead took notice, and one Marine from each Humvee took aim with his personal weapon in the vehicle's turret and began shooting the zombies through their skulls. Metzger heard gunfire from behind him as the Marine riding the truck bed behind him assisted his comrades. They missed their first few shots, firing from a distance and at an odd, elevated angle. Not until the undead staggered a bit closer did the rounds hit home. As one wave of the undead fell, their skulls spurting coagulated blood, a second line of their kind approached the vehicles, endangering everyone with their sheer numbers.

"There are dozens of them," Molly noted aloud.

"We're going to get overrun if we stay here," Metzger said. "Someone needs to distract them, or we aren't going anywhere."

"Run their asses over," Molly suggested firmly.

"You ever driven a vehicle after zombie guts get into the engine block?" Metzger countered. "You don't get far, even in a Humvee."

As though his thoughts mirrored those of his younger brother, Bryce stepped from one of the Humvees, taking aim with a pistol at a few of the undead, putting them down as the rest of the zombies focused their attention on a hot meal. In the distance, Metzger saw the cargo hatch open, revealing a ramp for the vehicles to enter the plane. One of the pilots stuck his head out, frantically waving with one arm for them to enter the vehicle. Both Humvees drove that way, and the Marine in the back of the truck pounded his hand against the roof, indicating he wanted to experience safety immediately.

Metzger gave a look to his brother, who ushered him to go while backpedaling from the undead, still continuing to shoot them. Stepping on the gas, Metzger found the truck unable to move as it lost traction in a soft area of the grass between landing strips. He pressed on the gas pedal once more, only to find the tires spinning, entrenching them further in the terrain.

Realizing the gravity of the situation, the Marine behind them tossed the prisoner off the side of the truck, jumping down behind him and jolting the man to his feet as they gave a wide berth around the zombies. Now some of the undead followed the Marine, breaking off pursuit of Bryce as they did so. With the undead faction divided, the Marines in the Humvees exited, taking their prisoners with them as they darted for the safety of the cargo plane. Each of them fired a few shots as they tried distancing themselves from the main cluster of undead.

"We need to move," Metzger said, worried they might get surrounded by the herd and trapped inside the truck.

Being left behind concerned him, but he wasn't about to let his brother take on the entire group of zombies alone.

Metzger and Molly exited the truck at the same time, quickly joined by Bryce, who brought the danger with him as they tried to reach the plane. Many of the undead staggering toward the aircraft turned to the group, attracted by the noise of truck doors opening. As quickly as Metzger sliced through the skulls of two zombies with his sword, another four of them were closing in, too close for him to use the weapon and hope to escape. He ducked under the groping arm of one of them, joining Molly on the other side. Bryce remained separated, and gunfire from the plane knocked a few of the zombies down, but there were still too many between Metzger and his brother.

"Go!" Bryce shouted. "I'll catch up!"

Metzger doubted the sincerity of his brother's words, because just under two dozen undead weren't going to stand aside and let his brother saunter onto the plane for a return trip to Virginia. Molly tugged at his arm, and as Metzger started backpedaling with her to guaranteed safety, he began to realize his brother wasn't intending to make a dash for the plane.

At least not yet.

Some of the Marines continued to shoot, trying to support Bryce as best they could, but Metzger began losing sight of his brother as the zombie horde surrounded him. Metzger reached the ramp of the plane, kicking a zombie aside as he ascended for a better view of his brother. He grew more concerned by the second, pulling his sword from its sheath to deal with a zombie that climbed the ramp, groping at Molly. To avoid striking her, he jabbed the carnivorous adversary squarely in the forehead, ending its second life instantly.

Continuing to hold his sword out defensively, Metzger backed up the ramp, finding his brother drawing more zombies in his direction while getting flanked from every side.

"We have to help him," he said to Molly, who started down the ramp.

Bryce continued shooting the undead closest to him, but his ammunition couldn't hold out much longer. Despite his best efforts to fend off the onslaught of the undead, Bryce failed to duck quickly enough as two zombies maneuvered behind him. One grabbed him by the arm, pulling him back as the other sank its teeth into his right trapezius muscle, dangerously close to his neck. Bryce's head arched back in pain before he slammed his elbow into one of them, prying free from both in an instant.

"No!" Metzger screamed as he lurched forward to help his brother, hoping the zombie's teeth hadn't penetrated his brother's thick uniform.

He felt strong hands clasp his elbows and shoulders, dragging him into the plane despite his kicks and protests.

"No!" he screamed a second time, holding the word at the top of his lungs. "Let go of me, you motherfuckers!"

Molly continued down the ramp, attempting to assist Bryce as the plane's ramp began ascending. Metzger locked eyes with his brother momentarily, seeing a fight in the Navy man's expression that indicated Bryce wasn't dead, or finished, quite yet. He fought against his attackers, even as the undead attempted to claw and bite at him. Bryce knocked several of them to the ground, and Metzger clearly saw a bloody spot on his brother's shoulder while he personally struggled against the Marines restraining him. A third military man came over to ensure Metzger didn't break free as the stream of daylight from outside the plane grew thinner with each passing second.

One of them snagged the sword from his right hand, and Metzger glanced to Molly, who'd exited the plane and now looked at him with confusion and mild fear as the undead turned to face her. Metzger felt dizzy, his legs rubbery, as though he might pass out from the overwhelming circumstances. Molly set to defending herself, and Metzger spied a blur pass along his left side as someone saw an opportunity to escape. Metzger wasn't positive, but he felt certain Fournier took advantage of the confusion and lack of manpower guarding him to leap from the side of the ramp before the door closed enough to confine him.

One of the Marines holding Metzger back started after him, but the leader put a stop to it verbally.

"Let him go! We have the paperwork, and the secondary objective is secure."

Metzger turned, staring the man in the eye, and he immediately realized *he* was the secondary objective based on the fact that the man looked directly at him when he spoke the words. They had just sentenced his brother and Molly to almost certain death, and let one of the worst people on the planet escape. Although he locked eyes with Metzger momentarily, the Marine leader looked away and walked to the front of the plane to carry on with his objectives.

Not until the cargo door slammed shut, sealing Metzger's fate, did the Marines let go of him. Bathed in the artificial interior lighting of the aircraft, Metzger couldn't possibly learn how his brother, Molly, or Fournier fared outside because the only windows were in the cockpit. Even if the engines hadn't roared to life within a few seconds, he couldn't have heard noises beyond the metal hull of the aircraft. He eyed his sword lying on the ground, but temporarily ignored it, walking absently to one of the seats along the side. Plopping down heavily, he felt overwhelmed by the sudden turn of events, certain he'd seen his brother as a living being for the last time while his only remaining ally was cut off from assisting him any further.

Confused, shaken, and angry, Metzger sat as the plane taxied, burying his face in his hands. He worried about the fate of his brother and his friend, feeling helpless because he wanted to be on the ground with them. Instead, he sat on a plane, destined for Virginia where he'd be lucky if they let him break the terrible news to his sister-in-law because the military obviously found some use for him.

He watched as the Marines secured their remaining prisoners, his body numb at the thought of losing his brother after fighting so hard to reach Virginia in the first place. He felt partly responsible for tagging along, but in the end the military made decisions that cost him the remainder of his family.

And though he felt a tear slide down his right cheek, Metzger decided he would get answers and hold the fragmented leadership of his country responsible if it was his last earthly act.

Twenty-Two

"We'd better have some weapons left," Driscoll said as he drove hurriedly toward the houses he and Sutton occupied, "or this is going to be a really short fight."

After a momentary reprieve when the pursuing vehicle lost them, the group heard squealing tires behind them as Dark Lady's people located them and made a sharp turn onto their current road.

Jillian questioned how much of what the gypsy woman spoke was true, because her people seemed to know exactly where to find them in South Hill at all times, and the pursuit came about rather quickly after they departed the property where Vazquez was murdered. To her, it felt as though their new adversaries might have conducted surveillance a day or two before making their move. She couldn't understand why the group escalated from being a common nuisance to outright murderers.

"You're going to have to park us right beside one of the front doors," Sutton said as Buster paced what little he could, confined within a car.

He sensed the tension among the four humans with him, which left him antsy as they raced to possible salvation.

Driscoll didn't say a word, but as the houses came into view, he directed the car into the yard of the closer residence, getting them as close to Sutton's house as possible without striking it. Everyone scattered from the car at once, like cockroaches in a bathtub when the overhead light is turned on. Buster followed his master into the first house, and both Jillian and Gracine chose the nearest house as well because their enemies drew closer by the second.

When Jillian entered behind Sutton, she found him heading for the kitchen, opening several drawers and pulling a semi-automatic pistol from beneath some old instruction manuals. Handing it to Gracine, he opened the refrigerator, then the storage tray near the bottom, finding another semi-automatic pistol he handed to Jillian. She ejected the magazine, checking the ammunition level, finding it just a few rounds short of full. Times like these made Jillian thankful for her father's guidance, and being lucky enough to find people who were helpful and like-minded during her travels.

"Some of the good stuff was in that truck," Sutton grumbled as he walked to one of the bedrooms further back, Buster right on his heels.

He emerged a moment later with an AR-15 in his right hand and a revolver tucked into his belt. Buster still sensed the group's anxiety, but wagged his tail and looked up to Sutton with wide eyes.

"What about extra ammo?" Gracine asked as they returned to the front of the house.

"None," Sutton answered succinctly.

When they stepped outside, the group didn't see or hear the vehicle that pursued them most of the way through the town. Driscoll stood on the front landing of the house he occupied, holding a rifle of some sort. He appeared ready for a fight, which came naturally to him, much like it did for Sutton. Firearms often sorted out predators and prey in the apocalypse, and Jillian knew if the group hadn't located the firearms, they wouldn't have stepped outside at all.

"Where did those motherfuckers go?" Gracine questioned aloud, her eyes panning the area around them.

"They're too dumb to retreat," Driscoll commented.

"Or they outgun us and they're waiting for us to let our guard down," Jillian said. "We should probably get to a better tactical position."

"Agreed," Sutton said, motioning toward an area down the street from them. "Come on," he called to Buster, who readily followed him.

Further down the road, a larger house sat near the base of a hill, offering them both cover and a topographical feature that prevented a vehicle from following their retreat if the battle didn't go their way. They all jogged down to the house, which remained unlocked like virtually every other building in the town. A truck and an SUV remained in the driveway, offering them cover outside of the house, and as Jillian reached the driveway, she ducked behind the truck for a look behind her.

Met by eerie quiet, she wondered why the group broke off the pursuit, because they certainly hadn't gotten lost in a small town like South Hill. Jillian looked to the eyes of her companions, and they appeared equally mystified, and nervous, until a sound reached their eardrums that caused all of them to stiffen.

As though a large jungle cat had been set upon them, the roar of a loud engine broke the silence and only a few seconds passed before the large vehicle meant for transporting humans and equipment raced directly at the group.

Like the others, Jillian realized immediately the truck wasn't slowing down for anything, aimed directly at them and their chosen cover. Either their transportation was capable of withstanding high-impact crashes, or they simply didn't care what happened to it, because they were about to strike two vehicles and possibly a house. All four of them scattered for cover in different directions, which certainly aided their adversaries, who created a ripple effect by hitting the truck and barreling it into the SUV behind it.

Jillian managed to keep her grip on the firearm Sutton provided her, knowing she couldn't fend off large carnie types with sheer will and empty palms. Rolling over to take aim at whomever emerged from the truck, she didn't have to fire because the truck backed away from the driveway. Perhaps their attackers thought better of their assault once they saw their prey armed, or their intent was simply to scare the four souls and one dog, but Jillian didn't want to give them an opportunity to regroup.

She looked to her colleagues, finding Sutton and Gracine had regained their footing while Driscoll was a little slower to rise, despite being further from the collision than the others. Buster snarled and barked at the truck from a safe distance, showing aggression Jillian had yet to see from the canine.

"Bastards," she muttered at the people inside the truck, taking aim at one of the tires before the truck could speed away.

One round took out the front tire, though it required two additional shots for Jillian to disable the rear tire on the same side as the truck turned to attempt a retreat. Sutton quickly caught on to her idea and attempted to flatten the other tires, but his rounds struck other portions of the truck as it turned away from him. Jillian striking two tires significantly slowed the truck, and she heard the rubbery thumps each time the bulging portion of the two blown tires slapped the pavement.

"I don't think they have weapons," Jillian called to her colleagues as Driscoll regained his footing and joined the others as they approached the partly disabled vehicle.

"Get out!" Sutton called to the people inside the truck as Buster continued to bark behind his owner.

Jillian looked over, taking more careful notice that Buster wasn't barking at the truck, but rather behind where Jillian stood, and to Driscoll's other side.

"Everyone, get to cover!" Jillian screamed as she darted to one of the smashed vehicles before a hail of gunfire rang out.

A single person emerged from the truck, rushing to the back of the vehicle as he fired rounds at Gracine and Driscoll. Sutton had already reached cover, calling Buster to his side as Jillian realized her intuition proved correct just in time. The truck had waited before coming at them because the driver let his passengers out for an ambush, knowing their targets were heading to an area with only one true exit road.

Jillian knew someone was on the hill behind her, but she wasn't going to leave her spot and become a target for the other potential gunmen. Her eyes desperately searched for the shooter, finding only overgrown grass and a few trees lining the hill until she saw some of the grass move. Wind wouldn't selectively blow blades of grass, and no creature with intact hearing would remain so close to the deafening noises below, so she took aim and fired.

Suddenly the grass stopped moving, but no yelp of pain or spurting of blood accompanied the stillness. Jillian wanted to run up the hill to see if her theory proved correct, but with shots ringing out around her, and from different areas, she decided to stay in cover.

Daring to look where her colleagues should have been located, she found each of them now ducked behind the vehicles, or trees, exchanging gunfire with their attackers. Although Sutton handled firearms better than anyone else in the group, Jillian found herself wishing Metzger were there for the briefest of moments. His instincts often kept them out of conflicts, because he knew how to resolve issues verbally, using force only when necessary.

Flanked by at least three sides, the group remained stuck behind the two disabled, smashed vehicles because no one on either side stuck any body parts out from cover. Although not a ceasefire, nearly a minute passed while both sides stopped shooting, waiting for an opening or a mistake by their adversaries.

"Why are you doing this?" Gracine called out, as though the silence caused a boiling point she could no longer withstand.

No one answered.

"We don't have to shoot one another," Jillian added, seeing that Sutton and Driscoll were acting too macho to request a truce.

Hearing the squawk of a radio, Jillian listened intently, knowing none of her allies carried any kind of portable radio or phone device that worked. A woman's voice said something, but she couldn't make out the words. If the man listening on their end answered, he did so in a murmur so no one else heard. Jillian suspected her nemesis was coming their way, and she wondered if blood would be spilled, or she could still talk some sense into Dark Lady. Jillian hadn't changed her mind about killing an alleged child molester, or his backers, but getting revenge for Vazquez meant staying alive long enough to formulate a plan.

Minutes felt like forever as everyone gave edgy glances in every direction, with no one opening fire again. Jillian felt certain the radio message caused the ceasefire on the other end, though she didn't like waiting to see what came next. Her options felt limited, but Gracine managed to crawl behind the disabled vehicles to join her.

"We can't wait around like this," Gracine said.

"I know, but they're all around us. If we run, they're going to shoot us in the back."

Jillian thought incorrectly about Dark Lady's group having insufficient firepower once, but they had obviously ransacked the main house and stolen plenty of firearms and ammunition. Running might be a more viable option if the group could coordinate a plan without their adversaries overhearing it, but Jillian wasn't sure the male members of their group wanted to flee in the first place.

"I say we pick a direction and go for it," Gracine said, thinking along the same lines.

"Not without the guys," Jillian said, waiting for Sutton to make eye contact with her when she looked in his direction.

He monitored the area around him like a hawk momentarily, with Driscoll pinned down just a few feet away from him. Buster also hunkered down, respecting the commands of his master, but audibly arguing that he wanted action because the canine wasn't accustomed to lying still for very long.

When Sutton finally looked over, Jillian pointed behind her, indicating with two fingers in a running motion that they could make a dash for safety. He contemplated her proposal momentarily, looking from the mostly open area behind her to the spots where their adversaries likely hid, and finally shook his head negatively. He obviously believed at least one of Dark Lady's associates was positioned in an area dangerous to their group.

Jillian liked their current odds at the moment better than if more circus types showed up with a variety of weapons.

"They're keeping us here for a reason," Gracine noted. "I don't like this one bit."

"Me either. Got anything to create a distraction?"

Gracine looked at her as though Jillian had lost her mind.

"Do I look like a magician?"

"You drove a truck. Can't you blow up a fuel tank or something?"

"Girl, this isn't the movies. Gas tanks don't blow up when you shoot them, and I don't have any fire arrows on me."

Jillian knew she should have felt nervous, or feared death far more intensely, but the culmination of her experiences, combined with surviving numerous harrowing situations, left her numbed to the prospect of death. Not until she heard the sound of an incoming vehicle did Jillian detect any emotion, and when she did, she felt pure hatred.

"That bitch," she muttered, knowing Dark Lady was about to show up once more and impose her will upon others.

"We need to find you a shrink if we survive this," Gracine said, motioning to Sutton that he needed to do something fast, causing him to respond with a shrug.

Momentarily, the car pulled to a stop and the sound of three doors shutting as people stepped out reached Jillian's ears. She couldn't see their new visitors, because the car parked behind the large circus truck.

"Cunt, what have you done with my Audie?" Dark Lady's voice beckoned from her unseen position.

"Bitch, I haven't done a thing with your child predator," Jillian answered, knowing only she could be the target of such verbal abuse. "Maybe someone finally put him out of his misery."

"I'm saving you for last," Dark Lady announced. "Your friends will all die in front of you, and you can watch. Then I'll do you nice and slow, maybe with a dull blade, or a few bullets in your stomach so you can bleed out."

"What's this bitch have against you?" Gracine asked just above a whisper.

"Long story."

Jillian heard footsteps around the car Dark Lady brought to the skirmish, sensing the violence was about to begin anew.

"Boys, surround them and open fire," Dark Lady yelled so all of her people could hear.

Jillian and Gracine heard more footsteps crunch in the untended grass, each looking in slightly varying directions to defend themselves against the incoming invasion. Feeling relieved that Luke and Samantha had escaped such a horrific ordeal, Jillian took aim at the rear corner of the large vehicle the first group arrived in, prepared to fire at whatever person emerged first.

Outnumbered, Jillian knew their group was capable of taking down several enemies before they fell, but such bloodshed wasn't necessary in a town the size of South Hill. Negotiations might have avoided any violence in the first place, but Dark Lady and her carnival employees sealed their fate when they murdered Vazquez. Jillian wasn't about to let his death go without some form of retaliation.

Stiffening, prepared to take a human life, Jillian waited and watched for her first target when a flash of orange shot down from behind her, causing an explosion to the large vehicle. White smoke mixed with orange flames mushroomed from the decimated vehicle after the quick boom pierced the air. Shrapnel flew in every direction, but Jillian avoided injury because Dark Lady's people hadn't parked incredibly close to their location. Yelps of pain and several screams pierced the air as everyone looked up the hill behind Jillian and her group, seeing a man standing there with a rocket launcher that billowed smoke out the front port.

"Thought you could use a hand," Gabe Keppler called down from above them, openly posing no threat to the group, though he addressed Sutton directly. "This'll be the last favor I do for you."

"You call that a favor?" Sutton retorted. "You almost got us killed."

Keppler scoffed, still holding the launcher firmly.

In the background, Dark Lady and her group bid a hasty retreat down the road. Some of them crammed into their car, but others took off on foot. Jillian glanced, unable to tell if the explosion actually killed any of them, or not. A small fire began to consume the synthetic materials within the vehicle, even running along the metal frame where leftover fuel droplets coaxed the flames.

Jillian saw complete confusion on the face of Driscoll, while Buster retreated several steps from the explosion, eyeballing the strange sight without making a sound. Gracine continued to glance behind them at the hill and the man standing above them, still wearing a military uniform so no one mistook his name, or underestimated his skills.

"How is that motherfucker still alive?" Gracine muttered.

"That's what I was wondering," Jillian replied, under the impression Sutton at least took care of *that* problem when he sent the group ahead once before.

"I've got your box truck," Keppler said, not bragging, but making certain Sutton knew he'd prevailed in the end.

Sutton scowled, openly unhappy about losing his truck, and seeing Keppler once again, but he refrained from saying anything, as though he didn't want the group to hear more open discussion between him and the disgraced lieutenant.

"What's wrong?" Keppler asked as though the silence offended him. "No thanks for saving your lives?"

"We had this," Sutton replied.

"Yeah. You sure looked like you had a handle on things until I came and fucked up your victory celebration."

"Maybe you should come down here and celebrate with us," Sutton provided an insincere offer.

"I'll pass. From the looks of this truck, I'll be days and days just organizing all the cool shit in the back of it."

Jillian noticed Sutton didn't take aim at Keppler, though he probably could've taken a shot before the man pulled a weapon on him, Buster, or anyone else below. Keppler possessed the high ground, and he stood in a spot where he could eyeball all of them at once and step back if anyone aimed a firearm his way.

"It's good seeing the rest of you again," Keppler said with a nod. "Sorry the military didn't let y'all stay, but I've learned they're kinda assholes."

"They sure are," Gracine commented, lifting her head to look at the uniform he still donned to make sure Keppler received her meaning.

He gave a grin in response.

"I'm going to get moving," Keppler said, thumbing almost casually towards the truck behind him. "Good luck fighting the crazy carnival folk."

Sutton said nothing, simply hanging his head in defeat momentarily as Jillian walked over to him, staring at the carnage around them once more. The large truck continued to burn, though the fire dwindled as it ran out of materials to consume. She didn't spot any bodies around the wreckage, assuming everyone ran, or limped, their way away from the blast. From the sound of their screams, some of them weren't faring too well after being burned or impaled with shrapnel.

"You left us," Jillian said as she approached Sutton, addressing him directly. "When we finally saw you again, you said you'd taken care of everything."

"I-"

Jillian cut loose with a hard slap across his right cheek before he could verbally manufacture an excuse. The sound of her hand against his skin sounded deafening compared to the nearby fire, and everyone froze, staring with wide eyes.

"You got my father killed, you let that maniac back into our lives, and you lied to us."

"I left him for dead," Sutton said firmly, trying to get a word in before Jillian laid into him further.

"You've become a liability, leading us into dangerous situations against dangerous people because of your ego and your precious box truck," Jillian said.

A car had managed to approach during the past few minutes, and only now did everyone look over to see Luke and Samantha emerge from the vehicle. Stunned expressions crossed their faces as they stared at the wreckage, obviously unsure of what transpired with any trace of Keppler and the box truck now gone.

"You need to go," Jillian said, blurting the words before she allowed herself to ponder her decision further, and possibly change her mind.

Sutton looked around, but no one said a word in his defense, including Gracine, who owed her life to Sutton according to his side of the story. A few awkward seconds passed before Sutton looked down to Buster, who'd settled down after the initial scare the explosion provided. He wagged his tail, looking up to his master with wide, dark eyes, wondering what came next in his canine life.

"Come on," Sutton said, calling Buster over to him with a defeated tone.

Jillian almost held back her next statement, but her blood boiled with infuriation over what Sutton had put her through.

"You should probably leave Buster with us," she said. "He'd be better off, because you'll probably do something reckless to get him killed."

Sutton flushed red, turned to her, and started to say something, hesitated a few thoughtful seconds, and held back his original statement.

"Buster comes with me," he said, walking in the direction of one of the nearby driveways, looking to secure a ride out of town. "We have a little business to take care of," Sutton added without turning around.

No one spoke a word until Sutton walked to the third house down the road with Buster by his side. Odors of burned seats, metal from the frame and engine block, and the pungent rubber of the tires wafted over to the group, reminding them of how a rocket could have easily incinerated them instead.

"What the hell did I miss?" Luke asked, openly stupefied about what he'd just witnessed.

"That asshole soldier came back and blew up this here vehicle," Gracine said, nodding at the smoldering circus truck.

"I thought Sutton took care of that guy."

"So did we," Jillian said coldly before turning her attention to Driscoll. "You're welcome to stay with us, if you want, or you can tag along with him."

Driscoll contemplated his future momentarily, but ultimately didn't take a step to leave his current group.

Gracine gave Jillian a knowing look before addressing her.

"We aren't leaving, are we?"

"No," Jillian answered. "We have to finish this."

"They're wounded," Driscoll noted. "There might not be a better chance."

"All this because one of them touched a kid?" Gracine asked without judgment in her eyes.

"All this because he laid his grubby hands on a family friend," Jillian said.

Luke cleared his throat.

"If it helps, they're down one carnie. The goofy guy who wore the skin and animal fur is no longer with us."

He looked uneasily at Samantha, indicating they had been through hell with the man up close and personal.

"That was him," Jillian said, openly relieved. "He was most of the threat, but if you want to kill a snake, you cut off the head."

"What are you proposing?" Luke asked as the sound of a car starting nearby caught their attention.

Everyone watched as Sutton backed the car out of the driveway, heading down the road and out of their lives.

In the distance, Jillian spotted a few undead staggering down the street, likely attracted by the noise of gunfire, vehicles, and the explosion. They remained a safe distance away, but more than likely, reinforcements of their kind weren't far behind.

"I'm not a coldblooded killer," Jillian replied. "I think I know a way to take care of our problem and keep our hands reasonably clean in the process. It'll also mean we can't stay here once we're finished, but at this point I don't give a shit."

Twenty-Three

During much of the return trip to Virginia, Metzger didn't dwell heavily on his brother's impending death because he kept envisioning ways to inform his sister-in-law of the tragic events in Buffalo.

None of the Marines went through the paperwork they confiscated during the mission, but they did talk on headsets after making certain Metzger's was muted, or on a different channel. His headset prevented the overwhelming volume of the plane's engines from reaching his ears for the most part, but he couldn't tell what the men were saying.

Metzger hadn't felt so alone in a long time, after losing his brother and being separated from Molly. When the plane finally landed, he was escorted by one of the Marines to a docked ship where a doctor had him strip down before examining him from head to toe for injuries. Metzger didn't feel like talking, much less asking questions, so he went along with whatever they said, his body and mind numbed from the gut-wrenching experience at the airport.

"You're lucky to have come through all of that unscathed," the doctor said as he drew samples of Metzger's blood.

During the checkup, he didn't think much about having his blood drawn once again, but that evening and the following morning he contemplated why no one else returning from Buffalo received immediate medical checkups.

Part of him wanted to talk to Isabella and Nathan to tell them in his own words how his brother sacrificed his life to save others, but Metzger figured the military had already made the notification to his sister-in-law. He didn't see much reason to stay at the base, but Metzger wouldn't leave the installation without saying farewell to the remainder of his family.

After a virtually sleepless overnight, Metzger got up from his bunk, got dressed, and grabbed a few belongings before heading outside. Civilians weren't allowed to possess weapons on the base, and his privileges were revoked when the plane landed as the Marines took his sword and firearms elsewhere for safe keeping. Feeling groggy, he stepped outside, seeing two soldiers immediately perk up when they spotted him. Not until he began walking around the base did he take notice that they followed him from a safe distance, never engaging him or speaking to him at any time.

He decided to forego causing any trouble, or asking questions, though he inquired where he might find Commander Mark Dascher from an enlisted sailor. The man didn't know, but he directed Metzger to an officer who respectfully walked with him to the commander on the *USS Ross*. Dascher shook Metzger's hand with a pained look on his face when the two finally met inside the commander's private quarters.

When the enlisted man opened the door, Metzger found the commander tidying up a few things inside his living space.

"I'm so sorry to hear about Bryce," Dascher said when he turned to face his guest, shaking his hand.

"Thank you," Metzger said, standing momentarily at the doorway.

"Please, have a seat," Dascher said, offering Metzger the chair across from his personal desk within the room. "I heard he drew the herd away from the rest of you."

"He did. We were getting overrun by the dead."

Dascher looked him in the eye before speaking again.

"Your brother was the best XO I ever had, and he made my job a hell of a lot easier," he confessed. "I can't tell my men that, because we officers aren't supposed to show cracks in the façade, if you get my drift."

"I do, sir."

"Mark. Call me Mark."

Metzger nodded, not entirely comfortable with being casual regarding his brother's direct supervisor.

"Has anyone talked to Isabella yet?" he asked.

Dascher nodded slowly.

"I did the notification last night with one of our chaplains," he said with a disheartened sigh. "She asked about you."

"I'm not sure I'm ready to face her just yet."

"What happened over there wasn't your fault," Dascher assured him. "You're a civilian, and I'm still not entirely sure they should've brought you along."

Metzger nodded again, knowing that his presence made their mission a great deal easier because he knew exactly where to lead them.

"How is Izzy holding up?" Metzger inquired, using his sister-in-law's nickname.

"It was a shock," Dascher answered. "I'm not sure how she's going to break it to Nathan."

"I know we live in different times," Metzger said hesitantly, "but they'll be taken care of by what's left of the government, won't they?"

"They're part of the family," Dascher said, his expression firm and protective, "so they'll be welcome here as long as Isabella chooses to stay."

"And what about me?" Metzger asked, mostly to gauge the commander's reaction to his question.

Dascher didn't give away any distinctive visual cues, which informed Metzger that the man knew something about why he'd been treated differently since the end of the mission.

"Are you wanting to stay?" the commander answered his question with a question.

"I'm not sure I have a reason to," Metzger answered, trying to frame his answers within ambiguous context. "My brother is gone, and I'm not sure my sister-in-law wants me here as a reminder of that."

"I'd hate to see you go," Dascher said, his expression indicating he spoke truthfully. "You've got a lot of Bryce's qualities, and you could be a real asset around here. Besides, it's dangerous out there."

"Believe me, I know."

"I reckon you do," the commander said, tapping his fingers on the desk momentarily before speaking again. "Are you thinking about finding your old group?"

"I'm not sure," Metzger answered. "I don't even know where I'd begin to look."

"Isabella could really use your support," Dascher said, as though slowly working into a sales pitch. "I can take you to her whenever you feel you're ready."

"Thanks," Metzger said, standing to leave as Dascher also rose to shake his hand.

"If you need anything at all, I'm available," the commander added before Metzger turned to leave.

He exited the ship feeling somewhat uneasy, as though everyone on the base except him knew some deep, dark secret.

Not quite ready to confront his sister-in-law, Metzger walked in the direction of the airstrip, finding the two military men continuing to tail him, and not being very discreet about their assignment. When he asked one of the stationed guards about Timmons, the man replied that the captain was flying for some assignment, and Metzger detected no deception in the response. The soldier added that he didn't think Timmons would be gone very long, believing the destination was nearby Washington, D.C.

Depressed and despondent, Metzger returned to his quarters where his body gave in and let him sleep for a few hours.

***

Early the next morning, Metzger watched a few crews depart the base on foot, with a few vehicles behind them, to further clean up Norfolk of debris, bodies, and animated bodies. He wanted to help, to keep busy in any way possible, but knew asking to leave the base's secure walls wasn't an option.

No one told him leaving wasn't an option, but at all times two soldiers monitored his every move, and shortly after breakfast that morning he was summoned to a lab for another blood draw. He complied without outward question, but internally, he knew they wanted something from the samples he provided. Playing dumb, he followed the soldier sent to fetch him into a building now converted into a scientific facility. From the looks of the interior, it might have originally served as a medical facility, or some kind of lab, so little renovation would have been required.

A man in a white lab coat drew two vials of blood from his left arm, and Metzger watched with indifference as the blood ran through the plastic tubing into the vials. Blood and guts never bothered him much in his previous life, and they certainly didn't faze him now that he'd cut into more body parts than a pathologist while battling the undead.

"What's with all the blood draws?" he asked the man conversationally once the vials were carefully set aside.

"Just testing for any changes in your blood after your visit to the hot zone," the man answered casually.

He wore bifocals, but Metzger found no other identifying objects on the man like a nametag, wedding band, or any insignias. Clean-shaven, the man possessed a head of thick, black hair, and Metzger felt certain he hadn't met this particular doctor or scientist previously. Quickly looking beyond the man, Metzger scanned the isolated room for clues, but it appeared blander than any doctor's office he'd ever visited. No posters lined the walls, no paperwork appeared atop the nearby desk, and no laptop or tablet awaited patient information entry.

"You guys drew blood from me yesterday," Metzger decided to press. "Did they lose the sample?"

"Nah," the man said, waving off the notion. "It's just a follow-up lab to look for any changes. Everyone aboard your flight is being tested."

Except for Bryce, Metzger thought, recalling the swarm of zombies attacking his brother just short of the plane's ramp.

"Anything else?" Metzger asked, acting as though he were anxious to leave the facility.

"You're free to go," the man answered. "Thanks."

Metzger got up from the chair where he'd been sitting, touched the cotton ball held against the inside of his elbow by an elastic wrap, and exited through the door into the main hallway. Standing still momentarily, he listened and watched for any activity, deciding to move along before the man in the lab coat exited the room behind him. Spying a few cameras along key portions of the hallway, Metzger knew he couldn't move about undetected, because much of the base, and some of the town, now had power thanks to the aircraft carriers docked nearby. He wasn't sure the military possessed manpower enough to monitory security footage, but he dared not press his luck.

Even so, he walked along the hallway, glancing into each open door as he went, finding no useful answers. Taking a right turn, he passed a lab with numerous computers and scientific equipment inside, including microscopes. The door remained open, with no one inside, and he'd decided to take a chance and step inside to look for answers when a female scientist rounded the corner down the hall in front of him.

"Fuck," he muttered, simply walking past the room before giving her a courteous nod when they passed in the narrow hallway.

Nothing in the building was marked as a restricted area, so he was perfectly free to walk about without question. If anyone had asked what he was doing, Metzger would have replied he was looking for an exit.

When he stepped outside, Metzger exhaled heavily, taking in the morning air. He looked around, seeing his two personal shadows in the distance, before strolling over to the airfield once again.

He approached the guard a bit apprehensively, wondering if his privileges of seeing Timmons might have been revoked, but the soldier recognized him and promptly called someone in the hangar area without even acknowledging Metzger until he'd inquired about the pilot.

"He's here," the man said. "Come on through."

"Thanks," Metzger said, noticing the two men watching his every move didn't follow him inside the airfield area.

A few minutes later he was guided to the captain, who carefully looked over a smaller plane for any issues that might affect flight.

"Hey!" Timmons called upon seeing Metzger, wearing his green flight suit as though he might have reason to fly later in the day. "I heard about your brother," the pilot added, heartily shaking his hand as his expression grew somber. "I'm so sorry. They told me when I landed last night."

"Thank you," Metzger replied, suddenly realizing he didn't feel much like talking.

He supposed he simply wanted to be around familiar people other than the last standing members of his family. More so, he wanted to leave the base and never look back, because he didn't feel much like speaking with Isabella due to his lingering guilt.

"Want to go over this with me?" Timmons asked, pointing to the plane. "Might do you some good to be distracted."

"I still haven't faced my sister-in-law," Metzger said, following the captain around the sides and belly of the plane, looking for any hazards.

"You've got to talk to her, son," Timmons said, thumbing a corner piece of metal sticking up from its normal position before jotting down a note atop a clipboard. "What's the problem?"

"I just feel guilty."

"For not saving your brother? That wasn't your job. Sounds to me like he died a hero."

"Maybe I just feel guilty about being alive."

"Don't *ever* think that," Timmons said sternly. "Every day we're given on this planet is a blessing, especially now."

"What the hell do I say?"

"You don't *say* anything," Timmons said as though he were a coach. "She just wants some reassurance that her husband didn't die in vain. Besides, you've got that little nephew to protect."

"I'll talk to her," Metzger conceded, knowing the conversation was inevitable. "I'm just not sure I can stay here much longer."

"That's crazy talk. Where the fuck would you go if you left?"

"I've managed on my own before. And my group is out there somewhere."

Timmons scoffed.

"The military isn't going to boot you out of here, Dan. You should probably stick around for the sake of your family, and yourself."

"Everyone keeps telling me that."

"Well, in my case," Timmons said as he pulled a wrench from his back pocket and tapped on something underneath the plane, "it's purely selfish because I wouldn't have anyone left to give flying pointers to."

Metzger chuckled.

"Yeah. I'm a model student."

"You're easier to teach than some of the hotheads I've been assigned to over the years. These kids come to the military thinking they know everything."

Metzger understood how complicated the military jets and planes compared to the Cessna he flew during emergency circumstances. Their training required years of classwork and flying, causing him to question if another generation of military pilots would ever exist.

"And you were mature at that age?" Metzger asked skeptically.

"Hell, no. I was drinking and chasing pussy like everyone else when I got leave. Women were putty in my hands when I told them I was a pilot."

Metzger suppressed a laugh by covering his mouth, not because he doubted what Timmons said, but because the man before him appeared refined, settled in both position and life.

"I need to ask you something serious, Scott," he said to the pilot, leaning against a nearby toolbox, seeing no one else near them who could eavesdrop.

"Shoot."

"Ever since we got back from this latest mission, I've had two guys in uniform tailing me from a distance."

Timmons arched an eyebrow, openly questioning why anyone would follow Metzger around the base.

"Did you piss someone off?"

"No. Not like that. It's as though they've been ordered to track my every move."

"That seems odd. Sure you're not imagining this? You've been through a lot these past few days."

Metzger shook his head.

"I'm not imagining it. And what's weirder is the Marines on our mission got a call about some secondary objective, and I think I was that objective."

"Why do you think that?" Timmons asked, stopping what he was doing to give Metzger his full attention.

"Because they held me back from helping my brother, and when their leader said 'secondary objective secure' he looked directly at me. They've also drawn blood from me twice since I've returned."

Timmons appeared skeptical.

"I work for these people, kid. There's no reason they'd single you out like that. They've got bigger issues to worry about."

"Okay," Metzger said, not about to drop the subject, or confess to being delusional. "Walk with me to your guard's area. You'll see these two jokers standing outside, waiting for me."

Providing a doubtful smirk, Timmons pocketed the wrench and motioned for Metzger to lead the way. A few minutes later, the two approached the military guard, who gave a nod to each of them, and Metzger looked beyond the perimeter only a few seconds before finding the two men currently ordered to follow him for unknown reasons.

"See?"

"That *is* peculiar," Timmons admitted. "I can get to the bottom of this right now."

As Timmons turned to carry out an inquiry, Metzger caught the pilot by the arm, preventing him from walking away.

"Probably best if you don't," Metzger said. "No one's told me a thing, and I don't want you getting in trouble over me."

"What are they going to do, ground me?"

Metzger caught the double meaning of the pilot's words, but he didn't want Timmons to risk anything by helping him. He regretted telling the man about his woes, but he needed to speak with someone, because he couldn't make sense of the past few days in his own mind. As though divine intervention entered his life at that moment, he spotted Isabella and Nathan crossing the base in front of him. His sister-in-law looked as though she might be taking a walk to clear her head.

"I've got to go," Metzger said to the pilot. "Please don't say anything about all of this to anyone."

"Okay, if that's what you want," Timmons replied, though Metzger felt the pilot might still intervene on his behalf.

Once the two shook hands, Metzger exited through the posted guard area, trying to catch up as the two soldiers adopted a leisurely pace while following him. Within a few minutes he caught up to Isabella, who held Nathan's hand while they stood before the water, near a few of the moored ships.

"Hey, Izzy," he said, hugging his sister-in-law when she turned to him. "I'm so sorry."

"You?" she asked, her voice cracking a bit as she stifled back sobs and tears. "He was your brother. We *all* lost him."

Metzger knelt down to his nephew, who appeared to want nothing to do with human contact at the moment. He started to address Nathan, but decided not to begin a conversation when he couldn't find the right words to tell a child.

"Let me find someone to watch Nathan a few minutes," Isabella said with concern and mourning in her green eyes. "I want you to tell me everything that happened."

"You sure?"

"Yes, I'm absolutely certain," she answered with resolve.

A few minutes later, Nathan spent time in a daycare of sorts with other children and a few parents, while Isabella led Metzger to a building inside the base where they were provided some privacy. She'd taken notice that Metzger kept looking behind him at the two soldiers who didn't bother disguising the fact they were following him across the base.

"Why do you keep looking back there?" she inquired.

"I'll explain after I tell you about all of the other odd shit that's been going on," he answered, keeping his promise after he spent a fairly lengthy amount of time giving her details about the mission and the past day.

Due to limited seating options, they sat atop a trundle bed, facing one another before Metzger revealed the painful nature of the mission in elaborate detail. He tried several times to spare Isabella from some of the agony he felt, but she insisted on hearing each little piece. Both of them cried openly during his tale, and even hugged a few times, sharing their pain. When Metzger reached the part of the story where he returned to the base, however, they both turned serious and dried their eyes.

"I just got him back," Isabella said mournfully a minute after drying her eyes. "The Navy asks so much of us, and we sit back and wait for our husbands and wives to return. Until they don't."

"The undead would've stormed the plane," Metzger stated. "Bryce did what he felt was best to save the rest of us. There were just too many of them."

Isabella nodded, though his words brought no comfort to her.

"We haven't been out there," she said. "You know better than anyone how dangerous it is while we've been safely tucked behind these walls."

Both of them sat silently a moment, unsure of what to say until a thought came to Isabella.

"They've taken samples of Nathan's blood a few times this past week."

"Not yours?"

"No. And I thought it was odd, but I figured they had a reason if they were using limited resources to sample his blood."

"I'm not sure how long I can stay here if I can't trust these people," Metzger said. "But I can't really leave until I know a little something about what they want."

"You know you can trust me," Isabella assured him, clasping one of his hands. "I've been doing a lot of work around the base lately. Maybe I can slip into some of the right places and get some answers."

"You've got Nathan to worry about. Don't risk your status here over me."

"I've met Bryce's commander a few times," she said thoughtfully. "He always seemed like an up-front kind of person."

"I feel like he knows something," Metzger admitted. "It was almost like he wanted to tell me out of obligation to Bryce, but his sense of duty took over."

Isabella sighed a moment in thought.

"This place isn't exactly like Fort Knox," she said after a moment. "But they're getting power restored, and soon the town will be functioning again. If I'm going to find out anything, it needs to be soon."

"Please don't risk anything for me," Metzger insisted.

"It's not just you. Apparently whatever they want from you may also involve my son. I may test the waters and see how people respond if I say I'm thinking about leaving."

"You'll probably get the goon squad tracking your every move," Metzger half-joked.

"I'm going to get answers," Isabella promised. "They cost me my husband, and I'm not about to let them poke and prod my son."

Metzger knew she wouldn't be deterred.

"Just be careful, Izzy."

"I will. And don't you do anything to raise their suspicion. If we're going to find out anything, they need to think we're docile."

"We're anything but," Metzger said, forcing a smile as he stood. "I'll see you soon."

Walking outside, Metzger knew both of them were hurting emotionally, requiring time to mourn that their current situation did not allow. He spotted his two personal escorts in no time flat, curious what the military had in mind for him, knowing he dared not jump any fences to force action on their part.

Presently, both Metzger and the military played a dangerous game of calculated risks and nondisclosed secrets.

He felt certain the soldiers assigned to him were meant to ensure he didn't leave the base or begin searching for answers. Metzger understood he was a virtual stranger to the military brass, but he'd proven his worth a few separate times already, and deserved to know what they wanted from him.

At least in his mind.

Part of him wished he'd stayed with his original group, doubting a second mission would have existed if he hadn't given the military specifics about his time around Buffalo. Bryce probably wouldn't have made such a risky move against the undead if not for his brother's presence. Metzger stared at the ground as he walked back to his quarters, conjuring ideas in his mind about ways to depart the base when the time arrived. He might jump a fence at night, or steal a uniform, or even borrow a smaller boat. He knew Isabella spoke the truth about them getting the Norfolk area closer to civilization with each passing day, meaning time became an adversary for both of them.

When he reached his area of the bunk room, Metzger removed his shoes and socks after plopping down on his cot, feeling guilty for not mourning his brother properly. He felt terrible, because Bryce would want to be put down after his transformation into a zombie. Perhaps Molly assisted Bryce through the last moments of his life, or they ended up pursuing the coward Fournier throughout the isolated airport.

Despite the morning hour, knowing two sets of eyes monitored him from somewhere nearby, Metzger swung his feet up and curled up for a nap, feeling a tear dribble down his right cheek.

Twenty-Four

When Brad Weir left Buffalo at long last, he didn't expect such an arduous trek to see his family, but a number of complications slowed him and his buddy. They quickly realized that interstates and highways, particularly those that led into, or near, a metropolis, were often cluttered with cars. Streaks of blood across various vehicles, bodies beyond reanimation, and of course, the undead, were among the unsightly things they spotted when traveling in such areas.

He and Mike Mullins decided early on that they wanted to stay closer to the coast if possible, briefly considering attempting their journey via boat, but the Atlantic Ocean wasn't always accommodating. Without weather updates, they had no idea when hurricane winds, heavy rains, or other seafaring groups, might compromise their voyage.

Instead, they decided to cut directly east, across New York until they drew closer to New York City. People tend to think of New York in terms of *only* the city sometimes, but Weir knew the state as an anthill of sorts, its many state roads intersecting like the tunnels ants use to complete their work.

Strangely enough, the duo barely knew one another throughout their careers as city cops in Buffalo. Nearly eight-hundred sworn and civilian employees worked for the department, so the fact that their paths crossed only a few times wasn't unfathomable. Weir worked as a detective off and on during his twenty-one years, while Mullins went undercover, spent time doing drug busts, and eventually migrated to helping at-risk youth with specially created programs in the city.

At best, the pair recalled working on three particular cases together, and only one investigation required much interaction between the two. During the apocalypse, they met while responding to one last call from their dispatchers where parents had already been compromised after their undead daughter bit both of them. Unwilling to shoot the couple, or wait around until the situation deteriorated, the pair left the family to deal with the already dead daughter. They couldn't reason with the distraught parents to put down their child permanently.

After that, knowing the world wasn't getting better, the pair decided to team up to better their chances of survival, looking for Mullins' family locally after sending Weir's family to an area he hoped might be free of hazards.

During their current travels, Mullins often carried out navigation duties while Weir drove, and he decided to cut south about halfway across the state, taking several state highways into Pennsylvania because going too far east created a longer travel distance for the pair.

"I feel like this is taking forever," Mullins said from the passenger's seat, his trusty, tattered Atlas sitting between them with creases in every inch of its cover.

"That's because it *is* taking forever," Weir replied. "Every day we deal with moving cars out of the way and shooting the dead is another day my family might get killed."

Weir possessed one source of inspiration that Mullins no longer had, because he knew there was a chance his family made it to South Carolina with two dozen people from their church. He let them travel ahead because he felt they were safer in a large group, rather than staying in an urban area like Buffalo. He also needed to help his colleague find answers about what happened to his family. They found the answers, in between assisting any number of stragglers, and while Mullins wasn't surprised, he was disheartened to find his family already turned a few miles away from where he thought they'd be.

Currently driving a powder blue Chevy Cruze, the pair wanted gas efficiency after several various vehicle selections following their police cruiser, which they left roadside near the southern border of New York. They grew weary of siphoning gas for the marked police car, trying a truck and an SUV, which proved useful for clearing the undead out of the way, but terrible on fuel economy.

"We've got something ahead," Mullins said, looking ahead to the left, his eyes squinting from the sunlight glaring through the unwashed windshield of their latest car.

Weir looked, seeing a small band of travelers dressed for cooler weather, pulling something along with them on the side of the road. Most of them dressed like homeless people from before the apocalypse. Wearing colors and patterns well beyond their trendy days, the group donned a baseball cap, a winter hat, a scarf wrap, and even a floppy bonnet. Each of them wore a backpack, likely carrying personal items beyond what their larger bundle contained. He grew less excited about helping people during the quest to meet with his own family, partly because some people didn't want help, but also because some of them proved downright dangerous.

"They look like they're managing," he commented, seeing that they were heading north, in the complete opposite direction of South Carolina, and an inconvenience if they stopped.

"Up to you," Mullins said with a shrug.

Weir pulled past the group, none of whom flagged them down or even waved, but something nagging at him instinctively told him to stop. The car's brakes squealed when he tapped on them, causing everyone in the passing group to turn and look as though he'd stomped on the brakes suddenly.

Despite changing vehicles a number of times, neither man bothered to don new clothes. While a number of different options were available, they chose to keep their police uniforms, partly to make themselves recognizable as helpers, and because any new clothes would soon reek of the same body odor and display a variety of stains. They saved themselves the trouble and simply stayed in their same clothes, occasionally dunking them in water when possible.

Once the car drew to a stop, Weir opened the door and stepped out, seeing the haggard expressions written across the four people in the group before him.

"You folks okay?" he inquired, receiving affirmative nods in response. "Where you headed?"

"West," one of the two men in the group answered. "We're hoping to get settled before winter."

"Why west?" Mullins asked. "And why the timeline?"

Mullins had opened his door and stood on the floorboard of the car, using the vantage point to view the strangers and their surroundings. He kept one of his hands on the car roof as he looked over it, while the other didn't stray far from the sidearm holstered at his side.

"We're hoping the dead will freeze. And if we're being honest, we're looking for a place to hole up. Maybe a ranch, or some prepper's bunker."

"Bunker?" Weir asked with a hint of surprise. "What makes you think you'll find one out there?"

"Not to be rude, mister," one of the women said, "but we don't know you from Adam. Why are you so interested in us?"

"Sorry," Weir apologized. "Just trying to be helpful. Didn't mean to chat you up."

"Look, we're just dead tired from being on the road," the first man answered. "We can't trust everyone we meet."

"Understood."

Weir noticed Mullins hadn't said much, and his former fellow officer and detective spent his time studying the four people diligently.

"We were with some guy who said he owned some holdings he wanted to get to," the second man said. "He offered us shelter if we got him there."

Weir immediately thought of what they learned about the man named Nadeau in Buffalo, but Mullins tapped his arm, indicating that he not follow up on his instincts.

"What happened to him?" Mullins inquired, breaking his silence.

Each of the four looked to one man as though he was the group's designated spokesperson.

"He died in a car wreck trying to escape the dead," the first man answered. "We couldn't save him, but we snagged some of his maps and information. We're just trying to get settled somewhere before winter."

Based on Mullins' reaction, Weir decided to stay quiet about what he knew.

"What was this guy's name?" he asked instead.

"Don't know that we ever caught it," the same spokesman answered.

An awkward silence filled the air momentarily.

"Any reason you're not driving?" Mullins inquired.

"We did for a while," the leader answered. "We got tired of syphoning gas, so we're hoofing it for a while. Where are you two headed?"

"South," Mullins answered. "Trying to find family members."

"You guys really cops?" the second woman asked, though not looking particularly interested in the answer.

A game of cat and mouse ensued between the two parties.

"We were," Weir answered. "Now we're just weary travelers."

"We know the feeling," the first man said.

"Need any food for the road?" Mullins asked, reaching behind him for two cans of vegetables, taking a few steps toward the group, causing them each to take a step back.

"We're good," the first man said, stepping forward to intercept the former cop before he stepped any closer to the bundle of packed goods they dragged along the ground with them.

Weir assumed his friend wanted a closer look at the group for some particular reason.

"Okay," Mullins said, backing away from the foursome.

"Look, we really need to get moving," the second man said, openly growing impatient with the conversation.

Weir faked a smile.

"Understood. How much further have you got?"

"We think this guy's property was somewhere in Minnesota near the Canadian border," the second man stated, drawing a few raised eyebrows from his wording, as though he'd spoken something a little too close to the truth.

Closely observing, Weir noticed the stares weren't immediate, but rather a delayed reaction to his untrue statement. In his mind, sticking around too much longer endangered Mullins and himself as the group wasn't entirely what they claimed to be.

"Well, we'll be on our way if you folks are doing okay," he said.

"Thanks," the first man said. "Safe travels."

As he and Mullins settled into the Cruze, they exchanged knowing looks, both watching behind them to make certain the strangers didn't pull guns and open fire on them.

"What do you make of that?" Weir asked once they'd driven a safe distance from the group without incident.

"Fake as fuck. They're lying through their teeth."

"What did you see?"

"Did you notice their body language? They kept looking to the one guy to answer, because they were afraid of giving conflicting answers and tripping themselves up. Their eyes kept shifting, and the way a few of them stood indicated an unusual amount of nervousness for them talking to two random guys like us."

"Anything else?"

"Yeah. Inside their communal pack they had at least two rifles and some other heavy items. They weren't just squeaking by."

Weir glanced behind him, seeing no danger.

"Why were they really walking?" he wondered aloud.

"I think they were plants," Mullins answered. "They gave up some certain information awfully easily. They didn't give up Nadeau's name, but they certainly implied it."

"How so?"

"One of them was wearing a Maple Cleaning Solutions logo on his coat. That was one of Nadeau's companies before he blew up the planet."

"How do you know that shit?"

"I read all kinds of business magazines back in the day," Mullins answered.

"Was anything they said the truth?"

"Doubtful. While there are lakes near Minnesota, they'd have to hole up inside a bunker just to survive the winter. And I'm guessing they're heading more northerly than west based on their route."

"So, if we're running with the assumption Nadeau is alive and these people are his prophets, telling of his false demise, why bother? Obviously, the man planned this in great detail, leaving himself plenty of time to find a place to hole up and hide. I know the government is going to look for him, but they don't have the resources to search every square mile of our country and Canada."

"But if the government isn't looking for a dead man, he's free to run around and do what he wants."

Weir kept his eyes on the road, swerving gently around a few lopsided cars.

"Do you suppose he intended to create all of this, or just kill a bunch of people to make a point?"

"It was an act of terrorism," Mullins noted. "At worst, his efforts killed a few thousand outright, which is one hell of a statement when he gets away with it at first. But he's already hunkered down somewhere, and likely has been with the government looking for him, so I'm saying he knew what he was creating."

"Money can buy you a lot of security."

"Money isn't the currency these days," Mullins countered. "He must've had this plan in place before those trucks blew up. People trade in canned goods, weapons, ammo, and survival gear now. He's either holed up for the long haul, or he stockpiled a bunch of that shit. Either way, I'm saying that dude knew what his chemicals would do."

Mullins contemplated something in his thoughts momentarily.

"Why would these people cover for him?"

"They probably weren't lying about the sanctuary," Weir answered. "I highly doubt it's where they say it is, though."

Met with silence, he turned to Mullins a few seconds later.

"You think we should follow them, don't you?"

"My gut tells me they're part of something much bigger," his friend answered, "but following them is dangerous and it sets you back even further from seeing your loved ones. Even if we somehow tailed them to their evil lair, assuming we're correct about that, what the fuck would we do about it? And if they got one whiff of us, they'd change their plans anyway."

"What do you propose instead?"

"Maybe we should make a pit stop on our way to South Carolina to put the right people on the scent of that Nadeau guy."

Weir nodded. He believed he knew exactly what Mullins had in mind, so he nodded at the map.

"Plot us a course, sir."

Twenty-Five

Jillian put together a plan almost immediately, but her group required the full day following their skirmish with Dark Lady to get the necessary resources.

In the meantime, Jillian kept a close eye on the camp of their adversaries, finding one of the woman's followers mortally wounded, and another two suffering injuries that limited their mobility. She'd spent the entire previous day monitoring their activities, currently seeing a fire illuminating the backyard in the early morning hour.

A day and a half had passed since the incident that cost Sutton his spot in the group. The mortally injured man in Dark Lady's camp had passed away the previous evening, only after he lost consciousness and Dark Lady used a knife to draw blood from a nearby zombie and slit his forearm to infect him. She gave the order to stand him in their yard as an undead watchdog before his body stirred. Held by a chain tied off at a stake, the man eventually reanimated and continued to grasp at the survivors around him without stopping for one single second. Not susceptible to tiring, the zombie didn't blink or give up trying to grab a warm meal.

Now Jillian understood how the woman's group treated Vazquez once they stole him away from his familiar group.

She wasn't sure if Dark Lady stayed due to her stubborn nature, or because of the injuries to her people, but Jillian hadn't softened on her stance regarding her group. She wanted them gone, dead if necessary, because they supported Frost, even after what he did to that poor little girl in South Hill. Luke had filled her in about how the man met his end, which Jillian considered further evidence that he wanted inappropriate relationships with children.

Since sending Sutton packing, Jillian hadn't thought about him much, or where she might want to travel after she concluded her business in South Hill. Staying in the town might have been a realistic option if not for the deaths of her parents. She couldn't envision herself waking each morning with her first thoughts being how her folks were buried down the road.

During the day, several times over, she considered backing down from her plan, but Jillian kept reminding herself that these people condoned fondling a child, and they murdered Vazquez without provocation. In fact, his body was still visible in the yard where they continued to sit, stand watch, and tend to their wounded. Jillian watched Dark Lady take time to address each of them in turn through her binoculars, admiring how the woman cared for each of them, despite her twisted actions around other people.

With only her thoughts to keep her company, Jillian reflected on how her group changed from Buffalo to Virginia. They lost Albert, Luke's partner, before Metzger departed when they reached the base in Norfolk. Vazquez's death proved senseless in her mind, because he wasn't the kind of man who sought to harm anyone. As for Sutton, Jillian felt justified in her decision to excommunicate him from their group, because she couldn't take another incident where he nearly cost them their lives through being overly assertive, or not following through on his promises.

Holding the binoculars in her left hand and a .40 caliber pistol in the other, Jillian whirled around when she felt a tap on her shoulder. She found Luke crouched above her, staying concealed as best he could.

"We got what you wanted," he reported. "It took most of the day, but we got just over two dozen loaded up."

"Where is everyone?"

"They're parked where that crazy soldier guy blew up the vehicle."

"Good," Jillian said, looking to the sky, which began to show light from the impending dawn. "No better time than the present."

She walked with Luke to the car he'd parked nearby.

"Where's Samantha?"

"I left her with Gracine," Luke answered. "She's taken a shine to her lately."

"But Gracine isn't the one she's started calling 'Dad.'"

Luke's face reddened from being put on the spot.

"I think it's a little premature, but I'll accept the responsibility."

"You're doing fine."

"I just wish Albert was here to guide me along. He was always the one who knew what to do, and didn't buckle under pressure."

"His entire career was based on being cool under pressure," Jillian said as she reached the passenger door and opened it. "Think of this as living up to your potential and honoring his memory."

Appearing only partially contented with that thought, Luke opened his door and slid into the driver's seat.

"Watching over her keeps me going," he admitted once they were both seated in the car. "That being said, I'm going to admit I'm not thrilled about involving her in this, Jillian."

"None of you will be involved," Jillian said. "I can handle the legwork myself."

"I don't like seeing you act this dark," Luke admitted, starting the car. "You're going to have to live with this the rest of your life."

"These people are a cancer, Luke. I'm not saying that because of their chosen occupation, or what they did to Juan. Even before the apocalypse they caused trouble wherever they went, and the world is currently giving them a pass to do whatever they want, to whomever they chose. It needs to end here."

Luke drove her back to the group where Jillian spied a large pickup truck with a horse trailer hitched behind it. She stepped out, immediately hearing the groans and wails of the undead as they tried reaching through the openings to grab at anyone nearby. Odors of fecal matter, urine, and the decay of the dead reached her nostrils the moment she got downwind of the trailer. Examining the trailer as she approached it, she counted more than two dozen undead trapped inside, waiting for their time to walk freely again in search of prey.

Their wait was nearly over.

"We gathered them, just like you asked," Gracine said, shielding Samantha from seeing the undead or stepping too close to the trailer. "What now?"

"Now I drive this over there and take care of the problem once and for all."

"Have you pulled a trailer before, or opened the door on one?" Driscoll asked. "Both can be a little tricky if you haven't."

"It can't be that hard," Jillian responded, having driven trucks before, and understanding the mechanics of opening a gate.

"If you're in a pinch between circus freaks and the dead heads, it would help to have some experience."

He spent a few minutes going over some tips about how to turn the trailer, and how to undo the latch in the back without getting it caught or stuck under pressure from the structural frame.

"You shouldn't do this alone," he said once they completed the tutorial and returned to the group.

"He's right," Gracine added. "We haven't gotten this far by being rogues."

"There's a lot of risk to this," Jillian said, "and I know you haven't all been onboard with my plan because it seems callous to sic zombies on these people when they're down. But *they* didn't care when they turned Juan into a lawn ornament. They'll have a fighting chance to run from the undead and leave town. But I have to do this alone. I'm not asking any of you to be part of a plan that may kill people."

Gracine handed her a small radio the group had used to lure the undead into the trailer in the first place. The trailer was built with several gaps for cleaning and airflow purposes, which allowed them to set the radio inside without risk to their limbs. Jillian wasn't sure it served a similar purpose for her, because she needed to throw it to a designated area and wasn't certain it would survive the impact. As though knowing this, Gracine produced a culinary timer from behind her back, placing it in Jillian's free hand.

"Girl, I hope this works, because you only get one shot, and the dead won't care who they chase around that yard."

"It has to work," Jillian said, partly to assure Gracine of her safety, but also to convince herself the idea wasn't rash.

While the others backed off to give her some space, Jillian stuffed a semi-automatic pistol along the small of her back. She made certain the two small knives she'd placed in various parts of her jeans remained intact, because she tried to envision every conceivable issue with her plan from start to finish beforehand. Not only the dead threatened her, but she knew enough of Dark Lady's camp remained to pose a threat to her and possibly dispatch the dead inside the trailer.

Tossing the radio and the timer on the seat beside her, Jillian climbed in the truck, started the engine, and gave a quick wave to her comrades before taking a wide turn and heading for the encampment down the road.

She second-guessed her decision the entire way, wondering if kicking Sutton from the group was a good idea while questioning if her current motivations made her just like him. Stopping short of visible and audible range, of Dark Lady's location, she set the timer for three minutes, knowing she could turn the dial again for adjustment before throwing it at her targets if necessary.

A nagging feeling that something was destined to go wrong tugged at her reasoning, so she checked her weaponry one last time before hitting the gas and heading for the residence Dark Lady and her people called home.

She recalled the layout of the neighborhood, knowing fences surrounded quite a few of the houses, but Jillian also knew the fence along the one side of the property had been compromised. Ideally, she would back the truck and trailer up to the opening and release the zombies into an area where they would be basically herded into the yard. Backing up would take too long, and she needed at least a little element of surprise for her plan to work.

Surveying the area from the driver's seat, which sat higher than most, Jillian plotted a course quickly as she drew near the houses, knowing at least a few of Dark Lady's people heard the truck's approach. Instead of trying to finesse the truck and trailer perfectly in the yard, she barreled through the neighboring yard, pulling past the compromised fence, knocking down another section of fencing that wasn't attached to Dark Lady's encampment. Trying to judge by sight in the rearview mirror, Jillian got the trailer reasonably close to the fence opening. She jumped from the driver's seat after snatching the kitchen timer, hitting the ground running.

Stealing a glance as she ran to the back of the trailer, which ended up being just a few feet from the fence opening, Jillian saw several pairs of eyes looking her way. Several of them attempted to gain their footing, or reach for weapons, so she hurried in her effort to undo the latch on the trailer. She dropped the timer as the latch required both hands to pull, and unfortunately for her, it began ringing, stirring the dead trapped within the makeshift prison. Managing to yank the latch open with one swift pull, Jillian swung the door wide, trapped between the opening where Dark Lady's people angrily approached her, and the dead staggering out of the trailer behind her.

Taking a quick, deep breath, she bent down to pick up the timer and darted through the fence opening where the eyes staring at her grew fearful when they saw the army behind her. Some of them possessed injuries from the rocket launcher blast, unable to easily scurry into the house, or jump the fence surrounding the house to safety. Jillian threw the timer directly in the middle of their group, ducking to the right behind the fence so the undead didn't focus on her, as they often seemed distracted by movement.

Skirting along the inside of the fence, Jillian intended to make her way to the back, undetected by the zombies, before jumping over and making an exit. She glanced back once, seeing none of the undead staring her way, because movement from Dark Lady's people, along with the blaring timer, kept their attention. She made her way to the far corner, attempted to scale the wooden fence, and felt a firm hand grasp her belt and pull her back, stripping her of the firearm in the process.

Jillian felt her back strike the ground forcefully, knocking the wind from her lungs as her assailant mounted her. Her eyes spun momentarily, but when she finally regained her senses, she found him mounting her at the waistline to keep her pinned down as he pulled his belt from the loops in his pants with a yank.

"It's time for you to learn a lesson, missy," he said with a smile that displayed yellow teeth, and particles stuck between them.

Hearing the screams of a man in the distance, Jillian felt some satisfaction that the undead found their mark on at least one of the unwelcome inhabitants. She heard more panicked yells in the distance as she reached for the knife along the right side of her blue jeans, requiring the man atop her to move his own leg just slightly so she could slide it out without notice.

"Shouldn't you be helping your friends?" she asked as she struggled against him with her left hand, keeping his eyes and hands occupied as he shoved back.

"They'll fend for themselves," he said, slapping her across the face with force enough to nearly knock her unconscious, giving him time to unbutton and unzip his pants.

Jillian couldn't see his underwear very well, but from the appearance and odor of the rest of the man, she envisioned them being yellow and grungy. She struggled to keep her consciousness and focus, and when the man went to pull down his pants, she freed the blade from her jeans and thrust it upward, toward the side of his neck.

Unfortunately for her, the man saw her move from the corner of his eye and blocked most of it with his elbow, receiving only a bloody scratch for his trouble. Jillian struggled as he pried the knife from her fingers, tossing it far enough away that she didn't have a prayer of recovering it. Her gun also remained too far out of reach to be of any use, and for a moment she prayed one of the undead would stagger her way, rather than let this man rape her during what she hoped to be her moment of triumph when Dark Lady's crew left South Hill forever.

Jillian continued to struggle, hearing gunfire in the background. She assumed it was Dark Lady's people fighting back, but she was forced to focus on the man pinning her to the ground, beginning to undo her jeans with a delighted, fiendish smile. Not a complete simpleton, but not moral enough to keep his desires in check, the man openly grew excited at the prospect of having his way with Jillian.

When he lifted one of her hands, Jillian managed to bite one of his fingers, despite the putrid taste, and received a slap for her trouble. Her resistance served only to excite him even more, making him more aggressive in his efforts. Laying his torso atop hers, he kept her still while his hands reached back, working on undoing her jeans once again. Jillian felt her pants, and her last knife, slipping away from her desperate fingers with each gentle tug as she struggled to draw breaths with his weight bearing down on her.

She felt a tear begin to form in the corner of her eye, because the outside world, and the events surrounding her, felt as though they were slipping further away and she was trapped in absolute isolation with this despicable man. Jillian bought time by trying to strike him with her fists, but he simply pinned her to the ground and punched her in the face this time, causing her to see stars.

Her left hand groped for the last remaining knife in her pants, and she attempted to contort her body to reach it, but his weight kept her from stretching far enough. She was about to give up all hope when she heard a female voice behind her address the man.

"Hey, asshole," Gracine said, drawing the man's attention before firing a bullet into his right shoulder.

As he recoiled, Jillian managed to reach just far enough to grasp the blade and swing it upward into his exposed neck. The blade struck its mark, causing the carotid artery to spurt blood from the right side of the man's neck as he gurgled until his eyes rolled back in his head and he slumped over.

Jillian quickly stood, zipped up her pants, and collected her weapons as she and Gracine assessed the scene before them.

"You came?" she asked of Gracine, somewhat surprised the group didn't honor her request.

"You really think we were going to leave you here with these freaks by yourself?"

Most of the undead began heading for the house, where the remaining members of Dark Lady's group sought shelter. Most of the zombies filed through the open sliding door, but a few turned to see the women chatting, and staggered in their direction. Gracine walked up to deal with them using her knife, while Jillian used one of her blades to jab the fallen member of the circus group in the skull, making certain he couldn't reanimate.

And partly out of spite.

"Where is everyone else?" she asked when she and Gracine locked eyes once again.

"They're out front, backing me up and making sure the circus people don't escape. That was a bad ass plan you had by the way."

"Thanks. It almost backfired though."

Jillian wished she knew the extent of the injuries to Dark Lady's people, but her preoccupation with avoiding a bodily violation kept her from observing her surroundings. Momentarily they heard gunfire in front of the house, likely meaning her allies cut off Dark Lady's people from making a hasty escape. The best their adversaries might hope for was locking themselves inside a bedroom, holing up against the numerous undead.

Two bodies were lying in the yard, indicating only a few men remained to protect Dark Lady. Chances were good that they suffered bites or other injuries trying to escape the invading dead, and Jillian didn't want to prolong the skirmish between the two factions any longer.

"I say we burn the place down," she suggested as Gracine stood beside her.

"You sure? This is your home."

"The sooner we end this, the better. They either burn or they run."

"Okay," Gracine said with a turn of her head before heading to the front yard.

A few minutes later the group found adequate materials to light a small torch on fire, which they planned to throw into the far bedroom window. Although they couldn't see what happened inside the house, they conjured a few good guesses, most of which placed the survivors isolated in one room or another. Any fire would produce smoke, and either the heat or smoke would eventually chase the living from the house, or into the arms of the undead.

All of them stood in the front yard, and Driscoll held the small, makeshift torch in his right hand. It remained unlit, and everyone stalled as though waiting for someone to make the morally objectionable call.

"If any of them were bit, they'd eventually die and turn," Luke said. "They're probably doomed whether we do this or not."

"This does seem a little Old Testament," Gracine acknowledged, agreeing with Luke. "We aren't cold-blooded killers."

Jillian looked to Driscoll, who simply stood there holding the torch, openly unsure of what to think. He possessed little emotional tie to the situation, or his new group for that matter. He hadn't given Jillian a reason not to trust him, but his former allegiances made him a sketchy character in her eyes. She supposed some people simply carried out dark necessities to survive the apocalypse.

"I'm not rescuing them," Jillian said, proposing a counteroffer.

"No one's asking you to," Gracine said, touching her arm in an attempt to comfort her after their ordeal.

A gunshot rang through the air, and Jillian actually felt the bullet pass dangerously close to her left shoulder as she whirled to see who fired the gun. Pulling her own firearm from behind her as she turned, a rather natural reaction by this time, Jillian couldn't believe a woman was crossing the yard, heading directly for her. Holding the gun outright with a stiff arm, Dark Lady stepped purposefully forward, directly toward Jillian.

"You murderous bitch," Dark Lady sneered as she squeezed the trigger again, but Jillian had already evasively moved her torso to one side.

Her adversary wasn't skilled with firearms, based on her stance and the way her right arm shook when she held her pistol outward.

Already gripping her firearm, Jillian took quick, precise aim and shot Dark Lady in the upper leg, downing her immediately. By now everyone else had their weapons drawn and aimed at the gypsy woman, forcing her to drop her own gun. Gracine moved forward, stepping on the gun before kicking it off to one side.

"I hope you're happy," Dark Lady said with a hateful look in her eyes, staring directly at Jillian.

"How are you not in that house?" Jillian questioned.

"I got out before you trapped the boys in there. Happy?"

"No," Jillian answered honestly. "There is no happiness in this world, but I would've been content if I'd never seen you and your people again."

She turned to the others.

"You can go," she said, looking to each of them. "I've got this."

Gracine raised an eyebrow, questioning Jillian's decision to go solo a second time.

"I'm good," Jillian promised, prompting Gracine to lead the others away as they piled into a vehicle and slowly started down the road.

Dark Lady continued to grimace in pain as she remained on the ground, fighting through the agony to look Jillian in the eye.

"Do what you want with me and finish it."

"I wish you'd given my friend a choice," Jillian said, kneeling down with the gun in one hand. "Juan didn't want to die, but you let your boys have fun with him. How did you put it? Like cats playing with a mouse?"

"You'll understand someday," Dark Lady said, her eyes softening just a bit to convey the truth in her voice. "When you lose enough people, you'll do whatever it takes to keep the rest alive."

"I've lost more than you know, lady."

"And yet you fight for a ghost town with nothing left to offer."

"This was my *home*," Jillian stated sternly. "You people came in and you ransacked it, you killed my friend, and you've left me with the memory of your worker molesting a little girl."

"There was no proof," Dark Lady said, trying to refute the words of the media, the police, and the court system.

"And there's no helping you."

"What does that mean?"

"It means I can't change you when you defend murderers and pedophiles."

Both of them locked eyes for a moment, neither yielding their position. Finally, Jillian stood and walked to the front door of the house, looked to Dark Lady one last time, seeing no change in the woman's harsh demeanor, and opened the storm door. From there, she turned the knob to the front door, shoved it inward, and stood to one side to await the inevitable.

Something inside the house preoccupied the undead until the moment they saw light streaming through the front room. Following the beacon, they poured through the front door, not seeing Jillian, who stood safely behind the storm door as they locked their pale eyes on Dark Lady. Her cold expression quickly turned to terror at the thought of being devoured by the legion her own sister chose to join over a month ago.

"No!" she screamed as the undead drew close. "You bitch! Save me!"

Dark Lady attempted to stand with her injured leg, but collapsed quickly. She clawed at the ground, trying to crawl away from the danger, but even the lethargic pace of the undead allowed them to catch up within seconds. The first few fell to their knees, sinking their teeth into her arms and neck, causing her to wail enough that even Jillian felt some semblance of pity for her.

Within a matter of seconds, the undead pulled entrails from their victim, munching on them like ravenous cavemen delving into raw fish. Their hands and forearms appeared covered in blood, droplets falling to the ground, or onto their victim. They bit into parts of Dark Lady's body that looked agonizing enough to force Jillian to turn the other way momentarily. The woman's screams went on for quite some time as more undead piled atop her like a comedic football video where all of the defensive players keep jumping on the downed ball carrier.

When the screams finally stopped, Jillian began moving away from the house, knowing her movement would catch the attention of the undead. A single zombie emerged from the house, immediately staggering after her, but Jillian drew her gun and fired into its skull. Their numbers were diminished by Dark Lady's people, and Jillian knew she could handle the small cluster of undead if her gun didn't fail her.

One by one, the zombies stood from Dark Lady's corpse, and Jillian put them down, feeling overwhelmed by the recent emotions stemming from multiple losses. Metzger's departure, her father's death, and Vazquez's murder all ran through her mind as she shot them one by one. Two undead remained when her firearm ran out of ammunition, and for a fleeting second, she wondered if allowing one of them to bite her might remove her pain. She remembered the agony Albert and others endured as their lives faded away, and Jillian chose to reload her gun when she heard a gunshot from behind her. One of the undead fell at her feet, its pale eyes looking permanently at the house where it had just exited.

Coming to her aid, the group rallied around Jillian, finishing off the last of the undead before Driscoll walked up to the house and shut the door, essentially imprisoning the dead and any survivors from Dark Lady's camp who might still be alive.

"We got you," Gracine said, her expression indicating she understood the dark place Jillian's mind traveled to just seconds before the group arrived.

"No matter where we go, there's only pain and disappointment waiting for us."

"I know," Gracine said, pulling her into a hug. "We can't stay here. It's not good for you."

Jillian nodded, knowing her friend spoke the truth.

"I have nothing left to search for," she said. "Does anyone else?"

Everyone slowly shook their heads negatively.

"You need to check on him, don't you?" Gracine asked, and Jillian immediately knew she spoke of Metzger.

"Is it unreasonable to think he might have changed his mind?"

"Living with those uptight assholes would probably change *my* mind."

Jillian chuckled, feeling guilty immediately with so much carnage surrounding her, but the thought of seeing Metzger brightened her day.

"Yeah," she said. "Let's give Juan a proper burial. Then we head east."

Twenty-Six

When Sutton left his group, he expected to track down his box truck with little issue, but Keppler proved a worthy adversary when it came to stealthy maneuvers.

Sutton searched for the man, backtracking several times after securing a truck as his personal ride. He finally realized Keppler wasn't running from him, but rather playing a game of hide-and-seek where he'd stash the box truck and settle in somewhere, likely watching with delight as Sutton attempted to locate him.

Being left alone with his thoughts hadn't proven beneficial, or healthy, for Sutton. Despite Buster's companionship, he kept dwelling on Jillian's father and the group he accidentally traveled with to South Hill. He didn't hold himself responsible for the man's death, or Vazquez's death for that matter, but he wasn't about to go crawling back to the group to ask for forgiveness. No one stuck up for him the first time, and Jillian made it clear she called the shots, at least in her hometown.

On a few different occasions, Sutton spotted his box truck on the other side of divided roads where he couldn't easily turn around, and by the time he did, Keppler had always found a place to hide. Sutton couldn't believe the man knew how to hide a box truck so well, and he realized the lieutenant simply wanted to taunt him, but he quickly grew tired of the game.

When Sutton finally did learn Keppler's location, or at least the location of his box truck, Sutton scouted the area where the man parked it. An old, small church with stained glass windows appeared mostly intact in an area just outside of a nearby town. A few houses dotted the surrounding area, and the undead weren't much of a factor. Sutton cleared one of the nearby houses of three undead and decided to keep watch over his truck.

Approaching it might give Keppler what he wanted, and spring some sort of trap, so Sutton decided to simply wait the man out and take him by surprise. The chimney along the far side of the church produced smoke, which indicated Keppler might be cooking, staying warm, or drying his clothes. Sutton remained inside the house, trying to keep Buster calm when the dog simply wanted to run around outside, get some exercise, and sniff out zombies.

"What's his plan, Buster?" Sutton asked his dog, causing the pit bull to simply tilt his head sideways with a curious look.

Sutton's thoughts occasionally returned to Jillian and the others, and he couldn't entirely blame her for excommunicating him. Several times over he brought trouble to the group, but he'd also saved their lives a few times. If he ever decided to reconcile with them, he needed to have any and all baggage out of the way, which included Keppler.

Buster eventually whimpered to go outside because he needed to relieve himself, and Sutton decided to use the rear door so they wouldn't be visible to anyone else. Sutton grabbed the AR-15 he'd brought with him from South Hill, missing some of his other firearms. The box truck held a few interesting pieces, like the military sniper rifle with the night vision scope. It also contained food, camping supplies, sealed water, and batteries enough to last for months, possibly up to a year.

Monitoring the area while Buster squatted to deposit his previous day's supper in the yard, Sutton strolled to the corner of the house, daring to peek around the side. He saw no activity from the church, causing him to wonder what kind of plan Keppler cooked up when the man could easily have been a state or two away from Virginia. The thought crossed his mind that the man might be using the sniper rifle with the night vision scope to monitor the nearby area, so Sutton didn't linger.

Looking to the sky, he found dusk growing close, and decided he might take a closer look at Keppler's setup under the cover of darkness. He returned to the house with Buster, opened a can of corned beef for dinner, and bided his time after that by starting a novel he'd found inside one of the house's bedrooms. When daylight left the windows, and Sutton dared not light a candle or use a flashlight, he peered out the window, seeing no change across the road. Continuing to exercise caution, he exited through the back door again, taking Buster outside with him, but ordering the canine to stay at the house.

With the last of the setting sun behind him, and a campfire in the side yard at the church ahead, Sutton carefully walked forward, holding the AR-15 in a ready position, his eyes darting left and right. Suspecting a trap, Sutton figured Keppler knew he was across the street, as though that's exactly where he *wanted* Sutton to be. His conscience told him he should have killed the lieutenant when he had the chance, instead of leaving the man's fate to chance.

A moment later he neared the fire, but opted to look around the church first. All of the stained glass windows were high enough that Sutton wouldn't be able to peer through them, even on tiptoes. Several plain windows lined the sides of the church along the ground, indicating egress from a basement, but Sutton saw no lights emerging from within.

Standing in front of the church momentarily, he waited for sound or movement, but nothing emerged from within. He stepped up the concrete stairs to the double wooden front doors, reaching for the lever handle doorknob on the right. Stopping just inches from touching it, Sutton hesitated, prepared to let the matter be, even if it cost him his box truck. He couldn't resume looking for his sons if Keppler killed him or occupied more of his precious time. In his mind, the risk no longer outweighed the reward when he was confronted with reality and potential consequences.

Taking a step back down the stairs, his eyes still locked on the front doors, Sutton felt a piece of cold metal pressed against his right temple. A sideways glance revealed a sidearm like the one Keppler would have used before becoming a disgraced lieutenant.

"Gun down, please," Keppler ordered more than requested. "It's time for us to have a long chat."

"Couldn't you just shoot me?" Sutton asked, still not complying.

"I'd rather not. But I don't want you shooting me, so gun down."

Sutton knelt down, gently setting the rifle on the concrete walkway before slowly standing to look Keppler in the eye.

"Let's go have a fireside chat," Keppler suggested, not foolish enough to lower the pistol he held for one second.

Both men made their way over to the makeshift fire pit, sitting on the logs Keppler, or someone before him, placed there for just such a purpose. Neither said a word for about a minute as they sized one another up, Keppler loosening the grip on the gun. Sutton didn't dare make a move, because the distance between them left the former soldier enough time to raise the weapon and squeeze the trigger.

"This is nice," Keppler said as though thoroughly enjoying their one-sided fireside chat.

"What do you want from me?"

"You and I are so much alike," Keppler said reflectively. "I really didn't see it at first, but the more I see of you, the more I know we're both survivors."

"You killed a man in cold blood," Sutton pointed out. "That's not who I am."

"But you've killed, haven't you?" Keppler pressed, obviously taking a guess since he hadn't witnessed any such action from Sutton.

Sutton said nothing, simply staring into the fire.

"I've always gotten things done," Keppler stated. "After working around so many weak-minded fools it just got tiresome. You give people simple orders and they can't even follow them, so you have to make examples of them."

Sutton got the meaning of the words, because the man had executed the soldier who let Sutton get the slip on him and take back his box truck outside of Norfolk.

"This world is custom-made for us," Keppler said. "You're on your own again and you don't need to be."

"What are you suggesting?" Sutton asked, already suspecting what the man was leading up to.

"I'm suggesting we team up. It's not safe out there alone."

"What makes you think I'm alone?"

"Come on," Keppler scoffed. "Either they kicked you out, or you left them for your precious truck. Either way, they aren't taking your shit much longer."

"How could I ever trust you?" Sutton asked, looking directly to the man. "The things you've done can't exactly be forgiven."

Now the former lieutenant laughed briefly.

"I could've killed you several times over," he said, shaking his head. "When I took the truck, I wasn't after your collection."

"You just wanted me alone."

"Talking some sense into you wasn't possible while you were with those yuppies."

"They're better people than either of us."

"I beg to differ," Keppler said, his body stiffening at the notion. "We're the top of the food chain."

Sutton contemplated his options, which didn't seem numerous at the moment. He couldn't envision a future where he scoured the country with a narcissistic murderer, but very few alternatives presented themselves.

"Where would we go?" Sutton inquired, feigning interest.

"Where do you want to go?"

"I have two sons," Sutton said, not entirely certain why he told the truth. "I need to find them."

Keppler's face registered some confusion.

"Sons? And you haven't looked for them sooner?"

"We did, but they weren't at our family meeting place."

"Meeting place?" Keppler asked with a furrowed eyebrow.

"We had a camp off the lake. The place was ravaged when we arrived, and my boys weren't anywhere to be found."

"Maybe you just had the wrong people helping you search. We can clear that place of the dead and leave some kind of marker if you think your boys are alive."

"I feel like they're alive," Sutton said honestly, knowing he'd trained them to survive.

"Then let me help you with this," Keppler said firmly, trying to persuade Sutton like he might with one of the young men under his command.

"You don't need me," Sutton countered. "Why are you so reluctant to fly solo? You know I'm straight, right?"

"As am I," Keppler answered, appearing slightly insulted, if not angered.

"So what would we do on this adventure of ours?" Sutton asked. "Break into some camps and loot? Shoot people trying to keep order in a violent world? Maybe rape some women?"

"Now you're just being insulting," Keppler said, openly irritated. "For a man with no gun, that's not your smartest move."

"I'm just testing our compatibility before I commit to anything. It seems to me you regard other people as insignificant insects."

"That's because they are," the former lieutenant said. "I'm betting one percent of the world's population is still alive, and we're *part* of that elite number. Join me. We've both been liberated from our former clans."

Sutton could tell Keppler still wanted him to form an alliance, but the more he heard, the more he disliked the man. Keppler couldn't be saved or redeemed, and his sociopathic view of others, including his own military brethren, made him deplorable. His existence endangered scores of good people, including Sutton's former group and others traveling the highways and interstates in search of a better future.

At the start of the apocalypse, Sutton ventured down a similar path, though not nearly as sadistic. Finding Gracine and the others preserved the human side of him, keeping Sutton from taking everything for himself at the expense of others.

Now, staring at what he considered a life and death decision, Sutton knew he couldn't walk away from this conversation with his freedom, and if he declined, he wouldn't walk away at all. Even if he pretended to accept, Keppler wasn't going to hand him back his firearm and trust him implicitly.

"If I agree to this, we go straight to my camp in the morning," Sutton offered, further testing the waters of Keppler's promises.

"I don't have any other plans," the disgraced soldier responded. "Get a good night's sleep and come back in the morning."

Sutton tried not to show his surprise that Keppler opted to let him leave the area. He figured the man might sleep with one eye open to make certain Sutton didn't sneak off, but the former lieutenant possessed the one thing that kept Sutton coming back.

"My truck?" he asked.

"I'll keep an eye on it tonight," Keppler said with a wink. "Wouldn't want any filthy marauders taking off with it."

"How kind of you," Sutton remarked sarcastically. "And my gun?"

"I'll need that to guard the truck."

Sutton nodded, openly unhappy about being stripped of his truck *and* his weapon.

He realized Keppler's life revolved around him being in control of everything, and Sutton could never make a decision with free will again if he teamed with the man. Standing, he gave the man a nod and walked halfway back to the house where he spotted Buster waiting patiently for him at the edge of the yard. Scratching his pet's head, he walked inside the house, grabbing the .40 caliber Smith & Wesson he'd left behind intentionally when he strolled across the street.

Stuffing the gun behind his back, he returned to the cool night air, spotting Keppler seated at the fire across the street. He walked directly toward the man, who never looked his way, obviously lost in contemplation of his future. Sutton motioned with his right hand for Buster to take a wider route, and the dog understood the command, walking a wide arch from his master in the same general direction.

Sutton thought he might have the drop on Keppler when he drew within shooting distance, but as he started to reach behind him for the gun, Keppler heard a noise and snatched up the AR-15 beside him, aiming it directly at Sutton. From the corner of his eye, Sutton saw Buster grow agitated at something about Keppler as he continued to walk stealthily on a parallel path.

"That was quick," Keppler said as he looked from Sutton's face to his right hand, which was quickly at Sutton's side. "You having second thoughts about our agreement?"

"I've had second thoughts about you since we met," Sutton replied.

"That doesn't sound like a good start to a partnership."

Sutton provided a grin that indicated he was kidding, though he wasn't.

"I'm just playing around," Sutton said with an airy wave of his hand. "Just knew I wasn't going to be able to sleep."

"Oh," Keppler said, turning to set the AR-15 aside, dropping his guard almost instantly.

"Buster," Sutton said, getting his pet's attention. "Stellen!"

Sutton used a Dutch word for 'attack' that sent his pit bull into action. What seemed like a lifetime ago, he'd asked a friend and K-9 officer on the local police department to teach Buster a few commands and actions. Despite being sweet and adorable to most everyone he met, the canine listened to his master first and foremost.

As fast as Keppler tried reacting to the move, reaching for the rifle, Buster was already leaping at him, snagging his left arm and dragging him away from the gun immediately. Keppler had the option of moving with the dog or watching his arm get torn to shreds by the dog's powerful jaws.

Now Sutton pulled the firearm from behind him, taking aim at Keppler after commanding Buster to stop his attack.

"Why would you do this?" Keppler asked, genuinely surprised that someone didn't want his guidance and companionship.

"You haven't left me much choice," Sutton said. "All these head games, stealing my truck, and trying to pin a murder on me that you committed. I can only take so much."

He shook his head.

"You're going to murder me in cold blood for a few indiscretions?" Keppler asked incredulously.

"You act like you had a lapse in judgement," Sutton said angrily. "This is who you are! You control, and you kill, and you don't give a shit about anyone as long as you get what you want!"

Keppler looked to the ground as though remorseful, but Sutton wasn't buying his act again.

"I don't want to kill you, but I can't be looking over my shoulder forever."

"I could make my way west," Keppler suggested, showing just a hint of desperation as he fought to keep his composure. "You'd never have to see me again."

Even if the man spoke the truth, Sutton knew lives, innocent lives, would certainly be taken if the man were left to roam the highways on his own. Although he'd killed a number of people personally, Sutton didn't target undeserving people. He knew he shared some kind of odd kinship with Keppler, and the longer he waited, the more dangerous it became as his moral compass suggested he not take a human life.

He stared at the man who held his bleeding left arm, Buster still giving a low growl nearby, attempting to decide his own future. Loyal almost to a fault, Buster wasn't a violent animal, but he judged people very well, in addition to sniffing out the undead. Sutton wasn't about to base his decision on the emotions of his dog, but he provided Keppler one chance at a new life and the man followed him instead, stealing his belongings.

Looking forward, Sutton knew what he wanted personally, and he knew the journey he needed to take to meet that goal. Nothing he pictured involved Keppler, or dealing with the man a fourth time, so he raised the Smith & Wesson, firing a round into the center of the man's forehead, securing his own future while saving the lives of strangers Keppler would never encounter. The lieutenant fell to the ground, his eyes still wide with surprise because he didn't anticipate Sutton pulling the trigger.

Buster immediately relaxed, assuming a sitting position, looking to Sutton, and giving a brief whining sound.

"I know," Sutton said. "We're getting out of here as soon as I find some keys."

Sutton gathered every loose weapon he found, discovering the box truck's keys within the confines of the church, which remained incredibly intact on the inside. Finding a few canned goods, bottles of water, and other supplies, Sutton put them in the back of the box truck after opening the back hatches for a look. His property appeared intact, either because Keppler simply used the truck as bait, or hadn't found a need to use any of the supplies stored there.

With everything loaded and secured, he ushered Buster into the passenger seat of the truck before taking one last look at Keppler's body crumpled beside the camp fire. The sound of gunfire would surely draw the undead to the church, so Sutton kicked some dirt on the fire, snuffing the flames. He joined Buster in the truck, glanced at the map lying atop the dashboard, and ignored it, already knowing their next destination.

"Buckle up, buddy," he told the dog. "Time to find some old friends."

Twenty-Seven

Isabella wanted to grieve her husband, but a nagging feeling about the mission that claimed him stayed with her. Her brother-in-law seemed like a prisoner on the base, and the combined military forces did little to disguise the fact because two armed soldiers followed him closely wherever he went.

Daring not communicate with him directly, she often had Nathan create a drawing, a card, or some other form of artwork before she inserted a subtle message for Metzger inside. Often, she wrote in code on the back of the paper so her scribblings looked like random letters until held up to light from the other side. Sometimes she scratched across certain letters in a crossword puzzle to spell out a message. In return, Metzger often handed Nathan a flower, or some trinket, with a note folded numerous times, for Isabella to read.

He informed her that they continued to draw his blood every day or two, possibly worried his blood cell counts might suffer. Each time they appeared to draw a little more, he reported, causing her to wonder if they found some kind of marker in his blood that resisted the undead infection. No one else received so much attention from the military, and they stopped asking for Nathan's participation after two draws. The bizarre mystery occupied time for both Isabella and Metzger, giving them something to focus on that wasn't the death of Bryce.

Making herself indispensable, Isabella told people on the base that she wanted to keep busy rather than dwell on the death of her husband. In a manner of speaking, she spoke the truth, but she wasn't carrying out busywork after taking Nathan to classes on the base. She took up several side jobs that provided her with access to numerous buildings. As expected, several higher ups in the military eyed her warily, but she busied herself with cleaning various buildings, assisting in the medical bays, and occasionally boarding the ships to unload or organize supplies because the sailors had assignments that kept them on land more often.

On what she believed was the eighth day since learning of her husband's demise, Isabella helped push a cart of supplies onto *Ross* with a fellow civilian. Roles changed often around the base, and many of the officers and enlisted men and women were occupied with clearing the town of Norfolk. She wondered how many of the military personnel were proficient with firearms, considering the majority of the people housed on the base were Navy folks. Ships only housed a handful of guns while at sea, and most of the enlisted personnel hadn't fired a firearm since basic training.

Even worse, ammunition would eventually run out, meaning those in charge allotted only so many rounds for target practice before their soldiers headed out to confront the undead.

While assisting her partner with putting up the supplies in various parts of the ship, Isabella casually scanned for any folders, computers, or tablets that might contain information. In particular, she wanted to know about the Buffalo mission, or why the military suddenly took a major interest in her brother-in-law.

Nothing caught her eye, and the joint leaders of the combined military force typically conducted business inside one of two particular buildings on the base. On her way off the ship, however, she spotted Mark Dascher walking the deck and drinking from his coffee mug. He spotted Isabella too late to turn around and act like he hadn't seen her, and she knew the commander hadn't been comfortable around her the few times they'd met since the Buffalo mission.

Wearing his dress white uniform because the winter changeover wasn't for another week, Dascher evidently had a function to attend. He approached Isabella without hesitation, giving her a courteous nod.

"How are you doing?" he asked.

"Staying busy keeps me from thinking about it," Isabella answered. "How are things with you?"

"Good," Dascher answered. "We're slated to be moved into a set of apartments near the base once they're cleared."

"It's hard to think we're going back to anything close to normal."

Dascher shook his head.

"I don't think we'll see *normal* for quite some time. Having electricity is a fringe benefit to living in Norfolk though."

Isabella already knew the commander returned to find his wife, son, and daughter alive and well when his ship docked in Norfolk. He remained close to them, safe and cozy on the base while her husband took on hazardous missions to Buffalo, twice no less. She didn't blame Dascher, or begrudge him, but Isabella didn't appreciate the man dodging her. Granted, Bryce was never officially witnessed as dying in the line of duty, but everyone knew what a bite from the undead meant. Dascher could have done more to honor the memory of his executive officer than offer kind words, even in the apocalypse.

"I know you're not allowed to talk about much," Isabella said cautiously, "but what is going on with my brother-in-law?"

"What do you mean?" Dascher asked, openly confused, or doing a phenomenal acting job.

"I'm talking about the reason he has two armed soldiers following his every move, every minute of the day."

"Oh, that," Dascher said, his eyes averting to the ground momentarily. "That's classified."

"Don't give me that classified bullshit, Mark," Isabella said firmly. "Did he undermine the mission? Did he get my husband killed?"

"No," Dascher said as though such a notion were preposterous, taking a quick glance around them to ensure no one eavesdropped on their conversation.

Isabella knew Metzger wasn't being followed for any kind of criminal reasons, but she needed to play the information game with Dascher and slowly coax facts from the man.

"What else could he have done to warrant that kind of attention?"

Dascher hesitated, rubbing his face nervously a moment with his free hand. The other still held the mug of coffee he hadn't consumed since meeting up with Isabella.

"My husband died for his country, for the survivors here," Isabella pressed. "I can't get answers about what happened because I can't even talk to Dan. Please, tell me *something* that can give me some closure over this whole ordeal."

"I know Dan is important to them," Dascher answered. "Bryce was, too, but I don't know exactly why. Let's just say that kind of information is above my pay grade."

Isabella believed him, but his words did little to assist or comfort her.

"Where do I go for answers?" she asked firmly, rather than plead, because she wasn't about to show weakness to a man who governed youngsters on a ship.

Again, Dascher took a look around before answering.

"You're going to have to get creative. I've already told you too much, and the people who outrank me aren't going to say a word about any of this."

"I'm not even sure why I'm staying here," she vented her thoughts. "Part of me wants to leave with my son and Dan and never look back."

"They won't let your brother-in-law leave," Dascher assured her. "He's too important if they're devoting this much attention to him."

Isabella got the sense that the brass left Dascher out of the loop regarding certain information because he was personally tied to Bryce. Although not fiercely independent, the man struck her as very intelligent and disciplined. The fact that he slipped any information to her at all showed good human nature on his part, and a few ideas hatched within her mind about how to obtain additional facts.

"I know you have a sense of duty," Isabella said, "but why do you stick around? You could make a go of it out there."

"Out there, we don't have walls and warmth," Dascher replied, losing a bit of the gleam in his eye, as though imprisoned within the base himself because of his family. "If the world is going to get rebuilt, it's going to start here."

"You say that, but a lot of people live here. Food, fuel, hell, even toilet paper will eventually run out."

"We have some great minds here," Dascher said confidently. "We'll get things figured out, and until then, we'll get by."

He finally relaxed enough to provide a grin.

"Hell, with some basics like coffee, anything is possible," he added before lifting the mug momentarily and taking a sip.

"Thanks, Mark," Isabella said before giving a nod and walking to the closest means to exit the ship.

"Isabella," Dascher called as she neared the halfway point down the ramp.

"Yeah?"

"I could see about getting you and Nathan some more conventional housing once the town is cleared. If that's something you want."

"Thanks," she called back. "I'll think about it."

In her mind, Isabella didn't envision leaving the base until she learned some answers about why Metzger was being monitored so closely, and why the military took such an interest in him, and perhaps her husband. Several strong ideas crossed her mind, but she needed definitive proof before taking action.

If Dascher had meetings to attend, then perhaps other officers were about to head off to similar gatherings. She began formulating a plan to learn about their objectives without them ever knowing better, or detecting her presence. Figuring the window of playing the grieving widow and speaking to officers directly was closing, she needed to make a move rather quickly before deciding her immediate and distant future.

Part of her wanted to write Metzger a note, telling him to run, regardless of whether she and Nathan went with him. Heading for her current living quarters, Isabella wondered if her brother-in-law fared any better.

***

Across the base, Metzger went for a run, trying to keep his cardio in prime condition, knowing he might need to utilize all of his skills in the near future. His guardians kept pace from a distance, both possessing holstered pistols, looking a bit strange as they jogged in full uniform across the base.

He noticed six particular men worked in shifts to monitor him at all times, each young and rather indiscriminate from the others. They didn't seem particularly unfriendly, but rather dutiful soldiers carrying out their orders. Each time Metzger neared a fence, or one of the exit points, he considered making a dash for freedom, questioning what might happen if he dared. Like Isabella, he wanted answers before making any attempt to leave the safety of the base, because a few things didn't add up.

Looking to the red dot on the inside of his elbow, he was reminded of how many times he'd donated blood samples over the past few days. The speck of dried blood caused him to wonder if they were testing his DNA or seeing how his blood reacted to whatever virus caused the zombie outbreak. His blood wasn't being used for transfusions, and if the military had simply used that ruse, Metzger would have volunteered as often as possible to donate, alleviating the need for spy games.

By not asking questions, Metzger wondered if he received more scrutiny from the military. He didn't care at this point. He simply knew he wanted off the base if they were going to watch over him night and day, basically making him a prisoner. He worried if he asked too many questions, or spoke of intentions to leave, they might truly imprison him.

Each day he watched several armed military personnel and civilians leave the base to clear the city of Norfolk of the undead before carrying out cleanup and construction duties. Much like the push west after the United States was founded, these brave souls pioneered a new land all over again. The sounds of drills, jackhammers, and saws filled the air just outside the base, reminding Metzger of normal times, and sinking his heart because he couldn't participate. At night, lights from several houses, apartment buildings, and businesses were visible from the base. The stars, too, shone brighter than Metzger could ever recall, because smog and pollution didn't create a hazy filter between the sky and human eyes.

A part of him liked being on the base, near the heavy, sloshing water that could carry a man, living or dead, out to sea. The sound helped him drift off to sleep at night amongst the steel and concrete surroundings in the form of ships and walkways. Having secured borders felt nice for a while, but Metzger grew to miss the personality his group provided as he bonded with them. Having the best of both worlds would mean having them stay at the base with him, but it seemed only so much room remained for new tenants.

Jogging near some of the security entrance points, Metzger saw a vehicle approaching that didn't look familiar. Not a green, black, or beige military vehicle, the powder blue car caught everyone's attention, and nearby soldiers snapped to attention, keeping their firearms in a ready position as the car pulled to a stop. Two men dressed in police uniforms stepped out, holding their hands halfway up to indicate they meant no harm, and Metzger immediately recognized them, though he couldn't believe his eyes.

"Hey, guys," Metzger said, drawing incredulous stares from everyone around him.

"Dan?" Mullins asked, stepping forward hesitantly as several guns pointed his way. "You made it back."

"Twice. You could've saved yourselves some trouble and caught a flight with us."

"But it's been so scenic and fun," Weir commented sarcastically.

"I can relate," Metzger said. "So what brings you here? I thought you were heading to South Carolina."

A few of the soldiers considered stepping in, but Metzger moved forward, indicating he knew the men personally. He knew putting his own body between them and the soldiers would keep the two former cops safe.

"We learned something about that Nadeau guy you were looking for," Weir said. "It seemed important enough to deviate from our trip and tell some of the brass here, if they want to hear it."

Metzger looked to a few of the soldiers, who returned slightly confused stares.

"They're talking about the asshole who blew up those factories and started all of this," Metzger explained, turning to address each of them. "The same ones who cost some of us our families. You guys might want to find some of your officers."

One sailor finally broke away to head into the base to locate someone with sufficient rank to make a decision.

"How've you been?" Mullins inquired of Metzger.

"Not bad."

"Where's your brother?" the former cop asked, as though hoping to meet the lieutenant commander during his visit.

"We lost him during a second trip to Buffalo," Metzger answered with a tone that indicated Bryce would never be coming back.

"Sorry to hear that."

"He died saving us," Metzger added, mostly for the benefit of the military personnel around him. "So what did you find?" he asked the two former cops, trying to change the subject.

Mullins explained their encounter with the strange group to Metzger, stating that they didn't believe the group's story, and that he believed they were heading to find Nadeau.

"Sounds like they were creating misdirection," Metzger surmised. "But why? The guy probably has some kind of underground bunker somewhere, kicking back with martinis beside his heated pool."

"That's what we thought," Weir chimed in. "It appeared they were heading north, possibly meeting up with him or his people somewhere."

Before their conversation could continue, an Army man dressed in a captain's uniform walked up with the sailor who'd left, causing the sea of military personnel to part as he approached the two men dressed in police uniforms.

"You two, please come with me," he ordered more than asked of them.

Metzger watched as the two men were led inside the base, across the open area to the buildings where the brass conducted their business. He feared for their safety, or at least their freedom, after his experience since returning from Buffalo. Everyone around him slowly dispersed, with jobs to carry out, and Metzger eventually resumed his run, though his personal escorts seemed to eye him a little differently. He didn't know what they'd been told about him, but they appeared to think him a bit more human after his interaction with the two travelers.

Metzger continued to jog around the area until the two men emerged from a building about half an hour after they were escorted across the base. He stopped to speak with them momentarily before they continued their journey south.

"Were they interested?" he asked once he stopped jogging, trying to catch his breath a moment as he hunched over slightly.

"Sounds like they aren't done hunting for him," Mullins answered.

"I'm beginning to question some of their motivations around here," Metzger said quietly enough that no one nearby could hear his words.

"What's with the two goons following you?" Weir inquired.

"You noticed, huh?"

"Hard not to," Mullins answered.

"I'm still not sure what I've done to provoke the powers that be. Them, or their buddies, watch me whenever I'm out of my barracks."

"Need us to spring you?"

Metzger chuckled.

"I've got things handled. You two need to finish your journey."

"We intend to," Mullins said. "This one needs to find his family."

"I wish you both luck."

"Back at you."

Metzger shook hands with both men, who looked like they'd been to hell and back.

"You guys considered getting some clothes off the dead?" he asked. "Might be an improvement."

He drew smiles from both of the former officers.

"We're trying to present ourselves as helpers, not harmers," Mullins said.

"Then maybe do some laundry. You guys smell like shit."

Both broke out into laughter before giving Metzger a goodbye wave and heading across the border Metzger couldn't cross, climbing into their most recent vehicle.

Watching them drive off, Metzger envied them more than a little for having the freedom to drive anywhere. He suspected their journey would have perils, and they might encounter assholes the likes of which he'd seen, but they seemed capable. Having a purpose kept Metzger going during some dark times, and he imagined the two armed men would reach South Carolina in a reasonable timeframe.

About to begin jogging again, Metzger noticed stares from the military personnel around him, as though they hadn't really noticed him before. One soldier dressed in fatigues walked up and offered to shake his hand.

"I just wanted to say I appreciate your brother's sacrifice," the younger man said as they shook hands. "I'm sorry for your loss."

It dawned on Metzger that he hadn't heard many supportive words since returning to the base. He didn't feel as though anyone disliked him, but rather they didn't know what to say, especially after it became apparent soldiers were being assigned to keep tabs on him at all times. Even they likely didn't know exactly why they needed to follow him around, but Metzger decided he wanted to know. If he wanted answers, asking directly wasn't the method to use, but rather stealth, and Isabella was already working on that angle.

"Thanks," Metzger replied to the soldier, noticing a bit more sympathy from the nearby personnel.

Perhaps many of them didn't know who he was because hundreds of other civilians occupied the base, but enough of them knew Bryce, or about his actions, after the last Buffalo mission.

Metzger felt his time on the base had nearly reached its end, but he needed some answers before planning an official departure. Eluding the military personnel wouldn't be difficult, despite them changing his living quarters to keep tabs on him a bit more easily. He'd played along to give them a false sense of docility on his end, but he constantly, with much scrutiny, viewed his surroundings with the endgame of forming an escape plan.

He hoped the answers he needed might fall into his lap through one of his few trusted sources, or Isabella might learn why the military took such an interest in him very soon. Several notions entered his mind, but he dismissed them because he wasn't being kept under lock and key, and because he shared the same bloodline as his brother. In his mind, the military would have made greater efforts to save Bryce if the lieutenant commander's blood possessed an equal value to Metzger's.

Wouldn't they?

Twenty-Eight

Isabella woke early the next morning, leaving Nathan with a trusted friend before initiating her plan to finally get answers about why Metzger was an unofficial prisoner inside the base. She risked quite a bit, personally, to learn answers from the secretive military. If soldiers caught her, she had already planned to use emotional distress from the death of her husband as her reasoning for seeking the truth.

Even so, she didn't plan on getting caught, because security on the base wasn't nearly as effective as it had been before the apocalypse. Despite power restoration to the entire base and a portion of Norfolk, several security cameras broke and couldn't be replaced, guards were sometimes reallocated to other tasks, and many soldiers weren't as dutiful. Widespread depression over losing friends and family took a toll on many of them, and though Isabella didn't address this with the military personnel personally, she heard stories from their spouses, and through office talk when she helped clean and resupply the ships and buildings.

She learned that the *USS Carter Hall* housed the medical research facilities for the base, keeping their findings safe from everyone living and working on the base. Isabella managed to dress the part and join with a resupply party the previous evening, and though she couldn't enter any of the labs, she spied a schedule that indicated the scientists met with the military commanders each morning to update them on any new findings or needs arising from their research.

Most of the ships returned from their deployments after the apocalypse struck. A number of vessels docked in Norfolk, and a slightly smaller amount in

San Diego where another group of military combined forces made a stand with their families.

Isabella felt bad for the poor souls who lived in Norfolk and the surrounding communities that tried coming to the base for assistance and protection, only to be turned away. As cold and calculated as it might sound, the military used their records and information from their personnel to weed out direct family members from those trying to enter the base using deception. Food and supplies began to run low within a few weeks and having extra mouths to feed only made survival that much tougher.

Soldiers and sailors initially took incredible risks to retrieve family members within Norfolk city limits, and Isabella personally felt thankful for their sacrifice, though she'd handled a few of the undead personally before they arrived. Having her husband at sea, and no other family nearby, kept her worried the first few days, and being ushered into the base provided little comfort. Groups of strangers were suddenly forced to live together in a setting that felt akin to a sadistic summer camp with late summer heat, crowded and uncomfortable sleeping conditions, and no real answers about their loved ones. Bonds were eventually formed, but the first few weeks were tense for the survivors until they received good news about their family members at sea.

Now she stood inside the building where the meeting would take place within the hour, trying to decide where to place the cell phone in her back pocket. While the cell phone provided little use other than a reliable source of date and time most of the time, Isabella wanted to use its video recording capabilities to learn as many details as she could from the meeting. Having studied activities on the base, the past week in particular, she knew the major players in command of the unified military.

Unlike meeting rooms of the past, there weren't decorative features lining the conference table or the surrounding furniture. She couldn't exactly place the phone in a floral arrangement or hide it in some tablet case. Even worse, she used a janitorial cart to move around the building, looking the part as she'd occasionally dust something or empty a trash can in case cameras were recording her movements. Fortunately for her, a rear door was propped open while a legitimate custodian or maintenance person stepped out to smoke or fetch some tools.

Trying to avoid looking suspicious, she looked around the room, taking note of several portraits of Navy leaders and the President of the free world, whom she suddenly realized she hadn't seen, despite him supposedly being housed somewhere on the base, or one of the ships.

Below the portraits were mounted gold name placards used to identify the subjects of the portraits. They were mounted about six inches below the portraits, separately, along dark, stained walls. Isabella had charged the phone fully overnight, glad she kept the device despite its otherwise useless nature. Dates and times didn't feel so important when one counted waking up each morning a blessing.

Isabella continued to clean and dust the room, knowing exactly where she planned to place the phone, and as the first footsteps echoed in the hallways, she turned on the device's video recording mode and set it between a placard and portrait where it blended in with the dark walls behind it. She prayed the battery would hold out, and that she would be able to retrieve the device without any issues later that day.

Sounds of more footsteps and doors opening and closing reached her ears, however, and Isabella knew she couldn't escape the area without being recognized by someone among the incoming group. She used a side door and took a lesser-used hallway to a custodial closet where she wheeled her cart, hiding inside with it and shutting the door behind her. She waited inside, accompanied only by the sounds of her breathing for nearly an hour as people filed inside, carried out discussions in the main conference room, and slowly departed the building after their meeting concluded.

Unable to make out specific words or conversations, Isabella held out hope that her phone picked up most of the meeting with audio and video clarity. She eventually opened the door, looking up and down the hallway before casually walking to the meeting room area. A few officers in uniform lingered at the main double doors, talking about family issues before switching to a different subject. Both men wore hats with what Navy personnel called 'scrambled eggs' on their brims, which meant they held distinctive ranks.

"How much longer can they keep the secret?" a man with graying black hair asked the other as they slowly sauntered down the hallway. He spoke with an accent that indicated he came from the south, though Isabella couldn't place his drawl.

Isabella glanced around her, seeing no one else, so she removed her shoes before following them down the hall. Words and footsteps echoed throughout the facility from her experience, so she didn't want to give herself away.

"Which one?" the older man with pure gray hair scoffed because the military obviously kept many secrets from its own people during such bleak times.

He held a wrapped binder in one hand, and an unlit pipe in the other. He appeared weathered, possibly from years of service, but also from an apocalypse that denied him retirement into a normal life.

"The President, and what's left of the government, are holed up in the Midwest, so we're the voice of the people now?"

"Tom, we're the only thing left," the older officer answered, stuffing the binder under one armpit so he could pack his pipe with tobacco. "If we crack, everything falls apart. Our people are hanging on by a thread as it is."

"San Diego has it far worse than us, Carl. Californians weren't as well-prepared, and there are a *lot* more of them."

"Glad we're *here*. Even if we cleared the dead across the nation today, we'd be years before we got things back to normal. I know we saved some good minds, but just a few months off the grid has crippled the country. We'll be hard-pressed to make fuel and grow food anytime soon. Our fearless leader is calling the shots from his cozy, safe bunker and we're the ones who have to make the real decisions around here."

Isabella found their conversation interesting because no pretense existed in the form of saluting, or formally calling one another 'sir' or by their ranks. Hidden from public view, and the other military branches, the two men acted like friends, rather than colleagues. Several juts in the wall and pieces of artwork atop pedestals had provided her with cover thus far, allowing her to hear their conversation without muffled echoes. She reached an area in the hall where she dared not follow the two men because she'd be spotted instantly if they turned around. Fortunately, they didn't seem rushed to leave the facility as they talked and stopped occasionally in the corridor.

"It doesn't feel like we're any closer to finding Nadeau," the younger officer with the drawl said, openly unhappy about that particular situation.

"Our guys letting his accomplice loose didn't help matters," the older man said with a hint of disdain. "I realize that Metzger kid is important to us, but he's not the key to locating that asshole Nadeau."

Isabella perked up when she heard them speak of her brother-in-law, wondering how he'd become a household name among the military brass.

"I don't like our resources being divided," the younger officer said. "We're hanging on by a thread around here and yet we send our people all over the country searching for a man who isn't going to cooperate if and when we find him. Hell, he may not even have a cure to all of this, even if we *do* locate his compound."

"At least when we found bin Laden we had technology on our side. This is literally searching for a needle in a haystack."

"Even worse, most of our potential witnesses don't have heartbeats."

"I'd just like to know where we stand," the older officer grumbled. "This unified military doesn't always feel balanced to me. They ask us our opinions as a *council* then do whatever the fuck they want anyway."

He hunched over to light his pipe with a match after striking it against the matchbook.

"Sure you should be doing that in here?" his fellow serviceman asked without judgment.

"Fuck smoking laws," the older officer chuckled, since virtually every rule went out the window when the apocalypse struck.

Isabella watched the two men continue down the hall, their words eventually becoming indistinguishable echoes. Lingering just a few seconds, she caught a whiff of the cherry pipe tobacco and she was transported to her childhood when her grandfather smoked a pipe before smoking became so taboo in public.

She felt surprised that her country was run from afar by a President hidden in some secret bunker. Other than reasons of morale, or to serve as a red herring, Isabella couldn't fathom why a body double was brought to the base. It sounded to her as though the military men ran things locally, like territorial governors, though she wasn't certain she trusted their judgment in all matters. She'd heard rumors that many important politicians were rescued in the early stages, but thinking back, Isabella hadn't really seen many civilians aside from the military families.

Bryce told her of protocols to save important government officials several times before the apocalypse, and he indicated the government constructed bunkers in secret locations, mainly in the central portions of the country. Isabella questioned if these men and women were much better than Nadeau if they remained underground until their supplies ran out, or they deemed it safe to return to the surface.

Wasting little time dwelling on situations she couldn't control, Isabella returned to the main room and collected her phone, knowing she'd be compromised if anyone reviewed the building's security footage and saw her spying on the two officers. She discreetly placed the phone in her back pocket to review once she left the building, and Isabella wasted no time heading for the closest exit, worried about the future of the military installation.

***

Before Isabella could review the footage on her phone, her friend said Nathan hadn't been very cooperative, so she collected her son and crossed the base, holding his hand as she walked. The sky above appeared foreboding with ominous gray clouds in one direction, and the sun piercing white, fluffy clouds behind her. She wasn't sure if a thunderstorm might dump an inch of rain on the base, or if the pleasant weather within her view might win out.

Deciding she didn't want to appear suspicious, Isabella carried out some of her regular duties after settling down her son and leaving him in the hands of familiar instructors and aides at the school. Today wasn't an instruction day, but parents were able to drop their children off daily when they worked their base jobs, or simply needed a break.

She spied Metzger jogging along the perimeter of the base, and the two made eye contact only briefly as though both were afraid to acknowledge one another and the secret alliance they'd formed since Bryce's death. Isabella considered them avoiding one another even *more* suspicious than conversing every so often, but when people asked about their family situation, she simply dismissed it as though she blamed her brother-in-law for her husband's death.

In truth, she felt relieved that Metzger witnessed the events in Buffalo because Dascher and the chaplain hadn't provided specific details during the death notification.

Following an assignment, she helped move supplies from one of the base entrances to a building being used as a warehouse. There she helped unload boxes and bulk goods, unable to find an opportunity to view the footage. With privacy at a premium on the base, Isabella needed to find a building with no one around to play the video. After her second job of moving supplies from the warehouse to one of the ships, she found such an opportunity because the officer of the deck and the duty section remained near the ship's bridge.

It seemed most of the docked ships served as additional warehouses because they weren't patrolling the seas looking for pirates or terrorists in an age where nuclear weapons no longer posed a threat. Crews remained aboard the vessels in case some threat forced them to move out to sea in a timely manner, but they were no longer weapons of war, per se. Isabella couldn't fathom why any world leader might use weapons of mass destruction when the job had already been done for them.

She began to question the future for mankind as her own government appeared shattered, and leadership in other countries couldn't possibly have fared better. Although the military didn't appear to be deceiving its citizens with malicious intentions, the reality of their current state wasn't the pretty picture they painted for base residents.

Before, Isabella held out hope that the remaining political leaders and the brilliant scientific minds the military claimed to have saved would put the world back together, but now she wasn't nearly as optimistic.

Holding the phone in both hands in front of her, she pressed the play icon on the screen to start the video, turning down the phone's volume to avoid drawing attention.

She skipped past the part where officers filed in, conducting small talk before the meeting began. Their first orders of business dealt with issues around the base, and taking back Norfolk from the dead and any unwanted inhabitants. Isabella heard them speak of shooing survivors from the city under the threat of execution because they didn't want the burden of feeding prisoners. They reported no one resisted, which alleviated some of her fears that the entire world turned barbaric, but she didn't like the idea of leaving people behind.

Trying not to judge too harshly, because she didn't know the entirety of their food supply, or how many mouths the military fed on the base, Isabella continued to watch.

A general briefed the group about orders from the President, which didn't sound very specific in nature to Isabella. She couldn't imagine how a person hundreds of feet underground could command a nation, and apparently the President opted to let his people taking the risks make most of the decisions.

Several Navy officers reported the status of their ships, and an Army colonel said their personnel continued to communicate with several installations, including San Diego. Isabella considered their reports interesting, but she grew bored waiting for what she wanted to view. Not daring to forward the video for fear of missing important material, she managed to monitor her surroundings while absorbing information from the phone.

Near the end of the meeting, two scientists stepped forward after a brief introduction from the only general in the room.

"What have you learned?" the general inquired once the two men took center stage before a room of nearly twenty officials.

"We've been testing the blood samples on a daily basis," the first scientist reported, wearing a dressy plaid shirt and black jeans, rather than a lab coat.

"And?"

"We're making headway," the second man said. "We have a few sample serums ready for testing."

"Have you found additional subjects who fit the profile at the other installations?" the first scientist requested.

"Negative," the colonel replied. "San Diego has one, but the subject they found in Florida was killed when the dead overran her and her escort assignment."

As she viewed the footage, Isabella felt as though a dozen questions enter her mind at once.

Test subjects?

Sample serums?

Was Metzger a guinea pig, or was he a part of their unspoken solution?

"We've tested virtually everyone on the base," the second scientist noted aloud. "Only the Metzger brothers provided a valid match, and now one of them is gone after the miscommunication during the Buffalo mission."

"It would be ill-advised for you to talk about mission parameters you weren't part of," the general admonished him with a stony stare. "You'll simply have to work with what you've got."

"He's beginning to ask questions," the second scientist stated. "How do you propose we proceed if he grows agitated with the blood draws?"

"We can't tell him the truth," one Navy officer said.

"Maybe we should," another suggested. "He and his brother have been nothing short of loyal."

"With his brother gone, he may turn on us," an Army major said.

"And if we treat him like a prisoner, he'll begin to look for an escape route," the general grumbled. "We can't afford to lose him, and our security is divided between the water, the town, and the base right now. It wouldn't take much for him to slip out if he chose to."

"If he learns the truth about his brother, we'll lose him for sure," the colonel said. "Maybe it's time to put him on lockdown."

Isabella wondered what 'truth' the man spoke of, since everything she'd heard from Metzger and others in Buffalo sounded consistent.

"He doesn't deserve to be a prisoner," the older officer Isabella saw in the hallway earlier said during the meeting. "His brother was a patriot and risked a hell of a lot more than any of us in this cause."

Although the man's words fell on deaf ears, his point was made because the room fell into silence momentarily. No one could deny that Bryce didn't risk life and limb for a cause that now appeared impossible to champion. Fournier escaped, and no other known links to Nadeau existed.

After nearly half a minute of silence, the general spoke once again.

"Perhaps Captain Timmons can shed some light on the mindset of our *guest*."

Wearing a leather flight jacket, and appearing somewhat uncomfortable in a room filled with people who outranked him, the pilot hadn't sat down the entire time. Instead, he leaned against a wall, reasonably close to where Isabella planted her phone to record the military meeting. He stood erect at the mention of his name, still uneasy around the brass, or perhaps the situation they discussed.

"He's curious why he's being followed constantly," Timmons said forwardly. "It looks a bit odd when he's the *only* civilian in this place receiving that kind of attention."

"And what have you told him?" a Marine officer inquired.

"Nothing. I've followed your guidelines."

"We've kept you in the dark about his status for your own good, Timmons," the general said. "We wouldn't want you to accidentally slip regarding crucial information."

"He trusts me, but I don't appreciate a genuinely forged friendship being used for tactical gain, sir."

"I'll advise you to watch your tone, Captain," the general said, staring coldly at the pilot. "It's bad enough you've been providing free flight lessons. We've only allowed this to continue because we trust that you'll keep your new friend motivated to stay here, where it's safer for everyone."

"Yes, sir," Timmons said, his words just short of biting.

Now the general turned his attention to the entire room.

"For the sake of a few new members to our council, perhaps we should address our current science project in detail. Council members only, please."

Over the course of the next few minutes, the remainder of the officers filed out of the room, though Isabella noticed Timmons lingered, as though he might try and eavesdrop on whatever secret meeting the higher-ranking officers were about to hold. She felt insulted that Bryce had never been invited to the council, though she supposed he wasn't at the base during the formation of the exclusive club.

Isabella listened in shock as the details of their scientific experimentation unfolded over the course of the next five minutes. A tingle of excitement and renewed hope ran through her veins as the meeting came to a close, and she knew what her next course of action needed to be. Even if it brought significant risk to her and Nathan, she needed to leave Naval Station Norfolk as soon as humanly possible.

And she needed to somehow bring Metzger with her.

Twenty-nine

Had Metzger been dense enough to not notice the military's sudden interest in him before, he certainly knew it when they provided him with his own private quarters. A shack of a building, used for punishment perhaps when the base was fully functional, the tiny facility provided only one window, and one exit. With the window nailed shut, and the door constantly guarded by two uniformed men, Metzger's chances of escaping notice were nonexistent.

Inside his unofficial prison he possessed a few changes of clothes, a few food rations, and the satellite phone he found during the last Buffalo mission. He wasn't entirely sure why they let him keep the phone when they wouldn't let him keep his firearms and sword. Their rationalization about the weapons was that civilians didn't need weapons as trained military personnel would defend them while they were on the base or working outside of the installation.

Metzger felt he'd lost his sense of purpose because the military didn't let him work inside or outside of the base. He spent his days stewing, waiting for the next blood draw, or random encounter with someone who might speak with him a moment. He missed his friends, and he wondered if he'd stayed with them if Bryce might have survived a second mission in Buffalo, or avoided going altogether.

He didn't want to dwell on the infinite number of possible outcomes, but his mind found little else to occupy it.

Now, as night fell across the base, sounds of work fell off and Metzger sat quietly in his bed, wondering what he wanted to do next. Isabella's communications felt like they took forever to come, especially when he required a response to questions he asked of her.

Feeling despondent, he debated whether to make a run for freedom, or stick around to protect his sister-in-law and nephew from a military that obviously had an agenda. He initially thought the walls meant safety, food, and a barrier from the undead, but the base felt like a prison sentence.

While the door to his residence wasn't locked, he certainly didn't feel free to walk about as he pleased. Other civilians were being relocated outside the base as housing became available, and he questioned whether it was to keep them from certain truths, rather than protect them and provide them with a sense or normality.

Even though Virginia was merely an hour past dusk, Metzger considered laying his head down and sleeping to escape reality until the next monotonous morning arrived. He was about to stand to switch off the single functioning light in the room when the door burst open and a familiar face stood at the threshold, openly relieved to see him.

"Colby?" Metzger asked in shock, standing to usher his friend inside and close the door quickly behind him. "How the hell did you get in here?"

"Buster makes a good distraction sometimes," Sutton said. "Your soldiers love dogs."

"Shit. You didn't kill anyone, did you?"

"No," Sutton said defensively. "Well, not today."

Metzger paced the floor momentarily, concerned that the military would discover both men and lock them away forever.

"Why are you here? How the hell did you get inside?"

"The security here is a little thin," Sutton said with a smirk. "And I need your help."

"My help?" Metzger questioned, a bit surprised anyone required his assistance nowadays.

Sutton shrugged.

"Well, the group needs your help."

Metzger said nothing, raising an eyebrow because he didn't picture Sutton going through so much trouble to assist others.

"What's really going on?"

Sutton sighed heavily.

"Fine. Your girlfriend kicked me out of the group, completely without reason I might add, and, well, you're my ticket to making amends."

Metzger rolled his eyes and threw his arms in the air before cupping his face with his hands as he continued to pace the floor in frustration.

"Let me get this straight," he said, keeping his voice low so he couldn't be heard outside of the shack, but growling his words. "You and Jillian had a playground fight and you want me to square things up between you?"

"It's more than that," Sutton virtually pleaded. "And I thought you'd be happy to see one of us after being cooped up in here."

"You're not wrong about that," Metzger admitted. "And why would you call Jillian my girlfriend? We barely knew each other."

"Well, she kind of let it slip that you guys, well, you know."

Sutton made a sexual gesture with both of his hands, forming a penis with one and a vagina with the other before a brief demonstration.

Metzger hung his head and groaned.

"Why the fuck do they have two guys watching you?" Sutton inquired, obviously wanting to get his plan into motion.

"How do you know about that? And where are they?"

"They're being distracted by Buster's adorable nature. And I've been watching this place since noon. I managed to get a game plan together once I saw where they were stashing you."

"I can't," Metzger said.

"Why would you stay?" Sutton questioned. "I overheard some workers talking about your brother. I'm sorry about what happened, Dan, but there's nothing left for you here."

"My sister-in-law and nephew are here, Colby. I can't just bail on them."

"What good can you do for them while you're being treated like a prisoner?"

Sutton made a good point, and his words echoed what Metzger began to contemplate the past few days.

"Even if I agree to this, how the fuck do we get out of here without being spotted?" Metzger asked.

"The same way I came in. They've got people patrolling the fences, the sea, and the town, but there aren't enough soldiers to cover every inch."

"It's still a huge risk."

"We can come back for your family," Sutton suggested. "It looks like it's you the government wants, not them. We get clear and recover them at a later date."

"No," Metzger said. "I made my choice. I have to live with it. You and Jillian will have to make up some other way."

Sutton appeared disappointed, not because Metzger turned him down, but because he genuinely wanted a friend at the moment. For his part, Metzger needed to ensure the remainder of his family was safe, and running away might cause them additional problems.

"For once in your life be selfish," Sutton requested, his eyes showing his anguish over Metzger's answer. "Trust me, you'll live longer."

"But there are consequences, Colby. You probably know a little something about that."

Sutton was about to answer when the door opened again, causing both of them to assume attack stances, but a confused Isabella poked her head inside.

"Who's this?" she asked of Sutton.

"An old friend," Metzger answered quickly. "How the hell does everyone keep sneaking over here?"

"Your bodyguards were distracted," Isabella answered before turning her attention to Sutton. "Why exactly are you here?"

"Good to meet you, too," Sutton responded. "Actually, I was trying to break him out of here."

"Me, too." She faced Metzger. "Dan, we have to leave immediately."

"Why all the sudden?"

"There's a very good chance Bryce is alive."

Metzger felt his heart sink. He didn't like seeing Isabella with false hope more than a week removed from the Buffalo incident.

"Izzy, I saw what happened. He would've died within a few days at most. He wouldn't be the Bryce we remember."

He went to give her a supportive hug, but she shoved him away rather forcefully.

"I know the difference, Dan. There's a reason why the military has kept tabs on you, and if Bryce had come back they would've done the same with him."

"I have no idea what you're talking about."

"There's no time," Isabella said, taking hold of both of his hands. "I've got Nathan packed, and I have a plan to get us out of here. Can you trust him?"

She bobbed her head towards Sutton when she posed the question.

"I'm right here," Sutton said, growing irritated, holding up his hands as he looked at Isabella.

"I trust him," Metzger replied, wholeheartedly believing his words.

"We need to go, now," Isabella insisted as the door opened, and someone entered holding a gun in his right hand that he aimed at no one in particular.

"Scott?" Metzger asked, surprised that Timmons left his runway area for any reason other than meals.

"I heard a voice I didn't know," Timmons said, aiming his sidearm directly at Sutton.

"He's a friend," Metzger said. "Are you in on this plan, too?"

"Against some of my better judgment, yes," Timmons answered, lowering his firearm and holstering it. "Your sister-in-law made a compelling case."

Timmons ushered Nathan into the shack from behind him, letting the door close to conceal their secret meeting. Wearing blue jeans, the brown shoes issued to pilots, and a button-up shirt, the captain appeared to mix uniform pieces with clothing he'd wear outside of the base.

"Fine," Metzger said, keeping his voice low. "If we're leaving, we need to do it quickly before they discover this little slumber party."

He knelt down beside his nephew, who appeared confused by the sudden change of events.

"You doing okay, Nate?"

The boy nodded bravely.

"Good," Metzger replied. "We're going to play a little game where we sneak off the base without any of the soldiers seeing or hearing us. Think you can be super quiet for me?"

Nathan nodded affirmatively again, eager to please.

"Good boy," Metzger said, giving him a quick hug.

"The two guards were messing with a dog out there," Timmons commented.

"Buster," Sutton said. "He's mine. And he knows to keep them busy until I call for him."

"That helps," Timmons said, "but we still have to time our departure just right, and even packing light like we did, that won't be easy."

He opened the door for a peek outside, closing it quickly.

"They're still preoccupied," he reported. "Most of the base is quiet this time of night, but we'll still have to slip past the patrols."

"That won't be easy with five of us," Metzger noted.

"I memorized their movements and timing this afternoon," Sutton said. "Do they keep the same routine at night?" he posed his question to Timmons.

"So far as I can tell. Even in this world the military still does things by the book."

"How would you not know?" Sutton questioned. "You work here, don't you?"

"Hey, I spend more than half my time in the air, or landing in some undead hot zone so we can try and rebuild this world."

"Sounds like you're still a company man to me," Sutton commented.

"Colby," Metzger said, motioning with his hand for his friend to settle down. "If the captain wanted to turn us in, we wouldn't be having this conversation."

Isabella stepped in the middle of everyone, covering her son's ears when she spoke.

"We don't need bickering. This isn't what any of us expected, but it's the hand we've been dealt. Now let's get the fuck out of here before something goes wrong."

Metzger stepped toward the door.

"Let me go first," he said to everyone. "If my stalkers are being attentive, I can pretend I'm going for a jog and get out some other way. It'll buy the rest of you time."

"I'm parked about a mile away at some sports bar," Sutton said.

"I think I know it," Metzger said, recalling the layout of Norfolk from visits before the apocalypse. "Or at least the area where most the bars were located."

He gave a nod before opening the door, expecting to draw the attention of two dutiful men assigned to watch him at all times. Instead, they were around the corner trying to get Buster to come to them, but he was playing hard to get. The closer they got, the further he trotted away, keeping his eyes on the soldiers and his position so he didn't get cornered. Avoiding the undead provided him with excellent senses and instincts.

A glance around the shack showed no other personnel walking through the base in the vicinity, so Metzger took a step outside, motioning behind him for everyone else to follow. They did so, and he led them to the side of the shack where the two men couldn't see them, even if they looked away from Buster momentarily.

Seeing several duffel bags packed with belongings and supplies, Metzger motioned for Sutton to lead them to safety since he seemed self-assured that his surveillance was accurate. Each of them picked up a packed bag, and Isabella handed one to Metzger personally. He looked at her strangely until his right hand felt what he believed was a sword handle through the canvas material.

He gave her a smile and followed Sutton to the area where numerous ships remained docked since their arrival to Norfolk. Unfortunately, all of the buildings were further back on the base, leaving them completely exposed in a wide-open area if anyone spotted them. The group moved quickly, however, staying in the darker patches where the light didn't leave them readily visible.

Some of the personnel guarding the ships stayed at the bottom of the ramps, while others loomed above on the ships. Sutton slowed to monitor each ship as they passed, finding the dock area dark unless patrol boats came by with their spotlights. They sent a beam along the water and the shore when the armed men turned it. One of the docked ships had a yawning soldier at the base of the boarding ramp and Metzger didn't see a way around him without backtracking. Before they drew too close, Sutton whistled for Buster, who broke away from the two soldiers outside of Metzger's residence. Barely visible, the two men appeared upset that the canine bolted from their location, but they dutifully turned their attention to the shack they were assigned to.

No signs remained that the resident had departed, and Metzger prayed the group could slip past the remaining watchmen and posted guard shacks.

Buster returned to Sutton, wagging his tail before immediately darting to Metzger for some attention, remembering his former travel companion. Metzger rubbed the dog's back a few times and scratched his head before Sutton whispered a command to the canine with a finger pointing out a direction. Buster immediately took off and distracted the sailor at the base of the ship moored closest to the city. If the group slipped past this man, they simply needed to wait for an opening at one of the guard shacks, hopefully passing unseen by the guards or anyone walking the perimeter.

"Who trains their dog to distract people?" Metzger whispered to Sutton.

"It's a natural talent because he's so cute," Sutton answered. "He's also highly trainable."

Carrying out his task perfectly, Buster ran up to the sailor, who couldn't resist bending over to pet him. Buster allowed a few gentle scratches behind his ears before moving in the opposite direction of his owner, allowing Metzger and the others to move forward without detection.

Each of them scoured in every direction, and Metzger was impressed how quiet his nephew remained, as though the boy knew the importance of them exiting the base. He worried that Nathan didn't understand the gravity of what awaited them beyond the small city, because Isabella was savvy enough to shelter in place until the military came and got her.

Staying in the shadows, along the side of the base, the group stopped twice when random people drew near them, simply walking within the base. Foliage and buildings were scarce near the front of the base, so they hoped darkness was enough to keep them hidden. At one point Sutton executed his unique whistle sound, summoning Buster, who left another military man heartbroken because he couldn't follow the dog.

Scampering even half the distance of the base was exhausting under ordinary conditions, and the group had added weight in the form of duffel bags and mental fatigue from fear of being spotted. When they reached the far corner of the base, the group stopped in a precarious location as the gate guards stood just outside the base speaking with a patrol unit consisting of two additional soldiers.

"We could make it," Timmons urged, nodding toward the guard shack.

"Then we'd be forced to run that way, which puts us in the sight of the next shack," Sutton replied. "We're better off waiting for this little soiree to conclude."

"What then?" Metzger inquired. "We still have two guards to deal with."

"Hopefully Buster can work his magic," Sutton said, scratching the dog behind the ears.

Closing his eyes in a canine form of ecstasy, Buster devoured the attention, and Sutton finally gave him a treat which he appeared to eat in one gulp.

"And if he can't work his magic?" Metzger pressed.

"Then we get a little physical," Sutton replied. "No one dies, I promise."

Silently, the group waited nearly five minutes for the patrol and the guards to talk about little of importance. Metzger breathed in the cool night air, realizing the one thing about the base he'd miss was the fresh odors of being near the ocean. While the winds and weather weren't always accommodating, not once had he smelled death on the base. The military carried out an efficient extermination of the nearby undead, and kept their home clear.

When the patrol left, they drove in the direction of the next guard shack, which left the group home free if they managed to get past the guard shack within their view. Sutton whispered to Buster once again, and the dog trotted off to distract the two guards, who eyed him warily, rather than coax him to the shack.

Metzger watched their actions, and they seemed to question how he got inside the base, and if he was healthy enough to handle.

Soon enough, the two men called Buster over, but he walked in the other direction, trying to get them to follow, despite their repeated calls to him. One soldier took a few steps toward the dog, but neither man left the vicinity of the guard shack.

"So much for that," Metzger said with disappointment. He turned to Timmons. "Are there any weak links to this fence?"

"How would I know?" the pilot retorted. "I'm always on the other side of the base. You already know they aren't going to leave weaknesses for the dead or scavengers to sneak through."

Metzger concurred.

"I'm not going to ask you to hurt your own people," he told Timmons. "Hell, I don't even want to do this, but me and Colby will deal with the guards."

Timmons provided a thankful nod.

Metzger followed Sutton along the inside track of the fencing that separated the base from the outside world. Both soldiers kept their focus on Buster, which made reaching the guard shack rather easy, but as Sutton approached the first soldier, the man turned, spotting him before Sutton was fully prepared to assault the man. The soldier tried swinging his rifle at Sutton, but the larger man caught the firearm with both hands, keeping it from doing harm. Metzger dropped his bag beside the fence, prepared to assist his friend.

Sutton managed to throw a punch that caught the man under the jaw, staggering him. Metzger dashed up to the now distracted second solider, catching him off-guard, but the man wore a helmet, making a blow the head rather useless. Instead, Metzger raised his knee, striking the man in the nose before throwing a solid right hand that caught the man along the jaw, knocking him to the ground. Pinning him down, Metzger found a set of zip ties along the man's belt. He grabbed one and secured the man, who continued to struggle. Fortunately, the man wore a handkerchief in his front pocket, so Metzger snagged it and stuffed it inside the soldier's mouth to keep him from calling for assistance.

Metzger felt bad for leaving his victim a bloody mess from the nose area, but he couldn't risk any shooting or screams for help so close to their escape.

He looked up, finding Sutton had rendered his adversary entirely unconscious, already dragging the man back to the guard shack. Sutton dropped him next to the other soldier, slightly winded from the brief encounter.

"Here," Metzger said, handing him a zip tie. "Find something to gag him in case he comes to."

Sutton searched the guard shack, quickly locating a rag of some sort that he stuffed into the man's mouth.

"That was a quick knockout," Metzger commented, motioning for the others to join them.

"Glass jaw," Sutton said before whistling for Buster.

Catching the men unaware of impending danger helped their cause, and Metzger felt certain that adrenaline aided his attack. Dragging the two soldiers into the shack, Metzger and Sutton emerged to find everyone ready to exit the base. Metzger retrieved his bag, taking up the rear, but his mind kept reliving the words his sister-in-law spoke about Bryce possibly being alive. He believed her, and Isabella wasn't someone who fell for tricks or flimsy evidence, so something she discovered backed her words.

Once they cleared the guard shacks, the group picked up their pace, heading for Sutton's box truck. Metzger hadn't asked how they were all supposed to fit inside, but he knew only one viable solution worked for transporting five people.

Some of them rode in the back.

"Where are we going?" Metzger asked of Sutton and Isabella while they all took brisk steps.

Both gave completely different answers, Sutton indicating their old group, while Isabella replied 'Buffalo' without hesitation.

"We don't have time for both, so I need to hear what you have to say, Izzy, if we're going to make a run for Buffalo."

"You're going to want Buffalo," Timmons assured him.

Metzger assumed his sister-in-law hadn't recruited the pilot, asking him to break an oath to the military, for no good reason.

"I can't promise Bryce is alive," Isabella said, stopping in the middle of the street, "but I wouldn't put Nathan through all of this if there wasn't a good chance."

"I just don't understand how," Metzger muttered, shaking his head.

Isabella unzipped her duffel bag and pulled out a box containing several vials of various solutions in a variety of colors.

"These are samples of some antidotes they've been working on," she said, not removing them from the packaging.

"Where did those come from?"

"They're stored on one of the ships."

"How the hell did you get them?"

"I've had a very busy day," she said, exasperated because of her day's activities and Metzger asking so many questions.

"You're asking the wrong questions, son," Timmons finally stated, looking to one side, acting a bit paranoid that they might be followed or spotted at any moment.

"Those have something to do with Bryce?" Metzger asked slowly.

Sutton and Buster both stiffened at the noise of a nearby vehicle and headlights illuminating the pavement just a few blocks away.

"We need to move," Sutton said, ushering everyone in the direction of his box truck.

"If they pursue us, your box truck isn't going to make a good escape vehicle," Metzger commented.

"How do you know I still have it?" Sutton asked, picking up his pace to a jog.

"You'd die before you'd let that thing out of your sight."

"Well, I almost died for it a few times, and I can assure you I consider my life more important than a few supplies."

"But you still have it."

"Of course I do."

Within a few minutes the group reached a parking structure where Sutton had cleverly hidden his vehicle behind some concrete partitions where it wasn't easily visible to passing soldiers. Metzger imagined the patrols focused on locating the undead and seedy people, rather than parked vehicles.

"Where are we going?" Metzger questioned as Sutton popped the back of the truck open, revealing just enough space for a few people to squeeze in with his belongings.

"We're getting the fuck out of Norfolk first," Sutton replied.

"Language," Isabella chimed in.

"How much of a head start do we have on the military if they track us?" Metzger asked no one in particular.

"Maybe two hours," Timmons said. "If we're flying anywhere, we need to beat them to the airports or get creative."

"Are they really going to come after us that hardcore?"

"Dan, they aren't going to let you leave," Timmons said solemnly. "They could give two shits about the rest of us. Even me, when compared to what you can do for them."

Metzger stared at him, waiting for an explanation, but Sutton ushered everyone except him into the back of the truck.

"Jump in, everyone. I'll get us out of here and find a second vehicle."

Everyone looked to Metzger, who gave an approving nod regarding the plan.

"It'll be okay," he said to Nathan in particular. "It'll be dark in there, but just stay calm and we'll be safe real soon."

He handed his nephew the flashlight he usually carried.

"I'll be okay," Nathan assured him.

"Good," Metzger said, kneeling down beside his nephew. "Keep your mom and the captain safe, because they don't like the dark either."

"That's for sure," Timmons grumbled more about the plan than any fear of darkness.

Once everyone climbed inside, Sutton closed the doors and used a steel bar to keep them secure. He looked to Metzger.

"Ready for this?"

"An hour ago, I was ready to call it a night, so no."

Both men climbed into the front of the truck, with Buster sandwiched between them, and Sutton managed to get them clear of the garage rather quickly. He navigated the streets of Norfolk without using the headlights, and whenever he or Metzger spied headlights nearby, Sutton either stopped or changed direction. Before long, he reached the town limits, and only a few bridges separated the group from Naval Station Norfolk and complete freedom.

Metzger's mind kept wandering to Isabella and the vials of serum. He began to guess his importance to the military based on her revelation that his brother possibly survived a zombie bite.

"You okay?" Sutton asked as they neared the first bridge.

"I'm not sure anymore. Surviving the apocalypse is one thing, but this feels like living in a soap opera with plot twists."

"Look, I can't leave the area," Sutton confessed. "Even if I can't patch things up with your girlfriend, I've still got to look for my boys."

"I understand. Have I missed anything these past few weeks?"

"You wouldn't believe me if I told you," Sutton said with a chuckle. "That's a story for another time."

Metzger sat silently with his thoughts a moment.

"Colby, am I going back to New York just to see my brother as a zombie?"

"That spunky sister-in-law of yours seems to think he's alive," Sutton said with a shrug. "What happened up there?"

"Bryce died saving the rest of us," Metzger said, feeling numb all over again. "He got a bite from one of the undead."

"You're sure?"

"There was blood," Metzger said, feeling as though he personally hammered a nail in his brother's coffin.

If only Bryce were given the benefit of a casket.

When Sutton entered the tunnel that went beneath the waters leading to and from Norfolk, he found a line of cars and trucks parked to one side, cleared so traffic could move freely. Done mainly for the military's benefit, the line of cars provided a used car lot of sorts for the group to peruse once Sutton freed them from the back of the truck.

Although sweaty from being locked inside, the trio appeared otherwise unscathed.

"We can't linger," Metzger said. "Let's pick a vehicle and Colby can lead us out of here."

After selecting a car and a van, the group discovered neither would start, so they settled on a dark blue Ford Expedition that started, though it immediately indicated the fuel level was dangerously low.

"Beggars can't be choosers," Timmons commented as he slung his duffel bag in the open rear compartment.

Everyone else followed his lead, placing their makeshift luggage inside. Isabella found a handful of maps inside, discovering one that covered the local area.

"Sure you won't come with us?" Metzger asked of Sutton, his mind continuing to stir regarding Isabella's statements.

He wanted nothing more than to get straight answers from her once they were safe from being pursued.

"I've got to stay in Virginia until I find the boys," Sutton replied.

"Sounds like we've got to find a plane," Metzger commented. "We can follow you out of here while we scour the map for airports."

"There are a few nearby," Sutton said, "if they aren't already picked over."

Everyone stood awkwardly a moment, as though uncertain how to go about parting ways.

"I'll lead you out, and I can get you some supplies for the trip," Sutton offered.

"Thank you," Metzger replied.

Sutton turned to jump into the driver's seat of his box truck when a pair of headlights came at them, aimed toward the Navy base. Metzger instinctively reached for a sidearm he hadn't worn in over a week, but he remembered the duffel bag that now held the firearm. He opened the rear hatch of the vehicle, rummaging through the bag Isabella handed him. Finding his sword and the .357 revolver his father gave him many years back, Metzger stepped forward, prepared to fight for his freedom if necessary.

A white van stopped a safe distance from Sutton's box truck, and as the passengers reluctantly stepped from the vehicle, Metzger began to see familiar faces. Luke, Samantha, and a male stranger emerged first, walking in his direction. He spied Gracine just behind them, and his worries subsided when he saw Jillian step in front of the group, bringing a smile to his face. She virtually ignored Sutton, and the man didn't say a word, taking a step back instead.

Jillian approached him and threw her arms around his torso. In her embrace he sensed she'd been through quite an ordeal the past few weeks. Perhaps Sutton had left some details out of his account of recent events, but Metzger could sort that out later. At the moment, he felt good holding Jillian, and he didn't want to let her travel without him again. As she released her grip, Metzger looked at the group, wondering where their adventures were about to take them.

"Looks like the band is back together," he said, feeling the happiest he'd been in weeks.

End Volume 2.

www.ingramcontent.com/pod-product-compliance
Lightning Source LLC
Chambersburg PA
CBHW060245210726
48292CB00002BA/505